I0725411

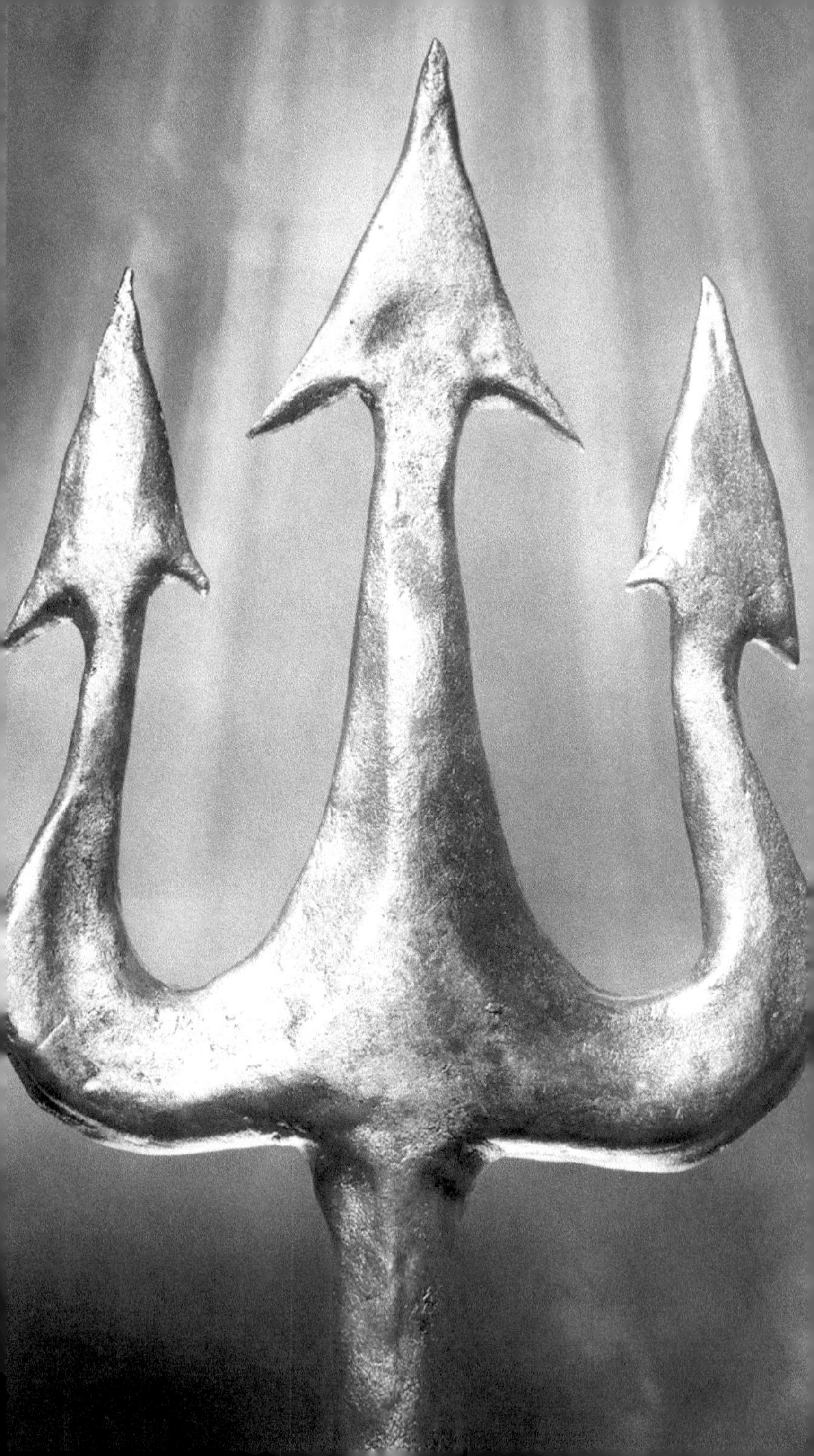

ABSOLVING
His Sins

Trident Security Book 9

SAMANTHA COLE

To my readers—without you, my world would be a lot dimmer.

ACKNOWLEDGMENTS

Here we go again! (Thankfully!)

To Jess, Jules, and Brandie—you ladies are there for me, day in and day out, and I am eternally grateful!

To my beta readers, Jen, Joanne, Charla, Debbie, and Allena—thank you for taking the time to help make my books the best they can be!

To my editor, Eve—I swear there are gremlins in my computer switching words around! Thanks for finding them and not laughing at me when I—I mean, *they* make stupid mistakes!

To my PA, Maria—thanks for helping with all the things that are too much for me to deal with by myself!

To Milynn—for answering my questions and righting any wrongs.

To the Sexy Six-Pack Sirens group—your continued

support and shout outs are appreciated more than you'll ever know. Keep cracking the whips and I'll do my best to keep the stories coming!

To my readers—thank you for loving my characters as much as I do. I hope you think I've done Carter justice.

AUTHOR'S NOTE

The story within these pages is completely fictional but the concepts of BDSM are real. If you do choose to participate in the BDSM lifestyle, please research it carefully and take all precautions to protect yourself. Fiction is based on real life but real life is *not* based on fiction. Remember—Safe, Sane and Consensual!

Any information regarding persons or places has been used with creative literary license so there may be discrepancies between fiction and reality. The missions and personal qualities of members of the military and law enforcement within have been created to enhance the story and, again, may be exaggerated and not coincide with reality.

The author has full respect for the members of the United States military and the varied members of law enforcement and thanks them for their continuing service to making this country as safe and free as possible.

***While not every character is in every book, these are the ones with the most mentions throughout the series. This guide will help keep readers straight about who's who.

Trident Security (TS) is a private investigative and military agency, co-owned by Ian and Devon Sawyer. With governmental and civilian contracts, the company got its start when the brothers and a few of their teammates from SEAL Team Four retired to the private sector. The original six-man team is referred to as the Sexy Six-Pack, as they were dubbed by Kristen Sawyer, née Anders, or the Alpha Team. Trident had since expanded and former members of the military and law enforcement have been added to the staff. The company is located on a guarded compound, which was a former import/export company cover for a drug trafficking operation in Tampa, Florida. Three ware-houses on the property were converted into large apartments, the TS offices, gym, and bunk rooms.

There is also an obstacle course, a Main Street shooting gallery, a helicopter pad, and more features necessary for training and missions.

In addition to the security business, there is a fourth warehouse that now houses an elite BDSM club, co-owned by Devon, Ian, and their cousin, Mitch Sawyer, who is the manager. A lot of time and money has gone into making The Covenant the most sought after membership in the Tampa/St. Petersburg area and beyond. Members are thoroughly vetted before being granted access to the elegant club.

There are currently over fifty Doms who have been appointed Dungeon Masters (DMs), and they rotate two or three shifts each throughout the month. At least four DMs are on duty at all times at various posts in the pit, playrooms, and the new garden, with an additional one roaming around. Their job is to ensure the safety of all the submissives in the club. They step in if a sub uses their safeword and the Dom in the scene doesn't hear or heed it, and make sure the equipment used in scenes isn't harming the subs.

The Covenant's security team takes care of everything else that isn't scene-related, and provides safety for all members and are essentially the bouncers. The current total membership is just over 350. The fire marshal had approved them for 500 when the warehouse-turned-kink club first opened, but the cousins had intentionally kept that number down to maintain an elite status.

Between Trident Security and The Covenant there's plenty of romance, suspense, and steamy encounters. Come meet the Sexy Six-Pack, their friends, family, and teammates.

The Sexy Six-Pack (Alpha Team) and Their Significant Others

- Ian "Boss-man" Sawyer: Devon and Nick's brother; retired Navy SEAL; co-owner of Trident Security and The Covenant; husband/Dom of Angelina (Angel).
- Devon "Devil Dog" Sawyer: Ian and Nick's brother; retired Navy SEAL; co-owner of Trident Security and The Covenant; husband/Dom of Kristen; father of John Devon "JD."
- Ben "Boomer" Michaelson: retired Navy SEAL; explosives and ordnance specialist; husband/Dom of Katerina; son of Rick and Eileen.
- Jake "Reverend" Donovan: retired Navy SEAL; temporarily assigned to run the West Coast team; sniper; fiancé/Dom of Nick; brother of Mike; Whip Master at The Covenant.
- Brody "Egghead" Evans: retired Navy SEAL; computer specialist; fiancé/Dom of Fancy.

- Marco "Polo" DeAngelis: retired Navy SEAL; communications specialist and back up helicopter pilot; husband/Dom of Harper; father to Mara.
- Nick "Junior" Sawyer: Ian and Devon's brother; current Navy SEAL; fiancé/submissive of Jake.
- Kristen "Ninja-girl" Sawyer: author of romance/suspense novels; wife/submissive of Devon; mother of "JD."
- Angelina "Angie/Angel" Sawyer: graphic artist; wife/submissive of Ian.
- Katerina "Kat" Michaelson: dog trainer for law enforcement and private agencies; fiancée/submissive of Boomer.
- Millicent "Harper" DeAngelis: lawyer; wife/submissive of Marco; mother of Mara.
- Francine "Fancy" Maguire: baker; fiancée/submissive of Brody.

Extended Family, Friends, and Associates of the Sexy Six-Pack

- Mitch Sawyer: Cousin of Ian, Devon, and Nick; co-owner/manager of The Covenant, Dom.
- T. Carter: US spy and assassin; works for covert agency Deimos; Dom.

- Jordyn Alvarez: US spy and assassin; member of covert agency Deimos.
- Parker Christiansen: owner of New Horizons Construction; husband/Dom of Shelby.
- Shelby Christiansen: stay-at-home mom; two-time cancer survivor; wife/submissive of Parker.
- Curt Bannerman: retired Navy SEAL; owner of Halo Customs, a motorcycle repair and detail shop; husband of Dana; stepfather of Ryan, Taylor, Justin, and Amanda. Lives in Iowa.
- Dana Prichard-Bannerman: teacher; widow of retired SEAL Eric Prichard; wife of Curt; mother of Ryan, Taylor, Justin, and Amanda. Lives in Iowa.
- Jenn "Baby-girl" Mullins: college student; goddaughter of Ian; "niece" of Devon, Brody, Jake, Boomer, and Marco; father was a Navy SEAL; parents murdered.
- Mike Donovan: owner of the Irish pub, Donovan's; brother of Jake.
- Charlotte "Mistress China" Roth: Parole officer; Domme and Whip Master at The Covenant.
- Travis "Tiny" Daultry: former professional football player; head of security at The

Covenant and Trident compound; occasional bodyguard for TS.

- Doug "Bullseye" Henderson: retired Marine; contract bodyguard.
- Rick and Eileen Michaelson: Boomer's parents; guardians of Alyssa. Rick is a retired Navy SEAL.
- Charles "Chuck" and Marie Sawyer: Ian, Devon, and Nick's parents. Charles is a self-made real estate billionaire. Marie is a plastic surgeon involved with Operation Smile.
- Will Anders: Assistant Curator of the Tampa Museum of Art Kristen Anders's cousin.
- Dr. Roxanne London: pediatrician; Domme/wife (Mistress Roxy) of Kayla; Whip Master at Covenant.
- Kayla London: social worker; submissive/wife of Roxanne.
- Chase Dixon: retired Marine Raider; owner of Blackhawk Security; associate of TS.
- Reggie Helm: lawyer for TS and The Covenant; Dom/boyfriend of Colleen.
- Alyssa Wagner: teenager saved by Jake from an abusive father; lives with Rick and Eileen Michaelson.
- Dr. Trudy Dunbar: Psychologist.

- Carl Talbot: college professor; Dom and Whip Master at The Covenant.

The Omega Team and Their Significant Others

- Cain "Shades" Foster: retired Secret Service agent.
- Tristan "Duracell" McCabe: retired Army Special Forces
- Valentino "Romeo" Mancini: retired Army Special Forces; former FBI Hostage Rescue Team (HRT) member.
- Darius "Batman" Knight: retired Navy SEAL.
- Kip "Skipper" Morrison: retired Army; former LAPD SWAT sniper.
- Lindsey "Costello" Abbott: retired Marine; sniper.

Trident Support Staff

- Colleen McKinley: office manager of TS; girlfriend/submissive of Reggie.
- Tempest "Babs" Van Buren: retired Air Force helicopter pilot; TS mechanic.
- Russell Adams: retired Navy; assistant TS mechanic.

- Nathan Cook: former computer specialist with the National Security Agency (NSA).

Members of Law Enforcement

- Larry Keon: Assistant Director of the FBI.
- Frank Stonewall: Special Agent in Charge of the Tampa FBI.
- Calvin Watts: Leader of the FBI HRT in Tampa.
- Colt Parrish: Major Case Specialist, Behavioral Analysis Unit.

The K9s of Trident

- Beau: An orphaned Lab/Pit mix, rescued by Ian. Now a trained K9 who has more than earned his spot on the Alpha Team.
- Spanky: A rescued Bullmastiff with a heart of gold, owned by Parker and Shelby.
- Jagger: A rescued Rottweiler trained as an assistance/service animal for Russell.

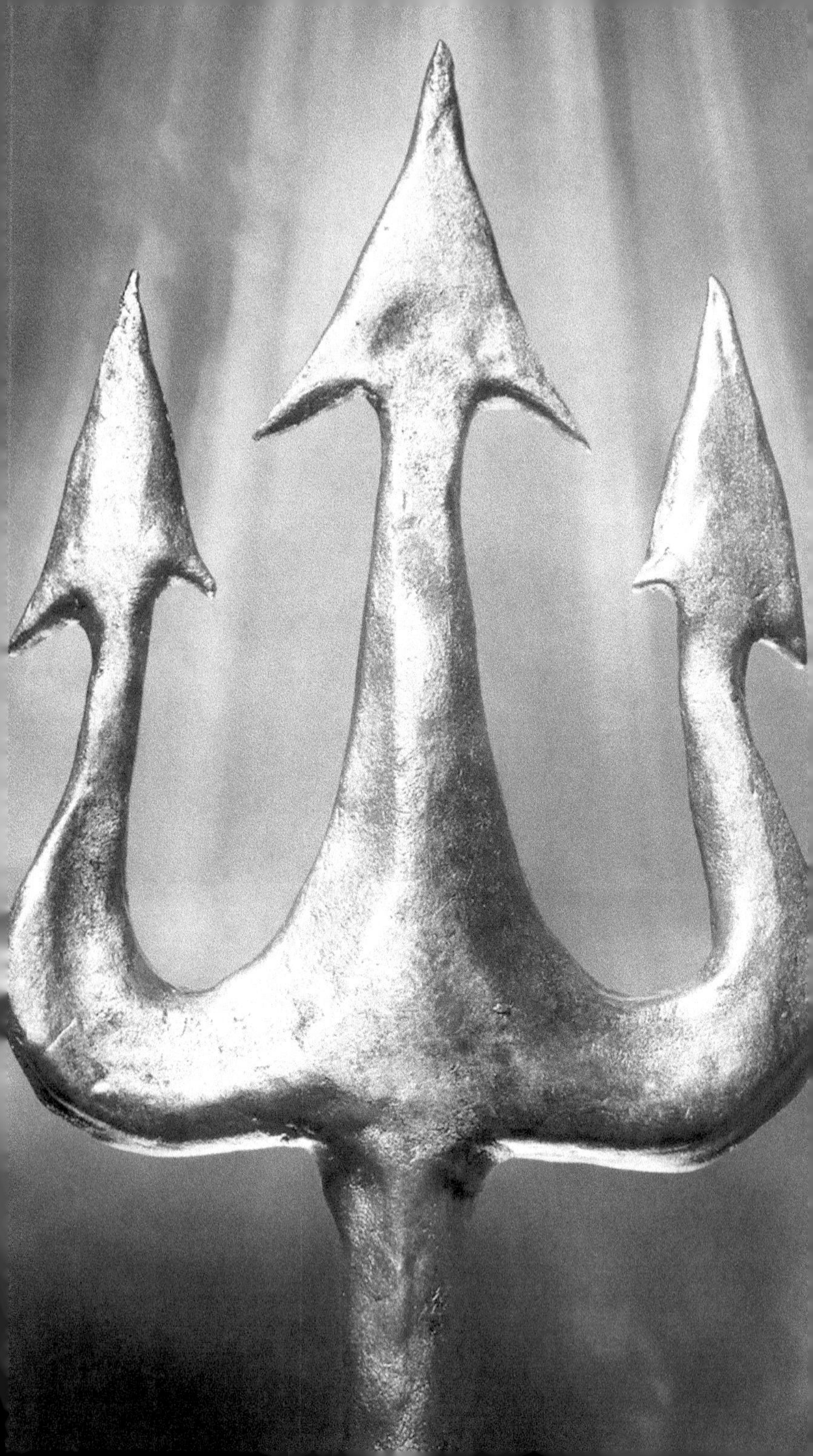

"**D**eep breath and let it out slowly."

"Get out of my fucking head, Carter."

"Not until I have you back in my bed, Jordy."

"Bastard," Jordyn Alvarez muttered to herself. You would think after all this time of hating the prick, she could rid him from her mind. But it was times like this, when she was about to dispatch a target, that Carter's voice would always flow back to her. It was smooth and sexy, and that just pissed her off even more because her body would remember what it was like to be in his arms.

One night. One fucking night that she would kick herself over for the rest of her life. If he hadn't been the one to train her, and killing the US spy would probably be considered an act of treason, she would have slit his throat a long time ago.

Trying to ignore his familiar, yet annoying, snark in her head, she concentrated on slowing her breathing and heart rate. Her job here was simple. Wait until her target came out of the restaurant, put a bullet in his brain, then hightail it out of there before his bodyguards knew what hit him.

Jordyn lay flat on the roof of a building in Kano, Nigeria, three blocks from where Mavuto Themba was having lunch with his mistress. The dirty, local politician had signed his death warrant when he'd become part of the pipeline supplying ISIS with funds and weapons. The US government had obtained proof that the Nigerian Minister of Defense was planning a coup of his own government. The fallout would have a devastating effect on the war-torn nation and could not be allowed to happen. Unfortunately, the United States could not reveal how they'd obtained the evidence against Themba, so Jordyn's bosses at Deimos, and probably POTUS, had been the judges, and she was here as the assigned executioner. That's what she and the others at Deimos did—the President's and the US government's dirty work. Not that anyone in power would admit to that fact.

Deimos was a black-ops agency very few people knew about. The operatives took care of things that the public could never know about to keep the US safe from terrorists and other world powers who wanted to see the leader of the free world fall flat on its face. Named after the Greek god of terror, it was the perfect name for an agency that excelled in torture and assassinations, among other things.

Assessing the wind speed and direction, she made the necessary adjustments on her Remington Defense CSR—a concealable sniper rifle. It was her baby. The design was lightweight and compact. With the NATO/.308 Winchester bolt-action, a carbon fiber-wrapped barrel, and a sound suppressor, the sniper carbine was one kick-ass piece of weaponry. She could break it down in less than thirty seconds, place the individual pieces in a case designed to look like it held a laptop, and be on the move a minute after confirming her shot.

Having been in the city a full week planning the assassination, Jordyn knew her escape route and two backup routes by heart. Between there and her hotel on the other side of the city, she would make several pit stops and clothing changes along the way. Within an hour, she would be Esmerelda Cortez, Quality Assurance Inspector for the World Health Organization—her chosen cover for this mission. Tomorrow, she'd be boarding a commercial flight and returning to the United States—her adopted home.

Heavy humidity hung like a wet blanket, coating her face and hair with sweat. It didn't help that she wore a long-sleeved shirt and black cargo pants to help her blend in with the shadows of a taller building to her left. She pushed the heat and sweat from her mind, shutting them behind a mental door, along with Carter—let him deal with them.

Through the scope, she saw the door to the restaurant open. Seconds ticked by before anyone appeared in the crosshairs. The first person was one of Themba's goon bodyguards. Next was the politician's mistress. A black SUV pulled up and blocked most of Jordyn's view of the restaurant's exit. *Fuck!* The goon opened the vehicle's rear passenger door for the woman and left it ajar while waiting for his boss. Finally, Themba stepped out of the building with two more bodyguards flanking him. He said something that had all three of them laughing. Jordyn could only see their heads and necks over the top of the SUV.

Center mass shots to the chest were best, but this time, she'd have to settle for a headshot and pray it was a direct hit.

She inhaled and slowly let the breath back out. Her target's face was large and ugly in the scope. She could make out the small mole just to the right of his nose and placed it in the center of the crosshairs. In between heartbeats, she squeezed the trigger with her index finger, smooth and steady. With a barely audible *pfft*, the bullet was on its way, taking death with it.

One Miss—

Before the rest of Mississippi registered in her mind, the projectile found its bullseye. Themba's head snapped back as his brains and skull were sprayed all over the bodyguard standing behind him. That man's head also jolted, and both of them dropped like stones.

Damn, two for the price of one. Not bad, Jordy, not bad at all.

Fuck off, Carter.

Jordyn was already disassembling her rifle by the time the other two bodyguards knew what happened and pulled out their weapons. There were shouts and screams, but she ignored them all. Thirty-seven seconds after the bullet was fired, she had the rifle concealed in the case, which was in her hand, and was running to the other side of the building. Without hesitation, she let one foot land as close to the edge as possible and leaped across the narrow expanse between the two buildings. She didn't even spare a glance down, instead hitting the next wooden roof with a muffled *thump*.

Pivoting, she headed for the northwest corner, where a trap door would drop her inside the apartment building. As she ran down the dimly lit stairs, her ears strained to hear shouts or sirens—anything that would indicate they'd figured out where the shot had come from. So far, she was in the clear.

When she reached the ground floor, she ducked into an unoccupied apartment. During her scouting adventures, she'd found out the old man who lived there alone worked in the food market every day, never wavering from his routine. It hadn't taken her long to break in after he'd left this morning. Now, she shut the door behind her, retrieved a large duffel bag she'd stuffed into a crawl space in the closet earlier, and opened it. Pulling out the black burka, she threw it on over her clothes and adjusted the cloak's veil to hide her head and face. The briefcase went into the duffel bag, which she then hid under the traditional Muslim clothing.

Jordyn was out of the apartment in under a minute, having practiced the whole routine in her hotel room until it had become automatic. Exiting the building, she fell in step with the moderate midday pedestrian traffic. She was just another local woman out running errands. Sirens sounded in the distance but weren't drawing nearer, so she still had plenty of time to disappear. Three blocks down, she merged into the outdoor food market, where she could blend in even more. The smells of bread, fish, meats, live animals, and Lord knew what else were overwhelming in the stifling cloak, and nausea roiled through her.

Striding into one of the overstuffed tents, she acted like she belonged there and cut through to the next row of vendors. Zigzagging her way through the huge market, she finally reached the other end as sweat soaked the fabric around her face and neck—how Muslim women wore these damn things without passing out in the heat was beyond Jordyn.

Her next stop was a chicken shed behind a restaurant. So many people were hurrying about, focused on doing their jobs, that no one questioned her when she snuck inside and shut the door. Grabbing a piece of wood she'd hidden in there a few days ago, she wedged it between the door and the rickety floor so no one could get in while she changed again.

Ignoring the clucking chickens, which were most likely on tonight's menu, Jordyn ripped off the burka, taking gulps of rancid air—at least it was cooler than breathing through the veil. Not needing the heavy cloak anymore, she tossed it behind the crates of chickens. This time, she pulled out a pair of khaki pants and a crisp, white T-shirt from the duffel, transforming into the visiting westerner she was supposed to be. A pair of glasses, which would give her a mousy look without hampering her vision, went on her face, and she quickly put her hair up into a messy bun. The cargo pants and black shirt went into the duffel bag, and then she adjusted the straps so it became a backpack.

Ready to go out in public as Esmerelda Cortez, Jordyn kicked the wedge from the door and cracked it open. The cook shouted at the workers through the backdoor of the restaurant's kitchen, but no one saw her as she exited the shack and hurried along an alleyway leading back to the street.

Ten minutes later, she sat at a table at the outdoor café across from her hotel and tucked the duffel under her chair. A waiter, who had been flirting with her over the past several days whenever she stopped in, hurried over with a bottle of sparkling water, which she always ordered. The café and hotel were located in the city's nicer section, catering to tourists, international businessmen, and diplomats. The WHO used this hotel for its inspectors and workers visiting the region, so it was perfect for her cover.

"Hello, Ms. Esmerelda. How was work today?"

As the waiter grinned at her, his stark white teeth contrasted with his dark skin. He was a handsome man in his twenties, but a white-and-pink, ragged scar from his temple to his lower jaw—the result of a knife attack, Jordyn guessed—was the first thing most people noticed about him. It didn't bother her at all.

Jordyn smiled back as she took the bottle from him. "Very good, Yabani. I finished earlier than expected today, so I'm free the rest of the day."

"Wonderful. Does that mean you will sit for a while and let me admire your beauty?"

Oh, he was a charmer. "With flattery like that, how can I refuse?"

"What the fuck are you doing here?"

Smirking, T. Carter stared down the barrel of the gun, not the least bit worried it would be fired. He lounged on the queen-sized bed in Jordyn's hotel room, with his back against a pillow, feet crossed, and arms resting behind his head, as his gaze trailed up and down her body.

Damn, the woman is fine.

Every muscle was toned to perfection, yet there was no mistaking her womanly curves. Curves he'd enjoyed only once before.

He'd anticipated and worried about her return for nearly an hour. Not knowing where she'd planned to take out her target, he'd been resigned to waiting for her there in her hotel room, and it had nearly killed him. The relief he'd felt when Ian Sawyer had reported spotting her at the café across the street had been palpable. She'd stayed there for a half hour, eyeing the hotel and its surroundings for anything or anyone out of place. The fact that she hadn't spotted Ian or any of his men didn't mean Jordyn wasn't alert—it just meant the covert team was that good. Now that Carter had eyes on her, he could relax even more despite the threat looming.

When he'd gotten the phone call from his bosses at Deimos that all hell was breaking loose, he'd immediately contacted Ian and his brother Devon, Trident Security's owners, whom he trusted with his life—and Jordyn's. Until a few hours ago, the men hadn't known which alphabet agency Carter had worked for—all they knew was he was a black-ops spy and assassin for the United States. But to get to Jordyn before she ended up dead, he'd called on the best team he knew for backup.

He hadn't been surprised when she entered with her weapon drawn. As he'd picked the lock to get in, he'd noticed a nearly invisible piece of tape she'd placed between the top of the door and the molding. It was one of the numerous tricks he'd taught her. She would've checked to see if it had been moved before entering, unsure if it was an intruder or the maid service.

"I asked you a question." Glowering at him, Jordyn lowered the gun but didn't re-holster it. "What the hell are you doing here, Carter? And how the hell did you find me?"

His grin grew at her attitude. She was a feisty little thing, and, damn, he loved feisty. "Easy, love. I trained you, remember?" He sure as hell did. Eight years ago, the lovely Ms. Jordyn had been recruited for Deimos after the international jewel thief had interrupted one of their missions on US soil. The powers that be saw the raw potential in her and gave her an option—go to prison or work for the government. Wisely, she'd taken Door #2.

From the moment Carter had laid eyes on his new apprentice, he'd craved her. But professionalism, integrity, and patriotism outranked his desire and lust. He'd trained her for months—twelve- to fourteen-hour days, seven days a week, with only occasional downtime. He'd enjoyed those times when she let down her hair and relaxed. More than once, the electricity in the air had crackled between them, but neither had made a move. He'd lost count of how many fucking cold showers he'd taken during that time.

She'd been turned loose once she'd excelled in weaponry, hand-to-hand combat, logistics, how to kill a man in numerous ways, and everything else she'd needed to learn. After that, Carter had been teamed with her several times. It was during one of those missions he'd let his desire take over and—

"Don't remind me," she spat, interrupting his thoughts. "And I'm not your fucking 'love.' Now answer my other fucking question, dammit."

He shook his head and frowned in feigned annoyance when, in fact, he was utterly turned on. "*Tsk, tsk.* Such a dirty mouth." He stared at that mouth, remembering what it felt like under his. His cock twitched at the thought. *Down boy.* "I'm here to extract you. Your cover's been blown."

"Bullshit. How?"

His gaze roamed her body, and his hands itched to follow. "I'll explain later, but we need to get somewhere safer."

"I'm not going anywhere with you." Still not relinquishing her weapon, or the duffel bag he knew held her sniper rifle, she cocked her hip as she glared at him. And, damn it, that just had his dick twitching again. If he didn't get her moving soon, he'd be hard as a fucking rock with no relief in sight.

He was about to tell her that yes, indeed, she was coming with him, whether she liked it or not, but paused, listening to the comm set in his ear as Ian's voice came over the airwaves. "We've got company, dude. Three guys packing, and it looks like they're on a mission. Getting on elevator. You've got less than thirty. Meet you out back."

Time to go. He tapped his comm set once to let the other man know the message was received. Grabbing his gun from where it sat within reach on the bed, Carter leaped up and strode past a gaping Jordyn on the way to the door. "If you don't want to go with me, love, then fine. You can deal with the hit squad on their way up here right now with orders to kill you."

"What?" she hissed, following him out the door, leaving behind the few things she had left in the room. He knew everything she needed was somewhere on her body or in the duffel bag—everything else could be replaced.

He glanced over his shoulder but kept moving at a fast, yet silent, pace down the hall. "Changed your mind?"

Her growled, unintelligible response caused the corners of his mouth to tick up in a smile.

They were almost at one end of the hall when the elevator dinged at the other end of the long expanse, and the doors began to open. *Shit!* They were spotted two steps away from the closed door to the stairs. Ignoring the shouts to stop, he burst through the door with Jordyn on his heels as gunfire exploded behind them. Splinters flew from the door jamb, narrowly missing them, and Carter pushed Jordyn in front of him as they ran down the stairs. They were two levels down, with one more to go, when the gunmen slammed the door above them open. More shouts and gunfire echoed through the stairwell. *Stupid fucks.* Not that he minded, but these guys were idiots. He and Jordyn were skirting the walls on their way down, staying out of sight, so those jackasses were just shooting for the hell of it. *Hmm.* Somebody didn't want to pay for an experienced hit squad or didn't care how much attention they attracted in the process.

The two spies hit the ground floor, and Jordyn ripped open the door leading to a hallway. She was about to go left when Carter grabbed her arm and pulled her to the right. "This way, love. Our chariot awaits."

He hurried through a set of swinging doors, into the laundry room, where the workers barely looked at them, and out onto the loading dock. Jumping off the dock, he still had Jordyn by the arm. A black SUV with smoked-out windows screamed to a stop in front of them. The rear passenger door flew open, and Carter pushed Jordyn into the back seat, jumping in behind her. The vehicle took off again before the door was even shut. The whole episode from the room to there had taken less than two minutes, and neither of them had fired a shot.

Leaving the hit squad far behind, Ian made three quick turns on the streets of Kano. When he slowed to a normal speed for the day's traffic, which was still close to neck-breaking, Jordyn put the duffel by her feet, shifted to face Carter, and glared at him. "Okay, Tristan, tell me who the hell they were and why they're after me."

"How'd you know my name?"

Carter hooted loudly as Jordyn glanced at the man in the front passenger seat, staring back at her with narrowed, wary eyes. "What are you talking about?"

"You said 'Tristan.' That's my name."

"And it's not mine," Carter added, still chuckling. "Sorry, McCabe. Every time the beautiful Jordyn sees me, she tries to guess my given first name. In seven years, she still hasn't gotten it—not that I'd ever admit it if she did."

A car pulled out in front of Ian, and he jerked the steering wheel sharply to avoid a collision. The sudden movement sent Jordyn flying across the seat into Carter's arms and practically in his lap. He grinned at his female counterpart. "Well, hello, love. And here I thought you didn't miss me."

Damn, her body felt amazing pressed against his, but it didn't last for long as she struggled to sit upright, her hand barely missing his groin, before shifting over to the other side of the vehicle again. If looks could kill, he'd be on his way to the morgue by now.

She growled at him again, but he understood what she said this time. "I didn't miss you, asshole."

"Jackass."

Jordyn's head whipped toward the front seat, and she glared daggers at the back of the driver's head. And, yup, Ian should be on his way to the autopsy suite too. "Fuck you!"

"Sorry, sweetheart, I wasn't calling you a jackass," Ian explained as he steered them toward the on-ramp of the highway leading to the airport. Fifteen more minutes, and they'd be taxiing down the runway. "It's a long-standing joke. Carter's the jackass, and our computer geek, Brody, is the asshole. That leaves my dear brother to be asshat."

"So, what does that make you—asswipe?"

"Ha!" Ian barked, slapping his hand on the steering wheel. "You were right, man. She does have grit. I think I might like her."

Carter eyed Jordyn smugly while she looked like she wanted to slice him six ways to Sunday. It was a good thing he'd been the one to train her, otherwise he might be in trouble. As it was, she'd hated his guts ever since they'd had a romp in the sack. And what a romp it'd been. The woman could kill a man in dozens of ways, yet in bed, she was submissive. Little Ms. Jordyn, assassin extraordinaire, was the hottest woman he'd ever enjoyed pleasuring—until the next morning when he'd woken to find her gone.

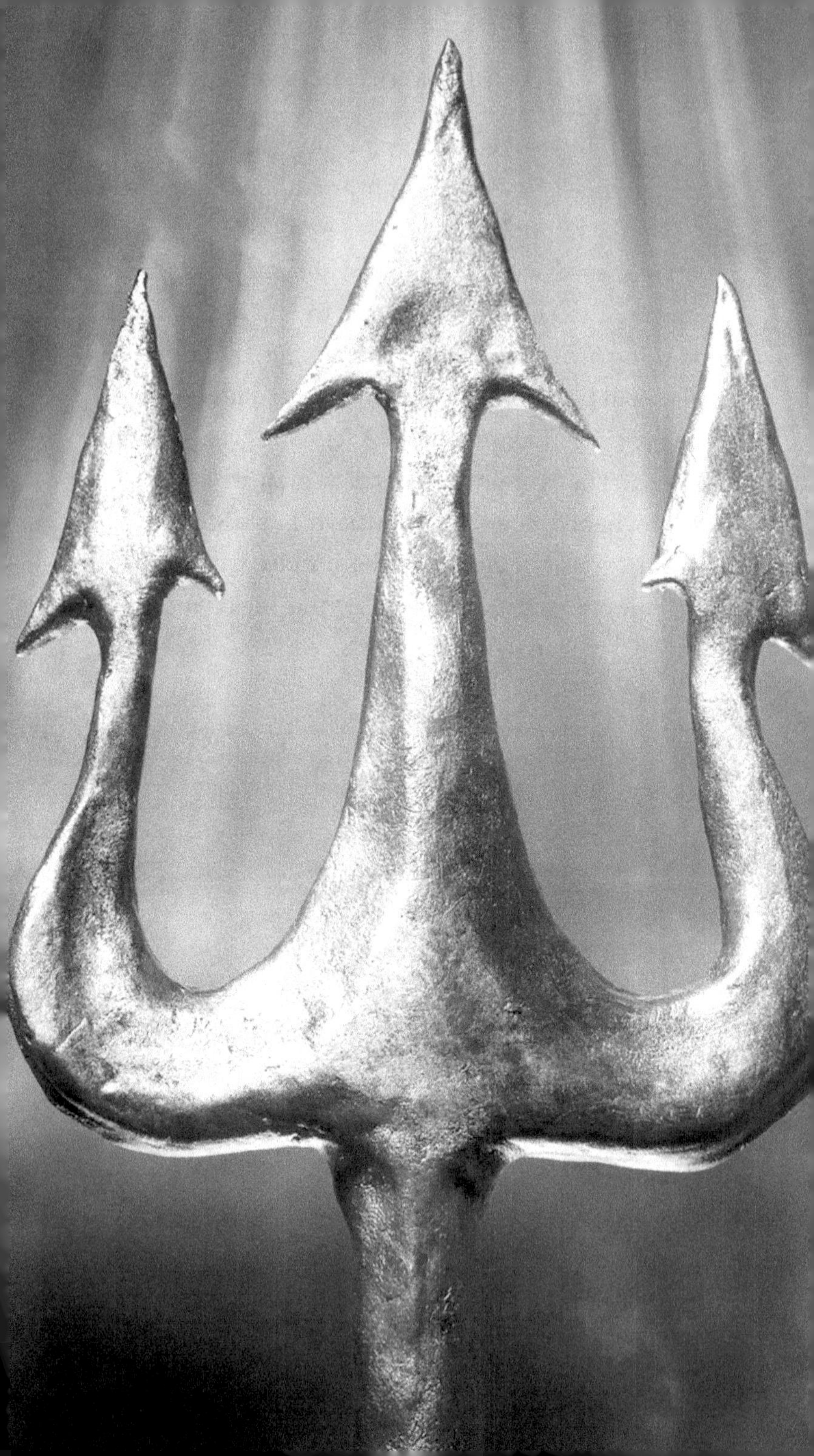

CHAPTER TWO

Seven years ago...

Laughing at something inane the ambassador from Bahrain had told the little group surrounding him, Carter tried to stay cool and not run off to find out what was taking Jordyn so long. She should have been back five minutes ago from the Iraqi ambassador's office in his embassy in Malaysia. The formal banquet had been the ideal opportunity to get into the man's safe and discover his contacts in the small Asian nation. ISIS had been spreading its radical wings into every country around the world, and some crooked politicians in those countries valued money and power more than their own people. But once Deimos had the names on the terrorist pipeline running through Malaysia, they'd be able to trace them back to those on the US military's most wanted list in Iraq and their current hiding places.

Carter had finagled an invite with his "date," Jordyn, through his fictitious import/export business with an office in Malaysia. In truth, Deimos owned and operated it as a cover for him and two other agents on the "Board of Trustees." Here, he was known as Carter Burke—a wealthy businessman—who didn't mind greasing some palms to get what he wanted.

Glancing around the ballroom, Carter feigned another sip of his champagne. While there were many attendees dressed in tuxedos like he was, others had donned the traditional formal dress of their nations. It was an eclectic mix of well over two hundred people, but the undercover embassy guards were easy for him to spot. All he had to do was look for a wire emerging from someone's ear or for them to talk into their wrists. They didn't have the sharpest tools in the shed running security in the embassy.

Another minute ticked by. *Damn it, Jordy. Don't make me come looking for you.* He was just about to do that when a vision in sparkling red fabric walked back into the ballroom. Carter inwardly sighed in relief.

Spotting him, Jordyn sashayed across the room as many pairs of lustful male eyes followed her seductive body. Her hair was pulled into some fancy updo, framing her beautiful face. The rest of her was poured into the floor-length sheath that accentuated every feminine curve. How she walked like a runway model in those five-inch heels was beyond him, but she made it seem effortless.

Upon reaching him, she laid a hand on his forearm. "Carter, darling, I'm not feeling very well. Would you mind terribly if we went back to the hotel?"

Before he could respond, the Bahrain ambassador spoke, using the last name Jordyn had taken as a cover for this operation. "I'm sorry to hear that, Ms. Dominguez. I'd be happy to send my doctor to your hotel to examine you."

The look on the man's face said he would be more than happy to watch the examination too. Taking Jordyn by the arm, Carter smiled at the man. "Thank you, Mr. Ambassador, but I don't think that's necessary. Jordyn has been fighting jet lag for the past two days. She's not used to traveling as much as I am."

Nodding, she agreed. "Yes, I'm sure that's all it is. Thank you very much for your kind offer, though."

The man gave them a respectful bow, but the lust in his eyes as he practically drooled over Jordyn was unmistakable. "Very well then. I look forward to meeting you again. Maybe you and Mr. Burke can join me for dinner the next time you are in Malaysia."

"That would be very nice. Thank you. Carter and I would love to."

After saying their goodnights to the others in the small group who'd been watching the exchange,

Carter led his "date" toward the embassy lobby. Valets waited outside the main entrance, and Carter handed one of them his claim stub. The young, uniformed man ran off to retrieve the vehicle.

"Did you have a fun time, love?" he asked Jordyn, keeping up their cover with his arm around her waist.

She looked up at him and grinned. "Absolutely, but it's definitely time to leave."

In other words, she had what they'd come for. *Excellent.* It was almost a shame their night ended so early, though, because he would love to spend more time with her in that incredible dress or, even better, with her out of it. The plunging neckline had given him, and everyone else, a generous view while the straps holding it up curved over her exposed shoulders.

Unable to stop himself, he raised his hand and cupped her chin. A flash of surprise in her eyes morphed into something different—something more. Lowering his head, he was about to kiss her when his cover's white Lamborghini pulled up with a roar. Carter froze, his mouth inches away from Jordyn's, his blue eyes fixed on her brown ones.

"This is going to happen tonight, isn't it?" she whispered. Sexual awareness, want, and need seemed to have taken over her facial features, and he was sure those same things were mirrored in his own expression. They'd been dancing around each other for a while now, and it was time they did something more than just a few steps, twirls, and dips.

"It's been coming for a long time, love. I was just waiting for you to give me the green light."

"How fast can you get us back to the hotel, Tyrell?" she purred as prettily as the 500 horses under the Lamborghini's hood did.

"In this thing? In a heartbeat. And no, it's not Tyrell." One of these days, she might say his real name, but she hadn't yet. Until she did, he was still unsure if he would admit it because he really hated it.

He stood straight despite wanting to kiss her senselessly. They needed to get out of the embassy compound before letting their hormones loose. A valet held the passenger door open for Jordyn while the one who'd retrieved the sports car stood at the driver's door waiting for Carter. After helping her into the low vehicle, he jogged around the back and handed the valet a tip in local currency. Within seconds, they were roaring through the gates and taking a left onto the city streets of Kuala Lumpur.

The slit of Jordyn's dress stopped just above her knee, and after shifting gears, Carter reached over and placed his hand on the exposed skin, pushing the fabric up another inch or two. Beneath his hand, he felt a shiver pass through her body, and he cursed when a car pulled out ahead of him, requiring him to remove his hand to downshift. He was as hard as the lever in his hand, and while the $300,000 vehicle was fun as hell to drive, the positioning of the driver's seat didn't give him much room for his throbbing cock. He repositioned his hips, trying to get comfortable, but comfort went out the window when Jordyn put her hand on his thigh and squeezed.

"Payback," she said with an unexpected giggle and another squeeze.

Damn! That woman turned him on more than any other had in a very long time. And that was saying a lot because, being in the BDSM lifestyle, he'd had more than his fair share of women from around the world who enjoyed the same kinks he did.

As he took a left onto the street their hotel was on, something caught his eye—or rather, someone. A man stood on the corner, seemingly with nothing better to do than watch the cars go by. Eyeing the white sports car, the guy lifted his hand and spoke something into his wrist.

Fuck!

Instead of continuing down the street, Carter took the first side street and sped up, needing to put as much distance between them and whoever the lookout had contacted. Jordyn's gaze shifted to him in confusion. "Problem?"

"Yup," he answered, keeping an eye on the road ahead and the rear and side view mirrors. "Hope there wasn't anything back at the hotel you wanted."

She glanced over her shoulder out the tinted back window, searching for a tail. "Damn. I really liked those black Louboutin heels I wore yesterday. Where was he or she?"

"On the corner, trying to look like he was waiting for a cab."

He downshifted and took another right, the car hugging the road like a dream. A black Mercedes was coming fast from the other direction. When Carter passed it, the driver slammed on the brakes and did a 180 in the middle of the street. The wheels spun for purchase, filling the air with smoke before they caught, sending the vehicle roaring down the street after them. "We've got company, love. Hang on."

Shifting again, Carter sped up, leading the chase through the city. He needed to lose this asshole and get to where he could let the horses run. On a highway, he could easily leave the Mercedes in the dust without worrying about pedestrians and other vehicles.

He glanced at Jordyn. Instead of looking scared or worried, the damn woman had a grin on her face. Like him, she lived for this shit. In her hand was the compact assault rifle from a specially-made cubbyhole hidden behind the glove compartment. While he knew there was also a small, concealed gun strapped to her inner thigh, this had more firepower.

Checking the rearview mirror, he noticed another vehicle fall in behind the Mercedes—a black BMW. "This party's getting bigger, babe. I say we blow this taco stand."

Taking another hard left, he sped up, heading for

the on-ramp for what passed as a highway in this country. They had about five more city blocks to go. At least, when they got there, he could open up the Lamborghini and let it do what it was designed to do —fly.

A tractor-trailer pulled out in front of them across the road and stopped in the cross traffic, blocking the intersection. With nowhere to go, Carter settled for the only option they had. "Um, duck."

Three things could happen. One—they'd be decapitated. Yeah, not a good thing. Two—they'd sheer the top off and ruin a sweet ride—a slightly better option. Okay, definitely a better option. Or three —they'd glide under the trailer with a hair to spare and lose their tails.

Taking a deep breath, they both ducked their heads, and thank God, number three was the winner. Tires squealed behind them, followed by a crash. *Sweet! Take that, you fucking cockblockers!*

Picking her head up, Jordyn began laughing. "I freaking love these James Bond moments! Breaks up the monotony. Nice driving, Double-O."

He couldn't help the grin that spread across his face. If someone had told him twenty years ago he'd be mimicking his movie idol, he would've thought they were crazy. But here he was, T. Carter, US spy and assassin, driving a car most people could only dream of, with an incredibly hot woman dressed in an evening gown while holding an assault rifle, running from people trying to kill them. He wished he could knock on a few doors from his youth at times like these. He would love to shove his life in the faces of those who'd either tried to bully him or told him he would never amount to anything. Too bad that wasn't an option, but damn, it would be so satisfying.

Their victory was short-lived as they picked up two more tails at the next intersection. Fuck, they were trying to box them in.

How many more assholes are out there?

One vehicle was another Mercedes—tan instead of black—and the other was a red Lamborghini. That was the one that was going to be trouble. Carter hit the on-ramp and floored the accelerator. Within seconds, they were cruising at 130 mph. Thankfully, at this time of night, traffic was very light. While the Mercedes fell a little behind, the Lambo gained ground as Carter dodged the few vehicles on the road.

Bullets struck the back of the car, shattering the rear window and causing him to push harder on the accelerator. Without hesitation, Jordyn rolled down her window and rotated in her seat, hiking up her dress in the process. And fuck him! Between the adrenaline, and the sexy-as-fuck woman's ass in his face, toned calves, and those "fuck me" heels, his cock twitched, making him groan.

A car changed lanes in front of him, and he swerved to avoid it, berating himself for getting distracted at 140 mph.

Get out of this mess, then get hot and horny, asshole.

But, damn, her ass looked delectable in the snug, red material, and his hand itched to reach out and give it a squeeze... or a nice, swift spank.

Gunfire from Jordyn's weapon sent his brain back into fight or flight mode. The driver of the other Lambo slammed on the brakes and then the accelerator again. Carter avoided another car and cursed when he saw what they were headed for. Brake lights appeared in the distance as traffic was backing up. *Fucking A!* The "let's fuck with Carter and prevent him from getting laid tonight" gods were out in full force.

"Gotta slow down a bit, Jordy. Can you get rid of the Lambo before the other assholes catch up?"

Instead of answering him, she released another volley of bullets, nailing the other sports car's front tire, which blew then shredded, sending the other expensive sports car into a violent spin. The driver lost control, careened off the highway, and rolled over several times.

One down, one more asshole to go.

Slowing down, Carter swerved left onto the shoulder of the highway, passing the backed-up traffic. Unfortunately, it allowed the Mercedes to catch up to them. Jordyn shifted in her seat, and now he had a great view of her cleavage as she aimed her gun out the missing back window. Hot lead spit out at Carter, and he ducked the flying cartridges as Jordyn eradicated the other vehicle's windshield, along with the driver and passenger. Just like the Lambo, the Mercedes flipped over several times onto the dirt median.

Flopping back into her seat, Jordyn gave him a sexy grin. Her dark eyes were filled with a combination of excitement, satisfaction, and lust. "I don't know about you, Double-O, but I'm horny as hell after that."

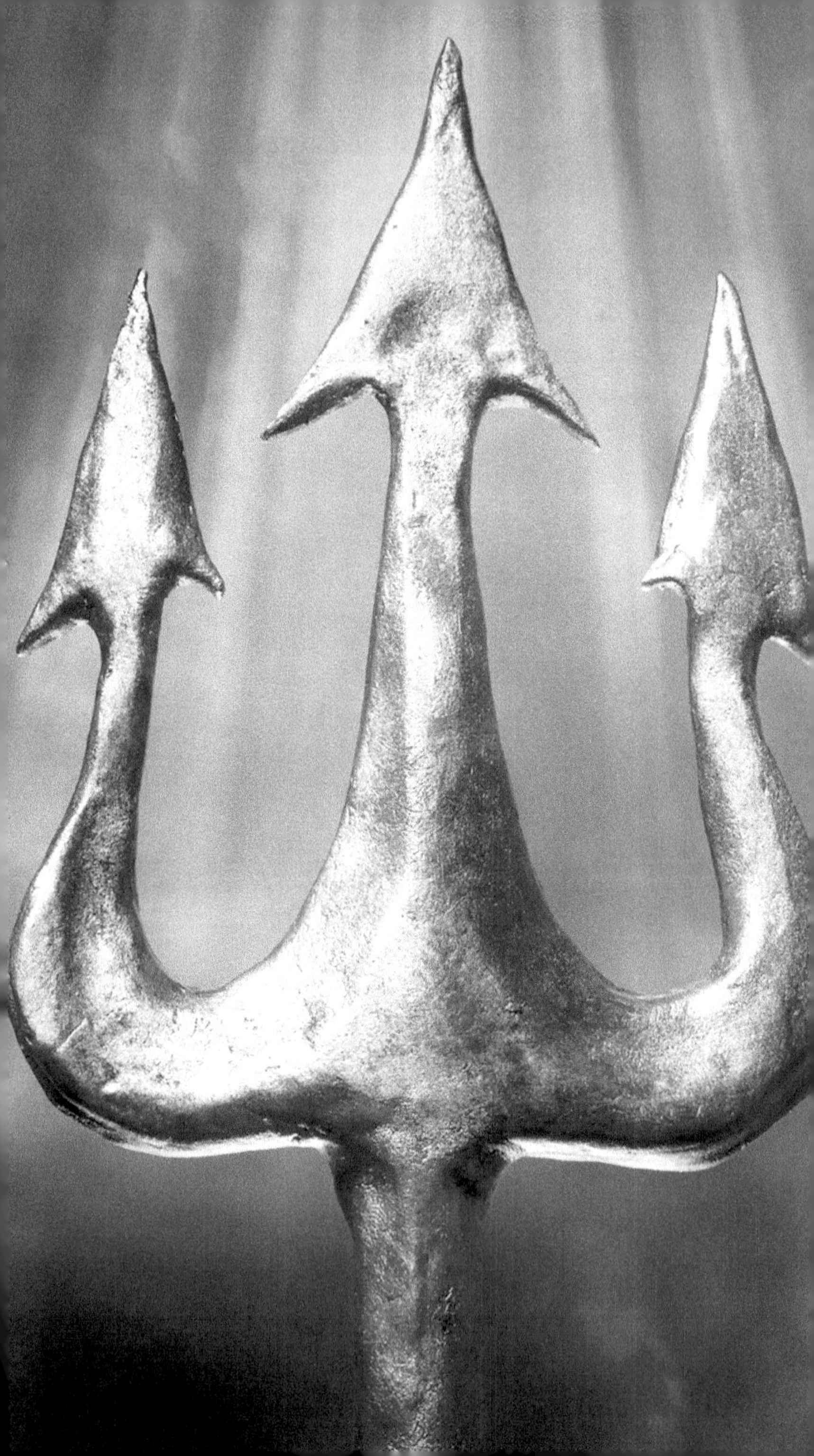

CHAPTER THREE

Present...

Ian pulled into the small airport for private jets and parked their SUV. The one following on their six for most of the trip stopped in the slot next to them. The area was quiet, and no one else was around. Bodies poured out from almost every door of the two vehicles, with the drivers leaving the keys under the floor mats for their contacts to recover. Devon "Devil Dog" Sawyer, Ian's younger brother and teammate, led the rest of the party toward the waiting Trident Security jet. Their pilot, Conrad "CC" Chapman, had already started the engines after being alerted to their impending arrival. A copilot, who Ian had borrowed from his friend and associate at Blackhawk Security for the transatlantic flight, lowered the jet's stairs for them.

"Where the fuck are we going, Carter?" Jordyn barked at him, trying to dislodge herself from his grip on her arm. No way was he letting go. The woman was faster than a jackrabbit, and he didn't feel like chasing her across the tarmac. They needed to get in the air as soon as possible before another hit squad tracked them down.

"On a vacation, sweetheart. Somewhere we can be alone." He winked at her and laughed when she glared back.

At the bottom of the stairs, she yanked hard on her arm, pulling him to the side. His backup let out a few chuckles as they kept their momentum up the steps. Jordyn was about to blast into him when the squeal of tires, barely audible over the whine of the jet engines, caught their attention. Looking back at the gate they'd driven through, they saw two black SUVs barreling toward it. *Fuck!*

Carter whipped around to throw Jordyn up the stairs to find she was already climbing them. Not wasting a moment to admire her fine ass, he flew up the stairs two at a time. When he'd reached the cabin, he and Ian grasped the handles for the stairs and pulled them up as CC started them rolling toward the runway.

Just as the cabin door shut, Carter saw the vehicles come to a screaming halt, and four guys with assault rifles climbed out. He shifted his view to the cabin window as Ian locked the door. The men raised their weapons, but an explosion rocked their world before they got a shot off.

"Yeeee-ha and hooyah!"

Carter laughed at the man cheering while staring out the window beside him. Boomer was Trident's explosives and ordinances expert, and in his hand was the remote that had sent the SUVs Ian and Devon had parked a few minutes ago up in a blaze of glory. "I fucking love blowing shit up!"

While the four men who'd been ready to pump the jet full of lead had been out of the direct blast zone, they'd still gotten thrown to the ground and had their bells rung from the concussion wave. Two of them were down for the count while the other two were rolling around, probably trying to figure out what the hell had just happened. Flaming pieces of metal and fiberglass landed in the parking lot and on the tarmac surrounding the men.

"Goddamn it!" Ian roared. "Now I have to pay for the fucking trucks! And I'm sure the price is going to be ten times what they're fucking worth over here."

Carter snorted at the head of Trident Security as the man dropped into one of the luxury, first-class-style seats at the front of the plane. "Oh, like those trust funds you and Devil Dog have couldn't buy a thousand of them every month for the next five years."

"That's not the fucking point, jackass.

Ignoring the other man's brooding, Carter pointed, one by one, at the men taking seats, preparing for takeoff. "Jordyn, this is Ian Sawyer, his brother Devon. You already met Tristan McCabe. Pretty boy over there is Val Mancini, and this here is Baby Boomer."

The latter rolled his eyes as he clicked his seatbelt shut. "Ben Michaelson and just Boomer is fine. It's nice to meet you, Jordyn."

"A pleasure." Her sarcasm wasn't lost on anyone as she disregarded them and stepped toward the middle of the plane, where there was a relaxed living room setup of couches and recliners. The Trident boys liked to ride in style when they could—it beat cargo planes any day of the week.

Carter followed her and sat in one of the recliners as she took another one after dropping her duffel bag on a couch and fastening a seatbelt through its handles. He'd barely clicked his seatbelt when the pilots started speeding down the runway. Evidently, the $500 in US currency Ian had given CC to pass onto the air traffic controllers to clear their takeoff trumped a measly explosion in the parking lot, which had probably been heard for a few miles. Boomer's unofficial motto was "Go big or go home." In this case, they'd gotten to do both, which was always good.

When the aircraft reached whatever altitude it leveled off at, Carter released his seatbelt, stood, and strolled to the back. He took two bottles of water from a stocked refrigerator and returned to the seating area, holding one out to her. It didn't escape his notice that the chickenshits were staying in the rows of seats up front. Clearly, he was on his own here to face her wrath. And, yes, she looked downright pissed.

Instead of taking the water from him, Jordyn stood and crossed her arms. Her eyes narrowed. "All right. We got away from the goon squads. Now, are you going to tell me what the hell is going on?"

He took in her exotic features. Born and raised in South America to a distinguished businessman and a former Miss Argentina, the thirty-one-year-old had inherited her mother's natural beauty. Her long, black hair was pulled into a messy but cute ponytail, and her olive skin complimented her soft brown eyes. Her body was exquisitely toned due to her constant training, yet she had curves in all the right places. And what he wouldn't give for another chance to explore each and every one.

Tossing the water on the couch next to her bag, he stepped toward her until there was only a matter of inches between them. As he'd expected, she stood her ground, but a flash of anger appeared in her eyes while her body rebelled against her mind. Her nipples pebbled beneath her shirt, and her carotid pulse increased in tempo at her neck. Lifting his hand, he stroked her cheek with his fingers and lowered his voice. "Are you going to tell me whatever I did so many years ago that has you hating me?"

To his surprise, her expression softened, and her

hands went to his chest. Electricity shot from her fingers through his T-shirt, lighting up the nerves just under his skin. "I don't hate you—"

He almost didn't see it coming. As it was, her knee caught him on the side of his groin instead of a direct hit. He'd shifted just in time but not fast enough to avoid a tremendous amount of pain. His breath fled his lungs, and he saw stars as he coughed and gasped for air. Bending at the waist, his hands on his knees, he tried to will the agony away.

Damn, that hurt! She not only hates me, she wants to make sure I never reproduce!

Standing over him, she growled. "As I was saying, I don't hate you. That's not a strong enough word. Try *abhor* or *detest* or *loathe*, you asshole."

A snort came from Ian when he approached them from the front seats. As he skirted around a temporarily disabled Carter, he said, "Don't mind me. Feel free to continue kicking his ass, Jordyn. I'm sure he deserves it."

Glancing up, Carter saw her smile pleasantly after the man. "I'm starting to like you, asswipe."

Without turning around, Ian waved to her over his shoulder on his way to the jet's head. "The feeling is mutual, sweetheart."

Carter hoped the bastard fell into the fucking toilet and got stuck. Taking a deep breath, he slid his hands to his thighs, then pushed himself up into a standing position and shifted his hips to give his aching cock and balls some room in his cargo pants. Moving slowly, he made it to a recliner, but lowering himself into it was torture—another reminder of why he would never submit to a sadistic Domme. He'd never understand why masochistic men would agree to have their junk tormented.

Gritting his teeth, he looked up at the woman who turned him on like no other, even though she wanted to castrate him for some reason. She calmly took a long drink from one of the water bottles as Ian returned from the back and, without saying a word, tossed him a bag of ice for his troubles.

Fucking gloating bastard.

When Carter was as alone as he was going to get with Jordyn again, he rasped, "Feel better?"

She plopped down on a nearby couch, crossed her shapely legs, and shrugged. "A little. Now, tell me what the fuck is going on. How was my cover blown?"

He placed the ice pack where it was needed and pushed back on the recliner so his family jewels had breathing room. He obviously wasn't going to get an answer to his earlier question and didn't dare repeat it at the moment—he was in enough pain. For now, he'd stick with the current problem. "Not just your cover— a hacker downloaded part of Deimos's NOC list before they could shut it down. As far as we know, a dozen agents were compromised. The first two targeted, Joe Aikman and Glenn Aldridge, didn't survive."

He grimaced, partially from the pain, partially

from the bomb he was dropping in her lap. The nonofficial cover list was something every covert agency had —information on their agents' true identities, which was an espionage nightmare. Deimos's was being used as an assassination list, which was ironic since some of the people on it were assassins for the United States. "And I'll give you one guess who's next on the alphabetical list."

"Alvarez," Jordyn said, a mixture of anger and obvious dread on her pretty face. "Me. Shit."

She took a deep, calming breath before standing and walking toward the front of the plane as Carter watched in confusion. Over the jet engines, he heard her clear her throat to get the attention of the five other men. "Gentlemen, thank you for coming to extract me. I appreciate it. Why don't you come on back so you can fill in all the blanks, *hmm*? I promise the only one who has to worry about an ass-kicking already got his. Well, actually, it wasn't exactly his ass that got kicked."

Boomer was the first to stand, grinning wildly. "I can't wait for the Trident women back home to meet you. Damn, woman. If I weren't already madly in love with my fiancée, I'd beg you to marry me."

And that had Carter wanting to plant his fist in the EOD specialist's face—which was weird, since he'd been a third in a few past scenes with Boomer and his fiancée, Kat Maier. But once he'd had his one night of incredible sex with Jordyn, the thought of her in any other man's bed had him seeing crimson. It didn't matter that it had been years ago and miles away from there. It also didn't matter that the man he currently wanted to hit was one of his best friends—in Carter's line of work, those were few and hard to come by.

The sexy-as-hell woman smirked as she sashayed her way back to the couch. "And if you weren't already madly in love with your fiancée, I might be taking you up on that offer, stud. I like a man who blows things up in spectacular fashion."

The others scattered around the casual seating area, settling in for the trip, except Ian, who retrieved a bottle of Jack Daniel's Single Barrel Select, lowball glasses, and ice. The fucking jet had everything, including a damn ice maker—which Carter's balls were grateful for.

Jordyn turned to Ian as he began to pour everyone a drink. "I heard your boys took care of that girl's perverted sperm donor last year. They saved me the trouble of returning to Tampa to do it myself. How's your brother doing? And the girl?"

The youngest Sawyer brother, Nick, had been shot while rescuing a teenager from the hands of her father, who'd been molesting her for years. He'd been backing up Ian's teammate, employee, and Nick's current boyfriend/Dom, Jake "Reverend" Donovan, on the case while on R&R from SEAL Team Three about a year ago. Jordyn had gotten involved in the action when Carter had asked her to use her cat burglary skills to break into the father's house and office safe to recover the vile pictures and videos he had of his daughter. In the end, the bastard had been killed.

"Nick's completely recovered and back on full duty with his team," Ian informed her as he handed her a glass of amber liquor and passed the others to the men. Their flight would be over six hours long, so a glass or two wouldn't be an issue for any of them. "He's got another six months in San Diego before he's going to retire from the Navy and come work with us. By that point, the West Coast team will be up and running, and Jake will hand over the reins to whomever we promote to team leader. They both want to come back to Florida. As for Alyssa, Boomer's parents were granted guardianship, and she started her first semester at the community college in Sarasota. She's going to be just fine."

"Glad to hear they're both doing well. Now, tell me about the hit squads and anything else you know about what's going on. Start with where we're going," she said to no one in particular.

"Scotland."

Her jaw dropped at Carter's response. "Scotland? What the fuck is in Scotland?"

"Castle Steel and a friend of mine." The corners of his mouth ticked upward. He knew that hadn't quenched her curiosity. If the expression on her face was any indication, his answer had conjured up at least half a dozen more questions, but she wouldn't give him the satisfaction of asking them. *Good.* He couldn't wait for her to meet Mic.

Before continuing, he took a much-needed taste of the whiskey Ian had given him. "About the hit squad. We had no idea if they'd tracked you down or not, but I wasn't taking any chances. The other two were both stateside when they were hit. Aikman took a sniper bullet to the head while sitting in his living room the other morning, and Aldridge had a car bomb waiting for him yesterday afternoon. Everyone else on the list has been pulled in already, except for Benito, Brennan, and Dartmouth. They have teams tracking them down on their assignments."

It wasn't uncommon for the operatives of Deimos to limit contact during a mission, even though their headquarters knew the bare basics. The less contact during an op, the less chance of their cover being blown. In this case, though, it had the opposite effect. Going black had almost gotten her killed. But now that she was under his watchful eye, he was going to make damn sure nothing happened to her. And after the threat against her was eliminated, he would find out, once and for all, why she had such a bug up her ass about him.

"Lady and gents, prepare for landing."

The pilot's announcement and the feeling of the plane dropping in altitude had Jordyn stirring from her sleep. After getting as many details about the leaked NOC list as the men had, she made herself comfortable on one of the plush couches since the recliners had all been taken. It hadn't taken her long to doze off between the combination of adrenaline crash and two glasses of whiskey. Usually, one was her limit, but Carter's announcement, on top of his constant heated gaze, despite his aching balls, had caused her to nod her assent when Ian offered her another glass.

Around her, the men all stirred or returned to their seats, and seatbelts clicking closed filled the small cabin. She glanced from one man to the next. They were all good-looking—what the hell was in the water in Tampa? Whatever it was, the women in that city were damn lucky if the rest of the male population looked anything like these hunks.

Even without meeting the two older Sawyer brothers before today, she could tell they were siblings. They had similar facial features, topped off with black hair that offset their matching blue eyes—their brother Nick had inherited the same family genes. While they were considered dark Irish, Tristan McCabe was a stereotypical Irishman—rusty blond hair with soft green eyes and a smattering of freckles over his nose. With broad shoulders, strong arms, and a chiseled torso, he was probably a big ol' teddy bear when he wasn't kicking ass. She wondered if he looked younger without his goatee and mustache—her guess was he had a baby face without them despite his mid-thirties age.

Boomer was a brown-haired cutie between his appearance and bubbly personality. His fiancée was a lucky woman, and Jordyn bet the man treated her like a queen. The last of the Trident men aboard the jet was Val Mancini. He had Hollywood pretty-boy looks similar to Jake Donovan—tall, dark, and panty-dropping handsome. Either one of them could be a movie star headliner with women swooning over them left and right. Since Jake was gay and in a permanent relationship, it wouldn't matter to him. Mancini, however, probably had a girlfriend in cities worldwide and many more women lined up to be among his harem.

Sitting up, Jordyn stretched her arms over her head before putting her own seatbelt on again. Glancing out the window, she saw dark clouds and raindrops battering the aircraft. The jet jolted and dipped as it hit a pocket of turbulence, but the pilot swiftly got it under control again. They descended and dropped below the clouds as the landing gear ground into position.

Her skin tingled, and without looking, she knew Carter was staring at her. What was it about the bastard that made her body so aware of him and crave to be in his bed again? Thankfully, her mind had more common sense than her body. Too bad she hadn't known what he was into before she'd let him fuck her brains out that night. He wanted to abuse women? Well, she refused to be one of them. Her mother had tolerated it, and look where that got her—six feet under, alongside the bastard who'd shot her and then himself—Jordyn's father.

Jordyn had been fourteen years old when her privileged life was thrown into shock and turmoil. Her father, a respected businessman in Buenos Aires, had abused his wife, a former Miss Argentina and a first runner-up Miss Universe, for most of their marriage. He'd been a jealous bastard. Jordyn would never know why her mother stayed with him, but she had. Regina Alvarez Huerta had become an expert in covering up bruises with makeup. Jordyn would be damned if she followed in her mother's shoes.

The jet bounced once before settling on the runway, and it jarred Jordyn from her memories of long ago. The pilot steered them across the tarmac into a hangar, and someone closed the huge doors behind them. Everyone stood and gathered their duffel bags and gear aside from Devon and Boomer. She raised an eyebrow at Devon.

"Boomer and I are heading home," he explained. "Ian, McCabe, and Romeo are sticking with you for now."

She nodded, realizing that "Romeo" must be Mancini—the moniker fit her earlier impression of him. Clearly, Carter and Trident had planned this out. She'd go along with the plan until she found out who was behind this mess. Once she knew who she had to kill for assassinating two good men, she'd return the favor, but not before she tortured the bastard. Then Carter would be out of her life again. Too bad he'd still pop up in her dreams without warning.

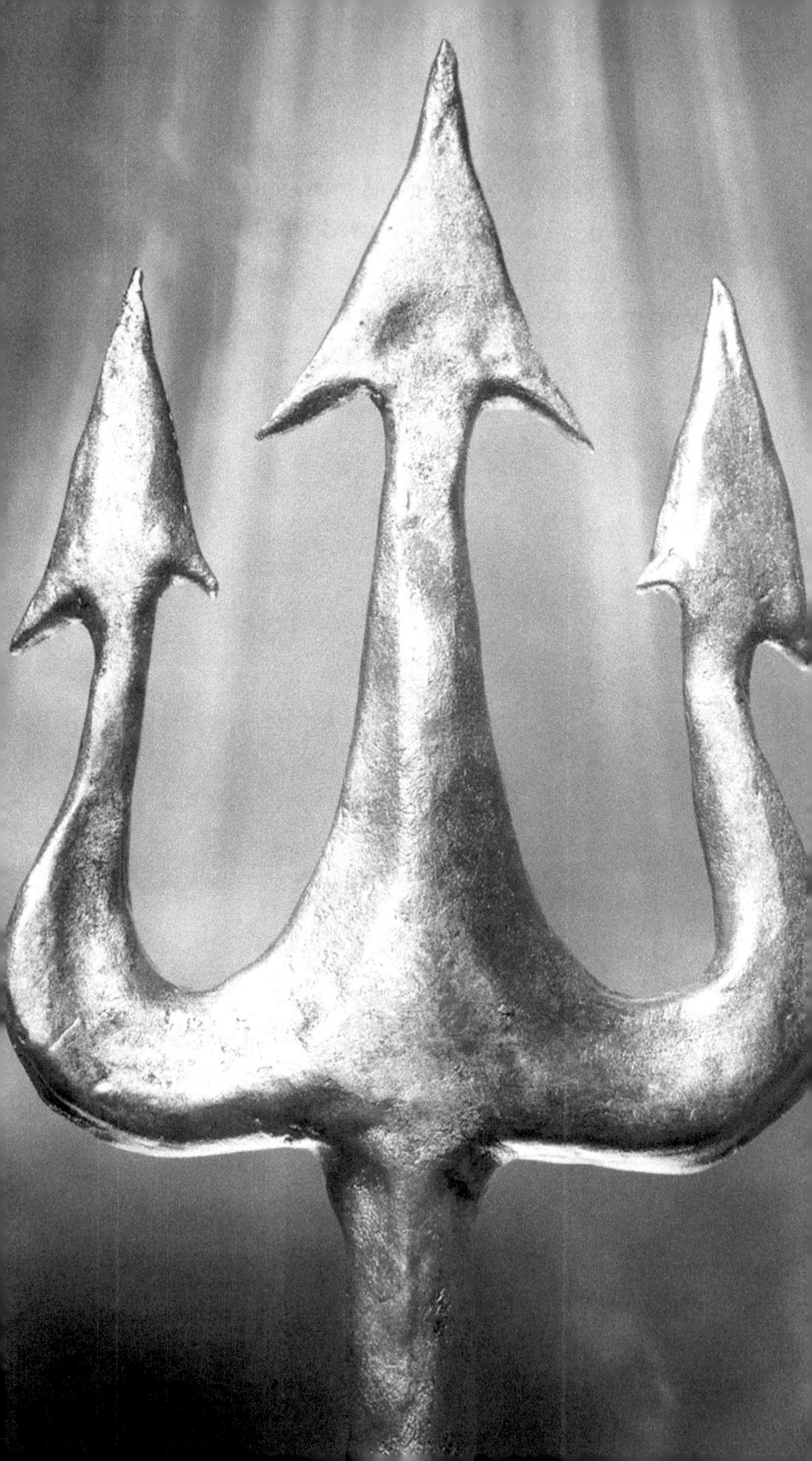

CHAPTER FOUR

Eight years ago...

Jordyn tapped on her thigh while waiting for Gene McDaniel to call her into his office. Her mind was still reeling over how she'd ended up sitting in a covert US agency's headquarters instead of a jail cell. She'd been caught red-handed stealing jewels from some rich bastard's safe during a huge party at his house in California. She hadn't been invited, yet had found a way to crash it undetected—or so she'd thought. Someone else had been targeting the same safe, but she was sure it was for a different reason.

The man who had interrupted her thievery had helped her escape when things went downhill fast after a rival of the arms dealer had also crashed the party and started shooting up the place. However, instead of letting her loose after there was no longer a threat, the man had kidnapped her—complete with handcuffs and a blindfold—and driven her to God knew where. In an underground parking lot, he'd handed her off to Gene McDaniel—head of Deimos, whatever that meant. McDaniel had interrogated her for hours, confirmed her information, and then given her two options—prison or come work for his agency. It'd been a no-brainer, so here she sat, still unsure exactly where that was.

The office level she was now on was much cheerier than where she'd spent the past two days and nights despite the armed guards standing in the hallway. While it hadn't been a jail cell, the room had no windows and only two doors, one of which opened into a bathroom. She'd been given clean clothes and whatever food and toiletries she'd asked for. A TV had been her only source of entertainment until one of the guards had brought her a couple of paperbacks and magazines. The only thing they wouldn't give her was an escape route.

She'd wanted to escape until McDaniel had come to see her last night after she'd eaten her dinner. He'd handed her the employment contract she was expected to sign. After reading through the entire thing twice, she'd agreed to become a spy for the United States, with an annual salary that had her counting the zeroes several times to ensure she wasn't imagining things. Her signature on the dotted line had ended her life of crime and started a new life, which was still a mystery to her.

The door to the office opened, and McDaniel gestured for her to enter his lair. Swallowing hard, she stood and walked into the room on wobbly legs. It was large enough for a desk, conference table, and a sitting area that could pass as a living room. Sitting in a wing-back chair was a man she hadn't seen before. He wasn't the agent who'd brought her here, nor was he one of the rotating guards she'd met. His elbows leaned on the chair's arms, and the fingers of one hand ran over his lips as he stared at her, giving no indication of his assessment. He appeared to be a few years older than her, but not by more than five or six. His long, dirty blond hair was pulled back into a ponytail, and his blue eyes were sharp, not missing a thing. A black T-shirt and snug, faded jeans did nothing to hide the well-defined physique underneath them. He was the hottest thing she'd seen in years, but it went beyond his looks—which she was sure had women panting over him all the time. It was his commanding presence. The air around him seemed to crackle with a combination of sexual energy and a deadly aura. She was sure he could kill someone with a flick of his wrist and not think twice about it.

His eyes narrowed, and she realized she'd stopped in the middle of the room and was staring at him. McDaniel had already sat in another wingback chair, leaving her to pick from one of the two loveseats in the sitting area. Neither of the men said a word as she sat down, and Jordyn fought the urge to squirm under their scrutiny. Her palms were sweating, but she didn't want to show her nervousness by wiping them on her jeans.

"My name is Carter, Ms. Alvarez," the younger man rumbled suddenly. The sexy timber of his voice shot through her and made her wonder what it would be like to have him talk to her like that while they were naked in bed. "I'll be training you over the next few months. Twelve hours a day, seven days a week. By the time I'm done and convinced you can do the job, you'll know how to defend yourself in any situation and how to kill someone in more than a dozen different ways, among other things. From what Mr. McDaniel says, you've already mastered the art of disguise, pickpocketing, and breaking and entering—all useful qualities. I'll still be testing those skills and adding to them. Any questions?"

Jordyn swallowed hard. She'd known a large part of the job included assassinations. Did she have it in her to kill someone and walk away? Her father hadn't had a problem killing her mother, but then again, maybe he had since he'd put a bullet in his brain shortly after murdering his wife.

"Is Carter your first name or last name?"

His eyebrows shot up. "That's the first question you have?" She nodded, and he barked out a laugh. "Well, then, I'll use the answer to that as an incentive for you to work your pretty little ass off. So, if you have no other questions, why don't I show you around? Your apartment in Los Angeles has already been packed up and delivered to the cabin you'll be staying in here." He ignored her dropped jaw and continued. "Your car's getting a tune-up and having some features added to it. I'll take you to the garage, and the mechanics can fill you in. Before we do all that, though, I'm getting kind of hungry. Let's grab some lunch and have a chat. I'm sure a few more questions will come to your mind by then."

A half-hour later, they sat at a table in the back of a little diner not far from the compound where she would spend the next few months training with the man across from her. On the ride there, she'd discovered they were still in California—albeit much further north than Los Angeles. The town of Bingham was about twenty minutes from the Deimos training headquarters, and Jordyn wondered if the small population of the tiny town knew they had a bunch of covert operatives driving around.

"Hi, Carter. Nice to see you again. Does this mean you'll be back in town for a while?"

Jordyn looked up to see a blonde waitress practically drooling over the man and totally ignoring her. Embroidery on her red shirt announced her name was Susan, and Jordyn was surprised the woman knew Carter's name. Didn't spies use aliases or something?

"Hi, Suzy-Q," he responded while grinning at the

woman, who blushed at the nickname. "Nice to see you too. I'll be working locally for a bit, so I'll stop in for your mom's great cooking whenever I can."

Jordyn snorted, which drew his attention. His eyes narrowed. "Problem, Jordy?"

"It's Jordyn," she corrected. "And there's no problem, but I thought this was going to be a working lunch."

He studied her for a moment before facing the blonde again. "My coworker is correct. We have some business to discuss. I'll have the turkey club with avocado, hold the mayo, and an iced tea. Jordy, what would you like?"

"Jordyn," she automatically said while gritting her teeth. The man was purposely pushing her buttons. "I'll have the same with the mayo, *Suzy-Q*."

Annoyance flared in the waitress's eyes at the nickname coming from her mouth, making Jordyn feel much better. *Score one for me.* She grabbed the menu from Carter's hand, added it to her own, and shoved them at the waitress. With a withering stare that didn't affect Jordyn at all, the blonde spun on her heel in a huff and stormed toward the kitchen.

The nervousness Jordyn had been experiencing earlier was fading fast as her confidence returned along with a heavy dose of aggravation. She'd been in quite a few jams and anxiety-filled moments in her illegal career as a jewel thief and had gotten out of every one of them basically unscathed. She would survive this jackass too. He wanted to push her buttons? She was more than happy to give it right back to him. "So, Double-O, tell me about yourself."

His eyebrows shot up. "Double-O?"

"Yeah, Double-O, as in James Bond. Don't we get a secret number or something like that, so we don't have to use our real names? What about a secret handshake?"

Carter shook his head and chuckled. "Oh, I'm definitely going to get back at McDaniel for sticking me with you."

Insulted, Jordyn frowned. "How did you get stuck with me? And how do we get you unstuck? If you don't want to train me, I'm sure someone else can."

He remained quiet for a moment when *Suzy-Q* returned with their drinks but never took his eyes off Jordyn. She fought the urge to squirm under his calculating stare for the second time in a little over an hour. When the waitress left again, Carter leaned forward, his arms crossed on the table. "I think I've changed my mind, Jordy. I don't want to get unstuck from you. I think training you will be the most fun I've had in over a year, and I'm looking forward to it."

"For the last time, it's Jordyn. And I'm glad to know one of us is looking forward to it," she snarked before sipping her tea. She grimaced at the taste. *Damn it. Didn't anyone put sugar in their iced tea in California?* She pulled two sugar packets from the little white caddy beside the salt, pepper, and ketchup. After adding them to her drink, she took another sip. *Not great, but better.*

Her gaze met Carter's. "Fine, you're training me. When do we start, and how long before it's over so I can get rid of you?"

When McDaniel had called him in to train someone, Carter hadn't expected this fiery woman who'd conjured up images of her under him in his bed since the moment she'd walked into his life. But for the next six months or so, he was her instructor, which meant she was hands-off. There would be a lot of cold showers in the near future for him. Thankfully, one of the private clubs he liked to frequent was less than an hour away. Whenever he got a chance, he'd be able to lose himself in a soft submissive for a few hours before returning to the training compound... and Jordy. Whether she liked the nickname or not, that was what he would be calling her from now on. Jordyn was too stiff for him. *Jordy* made her his... for now.

He studied her, just as he'd done in McDaniel's office. Five foot six, about 125-130, beautiful olive skin, long, black hair pulled up in a ponytail, and the softest brown eyes he'd ever seen, yet she was sassy and bratty, just the way he liked his women. He wondered what Ms. Alvarez would say if she knew about his sexual proclivities. Well, now was not the time to find out.

Glancing around, he made sure there was no one within earshot. "When do we start? First thing tomorrow morning, we're going for a five-mile run. Then, after breakfast, we'll see how you respond when someone attacks you. From there, I'll be able to figure out how much self-defense training you need. After lunch and a shower, not necessarily in that order, comes firearms training. By the time you're released out into the great big world again, you'll know how to operate, strip down, and reassemble every gun on the planet. And all of that is just for starters. Add in international geography, politics, customs, languages, military, infrastructure, economy, demographics, et cetera. How to eliminate a target and think on your feet if a situation changes. You'll be proficient at hand-to-hand combat, knives, and any other object that can be used as a weapon. You'll also know how to torture someone for information." He drew his bottom lip in between his teeth. "Hmm. Let's see, I'm sure I'm forgetting something in there, but those are the basics. Any questions?"

Her mouth gaped open. He could almost see the wheels spinning in her mind. "Holy shit. How long is this going to take? And is all that really necessary?"

Leaning forward, he stared at her with hard, deadly eyes. "Necessary? Yes. How long? You'll train until I think you're ready. It could be three months— it could be three years. But I'll be damned if I'm going to send you out before you're ready just to get yourself or another operative killed. So buckle up, Jordy, it's going be a bumpy ride." He smirked. "But I'll let you sit on my lap if you want to."

"Bastard," she muttered before straightening her back. "All right. So, when will you tell me if Carter is your first or last name?"

He shrugged his shoulders. "Since all you have to do is ask anyone else at Deimos, I'll tell you now. It's my last name, but I use it as my first when I'm undercover."

"So, what's your real first name?" she asked before taking another sip of her drink. Her lips wrapped around the straw. As she sucked the liquid into her mouth, his cock twitched again.

"T.—as in the letter of the alphabet." Only one person at Deimos knew what it stood for—Gene was the one who'd eradicated it from every public record at Carter's request.

Her eyes narrowed. "T.? What kind of name is that?"

"The kind you have when you hate the name you were given at birth."

"Hmm. Okay, now I'm definitely curious." A lazy smile spread across her face. "I'm going to have to do some research and find out what it is—track down your birth certificate or something."

A bark of laughter escaped him. "Oh, sweetheart,

that's never going to happen, so don't waste your time."

"Why not?"

"Because my given name was wiped clean from every database on earth when I came to work for Deimos, and there's nothing you can do to make me tell you. Let's just say I hated it growing up, and we'll leave it at that, okay?"

Jordyn shook her head and got a determined look in her eye, and damn if it didn't turn him on. Then she licked her lips, and he had to bite back a groan. Crossing her arms in front of her on the table, she leaned forward. "What if I guess it? Will you tell me if I get it right?"

He mimicked her last actions, then lowered his voice, adding a seductive lilt to it. "What will I get out of it if I do?"

A blush spread across her cheeks, but she didn't back down. Instead, she reached into the pocket of the sweatshirt she'd worn over her V-neck shirt and jeans and pulled out a black leather object, holding it up for him to see. "Maybe I'll promise to give you back your wallet. In the meantime, let's eat and get this show on the road."

Even though he was shocked, Carter couldn't help the grin he was now sporting, nor the hard-on. The woman was good at pickpocketing. He'd give her that. And now he couldn't wait to discover what else she was good at.

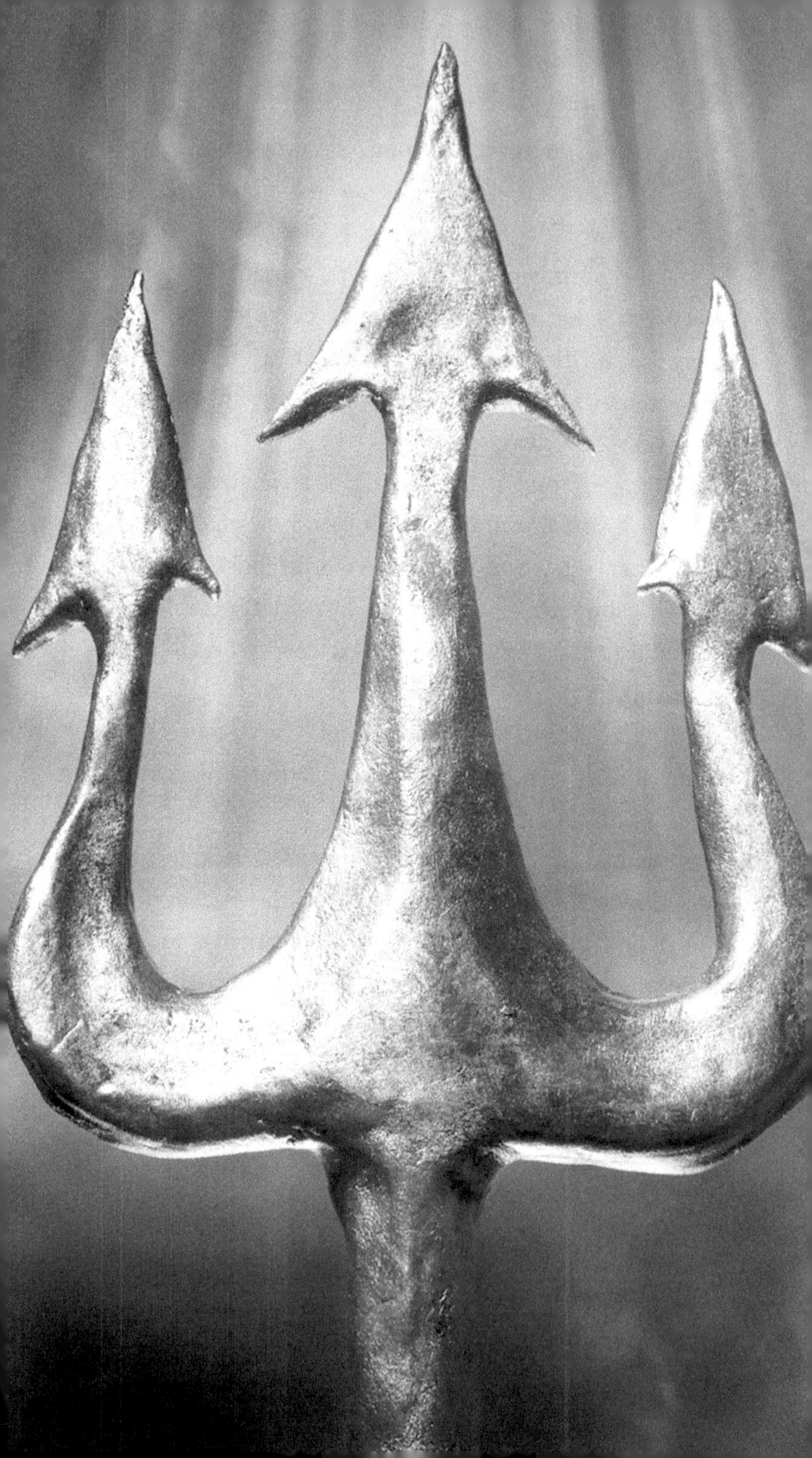

CHAPTER FIVE

Present...

Carter steered the SUV onto the long drive leading to the stone castle surrounded by Scotland's picturesque hills and valleys. Even though it was damp and overcast, at the beginning of November, the temperature was hovering around fifty-eight degrees—about ten degrees higher than average. The huge fortress was now home to Steel Corps, a covert team once sanctioned by the US government. Through minimal fault of their own, the members of the team were now branded as traitors and not allowed to step foot on American soil. While no international warrants were out for their arrest and extradition, thanks to the deal their former master sergeant, Fisher Jackson, had made with his superiors, the team was still persona non grata. But Carter and Ian knew better—they knew Mic better.

Army Staff Sergeant Bea "Mic" Michaels had been the team leader under Jackson. Carter and Ian had known her in Iraq, where she'd started in Army Intelligence before the spy had suggested to her superiors she would be an asset in terrorist interrogations. And he hadn't been wrong. After she proved herself there, in more ways than one, he'd passed her file onto Jackson when the man had been putting together his new black-ops team. Mic, Carter, Ian, and a few others had worked together in the early days of both Steel Corps and Trident Security to take down a large domestic terrorist organization. The New Order had been a bunch of neo-Nazis planning their own Oklahoma City-style bombing at several football stadiums in the US as well as in the UK, France, and Germany. Thankfully, the good guys had stopped it in time.

He parked next to several other vehicles in the circular drive and cut the engine. From the seat behind him, Jordyn gaped. "Um, when you said 'Castle Steel,' I didn't think you meant a real freaking castle. Holy crap, it's huge."

Carter chuckled, "It is that. Come on, I'm sure they already know we're here."

Opening his door, he climbed out and stretched while Ian, McCabe, Mancini, and Jordyn did the same. Despite her resistance, Carter was glad he'd grabbed

Jordyn a heavy jacket in one of the airport shops. While the rest of them had known they might be stopping in Scotland and had packed accordingly, she'd been dressed for much warmer weather.

"Don't you ever fucking call before you show up uninvited, asshole?" Chris Jordon asked as he emerged from the garden hedges on the castle's east side, his sidearm secure in its holster on his hip. The pissed-off glower he wore and the ugly tone of voice weren't unexpected. To say he wasn't a fan of the spy was a huge understatement.

Next to Carter, Jordyn crossed her arms and smirked. "See, I'm not the only one who thinks you're an asshole."

A loud snort came from Ian as he rounded the hood of the SUV. "It appears I'm starting to get outnumbered, but don't worry, Carter, you'll always be 'jackass' to me."

As Chris stopped a few feet away from the group, his glare not leaving the only person he knew among them, the large, ornate front door of the castle swung open, and Mic stepped out with a scowl that Carter knew she really didn't mean. "Carter, don't you ever call first before showing up out of the blue?"

"That's what your boyfriend just asked, sweetheart," he replied with a wide grin. "But you know me, surprising you is much more fun."

"And it'll also be too late for me to say no."

Damn, he loved Mic. Not as a lover, they had never

gone that far, but she would always occupy a large portion of his heart. Their relationship went far beyond friendship—it was more of a kinship.

Despite her words, the small but mighty blonde smiled as she hurried down the stairs and into his arms for a hug. As he held her a moment too long for her boyfriend's liking, the man snarled. "Enough, asshole. Get your hands off her."

Carter eased up and stepped to the side, keeping one arm around Mic's shoulders just to piss off Chris—and maybe to see if he could get a little jealousy out of Jordyn, too. "Bea Michaels, Chris Jordon, allow me to introduce you to Jordyn Alvarez—gotta love the Jordyn/Jordon thing we've got going on there. That'll drive everyone fucking nuts." He pointed to the two men standing beside the jeep, enjoying the show. "This here is Tristan McCabe and Val Mancini, two of Trident's new Omega Team. And Mic, you already know Ian Sawyer, of course."

"Of course." Ducking out from under Carter's arm, she hugged Ian. "Great to see you again, Sawyer. I hear there are more congratulations due back home. You Trident boys are dropping like flies down in Tampa, and I can't believe Dev and Marco are fathers now. Sorry I couldn't make it to your wedding."

"Completely understood. But we missed you." He held her tight against his chest in a brotherly embrace. Chris's jaw clenched further, but even he could see Ian's actions were harmless and sincere. "The team and I were sorry to hear about Phillips. He was a good man."

"He was," she murmured. "Thanks for the donation you made in his memory to the Veterans' Assistance Fund." Gary Phillips had been the second member of Steel Corps hired behind Mic and also a former Navy SEAL. He'd been violently murdered at the hand of a man who'd been bent on avenging the death of his drug lord father, who'd been killed during a Steel Corps mission. Like his father, the son had also been sent to Hell for his crimes.

"It was the least we could do." Ian pulled back a little to inspect her face. His hand cupped her jaw as his thumb brushed over the angry, jagged scar running down her cheekbone to the corner of her mouth—the result of a psychotic freak's knife months earlier. Mic had been lucky to get out with her life, and her assailant was lucky he was dead because there were plenty of people who wanted revenge for what he'd done to a woman they all admired. Ian's eyes hardened with rage as he studied it, which was good because Mic probably would have kneed him in the balls if his reaction had been sympathetic or anguished. His voice dropped to a near whisper. "It's a badge of courage, Mic. You never cease to amaze me."

Not answering him—it wasn't necessary nor expected—she blinked several times and swallowed hard as she pulled away. Pivoting, she shook hands with the other two men and then Jordyn while trying to swing the mood to something more pleasant. "Welcome to Castle Steel. Call me Mic. Come inside, and you can fill us in on why this dumbass dragged you to our humble abode."

"Jeez, anyone else want to throw insults at me?" Carter snarked. "Asshole, jackass, dumbass—everyone seems obsessed with my ass. And McCabe and Romeo, I suggest you don't put your two cents in. Not unless you plan on sleeping with one eye open for the next five years."

The two teammates grinned but wisely heeded his advice.

While Carter opened the rear end of the SUV so everyone could retrieve their bags, Chris shook hands with the rest of the men while giving the spy dirty looks. Heavy tension filled the air, almost all of it started with Carter. The last time he'd been at the castle, the two men had come to blows over Chris's jealousy—of course, the boy's buttons had been intentionally and repeatedly pushed up to that point. He was madly in love with Mic and far from thrilled with her close, longtime friendship with Carter.

Well, suck it up, buttercup.

While he really did enjoy busting Chris's chops, it was time to set the record straight and bury the hatchet with Mic's boyfriend.

Jordyn didn't know what to think about this place... about these people... about the woman who was leading her through a freaking castle of all places. Following Mic, she studied her. Five foot four, with short, blonde hair, the woman was in peak physical shape, just like Jordyn. Her muscles were long and lean, not bulked up like a gym rat. The only thing out of place was the lengthy, jagged scar on her cheek. Jordyn recognized a knife wound when she saw one, and she hoped whoever had done it was now six feet under. If not, she would gladly take them out for the woman opening her private lair to a stranger with a target on her back.

Mic stopped, and Jordyn realized they were in a large living room with plenty of couches and chairs, which didn't match the rest of the décor. They'd clearly been brought in by the new owners for their comfort and not for show. A roaring fire was ablaze in a stone hearth, and in the corner of the room was a suit of armor, more in tune with what should be in an old castle. It was kind of cool, and she would have left it there, too, if this had been her place.

Gesturing for everyone to take a seat, Mic said, "If you're hungry, I can have our cook, Maggie, reheat the stew from last night. It's awesome."

Ian answered for his group, "That sounds great, Mic. We all pretty much crashed after the first hour on the plane."

"Great." She nodded toward Chris. "Jordon, can you please let Maggie know?"

Yeah, Jordyn hated to admit Carter was right, but that Jordyn/Jordon thing was going to be a pain in the ass. She'd have to make sure it was her being addressed before answering.

As Chris nodded and left the room with a frown, two other men and one woman entered. Carter and Ian shook hands with the men but only greeted the woman with a smile. Jordyn could see why. The woman was as wide-eyed and wary as any forest animal when it heard a predator in its midst. Jordyn bet that she'd seen quite a few horrors in this world, and if she got any closer to the man who seemed to be her protector, she'd be under his skin.

Except for Carter, who'd already met them, Mic introduced the visitors to Ed Pierce, Matthew "Rook" Riley, and Roza—no last name given. The latter quietly nodded her head in a silent hello as the men shook hands with the newcomers.

"Where's the rest of the gang?" Carter asked as pretty much everyone settled into seats.

Rook sat on a loveseat with Roza by his side. He put a reassuring hand on her thigh. "Ran into town for supplies. What's going on?"

Striding to the bar, Pierce said, "Before you get into

it, we've got booze, beer, soda, and sweet tea. Anyone?"

After taking their orders, he prepared the drinks, but his ears were on the conversation.

"Part of Deimos's NOC list was compromised," Carter announced without preamble, and a stunned silence filled the air. Roza appeared to be the only one who had no idea how big a bomb that was.

With a bottle of scotch in one hand and an empty glass in the other, Pierce stepped closer to the group. "Come again? You've got to be shittin' us."

"I wish I was. Two operatives were killed, and we believe ten more are targeted. We yanked Jordyn out minutes before a hit squad arrived. As it was, we had to blow up a few things—"

"That I have to fucking pay for," Ian bitched.

"—and there was a lot of wasted ammo."

Mic shook her head. "I assume you mean it was wasted by the hit squad, so definitely not pros. Who the hell hacks a covert agency's NOC list and then sends a bunch of lackeys to do the job?"

Shrugging, Carter took the now half-filled glass Pierce handed him. "Got me, but Aikman and Aldridge were definitely hit by pros—one by a sniper, the other by a car bomb. I'm sorry to crash in on you like this, but there was little time to plan. Devon and Boomer headed back to the States in Trident's jet as a ruse in case anyone discovered the tail number back in

Nigeria. We'll be flying out to D.C. late tomorrow afternoon."

"What's in D.C.?" Rook asked.

Carter took a swig of scotch. "Hopefully, a clue or two about who wants Jordyn and me dead."

Jordyn's head whipped toward his, and he met her startled gaze. She'd been so wrapped up in the roller coaster ride that made up the past ten hours, from the moment she'd taken out her target, that she hadn't run the list of other operatives through her head. Carter was number eight on the alphabetical list. *Shit.* They were going to have to work this together—strength in numbers. Two heads were better than one. And all that other clichéd crap. *Damn it.*

"Do you mind setting up a secure line to Trident before we eat?" Ian asked Pierce as he accepted a bottle of beer. "We need to check on a few things."

The man nodded. "Sure thing. Give me five minutes. Do you want Evans or the new twerp? I've met some big geeks in my time, but that fucking kid must eat, sleep, breathe, and shit coding. I've only talked to him a few times on the phone and have this vision of a skinny runt with glasses held together by tape, wearing a button-down shirt with a pocket protector. Am I close?"

Ian's rumbling laugh filled the room, and Jordyn liked him more as time passed. If she had an older brother, she imagined he'd be just like the head of Trident—funny but with a take-no-prisoners attitude and fiercely protective of his friends and family. "Pretty close. Nathan's definitely a geek of the highest degree, but he's worth his weight in gold. Swiping him from the NSA was the best deal I've made all year—except for my marriage, of course. Anyway, Brody's waiting for us to check in."

Pierce headed for the door to the hallway, passing Chris walking back into the room. "Jordon, finish the drinks. Sawyer, I'll yell as soon as I've got Egghead on the line."

It wasn't long before Pierce called them into the combination computer/communications room. The man left the room without being asked as Ian, Carter, and Jordyn stood in front of the camera and stared at the video screen. Brody was sitting in his own war-room in Tampa, leaning back in his ergonomic chair. "Damn. Boomer wasn't kidding when he said Jordyn was hot. Nice to finally meet you, sweetheart." She'd received emails and texts from him during the op to help the girl, but they'd never met. "Next time you kick Carter's ass, can you make sure I'm there? I want to film it for posterity. Of course, I'll have to blur out both your faces, which kind of defeats the purpose, doesn't it?"

Each one of the Trident boys was more charming than the last, and she chuckled. Beside her, Ian pointed to the bottom of the screen, which showed part of Brody's desk. "What is that? Don't fucking tell me Fancy made pecan rolls today. Seriously? Tell your fiancée she's not allowed to bake those damn things when I'm out of town."

Purposely, Brody leaned forward, picked up the sticky treat, and took a huge bite out of it. "*Mmmmm-mmmh*. D-fwking-wiscous," he said with a full mouth, clearly savoring the taste of the pastry. He swallowed the bite, then slowly licked his fingers one by one. "Sorry about that. What were you saying, Boss-man? Something about *my* fiancée? The woman who bakes with only *me* in mind, and you're just lucky to get the leftovers." Ian opened his mouth to retort, but Brody cut him off. "And before you threaten me, just remember the 'Chicken Dance' ringtone and Siri calling you 'Princess Twatwaffle.'"

Ian growled. "Fucking bastard. I *will* get my revenge one of these days, you little shit. In the meantime, what do you have for us?"

Washing his breakfast down with a swig of coffee, Brody leaned back in his chair again. His expression went from playful to professional in the blink of an eye. "McDaniel sent me all the info I needed by courier." The head of Deimos had wanted an independent, high-clearance-level contractor to confirm what the agency's techs had already told him and had taken Carter's suggestion about having Trident do it. "I tracked the hacker through seven countries and twice as many IP addresses, only to land back in Washington D.C. in an internet café on Connecticut Avenue. Had one of our contacts go check the place out with no luck. The camera system in the place was hacked and erased while our UNSUB was there. When I called McDaniel a little while ago, he said that was exactly what his techs had discovered, so it doesn't appear any Deimos techs had a hand in the breach." He paused. "Um, by the way, Carter, have you checked in with him in the past two hours or so?"

Carter's eyes narrowed. "No. I was going to call him in about thirty minutes. Why?"

"Shit. Sorry to tell you, but Luis Benito was found dead a few hours ago in a hotel room in Paris. His extraction team made the discovery and said his throat was slit—body was still warm. Looks like he was sleeping and taken by surprise."

Anytime Jordyn had ever seen Carter pissed over the years paled in comparison to now. He looked like he wanted to tear apart Steel's castle, and the only thing keeping it from happening was a thin thread of restraint. Taking a step back, he ran a hand down his face, and Jordyn couldn't resist reaching out and touching his arm. She could feel the raw tension he was holding back. If he was surprised at her sudden tenderness, it didn't show. In fact, she had no idea why she'd touched him. Meeting his gaze, she said, "I'm sorry. I know you trained him before me. He was a great guy."

With his jaw clenched, he nodded once, then addressed Brody again. "Anything turn up in Deimos's history that seems like a red flag."

The geek snorted. "You mean, like practically every mission you guys have ever been on?"

"Can you narrow it fucking down and give me a place to start, damn it?"

Yup, barely hanging on by a thread, Jordyn thought.

"Yeah. I had Nathan run some names, dates, and places through NSA to see if we could match them up with any intercepted chatter. Got a few hits, but not sure if they have anything to do with this mess. I sent it all to Boss-man's computer so he can access it through Steel. I used Jones's preferred encryption— just have him open it for you."

When Carter didn't answer, Ian did. "All right. Anything else?"

"Yeah." Brody let out a heavy sigh. "On another problem we're dealing with. Tara O'Brien's body was found this morning—at the Tampa Zoo, of all fucking places. Same condition as the others."

Confused, Jordyn glanced at Carter and then Ian. "I don't understand. Who's Tara O'Brien?"

She didn't miss the silent exchange of stares between the two men and a subtle shake of Carter's head. Ian uncrossed his arms and leaned on the back of the desk chair. "Local case. Tampa's got a serial killer, and Trident's been helping the feds with it. It's nothing to do with the Deimos crap."

While she believed that last statement, she was certain there was something they weren't telling her. If she didn't have the NOC list situation on her mind, she'd be curious enough to do some research on the Tampa case. But right now, it was very low on her list of things that needed her attention.

Back in Tampa, Brody continued. "There's a task force meeting today with the profiler from Quantico—Dr. Suki Ralston. Anyone know her?"

"I do," Carter answered. "She's good."

"Hope her bedside manner is a lot better than Parrish's. I didn't think anyone could be a bigger dick than Stonewall. Anyway, that's all I've got."

After ending the video chat with Brody, Carter led the way through the castle halls until they reached the huge dining room. Well, Jordyn didn't think any of the rooms in the place could be described as anything but huge. Their lunch awaited them, and the two other Trident men had already dug into their large bowls of stew. Jordyn sat across from Romeo, and Ian and Carter took the seats flanking her. The latter passed her a basket of fresh bread, and she couldn't resist taking a piece and slathering it with butter.

They ate silently for a few minutes, but suddenly, Carter stood and stalked out of the room without saying a word. Jordyn glanced at his table setting. He'd barely eaten a bite. For the first time since she'd left his bed many years ago, she wanted to go to him, wrap her arms around his neck, and comfort him. Her heart said to do it, but her mind said no. And she always found it best when she heeded her mind over her heart.

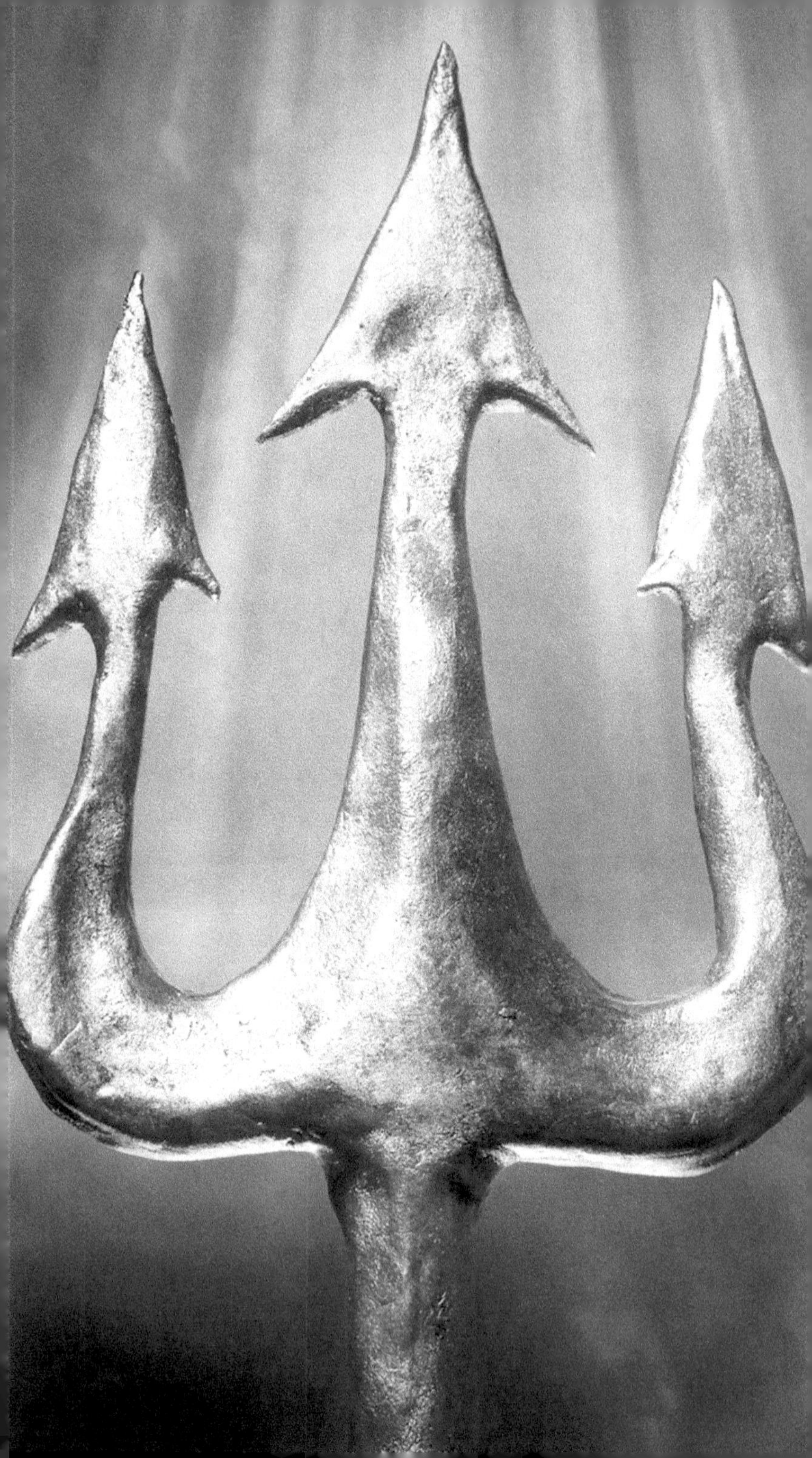

CHAPTER SIX

S itting on top of a picnic table near the back entrance of the castle's kitchen, Carter hung up the secure sat phone Pierce had let him use to contact McDaniel. He'd given the head of Deimos the rundown on Jordyn's extraction and then listened to his boss recount the details of Benito's murder. The body count was rising, and they still had no idea who had targeted Deimos and why. There wasn't much Carter could do from Scotland, but once he was back on US soil, he'd knock on a lot of doors, refusing to bury any more operatives.

His gut was in turmoil. Between the murders of the three agents, being so close to Jordyn, and not being able to touch her the way he wanted to, he was going a little nuts—which was putting it mildly. Add in someone torturing and killing submissives of the BDSM lifestyle in Tampa—a city he'd spent a lot of his downtime in—and he felt things were spiraling out of control. And that was something he couldn't allow to happen. He needed control in his life. Without it, he was afraid he'd become the type of man he despised—one with no honor, loyalty, or soul.

The number of dead submissives was currently five, but he feared that count would rise before they caught this bastard. The feds had been called in after the fourth homicide—or, at least, they thought it was the fourth. The first two alleged victims were never found, but it was assumed they'd met a similar fate. After the third victim disappeared, the killer started leaving them where their mutilated bodies could be found. The Tampa FBI's Special Agent in Charge, Frank Stonewall, had butted heads on several occasions with Trident and Carter. While the spy hadn't met Special Agent Colt Parrish yet, he'd already heard about how he'd been assigned to the Tampa office from Quantico with one goal in mind—find the BDSM killer.

Movement caught his eye, and he glanced up to see Mic strolling toward him with her hands tucked in her sweatshirt pockets and concern on her face. Neither of them said a word as she climbed up and sat beside him on the tabletop. Leaning back on her arms, she tilted her face toward the sky. "It's about time we had a sunny day. It's been rainy or overcast for the past five days, and tomorrow we're expecting more shitty weather, although it's better than snow."

"See what happens when I visit?" he asked with a wry grin. "I bring the sunshine with me."

Mic snorted. "Yeah, right. Along with a lot of fucking problems."

"Sorry." He mimicked her position and stared off at nothing in particular.

"Don't be. *I'm* sorry about your agents." He gave her sympathy a curt nod but wasn't sure she saw it as she continued. "I wish we could head back to the States with you to cover your six. Any idea who's behind this or what you'll do next?"

Carter sighed. "No clue who's behind it, but I've got a few things to check out in D.C. At least, it's a start." Silence descended between them again until he couldn't take it anymore. He kept his gaze on some clouds in the distance. "Say it."

"What?"

"Whatever's on the tip of that pretty little tongue of yours, sweetheart."

She paused. "What's the deal with you and Jordyn—yours, not mine? I already know what the deal is between you and Chris."

He didn't answer right away. Not because he didn't want to, but because he honestly didn't know what to say. He should be concentrating on trying to find out who the fuck wanted them dead, but the situation with Jordyn was starting to eat him alive. It had gone on far too long, and he had no idea what he'd done wrong. "I can't believe I'm going to ask this, but do you mind talking to her, Mic? I mean, shit. I trained her. Things were fine. There was sexual tension there from the start, but we didn't act on it until months later, when things got hot and heavy after a mission. She's hated me ever since, and I have no fucking idea why."

"Maybe you didn't rock her world, stud." Her snark made him chuckle and relax a little as she bumped her shoulder against his. "Although I doubt that. If you fuck the way you kiss, I'm sure rocking her world wasn't the problem. So, what did you say or do that was out of line? Did you pull the Dom card and freak her out?"

He shook his head. "Oddly, I didn't. Not really, I mean. I didn't tie her up and spank her if that's what you're asking, but I did use psychological ropes." He knew Mic understood the lifestyle a little better now than when she'd first discovered he was a Dom. While not into the BDSM scene herself, Mic had been curious since Ian and his team were also into it. When they'd worked the first mission Steel and Trident had been on together years ago, Ian and Carter had teased her about her personality being perfect for a Domme. They'd told her they'd be more than happy to show her how to dominate a submissive if she wanted to learn. She had passed on their offer but had still researched it a little after the mission and occasionally asked them questions about it.

"So you told her what to do, and she obeyed you." He nodded in agreement, and Mic tilted her head toward him. "You want me to take her out for a mani/pedi and a few Cosmos to see if she'll spill her guts?

True laughter burst from his chest for the first time all day.

Mic doesn't do manicures, pedicures, or Cosmos any more than I do. And neither does Jordyn... or does she?

His apprentice's missions required her to blend into many social settings, so she had to ensure her appearance always fit. Now that he thought about it—

"That was a fucking joke, Carter," Mic said, interrupting his thoughts. "Girlie chats aren't my thing, and I don't think they're your woman's thing either. But I'll take her to the range, and maybe we can bond over a few boxes of ammo." She paused. "So, did you ever think six years ago, when we had that conversation at the airport, that either of us would find 'the one'?"

"Nope. Did you?"

"Nope. But I think I'm glad we were wrong."

He wished he could say the same.

Jordyn followed Mic to the outdoor shooting range. The woman's invite had been unexpected—so had the change of warmer clothing—but Jordyn had accepted both, curiosity filling her. She'd seen Mic and Carter sitting on the picnic bench a half hour ago and felt the same pangs of jealousy as she did when the two had greeted each other with a hug earlier. And all that did was annoy her. She didn't want to be jealous of any woman over Carter.

Mic stopped at a small shack beside the shooting range, backdropped by a small, manmade hill. It was the perfect setup, as there was no need to worry about stray bullets hitting something beyond the targets— not that either one of them would miss. Jordyn may have just met Mic, but she knew the petite blonde was kick-ass without a doubt. The scar down her cheek made Jordyn curious to know how it was acquired, especially with Ian's reaction to seeing it, but it wasn't her place to ask. Whatever had happened, it'd been fairly recent.

Like Jordyn, despite Mic's size, she looked like she could handle herself in most situations. But unlike Jordyn, she had a team to back her up if need be. The Deimos spy was on her own. Yeah, if an assignment required more than one operative, she'd have at least one partner, but she flew solo by the seat of her pants for most of her assignments.

Opening up the door to the shack, Mic pulled out two paper targets with the blackened shape of a man's head and torso on them, a staple gun, and eye and ear protection. She placed them on a shelf nailed to the outside wall. Jordyn set down her sniper rifle bag and pulled the individual parts out, putting it together.

"So, how long have you known Carter?" Mic asked after she'd ducked back into the shed and returned with a box of ammo for each of them—.308 rounds for Jordyn's Remington and 9mm for her own Heckler & Koch MP5.

Jordyn arched a brow. While it wasn't an unexpected question, she'd anticipated a little chitchat before they got on the topic of Carter. "You mean you don't already know? I find that hard to believe, as close as you two seem."

Shrugging, Mic began to load her magazine. "All I know is you've known him longer than I have."

"And how long is that?"

"Turning the inquisition around won't get you out of answering my question."

Placing her rifle down on the shelf, with the chamber empty and the filled magazine next to it, Jordyn picked up the paper targets and began walking the half mile to the wooden boards they would attach them to. Mic grabbed the staple gun and followed.

"All right, Mic. How 'bout we do it this way? I answer your questions, and you answer mine."

"Fair enough. I asked first, so..."

"Eight years. He trained me when I came to Deimos. You?"

Since they were close in height, they had the same stride walking across the grassy field of the range. A light wind blew, bringing the scents of fall with it. "Over six. Technically, seven, although that first year had been over the phone lines. I worked in Army Intelligence in Iraq. Carter was the one who recommended me for interrogation training."

"Seriously? I've only taken part in torturing a target a few times, but I'm sure you got the same response I did when you first walked into the room."

"What? That 'check out this tiny piece of ass' look?"

Jordyn snorted. "Yup. It goes right along with that 'this isn't going to hurt at all' look."

They both laughed, and Jordyn felt herself start to relax. She held the paper targets against the wood while Mic stapled them. Once they were up, the women started the trek back to the shed.

"So, did you and Carter ever... um..." Jordyn's question died in her throat. She was curious as hell, but now that the words were almost completely out, she wished she could take them back. Another thought floated through her mind—was Mic aware of Carter's apparent penchant for abusing women? Jordyn doubted it. Mic didn't seem like the type of woman who would let that bit of knowledge slide.

Mic studied her, and Jordyn wondered what she saw—a rival or something else? After a good twenty seconds, the blonde woman finally said, "No, we never did. Could have, the attraction was there, but... I don't know. I think we both knew it would've screwed up the friendship we'd already built—and that was more important than a quick fuck or two. Carter was the first person who ever saw through me—which pissed me off and scared the crap out of me at the same time. He means a lot to me, but not in the way you're asking. I can't explain it, but until the day I die, I'll have his six, and he'll have mine, but we'll never have each other's hearts. And damn, I'm sounding like an actual fucking girl here, and that's so not me. Anyway, the short answer to your question is no, we never had sex. Kissed a few times for the cover, but that's it." There was a long pause. "So... what about you? Did you two ever... you know—do the nasty?"

The obvious question was asked in such a way that Jordyn wondered if the other woman already knew the answer. For the first time in her adult life, she found herself opening her mouth for a girl talk that wasn't part of a cover. Why, she didn't know. She wanted nothing to do with Carter—at least, that was what her mind kept trying to tell her heart. "Yeah... once. Years ago."

Stopping five yards from the shed, Mic crossed her arms and glared at Jordyn. "And... don't leave me hanging, Jordyn—I don't know how to do this fucking girlie chat thing any better than you do. And yes, it's obvious, but only to someone as experienced as me— or inexperienced, as it were. But come on, I've seen his bare ass—totally drool-worthy. So, give me details."

"What? We did it." She shrugged her shoulders. "It was fine. Story over."

Mic's eyes narrowed, and it was clear she knew

Jordyn was lying through her teeth. "Look—I don't know what your problem is with Carter, but I can tell you he's one of the most loyal, caring, protective men I've ever met, and he's hung up on you—big time. To my knowledge, you've managed to do something no other woman has done. You've tied that asshole up in knots. Either sit down, talk it out with him, then fuck like rabbits or when this shit with Deimos is over, let him go and walk away. He deserves someone to love, just like everyone else in this Godforsaken world. If that's not you, tell him and get out of his life for good. Don't make me fucking throw down with you. I'm starting to like you, so it would really fucking suck if we had to fight over him—with our training and backgrounds, it'd be bloody as hell. I'll always have Carter's six, no matter what or who it involves. Got it?"

Without waiting for an answer, Mic strode to the shed and took out two waterproof blankets so they could lie on the ground without getting wet or dirty. They dropped down and adjusted their ear and eye protection, then got to work eliminating the paper bad guys. While Jordyn had dead-on accuracy—her shots were an ultra-tight grouping in the heart—Mic wasn't far behind, her cluster a little looser but still kill shots.

Half a box of ammo each later, the women left their empty weapons on the blankets and removed their protective gear. Standing, they turned to the two men who'd walked up behind them a few minutes earlier. Both women had known they were there, and since Mic had ignored them, so had Jordyn.

Mic gestured to the men, who, judging by their well-built physiques, were the missing members of her team. "Samuel Jones and Jerimiah Flynn, this is Jordyn Alvarez, and yes, we already know that's going to be a pain in the ass with Chris and her in the same room. Jordyn works with Carter, who is here as well. Ian and a few of the Trident boys tagged along too."

"Damn, we go to town, and the fucking party starts without us," Flynn snarked. He then bowed at the waist in Jordyn's direction with a sweeping gesture of his arm. A playful grin spread across his face, and his eyes lit up. "If you'd like a tour of the castle, princess, I'm your prince."

"Fucking Flynn," Jones growled and rolled his eyes before smiling at her. "It's nice to meet you, Jordyn. Please ignore this idiot—he was raised in a barn." He glanced at Mic. "Something we need to know about?"

Mic nodded. "Yeah, go inside, and they'll fill you in. We'll clean up here and then be right behind you."

While the women walked across the field to retrieve their targets, Jordyn could feel Flynn's eyes on her ass before he turned and caught up to his teammate heading toward the house. "Does he always flirt like that?"

Inspecting her target closer, Mic gave her a quick glance. "Who, Flynn? Yeah, he can be an asshole, but I couldn't ask for a better team, and that includes him.

Feel free to put him in his place, in fact, please do—I could use the entertainment."

The woman's anger and wistfulness weren't hard to miss, and she wouldn't look Jordyn in the eye. "Carter mentioned you can't return to the States, but he didn't give me all the details. That sucks."

Mic shrugged and ripped her target down. "Yup, it does. Even more so, now that he has a target on his back, and we can't cover his six." She turned on her heel as Jordyn took down her own target. "So that means you'll have to watch it for me... and God help you if you fail."

CHAPTER SEVEN

Seven years ago...

After losing their tails, they switched vehicles twice. Spare clothes had been waiting for them in the first car, a Mercedes, and in the middle of nowhere, they'd changed from their formal clothes into more comfortable jeans and T-shirts. A half-hour later, the Mercedes was ditched for a nondescript Volkswagen, and another hour had passed before they reached their destination at 10:00 p.m. local time.

Carter steered the car down the dirt road leading to the home of a Deimos contact, who was waiting for them. The man was former CIA—which was an oxymoron. Like the US Marines, once CIA, always CIA. If you weren't, you were probably six feet under somewhere. His cover in Malaysia was that he was an expat turned information dealer. However, the information he tended to sell was stuff the CIA wanted leaked out in the first place.

The light glowing from inside the far right window of the farmhouse was their signal that all was well—if it had been out, they would have hightailed it to another location with a different contact. Carter slowed the car to a stop fifty yards away from the structure. Flipping the vehicle's headlights on and off in old Morse Code, he let their contact know it was them.

The light in the window switched on and off in response, signaling them to approach. While Jordyn had never used this location before, Carter had and knew exactly where he was going. They wouldn't go into the main house but instead to a small apartment in a barn not far past it. They would be safe there until morning, when they'd head for a private airport and a jet waiting there.

Pulling the car into the barn's wide open doors, Carter killed the engine, hopped out, and shut the sliding doors. Locking them in, he armed the alarm system as Jordyn retrieved her duffel bag and left the rear car door open for Carter to grab his. These were their go-bags, carrying clothes, weapons, money, throwaway phones, passports in various aliases, and anything else they would need if they had to run.

Hanging his bag on his shoulder by the strap, Carter shut the car door and led Jordyn to the one-room apartment on the other side of the barn. It was on the first floor with no windows, not that it mattered. The security system had cameras all around the property, along with trip alarms. Dropping his bag, Carter flipped a few switches on a computer console setup on one wall, and several images appeared on the monitor. If anyone infiltrated the inconspicuous farm, the occupants would know it. He pointed to a wall on the other side of the room. "Behind that picture is a switch to open an escape door. It'll dump us about a half mile away in another barn. A car is there if needed."

Jordyn set her bag down on a table and looked around. There was a couch, TV, kitchenette, bathroom, dining table for two, and computer desk—sparse yet comfortable. "The Hilton, it's not, but you know me, I love all the James Bond stuff, Taylor."

"Nope, not Taylor." Grinning, he strode toward the bathroom, in need of the toilet. "Give me a sec."

When he returned moments later, it was to see Jordyn's luscious ass as she was bent over, checking out the camera feeds. And just like that, his desire and lust were back with a vengeance. It was suddenly hot in the room, and he pulled his T-shirt up and off, tossing it onto the couch. With the adrenaline of the chase still coursing through his body, he stepped behind her and grabbed her hips, pulling her flush against his groin. She straightened and reached back to clasp her arms around his neck, then rubbed her ass against his growing erection. Sparks shot through him as he leaned down to lick her ear and then murmured, "We have unfinished business to attend to, love."

Jordyn arched her back, thrusting her breasts forward. Her breathing hitched as he brought his hands up to cup and massage each heavy orb. "*Business* or pleasure?"

The question caused him to chuckle as he nuzzled her neck and played with her tits. "Which do you prefer?"

He plucked her nipples through her shirt. She hadn't been wearing a bra under her evening dress and hadn't changed into one. Good, because it was one less thing he needed to rip off her body. A moan escaped her as her body brushed against his. "Pleasure... definitely pleasure."

"That was my choice, too." His hands dropped to the hem of her shirt and then under it. He was torn between removing it swiftly or agonizingly slowly. He chose the latter. His palms and fingers tingled as he dragged them up her torso, pushing the shirt higher and higher. Her skin was soft, like velvet. Up over her ribs, his hands paused to rub the underside of her breasts.

Jordyn's hands left his neck and reached down to pull her shirt over her head, but he covered them with his own hands. "Uh-uh, sweetheart. I've been waiting a long time for this. I want you to do nothing but feel while I have my way with you."

"Can—can your way be fast first and then slow for the second round?"

He nipped her earlobe, pleased to feel a shiver go through her spine. "Trust me. I think you'll find my way of doing things quite enjoyable. Think you can handle that?"

Not letting her answer, he spun her around and took possession of her mouth with his. Soft lips, a wet tongue, and moans of need fueled his desire. Her shirt was pushed up, scarcely covering her tits, and he edged it further until the beautiful flesh was bare. He slid his hands to her back, caressing her skin and pushing her chest into his. They both moaned into each other's mouth at the contact.

Bending his knee between her legs, he encouraged her to hump his thigh. Her hips undulated, and he could feel her heat and wetness through their two pairs of jeans. He was now painfully hard, but he wanted to savor each second of the first time he took Ms. Jordyn Alvarez. His mind and body stressed that this was the *first time* because he'd be damned if there wasn't at least a second and third time.

Wanting her bare, he pulled his mouth from hers just long enough to rid her shirt from her body. His tongue delved back in between her lips and dueled with hers. She tasted like heaven and spice. His hands dropped to her ass, and he picked her up, her legs immediately wrapping around his hips. Backing her up to a wall, he ground his erection against her mound. His mouth left hers. Kissing and licking, he made his way over her jaw, down her neck to those breasts he was dying to torture.

He sucked one of her nipples into his mouth and lapped at the stiff peak. Her hands dove into his hair, sliding the thin leather band holding his ponytail down until the blond strands fell free. She held him to her breast, moaning and gasping. Her native Spanish poured from her as she begged him for more. She'd come to live in the United States with her uncle at fourteen, and English had become her primary language. But there were times when she was excited or mad that words such as *oh Dios mío, por favor,* and *mierda* flowed from her pretty lips.

She pleaded for him to fuck her hard and fast. Jordyn didn't know about the lifestyle he enjoyed, and now wasn't the time to announce it, but that didn't mean he couldn't incorporate it into this scene without her realizing it. He cupped her ass cheeks and squeezed. She had him hotter than any other woman he'd ever been with, and they both still had their pants on—but not for long.

Carrying her over to the bed, he dropped her unceremoniously, and her body and breasts bounced a few times while she laughed. Leaning back on her elbows, she stared up at him seductively as he stepped back and crossed his arms. His voice was low and smooth like fine whiskey. "Finish getting undressed, Jordy. I want to see all of you."

Her gaze slid down to his bulging crotch, and she licked her lips. "The feeling is mutual."

God, she was going to be the death of him tonight. What he wouldn't give to have her call him Sir or Master? He could survive without it for tonight, though. "You first, love. Strip for me."

Biting her lower lip, she stood on the mattress and undid the snap of her jeans. Oh, so slowly, she lowered the zipper. He could hear the metal teeth separating one tick per second, and it was torturous and exhilarating at the same time. The glide of her tight jeans and black thong down her legs was more of the same, as inch by inch, her skin was revealed. He swallowed hard and mentally field-stripped his sniper rifle to keep from throwing her over his knees and spanking her ass. She was far from ready for that.

He was back in control when she finally stepped out of the jeans and thong, then flicked them to the floor with her foot. His gaze started at her polished, red toes and roamed upward, over her legs, hips, torso, and breasts, until it reached her face. Clothed, she was stunning. Naked, the only word he could think of was glorious. But then another word flickered in from the far recesses of his mind—*mine*. Well, at least, for tonight, she was.

Carter stripped off his pants and then circled the corner of the bed. He laid down with his head on one of the pillows, and Jordyn spun slowly as she watched him. Shifting toward the middle of the mattress, he crooked his finger at her. "Come here, love. I want you to sit on my face until I've had my fill of your sweet pussy."

Her eyes flared with heat and desire. Stepping toward his head, she placed one foot on either side of his shoulders, then slid to her knees. Her sex was inches from his mouth, and he ran his fingers up and down her thighs and calves. "Grab onto the headboard, Jordy, and don't let go. If you do, I'll slow down and start all over again. Understand?"

"Um, yeah, stop teasing. Just get on with it." She clutched the wrought iron headboard. Her breaths were coming in pants, and he hadn't even begun torturing her yet.

He chuckled. She may have said she understood, but he was certain she didn't—but she would soon learn he meant what he'd said.

Inhaling deeply, he drew her scent into his nose. Sweet, spicy, and something distinct that was all his Jordy. Putting pressure on her hips, he pulled her down onto his mouth. Her pussy was bare, her lips already swollen for him. With a swipe of his tongue, he took his first taste of her and fell into nirvana. She was delicious and intoxicating. Just as he'd suspected, it was going to be quite a while before he fucked her out of his system.

Her hips bucked as she cried out. "Oh, fuck! Give me more!"

His hands clutched her hips, holding her still for him. He ran his tongue through her folds as she begged and moaned. Using his thumbs, he exposed her clit and set about sucking the little pearl. Jordyn's hands flew to his head, and he slowed everything down as promised. Turning his head, he licked her inner thigh. "Put your hands back on the headboard, love. I won't go any further until you do."

"Damn it, Carter." She tried to lower herself to his mouth again. "That's mean."

When she realized he meant business, she huffed and grabbed the curled iron bars again. His tongue found her wetter than before as he licked and nibbled on her. He alternated from her pussy to her clit and back again, taking her higher and higher, but not enough.

"Please, Carter! *Oh Dios mío, por favor!*"

His hands slid up her torso to her breasts, and he cupped the bottom of them. His mouth left her for a moment. "Play with your nipples, Jordy. I want to watch while I eat this pretty pussy."

Her head fell back on her shoulders as she followed his command. Her fingers played with the pinkish, brown peaks. His gaze focused on them as his tongue lashed at her clit. Bringing one of his hands back down, he positioned it between her legs. With one finger and then two, he entered her tight passage. She clenched around him as sighs, gasps, murmurs, curses, and moans spilled from her mouth. Her wetness flowed, allowing each thrust of his fingers to ease further inside.

"Oh, fuck! Yes, more!"

Not yet. "Beg me, sweet Jordy. Ask me to let you come."

"*Mierda*! Oh, please! Harder. I need to—"

He nipped her inner thigh. "That's not what I said, love. *Ask* me to let you come."

Her chin dipped down, and her gaze met his. She was so close to falling into an orgasmic abyss as his fingers continued to fuck her, but he wouldn't let her go until she gave him what he wanted—what he needed.

"*Ask* me," he demanded.

"P-please. Would you please l-let me come?"

His tongue and teeth returned to her clit as he increased the intensity and speed of his fingers, thrusting deep into her core. He curled his fingers, searching for the spot that would have her screaming his name and her release. *Almost. Right. There!*

"C-Carrrrrterrrrrr! *Ahhhhhhhh*! Oh! *Ohhhhhhhh*!"

Her walls spasmed and clenched his fingers to the point they ached as her juices poured from her. Her entire body quivered as she came in wave after wave of ecstasy. The headboard shook violently, rattling against the wall. Jordyn coming apart in the throes of passion was nearly his own undoing. She was beautiful—beyond beautiful. In fact, he didn't think there was a single word spoken in any language on Earth to describe it. And he couldn't wait to watch her do it again.

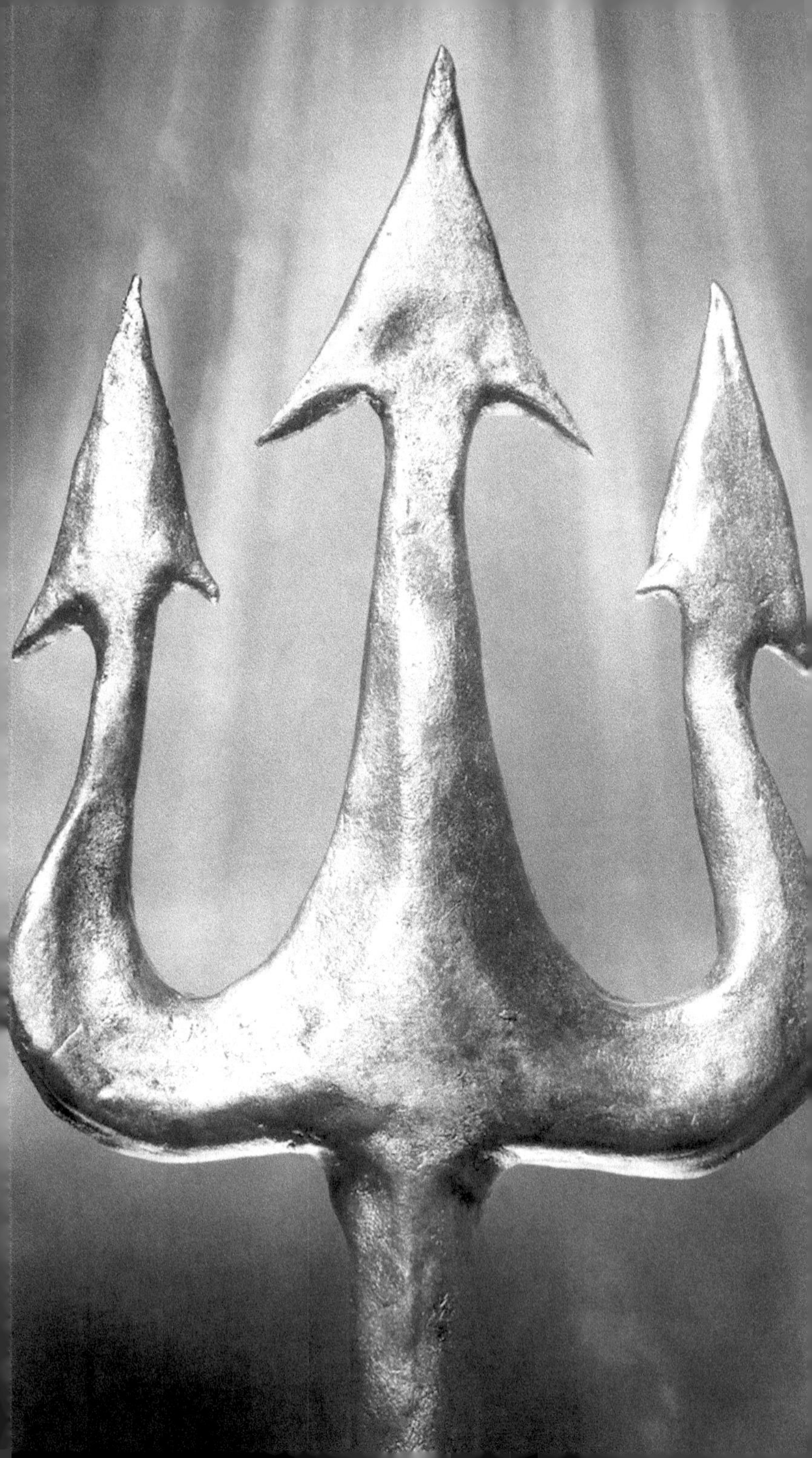

CHAPTER EIGHT

Present...

Striding into the large living room, Carter glanced around. It was late, and nearly everyone was asleep, but the person he wanted to talk to was the only one in the room, standing at the bar, pouring a glass of scotch. Chris Jordon's jaw clenched, and his shoulder muscles tensed at the intrusion, but he didn't say a word.

Carter approached him. "I'll take a double on the rocks if you can pour it without breaking the glass. And I wouldn't advise you to play poker. You can't bluff to save your life—or your money."

The younger man snorted as he filled another crystal lowball glass with ice and the hard amber liquor. "Poker's a different game, and I do just fine at the tables."

Taking the drink, Carter sat in a straight-back chair beside the fireplace and propped his feet on an ottoman. The fire no longer roared, but the embers still glowed brightly with heat. Chris dropped onto the couch with his own scotch, and the two sat in silence for a few moments. When the spy saw the other man's shoulders finally relax, he spoke softly. "I knew Mic long before I met her. She was working in Army intelligence at the time. There was something about her—something strong and confident, I could tell even over the phone. Smart as a whip too. She could take a jumble of intel and make sense of it before anyone else could. It took me a while to become almost positive she would make an excellent interrogator, but not knowing her well enough, I wasn't sure if she had the guts for it. Not because she's a woman, but because she's human."

Chris rested his glass on his thigh, his eyes on the fireplace as a piece of a log split and flames flared up again. But Carter knew the guy was listening... analyzing... so he continued. "Before I made the recommendation to her superiors, I did some digging—more than the Army would have done. I spoke to her recruiter, Alex Mitchell, and heard how she'd grown up. Ironically, her childhood was similar to mine, yet my abusers were foster parents, not blood relatives. After my conversation with Mitchell, I was even more convinced she was right for interrogation training. She overcame the horrors of an abusive childhood and was stronger for it. Most people would have sought revenge or resented people who'd had great child-hoods. Not Mic. She found something she was good at —something that made a positive difference in the world. As I've told her many times, she's a hell of a woman." He paused. "Did you know she saved my life once?"

With a furrowed brow, Chris's gaze shot to his. "How?"

"Does it matter?"

Shrugging, the man stared at the fireplace again. "Not really, I guess."

Carter paused for a sip of scotch, letting the familiar burn warm his core. Part of the reason he was telling the guy all this was because he cared about Mic, but the other part was he was willing to admit Chris was the right man for her as long as he didn't screw things up. Carter did like him, but pushing his buttons was so much fun sometimes. However, now was not one of those times. "Listen. As much honor and integrity as she has, though, it isn't enough. There was a time I regretted not being the man who could win her heart—a part of me will always regret it. But we would kill each other because we're far too much alike. Mic needs a man who will treat her as his equal, no matter what. While there are many times I would've been able to do that, there are others when I couldn't. It's my nature to want to shield all women from the horrors of the world. Mic would never allow me to do that—she's put me in my place more than once over my trying to do just that. And that's where you come in, Chris. Be the man who will stand beside her, no matter what. Let her fight her battles with you at her side… not in front of her or behind her. It's the only way it will work out for the two of you."

He stood and tossed the last of the scotch down his throat. "She loves you, dude. Don't throw that away because you're jealous of a man who cares for her but will never own her heart."

Setting the empty glass on the coffee table, he headed toward the foyer and stairs, but Chris's words stopped him cold. "What about Jordyn?"

Carter snorted and spun back around. "And here I thought Mic was the only dominant in your relationship." At the man's annoyed yet baffled expression, he clarified, "I'm not calling you a wuss—far from it. It's in a Dom's nature to worry about others, to want to protect them from the world, even if they barely know each other. As for the lovely Jordyn Alvarez, in many ways, she's a twin of Mic. But on the other hand, they're completely the opposite. And I don't stand a chance until Jordyn admits that to herself." He pivoted toward the doorway again, then glanced back. "Go to bed, Chris. Go sleep with your woman."

Before he reached the stairs, Carter's cell phone buzzed, alerting him to a voicemail. Very few people had the number to reach him, so it was probably important or an update about the mess they were in.

Walking through the castle's main floor, he headed to the kitchen, dialing the number to retrieve the voice-mail. Two other messages he'd forgotten to listen to played first. Both were updates from the Deimos head-quarters. The two other agents on the NOC list had been successfully extracted from their missions and were now in protective custody at the training facility in California.

The third message played as he sat on a stool at a huge butcher block counter. "Hey, T. It's me." He smiled at hearing Vicki's voice, but her next words worried him. "Can—can you give me a call as soon as possible? Um... I'll explain when I talk to you. Miss you. Bye."

Shit. That didn't sound good. He quickly calcu-lated the time zone difference and then dialed the number he knew by heart. He'd have to swap out this cell phone for a new one before they got on the plane tomorrow. To keep his foster sister and her family safe, he never called her from the same number twice. Maybe Mic and the boys had one he could use.

The phone rang three times before Vicki Underwood picked up. "Hello?"

She couldn't have known it was him since the cell had a Chicago area code. "Hey, beautiful. How's my favorite lady?"

"Oh, thank God, it's you, T.," she blurted out. "I-I was hoping you'd call right back."

The slight tremble in her voice had him stiffening in his seat. "What's wrong?"

"It's Justin." Carter's heart sank as she continued. "He's been admitted to the hospital. He hasn't felt well the past few days but said it was just fatigue. Then, this morning, he was in pain, so I called his doctor right away, and he said to get him to the ER. They're trying some new meds, keeping him hydrated, and have him back on dialysis for now. If he doesn't respond then..."

Fuck. He hadn't needed her to finish, knowing exactly what came next. If nineteen-year-old Justin's body was rejecting his mother's donated kidney, he would need another transplant. The problem was that the kid had one of the rarer blood types, and a compatible donor was hard to come by. Not for the first time, Carter wished he could give Justin one of his kidneys, but he wasn't a match. Four years ago, Vicki had given her son the only kidney she could spare, and now they would have to look elsewhere. Carter knew where to find one, even though it was from the last place he wanted to get it. "I'm overseas, sweetheart, but I'm heading back tomorrow. I have to stop in D.C.—if it wasn't important, you know I'd skip it. As soon as I can, I'll be there. And if it comes to that point, we'll get Justin what he needs, no matter what." He'd do whatever he could, even make a deal with the devil, to get a kidney. Hell, he'd rip it out of the devil himself if it came down to it. "Where's Joe?"

"He and his sisters are in Phoenix, dealing with their father's estate and getting the house ready for sale. I called him right away, and he caught the first flight he could. He should be here soon." Joe Underwood, her husband, was a great guy, and Carter couldn't ask for a better man to take care of Vicki and Justin.

"All right. Good. You call me if anything changes, all right?"

"Y-yes... T., I'm scared."

So was he. Except for Joe, Justin was Vicki's life. If she lost him, Carter didn't know if she'd survive. "I know you are, sweetheart. But I'll do everything I can to make sure he gets through this."

"Th-thank you. I love you."

"I love you, too, sweetheart. Give my boy a kiss and a hug from me. I'll call you when I land in D.C."

"Okay. Fly safe. Bye."

"Bye." Disconnecting the call, Carter took a deep breath. Of all the times for this to happen. Now he had to worry about Justin on top of worrying about Jordyn, Deimos, and the dead submissives in Tampa. *Damn it.*

Jordyn flipped over again. It wasn't that the bed wasn't comfortable, because it definitely was, but she couldn't shut her mind down. And whenever she let it wander, it took a hard left, right in Carter's direction. She'd been jealous as hell when she first met Mic, and that just pissed her off. She didn't want to be jealous of any woman over Carter. She didn't want anything to do with the bastard.

Throwing the covers off, she pulled on the sweatpants and jacket Mic had loaned her. They were about the same size, so the fit was good. The woman had also given her a clean pair of socks, which Jordyn also grabbed. She didn't want to put her shoes on but needed something to protect her feet from the cold castle floors.

A castle. Harrumph. She was still a little shocked that they were in an honest-to-goodness castle in Scotland. It was one thing to live in a mansion—she'd spent the first fourteen years of her life in one—but a castle was in a whole different category. It conjured up images of dashing knights saving damsels in distress or Cinderella and Prince Charming. Every little girl who'd seen the Disney cartoon, or one of the nonanimated versions, had dreamed of living in a castle with her prince at some point in her young life. At least until the reality of adulthood came crashing down on her.

Mic and the others had told her to help herself to anything in the kitchen, and a glass of warm milk might be just what she needed to get some sleep. One of her childhood nannies had gotten her hooked on the comfort drink when she couldn't sleep, and Jordyn still found it helped all these years later.

She quietly opened the bedroom door and stepped out into the hallway. Pausing, she listened for the sounds of anyone else being up at this hour but was met with silence. Trudging down the steps, she tried to remember how to get to the kitchen from the front foyer. *Was it a left, left, right? Or a left, right, right?*

After correcting one wrong turn, she spotted the swinging door that led to the kitchen. She was about to push it open when Carter's voice came from the other side. "Hey, beautiful. How's my favorite lady?"

Jordyn froze.

Beautiful? His favorite lady? Probably the gigolo's standard line for when he couldn't remember the name of a woman he'd fucked.

Turning on her heel, she took several steps toward the stairs but stopped short. Indecisiveness had her standing there for longer than she wanted to admit.

Should I forget about the bastard, go to bed, and try to sleep? Should I breeze into the kitchen like I have no idea he's there talking to one of his girlfriends? Orrrrr... should I eavesdrop?

If she weren't so damn curious, she'd be mad at herself for choosing the latter. Tiptoeing back to the door, she listened again.

"I love you, too, sweetheart. Give my boy a kiss and a hug from me. I'll call you when I land in D.C.... Bye."

The sound of a stool scraping across the tile had

Jordyn scrambling for a place to hide. Running on silent feet back the way she came, she made a left and tried the first door she came to on the right. The knob rotated easily, and she ducked inside, shutting the door behind her. It was pitch dark, and she had no idea which room she was in.

Waiting with her ear against the door, she struggled to hear any sign of someone walking down the hall. If it were anyone else, she'd probably pick up a footstep or the rustle of fabric. But Carter was a fucking ghost, moving around with as much noise as a piece of dust floating through the air.

I love you, sweetheart? Give my boy a kiss and hug from me? Carter has a son? And from the sound of it, he has a wife too—or at least a longtime girlfriend.

And why did all that piss her off?

Because of the way my cheek tingled when his fingers brushed over it. Because of the heated stares he keeps sending my way. And because of how all of that makes my blood boil and my core ache for him. Because I'll never forget the one night I spent in his bed. That glorious night rocked my world and ruined me for every other man. Damn it!

Hearing nothing, she waited for five minutes, counting each second off in her head, before she eased the door open a crack. Still, nothing stirred. Stepping into the hall, she turned and ran right into a wall. Well, not one of the castle's stone ones, but a solid, warm, and breathing wall of flesh. Large hands grabbed her shoulders to steady her, and Jordyn fought the urge to drop whoever it was to the floor. Looking up, she was glad she had.

"Any reason why you're coming out of the dark billiards room in the middle of the night?" Pierce asked, his expression unreadable.

"I... uh... I mean... um." She rolled her eyes and sighed loudly, her shoulders relaxing under his big hands. "Yeah, I've got nothing. At least, nothing I want to fess up to or that you'll believe."

The corners of his mouth ticked up in a grin, and amusement filled his soft, brown eyes. He was really good-looking, and not for the first time since she met him a few hours ago, she wondered why she couldn't fall for a guy like him. But no. Jordyn Alvarez's traitorous body only revved up to an eleven, on a scale of one to ten, whenever the man she hated was around. There had to be some sort of women's law about that—like craving chocolate is mandatory during that time of the month. If you despised a guy, your girly parts shouldn't get all tingly if he was near.

Pierce cocked his head to the side. "Try me."

"Yeah, like that's not a loaded statement."

It was his turn to roll his eyes. "That's not what I meant, although if you'd taken me up on it, I wouldn't have said no." Grasping her upper arm, he spun her around and walked toward the kitchen. "Come on. There's leftover apple pie in the fridge. I'll heat it up and add some ice cream. Maybe that'll get you talking."

Jordyn snorted but let him lead her. "Let me guess. You failed Torture 101, didn't you?"

"Nah... this is just more fun—plus there's pie. No one can refuse Maggie's homemade apple pie. Now, if you were some fugly third-world terrorist with a God complex, then, yeah, I'd probably start with the waterboarding."

CHAPTER NINE

The tension in the dining room was sky-high, but no one said anything about it. Jordyn and Chris, as usual, were glaring at Carter, who was glaring at Pierce—*not* as usual. The rest of them ate their breakfast in silence, their gazes bouncing from one angry person to another, trying to figure out what the hell was going on. Flynn and Pierce were the only two oblivious to the hostility flying around the room while Ian, Mancini, McCabe, Mic, Jones, Rook, and Roza looked on in a combination of confusion and amusement. Carter wanted to tell them all to fuck off, but Roza's presence had him biting his tongue—Mic and Jordyn wouldn't be offended, but the quiet, shy woman had his protective and polite inner Dom emerging.

About an hour after he'd left the kitchen and gone to bed last night, Carter had heard Jordyn and Pierce in the hallway. To Carter's shock and amazement, the man said something that made her giggle. It'd been years since he'd heard a flirty, little laugh from Jordyn, and it made him want to rip the other man's head off. Whether Jordyn knew it or not, she was off limits to any other guy. At least, until Carter figured out why she hated him so much so he could fix it. After that, he'd get her back into his bed until he had his fill. But for now, he wanted to pound on any guy who dared flirt with her. Jealousy was a new emotion for him, and unless he got it under control as far as Jordyn was concerned, there would be quite a few homicides in the near future—starting with Pierce.

Mic cleared her throat as she glanced back and forth between Carter, Jordyn, Pierce, and her boyfriend. "Soooo... what time are you heading to the airport?" she asked none of her guests in particular.

A knowing smile spread across Ian's face. "Smooth icebreaker, Mic. Can't get any subtler than that."

A few chuckles filled the air as she shrugged. "What can I say? It's a talent." She sent a scowl around the table. "You know, you assholes either need to fight, fuck, or let it go. The hostility is getting tiresome."

The buttered roll in Flynn's hand stopped halfway to his mouth, and his eyes narrowed. "Am I missing something here?" No one answered.

Ian threw his napkin down on the table and stood. "She's right. This is getting old very fast. Break out the paintball guns, Mic. I don't trust these assholes with anything stronger. We have a few hours before we have to leave. Let's take it out on the course until the last man... or woman... is standing."

Flynn jumped from his seat in excitement. "Yes! Get ready to eat my paint, bitches—that goes for both sexes. What do I win when I'm the last one standing?" Not waiting for a response, he ran from the room, looking like a kid in a candy store, presumably to gather up the equipment.

"Fucking Flynn," his team grumbled in unison.

Everyone finished their breakfast, then headed upstairs to throw on clothes they didn't mind getting ruined. Jones volunteered to monitor the property's security system while working on some computer coding. Roza also didn't join them, opting to remain indoors on the dreary, overcast day. The cool air out on the huge paintball and laser tag course did nothing to temper Carter's jealousy, but he had to admit that Ian and Mic were right. They all needed this "shoot 'em up and spit 'em out" release of energy and frustration to get back to the task at hand—figuring out who wanted the Deimos operatives dead.

Loading the gun with paintball pellets, Jordyn eyed the others doing the same. The red team consisted of Ian, Mancini, Pierce, Chris, and her, while Mic, Carter,

Flynn, Rook, and McCabe made up the blue team. Jordyn was looking forward to nailing Carter's ass. She wore her black pants from yesterday, and Mic had given her a clean, long-sleeved, black shirt. Resting her gun on the picnic table they were gathered around, she pulled a hairband out of her pocket and gathered her long locks into a ponytail. Without looking, she knew Carter was watching her every move, and unwanted goosebumps pebbled her skin.

Ignoring him, she checked out the landscape they were about to head into. The game course was a maze, spreading out over several acres with trees, eight-foot hedges, boulders, trenches, and small hills to hide behind. Jordyn knew she was at a slight disadvantage between having never been on the course before and it'd been a while since she'd engaged in this type of warfare. Urban assassinations and undercover ops tended to make up the majority of her missions. But sneaking around and being invisible was something she'd learned from her uncle and then from Carter, and she had plenty of tricks up her sleeve.

As everyone finished loading and put on their eye protection, Mic nodded at Ian to set things in motion.

"All right," he announced. "Since you're not a bunch of pansies taking time off from an office job to play cops and robbers, the rules are simple—there are no rules. You're on your own once the opposing team has been eliminated. The last person standing gets bragging rights."

"That's it?"

"Shut up, Flynn, or you're my first fucking target. Blue team, head out. You've got a three-minute start before we come after your asses."

After some challenges were laid down, a few fists were bumped, and one or two middle fingers were flashed, the blue team disappeared behind the first hedge. Ian set the timer on his watch, then leaned against the wooden picnic table covered with empty paintball boxes. His gaze fell on Jordyn. She looked away and then back at him. "What?"

He shrugged. "I just knew the woman who would tie that boy up into knots would be kick-ass."

Her brow furrowed. "What *boy*? What are you talking about?"

"Oh, please." He rolled his eyes. "I don't know if it's because you're giving him the cold shoulder or what, but, damn, woman, you have to know Carter's hot for you. And despite your words and actions, the feeling is definitely mutual. So why don't you bury the fucking hatchet, find the nearest bed, and get it over with."

"What? Screw you, asswipe! You have no idea what you're talking about. And that bastard is the last man I want in my bed."

Chuckling, Pierce stepped over and leaned against the table as well. "I tried telling her that last night and got the same response. Methinks the lady doth protest too much."

Seriously? Who do these guys think they are? They sure as hell weren't Dear Abby, and even if they were, she wasn't discussing Carter with either of them.

"Last night?" Ian repeated with unveiled interest. "Do tell."

"Yeah. Found her sneaking around downstairs and tortured her with apple pie, but she wouldn't fess up. I think she was avoiding Carter since he came up the stairs a few minutes before I went down. But that's just my guess." Pierce lifted his chin toward Jordyn. "Zip-lips over there would neither confirm nor deny."

"Well, that explains why he sent daggers your way at breakfast. You shared a fucking pie with his woman." Ian punched Pierce's shoulder in jest. "Don't you know that was added to the man code recently? I mean, it's *pie*, dude. You don't share *pie* with someone else's woman."

Jordyn gaped at the two of them. They were not Abbott and Costello, even though they seemed to think so. "I'm not his woman, asswipe. And let me tell you something else—"

Her words were cut off by the timer alert on Ian's watch. He pushed off the table and gave her a wink, which irritated her even more. "Sorry, sweetheart, you can finish that lie when we're done. Now, let's go have some fun."

Circling his hand in the air, he gave the silent signal for them to move out into the maze. Everyone pulled their goggles down over their eyes and merged onto the course. Ian and Jordyn went to the left while the others took the right. Covering the former SEAL's six, Jordyn listened for any signs of their playtime enemy nearby. They spent a good five minutes creeping around before Ian held up his fist, telling her, without words, to stop in her tracks. He swiveled his head toward her, pointed to his right ear, then at the row of tall hedges next to them. He'd heard someone on the other side that she hadn't. In complete silence, the man dropped to his knees, then to his stomach. She would never have known he'd moved if she hadn't watched him do it. Aiming his weapon between the bases of two arborvitaes, he edged it forward. With a slow squeeze of the trigger, he fired a single shot.

A split second later, loud cursing came through the branches. "Fuck! God fucking damn it!" Flynn roared. "Who the fuck was that? Shit! Don't tell me I'm the first one out!" He continued to curse and mumble as he left the playing field.

Ian got to his feet and grinned wildly at Jordyn. One down and four more blue players to go.

Mancini was the next person hit, followed by Rook, who was taken out by Pierce. The rest of them spread out. When a team was eliminated, the others didn't want to be in sight of their teammates when it became a free-for-all. To the maze's east were stairs leading to a wooden platform high above the playing field, where those who had been shot could watch the action. They wouldn't reveal any active shooter's position because that would be poor sportsmanship, but when McCabe was taken out by Jordyn, cheers and snarky comments filtered down.

Chris went down next. "Fuck, Mic! Seriously? You had to hit me in the ass?"

Creeping around a large boulder, Jordyn tried to figure out where the man's complaint came from. While she'd started to like Mic, all was fair in love and war out there on the course. A shuffle came from her left, and she ignored it to a point. There was no way any of the other four remaining players would make a noise unless it were to purposely draw someone in that direction.

Pierce was the next player eliminated, but Jordyn didn't know who'd hit him. He just announced loudly that he was out on his way off the course, so no one would hit him again if their paths crossed. Creeping around like this, without worrying about a real bullet, was really kind of fun, Jordyn thought. She'd have to do it again sometime.

"Son of a fucking bitch! Jackass, you're a dead man!" Ian was out, and from the sound of it, Carter had fired the shot.

A small rock landed behind Jordyn, and she rushed around the boulder for cover, realizing her mistake a half second before Mic's blue paintball hit her in the shoulder and exploded. The woman grinned at her and silently mouthed "bye-bye" with a dramatized girly wave of her fingers.

Mic was good, Jordyn would give her that. If she ever needed the woman to cover her six, she was confident her ass would be safe. Cutting through the hedges, she yelled out to Carter that she'd been hit once she'd put some distance between her and Mic. She didn't want to give the man any clues to her attacker's location. If Jordyn couldn't be the winner of this game, she was rooting for the other woman to win.

By the time Jordyn reached the top of the tower and joined the others, Mic and Carter were closing in on each other. As good as the Deimos spy was, Mic had the advantage of being smaller and more familiar with the course. She nailed Carter in the thigh through a heavy shrub in a move similar to Ian's earlier.

Carter dropped his head back on his shoulders and cursed up a storm like everyone who had been eliminated before him. But the game had done what Ian and Mic had hoped for. Both teams were now laughing, joking, and slapping each other on the back. A majority of the tension had faded away. Unfortunately, not everything could be fixed with a bunch of blue and red paintballs.

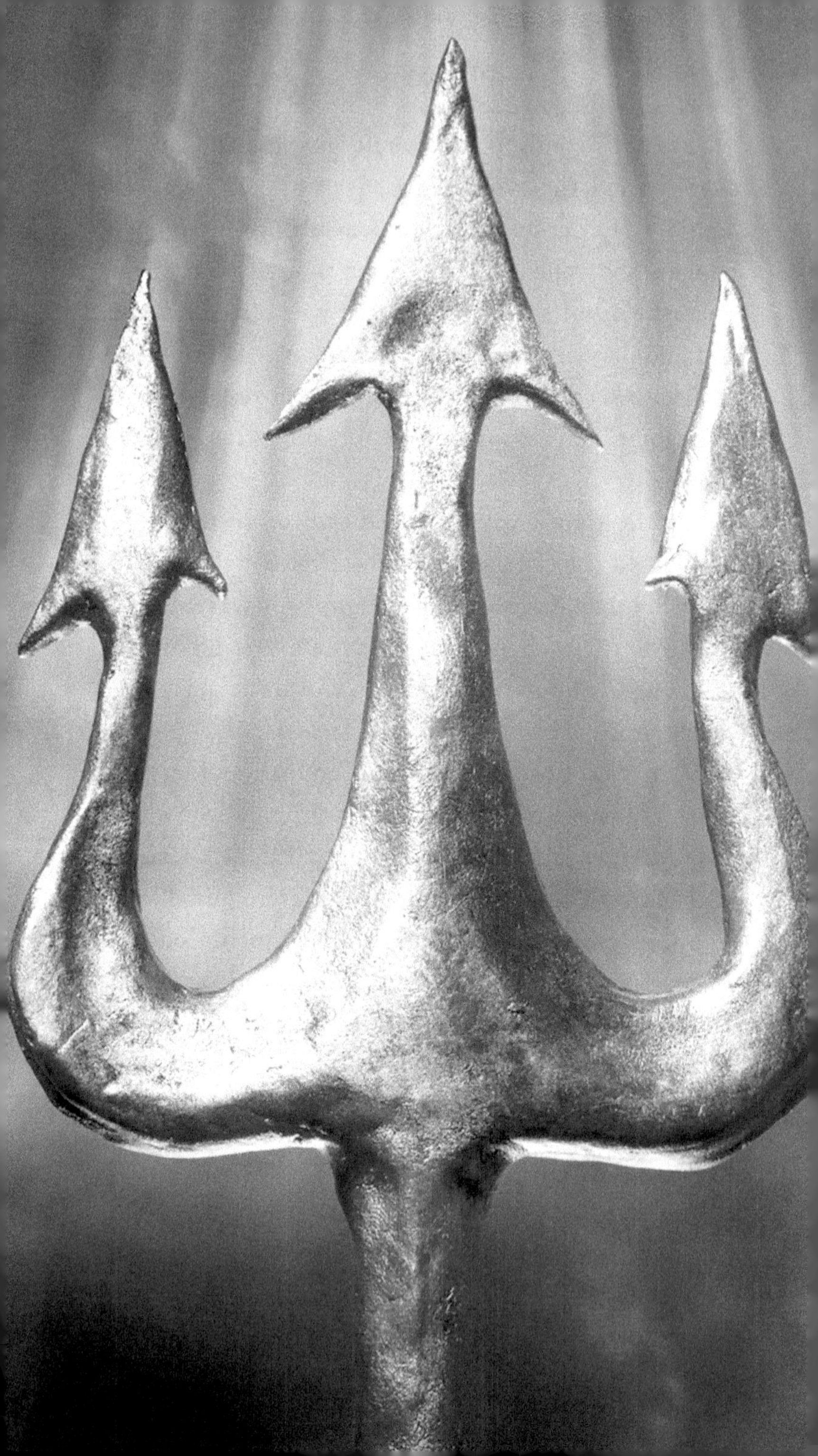

CHAPTER TEN

"Prepare for landing."

At the sound of the pilot's voice, Carter was instantly awake. On private jets, surrounded by people he trusted with his life, was where he got some of his best sleep. His mind knew he could relax, knowing that if anything went wrong, there was little he could do about it. Learning to fly a plane was one of the things on his bucket list he hadn't gotten around to yet. Now, jumping out of a plane or crash landing in one were things he'd already done, so actually flying one was kind of anticlimactic after those two.

They descended toward a small, private airport in Virginia, just outside Washington D.C. Minutes after the pilot's announcement, they touched down and taxied to a hangar. From across the aisle, Ian leaned over the armrest of his seat and smacked Carter's shoulder. "You sure you don't want us sticking with you? You know damn well my wife and the rest of the Trident women are going to give me hell if anything happens to you. For some fucking reason, they love your scrawny ass."

Pulling the leather tie out of his hair, Carter ran his hands through the strands, then redid the ponytail. "Yeah, I'm sure. We're going to need to go see a few people, and it may put some of your contracts in jeopardy—"

"Fuck you. Like I give a shit about that. Trident could fold today, and I'm still set for life, so don't give me that goddamned crap."

They both stood as he glared at Ian. "Dude, we've got it covered for now. I appreciate it, but plausible deniability is probably going to come into play at some point, and I'll be damned if you or anyone else at Trident goes down because of me." When it looked like his friend would curse him out again, he held up a hand, stopping him. "But I may need you for something else, though. I won't know for another day or two, but... it's important to me. I'll call if I need you."

Crossing his arms, Ian stared at him for several long seconds, clearly trying to decide whether to return to Tampa or not. Jordyn walked toward them from the back of the aircraft, the strap of her duffel over her shoulder, and she glanced back and forth at the two of them. "Problem?"

Finally, Ian relented. "No. No problem." He pointed

to his friend's chest. "But if you don't call if you're in a jam, I'm going to be fucking pissed."

Carter barked out a laugh. "Sawyer, name one fucking day of your adult life when you haven't been pissed about something."

"October 15. My wedding day." Ian shook his head. "Nope. Scratch that. I was pissed you almost missed the wedding, jackass." He pondered a moment while Carter's grin grew. "*Shit*. Let me get back to you on that. There's got to be one fucking day I wasn't pissed at something."

They disembarked inside the hangar behind closed doors. As Carter had requested, a black SUV with completely tinted windows waited for them sans driver. After saying goodbye and thanks to Ian, McCabe, and Mancini, the two Deimos operatives climbed into the vehicle, and Carter started the engine. Once refueled and a fresh flight crew took over, the Trident guys would take the contracted jet to Tampa.

When McCabe opened a roll-up door on the far side of the hangar for them, Carter drove out into the sunshine. They were out of the airport within minutes, cruising toward their destination.

Jordyn glanced at him. "Where are we going?"

"If I told you that," he said with a smirk, "I'd have to kill you."

Rolling her eyes, she let out an unladylike snort. "Well, you could try."

Not in this lifetime. The top spot on a list of things he never wanted to do on this Earth was to hurt Jordyn, but somehow, he had. While she wasn't trying to knee him in the balls anymore, something heavy still hung between them. Later, when they were safely hidden from the people gunning for them, he'd ask her again why she'd hated him all these years. And she would answer him even if he had to tie her to a bed and torture her with orgasm deprivation. Damn, that thought had his dick twitching. *Put your head on straight and watch for fucking tails, asshole. Deal with Jordyn and whatever's up her ass later.*

Silence filled the vehicle as Carter navigated the streets of Washington, D.C. Several blocks away from the White House, he pulled into a private parking garage. Stopping at a small box in front of a heavy metal gate, he rolled down the driver and passenger windows and entered a twelve-digit code. The gate rolled to the side, granting them entry. Not only had the code verification gained them access, but whoever was monitoring the security cameras with facial recognition software had also flipped a switch. One would not work without the other.

Steering down several ramps, he parked on the third lower level. Jordyn looked around. "Where are we? What's here?"

He pointed to what appeared to be a dirty-looking fire escape door. "Tunnel to the White House."

Her gaze shot to his face in disbelief. Most of the

members of Deimos had never been to the big house, but Carter was not among them. He'd gotten to know President Robert Jacobs quite well over the past year since the man had taken office. While they'd gotten off to a bit of a rocky start, that had quickly passed as the new POTUS realized the value of the covert agency he'd known nothing about until a few hours after being sworn into office. The power players of Deimos, the FBI, CIA, NSA, and every other agency in D.C. had to gain the trust of the new president every four or eight years and vice versa. Thankfully, Jacobs was as intelligent as his predecessor and had also been a Green Beret in the Army—a background that gave him a better understanding of black ops than most people.

"Th-the White House?" Jordyn asked. "What the hell are we doing there?"

"We have a meeting to attend. Leave your duffel here," he added as he opened his door and climbed out of the vehicle. "It's as safe here as it would be in the Oval Office, but it'll cause a lot more problems in there."

Still looking a little shell-shocked, Jordyn followed him to the door. He opened a small box on the wall and placed his right eye level with the retina scanner. It wasn't the last hoop they'd have to jump through to gain access to the head of the country—there were a few more waiting for them.

The door clicked open, and another heavy metal door behind it slid to the side. Jordyn chuckled in incredulity and amusement. "Definitely a James Bond moment."

"You're really hung up on him, aren't you?" Carter asked, leading her into the tunnel that was four city blocks from their destination. "Who was your favorite actor who played him?"

The door slid closed behind them, and he strode to one of two golf carts. Unplugging the charger, he turned the key and waited for her to climb aboard.

"Sean Connery, of course, but I must admit, Daniel Craig is a very close and yummy second."

Rolling his eyes, Carter hit the cart's accelerator and sped them toward the underground entrance to the White House. When they arrived at the other end, the only things different than where they'd entered were an elevator and two Marines standing guard, with a third sitting at a desk with several computers, phones, and video screens. With a nod toward the three men, Carter stepped over to several small lockers built into the wall. Removing all his weapons, he placed them in a vault, locked it, and took the key while Jordyn followed his lead.

The Marine at the desk stood with a metal detector wand in hand, and Carter spread his arms and legs. "How're you doing, Jansen?"

Running the wand over the spy's body, the Marine answered, "Good, man. Wife's due any day now with our new boy."

"Hey, congrats. I expect a cigar next time."

"You got it, and thanks." After the wand, he patted Carter down from ponytail to shoes. He then turned to Jordyn and repeated the procedure. Jansen never asked for her name or ID. In fact, he didn't know Carter's name, even after meeting him this way many times over the past few years. Like the other Marines who worked the same detail, all he knew was the covert operative had carte blanche access to the president unless otherwise notified.

When he was convinced neither was carrying something that could harm the big boss, he gestured to the elevator. "You're clear. Do your thing."

Carter went to another wall panel next to the elevator. He pressed a button and spoke into a microphone. "And so, my fellow Americans: ask not what your country can do for you — ask what you can do for your country."

Behind him, Jordyn chuckled, and he stepped aside to let her enter the elevator first when the doors slid open. "Jacobs is a fan of Kennedy," he told her with a shrug. "Garrett had us reciting the beginning of Lincoln's Gettysburg Address. Each president picks whatever quote he wants to use for security."

The doors closed, and as the car rose, Jordyn faced him, suddenly seeming unsure of herself. "Um, what's the protocol here? I don't want to say something stupid in front of the president. It is the president we're going to see, isn't it? I mean, anyone else, we could have met some other place."

"Yeah, we're heading to the Oval Office. McDaniel is meeting us too. The only two things you have to remember are to address Jacobs as 'Mr. President' or 'sir,' and if he's standing, you're standing unless he tells you otherwise." He paused. "Oh, and one other thing, during the meeting—don't stare if he rubs one out."

"What!" He smirked, and she punched him in the gut, sending an *ooof* from his mouth. "Jackass."

The elevator stopped, and the doors opened, revealing two Secret Service agents. Carter nodded hello and turned right out of the car. "Wow. I'm moving up in the world with you. Ian will be impressed. I've been promoted to 'jackass' from 'asshole.'"

"Sh," she hissed in a low voice from behind him. "We're in the White House."

He chuckled as he knocked on a door at the end of the hall. "What, you think the president doesn't curse?"

Jordyn opened her mouth to respond but was interrupted by a rumbling voice coming from the other side of the door. "Enter."

The color drained from Jordyn's face.

Well, what do you know? Meeting Commander-in-Chief Jacobs for the first time has her all flustered.

While part of Carter wanted to tease her about it, he thought it best he calm her down before she puked in the Oval Office. Reaching out, he cupped her chin.

"Hey. He puts his pants on one leg at a time and takes a dump in the toilet, just like everyone else. He won't bite."

Swallowing hard, she nodded. "O-okay. Not sure why I'm nervous... I'm never nervous... I mean, I've never met the president before... but—"

Her babbling was cut off by his lips meeting hers. Her eyes widened, then flared with heat, as he kissed her softly. The air around them crackled, and he would have sold his soul at that moment to be anywhere else with her—well, anywhere with a bed.

Suddenly, Jordyn stiffened and pulled away. Her eyes narrowed in anger at him. "What the hell—"

The door next to them flew open, and McDaniel raised an eyebrow at them. "Are you two going to stay out here all day, or are you coming in?"

"Just finishing a conversation, boss." With a sweep of his hand, Carter indicated for Jordyn to precede him. She gave him a deadly glare before letting a professional indifference fall across her face.

Shutting the door again, McDaniel gestured toward the sitting area by the room's fireplace. President Jacobs stood from his favorite wingback chair and held out his hand in greeting. "Ms. Alvarez, it's a pleasure to meet you finally. I've heard great things about you from Carter and Gene here."

"Th-thank you, sir."

As Jordyn shook Jacobs's hand, Carter's jaw clenched. Hearing her call anyone else "sir" grated on him, even if it was the President of the United States.

"Carter. I wish I were seeing you under better circumstances."

He accepted Jacobs's handshake. "So do I, Mr. President."

"Please, everyone, have a seat." With a tilt of his head, Jacobs indicated the couches in the sitting area. Jordyn sat on one with Carter while McDaniel took a seat across from them. POTUS sat back in his chair after handing the two US spies bottles of cold water with the presidential seal on them. "Gene has filled me in. I'm very sorry for the loss of the three operatives. Any idea who's behind this?"

"No, sir," Carter replied. "We have the Deimos computer wizards and a few contract agencies we trust trying to find a direction to point us in. Everyone's got their ears to the ground, trying to intercept some chatter, but there's been nothing so far. But there are a few things I want to check here in Washington."

"Such as?"

Carter settled into the plush cushions, resting his ankle over the opposite knee. He was about to push a button POTUS wouldn't like, but it was necessary. "I'd rather not say at the moment, sir."

Jacobs's eyes narrowed at him. "I could order you to tell me."

"You could," he agreed with a nod of his head.

"But you won't." They both knew that. Plausible deniability was coming into play again. When the time came, Jacobs would be given all the information needed to order the assassination of whoever was behind the deaths of Benito, Aikman, and Aldridge. There would be no trial—there couldn't be since, technically, like Carter and Jordyn, the three men hadn't existed. How did you hang murder charges on someone when the victims are governmental ghosts? "If nothing pans out, Jordyn and I will follow up with the crime scenes. Maybe we'll see something the locals missed."

"I'd rather put you in protective custody," McDaniel said. "But I know better than to try it."

He was right. Between Jordyn and Carter, they had the best chance of figuring this out, and neither of them would willingly sit around waiting for someone else to solve it. The other operatives on the list were cut from the same cloth. As the others had been located and extracted, McDaniel had teamed them up with those who weren't walking around with targets on their backs. Everyone would have someone covering their six, and they were all hitting up their contacts around the globe, trying to find a fucking clue as to who wanted them dead.

Jordyn shifted in her seat beside Carter, still seemingly uncomfortable being in the Oval Office with POTUS. "Um, have we heard about Brennan and Dartmouth yet? Have they been extracted?"

McDaniel nodded. "Yes. But, like you, it was a close call for both of them. We need to end this—and soon."

Something in his boss's tone bothered Carter. A lightbulb went off in his head. "Shit. Are you telling me there's a chance Deimos will be disbanded?"

"What?" Jordyn looked back and forth between Jacobs and McDaniel. Her discomfort faded in an instant. "Are you kidding me?"

Neither man answered her as seconds ticked by, and Carter could feel her tension growing. He subtly dropped his hand to the couch between them, brushing his fingers against her outer thigh, silently telling her to keep her cool.

Finally, Jacobs spoke. "Trust me, Ms. Alvarez. The last thing I want to do is shut Deimos down. The United States needs you and your fellow operatives more than ever. But *I* need you to find out who is doing this and keep it under the radar as much as possible. If any of this goes public, every Deimos agent will have to go off-grid until we can have you regroup under a new name and address. And we can't do that with your NOC list flapping in the wind. This isn't the CIA or FBI that every American knows about. Deimos is as black ops as it gets and needs to stay that way."

Faint, incoming thumps of a helicopter's rotors grew louder, and Jacobs stood. "That would be Marine One for me."

The others got to their feet. The president's staff would knock on the door any second, and the covert operatives needed to be out of the room before anyone else came in. Carter extended his hand to Jacobs and raised an eyebrow at him. "Free rein?"

His jaw tightening, POTUS nodded and shook Carter's hand. "Find the son of a bitch and make sure his body is never found again. Ms. Alvarez, do your best, and I'll do mine."

Jordyn's nervousness was replaced by determination. "That's all I ask, sir."

After retrieving her weapons, Jordyn hopped into the driver's seat of the golf cart. Carter eyed her but took the passenger seat without question. Despite the lingering tension from the meeting they'd just left, she giggled as she turned the ignition key and pressed down on the accelerator. The cart jerked forward, and Carter's hand flew to the oh-shit handle above his right shoulder. Jordyn eased up on the pedal until the cart moved smoothly. "Sorry about that. I've always wanted to drive one of these."

He laughed out loud at her. "I've taught you how to drive every fucking car and truck on the planet, and you're all excited about a golf cart."

When he put it that way, it did seem silly, but she was having fun, speeding down the dimly lit tunnel at a whopping 25 mph. Once they reached the other end,

Carter plugged the electric charger back in and hit a button on the wall next to the door. Someone buzzed it open for them, and they were again back in the parking lot. Climbing into the SUV's passenger seat, Jordyn clicked on her seat belt. "So… where are we going from here, Tyrone?"

Putting the vehicle in drive, Carter steered up the ramps toward the exit. "Tyrone is a no. And we're going someplace where we can shower, eat, get some information, and sleep—hopefully, in that order."

"Does this all-inclusive place have a name?"

He paused as if trying to decide whether to tell her or not. After a moment, he said, "Club X. Ever heard of it?"

Her body clenched as she remembered why she'd hated him all these years. Oh, yeah. She'd definitely heard of it, and there was no fucking way in hell she was going there with him—or anyone else for that matter.

CHAPTER ELEVEN

Seven years ago...

Pacing back and forth in her temporary bedroom in Deimos's secure Virginia headquarters, Jordyn bit her lip. Why she'd snuck out on Carter after they'd fucked each other senseless a few nights ago was something she hadn't figured out yet. She'd always suspected sex with him would be off the charts, but even that had been an understatement. After making her ask to come in his mouth, he'd rocked her world. Then before she could recover, he'd donned a condom, slid her down his torso, and impaled her with his very impressive cock. Within seconds, she had been trembling with her second orgasm of the night, and it had been far from the last one he'd given her hours later. She'd ridden him hard that first time. Then he'd taken her from behind. The missionary position. Reverse cowgirl. Against the wall. Bent over in the shower. And several other positions she had no idea how to describe or what to call them. She'd lost count of the number of times he'd made her body sing with ecstasy in between bouts of sleep.

But before the sun had risen, doubt had started to take over her mind. She knew she'd started falling for him during their training sessions, but neither had given the other a green light. In fact, the waiting had been fun in a way. Months of mental foreplay, her vibrator, and cold showers had reached a climax in that small farmhouse barn. But her body, mind, and heart's reaction to it all made her sneak out of there while Carter still slept. It hadn't taken her long to figure out how to turn off the alarms so she could open the doors without waking him. The expat, whose farm it was, hadn't asked any questions when she went looking for a ride from him. She hadn't wanted to leave Carter without a vehicle, and he would have heard her start it up.

The former CIA agent had dropped her off in a mid-sized town about twenty minutes from his place. From there, she'd gotten a taxi to the airport in Kuala Lumpur, then purchased a ticket for Virginia with one of her alias passports. Carter took the private jet back, and she'd left her favorite sniper rifle and other weapons with him, knowing he'd be able to get them into the US for her. The only weapon she'd brought to the airport with her was one of the revolvers she acquired in Malaysia, just in case she ran into trouble. Before approaching security, she'd made a detour to a bathroom where she'd stripped the gun down to its individual parts. Each piece had ended up in a different garbage can along the check-in concourse. She hadn't wanted to risk a child or criminal finding the completed weapon.

She'd arrived in Virginia yesterday and taken care of her reports. The flash drive with the data she'd garnered from the ambassador's computer and photographs of a few documents in the safe she'd cracked open had gone to the computer and intelligence divisions of Deimos.

Glancing at her cell phone, she couldn't tell if she was disappointed or not that Carter hadn't run after her and knocked down her door, demanding to know why he'd woken up alone. He knew where she would go, so that couldn't be why he hadn't found her. And he hadn't left any voicemails for her either. Well, what had she expected after doing the walk of shame from halfway around the world? Maybe he didn't feel the same way she did. Maybe it had only been a one-night stand that had taken months to develop, and he was done with her now.

Shit. Woman up, Jordyn. You have more than enough guts to kill a man, but you can't ask one you slept with how he feels about you?

Opening the bedroom door, she strode the halls of the large building until she reached the communications division. If anyone knew where Carter was right now, it would be these guys. He had to be in the Virginia/D.C. area since he needed to file his reports too. It was getting late, but if she tracked him down in time, maybe they could go to dinner or something.

Entering the room, she saw that Kenny Reardon was the only comm tech not currently on the phone. Walking over to his computer setup, she flopped down in a chair next to him.

"Hey, beautiful," he said as he finished typing an entry into his computer. "Long time no see. How've you been?"

Reardon was a sweet kid with bright red hair and a perpetual smile. A few years younger than Jordyn, he always flirted with her but had no illusions they were anything more than associates and maybe friends.

"I'm good—getting ready to get out of here. Listen, I was wondering if you know where Carter is. I need to talk to him about something and don't want to wait until he gets around to checking his messages."

Leaning back in his chair, the tech tossed a rubber stress ball up in the air and caught it before throwing it again. "Yeah, about that. Weren't you two supposed to fly back from the other side of the world together?"

That just went to show that no one in Deimos was completely dark—unless they went rogue—there was always someone who knew where you were and what you were supposed to be doing.

Not wanting to tell him the real reason she wanted

to talk to Carter, Jordyn lied as smoothly as she did on her missions. "I had some stuff to take care of..." She purposely lowered her voice to a near whisper. "...you know, woman stuff. And I didn't want him to have to wait around for me."

The guy's pale face turned beet red, just as she knew it would. Tell most men that you had to take care of "woman stuff," and there would be no further questions from them.

"I... ah... gotcha... I mean, I understand... no, scratch that. I don't understand. Nor do I want to understand... um... what was the question?"

Jordyn stifled a laugh at his embarrassment. "Where can I find Carter?"

He seemed to relax a little now that they weren't talking about "women stuff," and he eased back in his rolling chair. "He was here earlier, then left after filing his report. But I think he was heading for Club X."

Her eyes narrowed. "Club X? What's that, and where is it?"

"Where? In Georgetown. What? *The* most exclusive BDSM club in D.C." He waggled his eyebrows a few times. "Not that it's my scene, but damn, I would love to check that place out someday."

What? A sex club? What the hell is Carter doing there?

Jordyn didn't realize she'd asked that last question aloud until Reardon responded, "He usually stops in there when he's in town. From what I hear, all the movers and shakers into kink go there."

"Oh, so... he goes there for intel, right?" She hoped that's all he did there.

Shaking his head, Reardon leaned forward in his chair to answer one of the phone lines that had started ringing. "Well, sometimes, sure. But most of the time, he's there as 'Master Carter.' He's got memberships to kink clubs all over the world. To each his own, I guess." He punched the blinking button on the phone and spoke into his headset's microphone. "Comm desk. What's up?"

Her mouth agape, Jordyn stood and walked out of the room, too stunned to say goodbye to Reardon.

Master Carter? Memberships to kink clubs all over the world? He fucking liked to abuse women? That fucking bastard!

She'd fucking kill him if she ever got her hands on him again!

Present...

It had taken Jordyn days or weeks, hell, maybe even months, before she'd calmed down enough following that revelation. But then again, maybe she still hadn't since, right now, she wanted to beat the hell out of the woman abuser sitting next to her. After she'd walked out of the comm office that day, she'd managed to avoid the bastard for years. She'd focused on her missions and became adept at working independently. If she had to be paired up with someone, she'd requested anyone but Carter. If McDaniel suspected bad blood between his two operatives, he never questioned Jordyn about it—she wasn't sure if he'd asked Carter, though.

"Jordyn."

Her head whipped around at the sound of Carter's low timber. Not realizing the SUV had stopped, she had no idea where they were. "What?" she snapped.

His eyes narrowed at her. He opened his mouth to say something, then clearly decided against it because his mouth closed as he ran a hand down his face. "Nothing. We're here. Come on."

Without waiting for her response, he opened his door and got out. From the passenger seat, Jordyn eyed their surroundings. She'd been so wrapped up in the past that she hadn't even noticed when he'd pulled into another underground garage. Expensive cars occupied several parking spaces, but no one else was around. A white door, with simple black lettering on it, loomed ahead of her—Club X.

She jumped when her car door opened suddenly, and Carter stared down at her, his brow furrowed. "What's wrong?"

"I'm not going in there." She crossed her arms like

a petulant child and sat back against the seat, determination and anger set in her jaw.

"What? Why not?" When she didn't answer, he reached down and turned her chin toward him. She batted his hand away, not wanting him to touch her. "Jordy, what the hell is going on? Talk to me. I can't fucking fix it if I don't know what's wrong."

Gritting her teeth, she glared at him. "Stop with the fucking 'Jordy'—you know I hate that name."

"You didn't mind when I used it while fucking your brains out. How many times did you come for me that night? Huh? Don't remember that far back? I sure as hell do. I remember every single time you shattered around my fingers, tongue, and cock. Every. Single. Time. *Jordy*. I also remember how I woke up alone. So, tell me what the fuck changed between you screaming my name in ecstasy to when you decided you hated my guts."

Damn the bastard—she remembered that night far more than she wanted to, and like it always did when she thought about it, her body responded. Moisture pooled between her legs against her will. Glancing up at him, she saw his face was red in anger or frustration, and a vein at his temple bulged. Tension rolled off him in waves, and Jordyn suddenly realized she was at a disadvantage sitting in the vehicle with him hovering over her. If he lashed out at her because he was pissed, she had little chance of avoiding at least one punch. Pushing him out of her way, she jumped out of the passenger seat and put distance between them.

She held out her hand. "Give me the keys—I'll check into a hotel. I'm not sleeping here."

"What?" He threw his hands in the air. "Jesus, woman, you're going to drive me to drink. You're not going anywhere. The club has everything we need, and I have to talk to some contacts here later."

"It might have everything you need, but there is no way in hell I'm going into a fucking perverted sex club where men get their kicks abusing women. Now give me the fucking keys, you son of a bitch!"

Carter's lower jaw practically scraped the ground—he couldn't remember ever being that stunned. *Holy fucking shit! That's the bug she's had up her ass all these years? Well, knock me out and paint me blue!*

A laugh started deep in his belly, and as hard as he tried, he couldn't prevent it from rising and shooting out his mouth. His entire body shook from the force, and tears filled his eyes as he roared, his amusement echoing off the parking garage walls. Jordyn glared at him, warning him his death was imminent if he didn't stop, and that just made him laugh harder. He threw his head back with a loud guffaw and brought both hands to his face to wipe the tears away. "Oh, shit...

woman... what—what am I going to do with you, huh? This is too fucking funny."

A flick of her wrist and a faint but lethal *snick* caught his attention, and he froze. His voice went from amused to deadly in a heartbeat as his eyes narrowed at her. "Seriously, Jordy? You're pulling a switchblade on me? Not a wise move, sweetheart, and you know it."

"Give me the fucking keys," she spat, holding the blade in her right hand.

There were about five feet between them, far enough for him to react if she really came at him with it. He didn't want to hurt her, but he also wasn't letting her stab him—not that he thought she seriously would. Instead of giving her what she demanded, he grabbed the waistband of his pants and dropped the keys inside his boxer briefs—and damn, the metal was cold against his hot flesh. "Come and get them, sweetheart. Or better yet, come into the club with me and let me show you how wrong you are about everything."

Her jaw clenched as her gaze flickered to his groin and back to his face again, but she didn't answer him.

"The BDSM lifestyle is far from the image you obviously have in your mind. I have never..." He took a warning step toward her, his hands loose at his sides, ready to react to an assault if need be. "...*ever* hit a woman in anger. And I've only hit one in self-defense. Now, sparring with or spanking a woman who consented to it is something completely different." Well, there had been that time he'd had to hit Mic, but that had been for their cover on a mission—no way he was mentioning that to Jordyn. Mic had known it was coming, and Carter had hated to do it. Every time he'd looked at the bruise he left on her cheek until it was completely gone, he felt like puking.

Jordyn snorted. "Right, like women are begging you to hit them."

A heavy sigh escaped him. "All right. Evidently, I'm not going to be able to convince you of anything out here in the fucking garage, so let's make a deal, shall we? Hmm?"

"A deal? Why would I want to make a fucking deal with you?"

Damn, this was killing him. Somehow, she'd found out about him being in the lifestyle, and like most people not in it, she had visions of despicable, harmful abuse in her head. It wasn't the first time he'd come across someone who was severely misinformed about BDSM, but this was the first time it involved someone he cared about—someone he wanted with every breath he took. "Because right now, sweetheart, we need to be working together to find out who wants us and the others dead. One of the reasons I brought you here is because of all the contacts I have who are club members. Some, if not all, of the people I need to talk to will probably be here later, and I'm hoping one of them will point us in the right direction. Now, put away the knife and come inside with me. The club's not open yet, but I have a permanent room here. We can shower, catch some Zs, and have a bite to eat. And in between all that, I'll try to educate you a little about the lifestyle." He brought his right hand up and placed it over his heart. "Come on, Jordy. I think you know deep down I would never, ever hurt you. No one will lay a hand on you inside the club, and I swear to you, I would never do anything to you or anyone else in there that wasn't asked for. Trust me—*please.*"

That last word almost sounded like a desperate plea, even to his own ears. He stood perfectly still, waiting for her to absorb and analyze what he'd said. Seconds passed as she glared at him. Finally, she wavered—her hard expression softened just a tad, and her hand and the weapon dropped to her side. With another flick of her wrist, the blade disappeared. "This goes against everything inside of me."

"I know, sweetheart, I know. But I'm asking you— begging you to trust me. It's not what you think." They stared at each other for a minute, then Jordyn reached for the rear passenger door of the SUV and opened it. When she pulled out her duffel bag and nodded at him, he heaved a sigh of relief. Knots in his stomach he hadn't realized were there released. "Thank you."

Retrieving his own bag, he locked the vehicle and led her to the club's door. He flashed his wallet containing an electronic passkey over a sensor, and the door unlocked. They entered the small hallway, and he pushed the button for the elevator. "Look, I know you'll be tense in the club, but I need you to go into mission mode. Blend in. I'll introduce you as a new and still learning Domme, so you won't have to worry about Doms trying to negotiate a scene with you. Unfortunately, that means you'll probably have the submissive men, and maybe some women, asking you to spank them and stuff. Do not insult or embarrass anyone here." When the doors opened, she entered the elevator, leaned against the back wall, and glowered at him, crossing her arms over her chest. Carter punched the button for the first floor. "I mean it, Jordy—this is important. Not blending in will raise a lot of red flags for people here. I've spent years cultivating my cover in this club. If I get outed, Deimos will lose a lot of important contacts who will never trust me again."

The doors opened when they reached the first floor, but Carter blocked Jordyn's exit. He stared at her until the doors shut behind him once more. She raised her eyebrows at him, then threw a hand in the air. "Fine. Mission mode. Undercover. Don't embarrass or insult. I fucking got it, asshole, now get me out of this elevator."

"Great," he mumbled. "I'm back to being an asshole." Pivoting, he hit the first-floor button again, and since the elevator hadn't moved, the doors immediately slid open.

Stepping into the lobby, he spotted the first person he wanted to see. A man in his thirties, wearing a black

T-shirt and gray dress slacks, stood at the concierge desk, reading something on the computer in front of him. He glanced up and smiled. "Master Carter, a pleasure to see you again, Sir—it's been a while."

"Good afternoon, Paul. It's nice to be back in town." He gestured toward Jordyn. "This is Mistress Jordyn, a friend from California who is relatively new to the lifestyle. She'll be here as my guest tonight. Jordyn, this is Paul, Club X's assistant manager."

Having gone into mission mode like he'd asked, she tilted her head toward the other man. "A pleasure to meet you, Paul."

Like any respectful submissive, Paul lowered his gaze and gave her a bow of his head. "The pleasure is all mine, Mistress Jordyn. Welcome to Club X. If you need anything, please come see me, and I'll take care of it immediately."

"Thank you. I'll do just that."

"Actually, you can do something for us right now, Paul." Pulling out his wallet again, Carter withdrew two $100 bills and handed them to the man. "Can you call Le Appétit and order two dinners off tonight's specials, with dessert, and have them delivered to my room, please?"

"Certainly, Sir—I'll deliver them myself. Would you also like me to bring up something to drink?"

"Hmm. How about a bottle of Screaming Eagle Cabernet Sauvignon, 2009?" From the corner of his eye, Carter saw Jordyn raise her brow slightly at the mention of the $2000 bottle of wine, but she didn't say a word.

"Excellent choice, Sir. I'll put that on your tab and bring everything up when the food arrives."

"Thank you. Now, one other thing—is your mistress here yet?"

"Yes, Sir. She's at the bar checking the inventory."

Carter nodded his thanks once more, then gestured toward a set of double doors. Jordyn followed him, and he held one of the doors open for her. Low, smooth jazz flowed from the speaker system, and the scent of oranges filled the air as two employees wiped down the various leather couches and chairs in the bar area.

"Carter, my dear. I didn't expect you tonight, but as always, it's lovely to see you." Mistress Trixie came from around the bar and sashayed toward him, a glint of delight and sensuality in her eyes. With firm, surgically-enhanced breasts tucked snuggly in the top of a long, black dress, Trixie had a body most women would kill for. "And who's this beautiful lady?"

As the tall, auburn-haired Domme assessed Jordyn with a knowing eye, Carter introduced the two and used the same story he'd given Paul. "Trixie, this is a friend of mine visiting from California. Jordyn is new to the lifestyle, and I've been training her as a Domme."

"Really?" Trixie's throaty, whiskey-laced voice held more than a hint of disbelief. She'd been in the lifestyle for many years and could spot a true sexual submissive from a mile away, but she didn't question his bald-faced lie any further. In her place of business, keeping secrets was mandatory if you wanted to *stay* in business—and alive. Holding out a hand to the shorter woman, she said, "Welcome to my club, Mistress Jordyn. It's a pleasure to have you here. If you'll excuse the cliché, any friend of Carter's is a friend of mine."

Jordyn shook the proffered hand. "Thank you, and it's a pleasure to meet you, too. You have a lovely place here." She glanced around the room with an appreciative expression on her face as if she'd been in BDSM clubs all around the world for years. Not that this level had any play areas—those were located on the second and third floors.

Clearing his throat, Carter addressed the establishment's owner. "I was wondering if you could arrange for appropriate club wear for Jordyn. Despite flying first class, the airline lost her checked luggage."

Rolling her eyes, Trixie shook her head. "How they can't get a bag from point A to point B in this day and age is beyond me." She ran her gaze down Jordyn's frame. "Let's see, a size six for the clothing, and, what, a six and a half shoe?"

Surprised, Jordyn let out a little laugh. "Damn, you're good."

"Oh, you don't know the half of it, darling. I'll call

over to Toni's and have her pick something spectac-ular for you."

"Thank you. I appreciate it."

Carter took a step backward, indicating the conversation was nearing its end. "Put it on my tab, Trixie. We're going to my room to relax for a little bit before Paul has our dinner delivered. We'll see you later."

With that, he led the way out to the lobby again. Reentering the elevator with Jordyn on his heels, Carter pressed the button for the fourth floor. When the doors closed, she faced him. "So... Trixie?"

He chuckled. "Jealous?" Frowning, she glared at him, causing him to laugh harder. "Don't worry, there's absolutely, positively nothing about Trixie that's attractive to me. First off, she's a sadistic Domme, and I'm a Dom who will never submit to her. Secondly, underneath that black dress is an impressive cock and balls—or so I'm told."

Jordyn's jaw dropped. "She... she's a... guy?"

"Transgender is the politically correct term."

"Holy shit, I never would have guessed. He... I mean, she could be a supermodel or something."

"You're not the first person to say that over the years." The doors opened, and Carter led the way to his private room. It had taken him a few years to be eligible for one, and then he'd had to wait for one to become available, but now it was permanently his until he was no longer a club member. Swiping his wallet in front of another sensor, he pushed the door open after he heard a *click*.

Following him into the large room, Jordyn eyed the furnishings. It had all the comforts of a studio apartment but on a very expensive scale. There was a sitting area with a sofa and chairs, an entertainment center with a forty-inch flat-screen TV, a dining table for two, and a king-sized mahogany bed. The décor was done in earth tones and was quite comfortable. He pointed to one of the other two doors in the room. "The bathroom is in there if you want to take a shower before dinner arrives."

She nodded but said nothing. Her gaze was on the huge bed, and he couldn't decipher her thoughts.

"Jordy, I won't jump you, so please relax. I've never had another woman in this room—it's my sanctuary. I come here to unwind and sleep."

With a nonchalant wave, she said, "I couldn't care less if you've had hundreds of women in here. I'm sure as hell not getting in that bed with you. I'll sleep on the sofa."

With her duffel still hanging from her shoulder, she stormed into the bathroom and slammed the door. When he heard the lock engage, he sighed. "Damn, she's going to be the death of me."

A few minutes later, he sat in the recliner, flipping through the TV channels for a sports game, while the sounds of Jordyn taking a shower floated through the door. He wanted to walk in there and join her with every second that passed, but he had to start from scratch with her—beginning with explaining the lifestyle to her. How she'd found out didn't matter—it wasn't like it was a huge secret at Deimos. He wasn't the only operative at the agency to be in the lifestyle, either. But for some reason, Jordyn was blinded against the reality of BDSM. Hopefully, she would open her mind and let him educate her because if she didn't, he'd have to walk away from her after this mess they were dealing with was over. And he didn't think he'd be able to do that—not after the sparks he felt while kissing her outside the Oval Office.

A soft knock on the door caught his attention, and he stood. Opening it, he stepped back to let Paul enter, pushing a room service cart. Three metal-covered plates, salads in china bowls, bread and butter, two wine glasses, and a bottle of cabernet sat atop a white tablecloth. Crystal salt and pepper shakers, expensive silverware, and cloth napkins accompanied them. Paul set the cart next to the door and then moved the first course and wine to the dining table. He even lit a small candle Carter hadn't noticed and placed it on the table with the shakers. "Sir, the dinners are a porterhouse steak *au poivre* and sautéed Chilean Sea Bass in a caramelized lemon sauce. For dessert, there's cheesecake served inside Valencia oranges topped with Grand Marnier and fresh whipped cream. They look delicious." He opened the bottle of wine with the flair of a sommelier and poured a small sample into one of the glasses. Carter sipped it, letting the enticing flavors coat his taste buds. It was an excellent wine, and he nodded his approval for the man to continue pouring it into the two glasses.

Leaving the remainder of the bottle on the table, Paul stated, "Mistress said to tell you Toni will have Mistress Jordyn's clothing delivered shortly. Will there be anything else, Sir?"

Jordyn picked that moment to come out of the bathroom. She was dressed in blue, haute couture lounge pants and a matching pullover shirt she'd purchased at the airport in Scotland, and her hair was twisted up under a towel. Forcing his body not to respond to her freshly scrubbed skin, bare feet, and the lavender scent of whatever shampoo she'd used that filled the room, he addressed Paul. "Could you track down a hairdryer for Mistress Jordyn, please? Leave it with her clothing outside the door when it arrives since we'll catch up on some much-needed sleep after eating."

"Certainly. Anything else, Sir?"

Carter glanced at Jordyn, and she shook her head. Turning back to the male submissive, he said, "No, that will be all for now. Thank you, Paul."

"My pleasure, Sir."

As the man left and shut the door behind him, Carter pulled out one of the dining table chairs for Jordyn. She hesitated momentarily, then sat and placed the napkin on her lap. He took the seat across from her and waited for her to pick up her fork and dig into her Caesar salad before following suit. It was a part of him he didn't have to think twice about—like breathing—it was second nature. A woman came first, especially a submissive, before his needs were met—whether they were sexual in nature or not. He opened doors for them, pulled out chairs, fed them, brought them pleasure, whatever was required. He needed to show Jordyn that's what a large portion of the BDSM lifestyle was for him and not whatever false image she had in her mind.

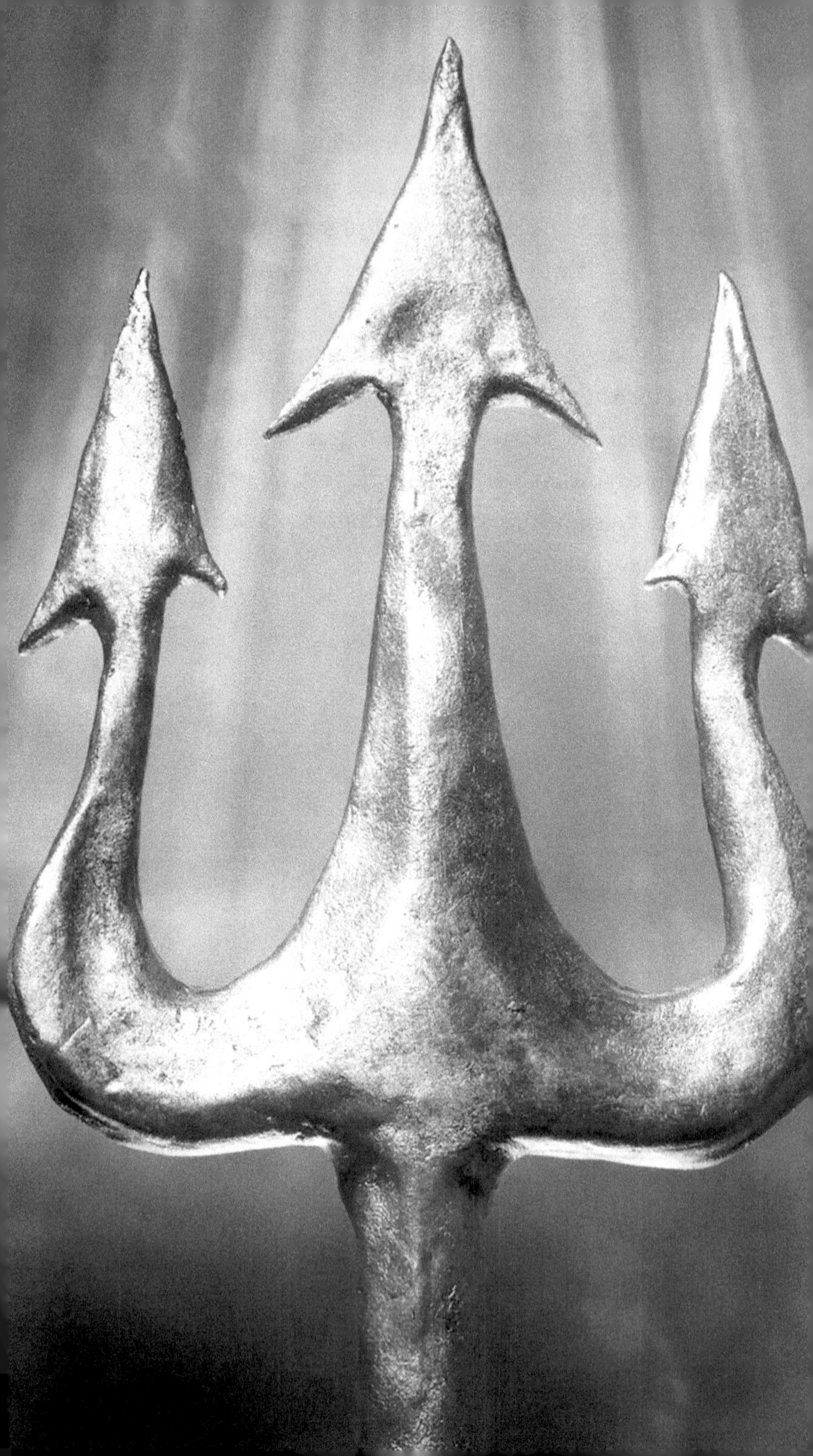

CHAPTER TWELVE

As hungry as she'd been and as much as she'd eaten, Jordyn couldn't remember tasting a single bite of the three-course meal. During their dinner, Carter had filled the silence with details of what they already knew about the breach and bounced a few hunches off her. She answered as best she could under his heated stare. Despite the conversation subject, the sexual tension in the room was off the charts, and she hated every second of it—at least her brain did.

Her lips still tingled from when he'd kissed her earlier at the White House. He'd caught her off guard, and she'd melted into the kiss for a few brief moments. Why, oh, why, did she have to be attracted to this man? He'd brought her to a fucking sex club of all places!

It hadn't been what she'd expected when they'd

entered the bar area earlier. Instead of a dungeon filled with ancient implements of torture, it was one of the most beautifully decorated clubs she'd ever been in, and that was saying a lot. In her undercover travels and missions, she'd been in high-end establishments worldwide, and Club X ranked right up there in terms of sophisticated décor. The black, gray, and burgundy colors had given the bar area a bold richness that reminded her of some of the rooms in Castle Steel that Mic and her team had left in the original décor.

Now, she paced the room as he took a shower, and every pass brought her face to face with that damn big bed. There were no whips and chains in the room, no restraints, just comfortable furniture—and that damn big bed. The blue and brown blanket with an unobtrusive, geometric pattern lay over blue satin sheets—she knew because she'd checked. And why she'd checked, she didn't know. She'd run her fingers over the cool material, and images of her and Carter rolling around on them had sent her hormones skyrocketing. An unwanted need pulsating between her legs was driving her crazy. She had to do something to quell her hormones. It'd been a while since she'd had sex, so that had to be the reason she was so horny, right? It didn't mean she was craving Carter—any man would do, right? *Fuck.*

Flopping down on the couch, she picked up the TV remote and changed the channel, not paying attention to anything that flashed on the screen before moving on. The bathroom door swung open, and Jordyn forced herself not to jump out of her skin. Her mouth watered as Carter, wearing only a pair of sweatpants, strode barefoot across the room to a small refrigerator and withdrew a water bottle. He held it up and raised an eyebrow at her. When she nodded, he grabbed another bottle and tossed it to her.

"Thanks." She opened the bottle and guzzled half as he sat in the recliner next to the couch. Reaching over, he took the remote from her and changed whatever show had been on to a seventies music channel. "Brandy" by Looking Glass filled the room, and he lowered the volume.

Shit, here it comes.

"We need to talk, love." She opened her mouth to respond, but he cut her off with a wave of his hand. "Uh-uh. This is long overdue. I just wish I hadn't waited so long to find out why you were running from me." He paused. "How did you find out I was in the lifestyle?"

She shrugged. "Does it matter?"

"Not really. How about *when* did you find out?"

Picking at an invisible piece of lint on her pants, Jordyn refused to meet his stare. "After I filed my reports about Malaysia in Virginia."

"*After* you left my bed." He leaned forward, resting his elbows on his knees. "Why'd you leave then, Jordy? Was it just a fuck and run for you?"

"No!" Her gaze flew to his face in anger. "I'm not

one of your fucking whores, Carter. I don't fall into bed with just anyone. It was just the adrenaline that night. Nothing more."

"I don't believe that, and neither do you. Adrenaline may have played a part in it, but there was so much more going on between us than just that, and you know it. And I never thought of you as a whore, Jordy—far from it. Tell me why I woke up alone, wondering why you left. What cardinal sin did I commit *before* you found out about the lifestyle? I gave you a few days to get over whatever you freaked, and then I called. And called and then called again. Finally, I gave up."

Swallowing hard, she stared at the floor. She'd deleted all those voicemail messages he left for her without listening to them. When he'd stopped leaving them, a small part of her had been disappointed—and it hadn't been her brain. No way was she telling him that she originally left his bed because she'd realized she didn't want to leave it at all—that she'd fallen for him hard. Their business wasn't conducive to normal relationships—no husband/wife deals or even co-inhabitants—live-in lovers. They'd be lucky if they saw each other every few weeks or months in between missions—not exactly a happily-ever-after situation. Then again, Jordyn didn't believe in happily-ever-afters. She didn't know anyone who'd ever had one.

Another thought popped into her head. She hadn't yet asked him about the kid he apparently had and whatever Carter's relationship was with the boy's mother. Was he still involved with her? Or was he just an absentee father who paid the bills and showed up on the kid's doorstep once or twice a year? It annoyed the hell out of her that she remembered what he'd said to the woman, word for word. *I love you, too, sweetheart. Give my boy a kiss and a hug from me. I'll call you when I land in D.C.* But each one of those words had cut her deeply because as much as her head didn't want to, her body desperately wanted to be in his bed again.

"Does it matter?" she asked again, not wanting to address the wife and kid issue right now.

Jordyn was surprised when he answered, "No, it doesn't. If you don't trust me, it'll never matter."

"I trust you." They both knew there was more to that statement—she trusted him to a point.

He ran a hand down his face. "You trust me to cover your six. You trust me to defend this country and Deimos with every breath I take. You *don't* trust me in your bed... and in your heart. If you give me a chance, I plan to try my best to rectify that fact."

Fidgeting in her seat, Jordyn didn't answer him— too many thoughts were swarming through her mind, and she couldn't focus—not when he was sitting there without a shirt. He stood suddenly and went to the entertainment center. Opening a cabinet door, he pulled out a laptop, disconnecting it from its charger. He sat on the recliner again and booted up the computer. "What do you know about BDSM, Jordy? Or better question—what do you *think* you know about it?"

"It's a bunch of people who get off on abusing other people," she spat out, her anger coming to the surface again.

Not answering her immediately, his fingers flew across the computer's keyboard. His head tilted from side to side in time to "Lyin' Eyes" by the Eagles, which was now coming through the surround sound speakers. She waited, wondering what he was up to. When he spun the laptop around, he handed it to her. "Some reading you need to do before we finish this conversation and most definitely before we go down-stairs. That'll keep you occupied for a while, so I'm going to take a nap. Try to resist taking advantage of me in my sleep, okay?"

"Wh-what? What's this?" Jordyn stared at the screen. *Was there really a website called BDSM 101?* From the looks of it, he'd had to log into the site. There was a list of pages on various subjects—*What is a Dom? What is a submissive? What is a power exchange? What's the difference between a submissive and a slave?* The list went on and on.

She glanced up at him with her mouth agape as he strode to the bed. Jumping into the air, he landed supine on the mattress, bouncing a few times. After releasing his ponytail from its band, he tucked his hands behind his head and gave her a wink before shutting his eyes. "Happy reading, love."

The sound of the hairdryer blasting in the bathroom penetrated Carter's sleep-filled mind, then the vibrations from the club's sound system thumping registered. Opening his eyes, he saw the laptop was still open on the couch, but at some point, Jordyn had retrieved the charger and plugged it into a nearby outlet. Standing, he stretched and strode over to it. The door to the bathroom was shut, and he took the moment of privacy to check the history of web pages Jordyn had been on. He was pleased to see she'd gone through dozens of "Frequently Asked Questions" on the site he'd logged her into, in addition to some community chat posts.

The hairdryer quieted, and he clicked the forward arrow to return to the last page she'd been on. By the time the bathroom door swung open, he was across the room, getting another bottle of water from the fridge. Turning around, he almost choked on his tongue when he saw Jordyn enter the room. Bug-eyed, he froze as his gaze went from her head to her toes and back again. *Fuck me* was the only thought that registered in his brain.

A black, spandex catsuit hugged the curves of her legs, hips, waist, and breasts while her bare shoulders and arms offset the high neckline. She was five inches taller in the knee-high, black leather boots, bringing her much closer to his own height of six foot four. She'd blown her black mane out in soft curls that framed her face and fell over her shoulders and down her back. Her makeup was expertly applied, causing her eyes and red lips to pop against her olive skin tone. But what made the whole outfit was the attitude pouring off her. If he hadn't known in his heart she was a sexual submissive, he would unquestionably accept the Domme in front of him.

She cocked her hip to the side and rested her hand on it. "So... do I pass inspection for this mission, *Master* Carter?"

Yeah, she may have read a lot on the subject, but her snarkiness said she still wasn't convinced that the lifestyle was safe, sane, and consensual. Reining in the urge to pull her into his arms and kiss her senselessly, he nodded. "Not bad." Yeah, that was an enormous understatement.

Snorting, she strode toward him, one sexy, drop-dead-gorgeous step at a time. He swallowed hard as his cock twitched in his sweatpants. Her eyes flew to his groin—yup, she couldn't miss the growing bulge the thin cotton material was doing nothing to hide. Stopping in front of him, she ran a manicured finger down his bare chest while licking her lips. He grabbed her wrist, halting her descent, and pulled her flush against his body. His other arm went around her waist and held her tightly in place. Myriad emotions flashed through her eyes as he dropped his voice to his Dom tone. "You're playing with fire here, little one. Don't start anything you're not willing to follow through on."

He felt a shiver go down her spine, exciting the shit out of him. For all her bravado, her body craved to submit to him—he knew it as well as he knew his own name. But just like that, her eyes narrowed, and she pushed him away. "Whatever. So, tell me what we'll be doing here tonight. Which assets are you targeting?"

After cracking open the bottle of water he was still holding, he guzzled half of it. The liquid quenched his parched throat. Getting himself back into mission mode, he took a seat in the recliner, trying to ignore the way she sat on the couch and crossed those long legs of hers. "First things first. What questions do you have about the lifestyle? I need you not to be shocked at what you'll see tonight. There will be people walking around half or completely naked. Spankings and floggings. Fucking in public. Some public humiliation. Women *and* men being submissive to the Doms. You have to remember that this is all consensual. There are dungeon masters who will intervene with a scene or negotiation if needed. They keep an eye on everything.

"Don't be surprised if both sexes are coming up to you, dropping to their knees, begging you to scene with them—especially with how you're rocking that outfit. Damn, woman." He took another much-needed mouthful of water. "Can you handle that? Any questions?"

Jordyn took a deep breath. He could see she was getting herself into the frame of mind needed to portray the character she would display to a large crowd. "I have a few questions. I found a lot on that site, but reading something and experiencing it are two different things."

"Absolutely. Ask away."

Swinging her foot, she said, "I'm still unsure about this whole thing. How is this not abuse, Carter? I mean, caning and flogging someone? I can't understand how that's consensual. Public humiliation? Seriously? And don't get me started on the fucking body-fluids play!"

"Well, you'll be happy to hear body-fluid play is on my hard limit list. Turns me off." He sighed, trying to figure out how to make her understand the lifestyle he loved. "Sweetheart, not everyone is wired the same way. That's nothing new to you. It's how you can analyze a target and figure out the best way to fool them to get what you need from them. Think of it this way—some people like horror flicks, and some hate them. Coke or Pepsi. Love coffee, hate it. Flowers and candy, or a new sniper rifle. Everyone has different likes and dislikes, that's what makes everyone unique. And everyone has their own kinks. There are things you like to do that turn you on, but they aren't the same things that turn someone else on." Putting the water bottle on the table beside him, he sat back and tapped his thigh. "Come here."

Jordyn froze. "What do you mean, 'come here'?"

"Come lay across my lap, face down—I want to show you something."

"You've got to be fucking kidding me, asshole." She crossed her arms and glared at him. "You want to try and seduce me when you've got a wife or lover and a kid you neglected to tell me about. Fucking classy. Well, it's not going to fucking happen."

Carter shook his head, total confusion on his face. "What the fuck are you talking about? I don't have a wife and kid. Where'd you get the idea I did?"

"I heard you talking to her—your 'favorite lady'— on the phone in Scotland. 'I love you, too, sweetheart. Give my boy a kiss and a hug from me. I'll call you when I land in D.C.'"

Whatever response she expected from Carter wasn't what she got. He roared with laughter, just as he'd done downstairs in the garage when she'd told him he was a perverted woman abuser. He threw his head back and rolled it from side to side against the brown leather of the recliner. "Oh, Jordy, Jordy, Jordy. What am I going to do with you, love? You are so entertaining... and misinformed." He lifted his head, and his amused gaze met her pissed-off one. "I do not... repeat... do *not* have a wife and son—or a daughter for that matter—no kids, no woman waiting for me in the wings. Vicki is my foster sister. Justin is her son—my nephew."

Her jaw dropped. "Y-you have family? They know you're alive?"

He knew what she was thinking—that was unheard of in Deimos. The black operatives had all "died" in their former lives. Their friends and family, if they'd had any at the time, visited empty graves. It sucked, but was necessary to keep everyone safe. The only reason Carter's sister knew he was alive was because she'd spotted him when he'd been checking up on her—something that had earned him a figurative ass-kicking from his boss afterward.

"Yes, I have family, but it's only Justin, Vicki, and her husband Joe—and I'm sure you understand why I've never mentioned them. Gene is the only person who can connect them to me. But I'll tell you about them some other time—we're veering off the subject, and I need you to understand what I'm trying to say about the lifestyle if you're going to be convincing down in the club tonight."

Taking a deep breath, he let it out slowly, trying to get back into the frame of mind he needed to be in—Dom mode. He lowered his voice. "Please, come here and lay across my lap. I promise I'm not going to do anything to hurt or humiliate you. I want to prove a point, nothing more. If you say the word red—your safeword—I'll let you stand immediately." He was taking a huge chance here, but if they were ever going to get past the elephant in the room, he had to do this. "Please, Jordy. Trust me to show you what I know your body's craving. As soon as I told you to lay across my lap, the pulse in your neck increased, your breath hitched, lips parted, nipples puckered, and I'd bet a thousand bucks you're wet and wanting right now. It's not a crime to be turned on, sweetheart."

Her jaw clenched as she stared at him. Her mind and body were dueling, and he prayed the latter was the victor. He held out a hand to her and waited. Seconds ticked by. He'd wait for hours or days if he had to, having learned long ago that patience was key in most situations on a mission or in the lifestyle.

Slowly, Jordyn uncrossed her legs and stood. She hesitated before stepping over to him. Carter stayed perfectly still, his heart pounding in his chest. His relaxed gaze remained on her apprehensive one. She had to do this on her own. Her mind had to learn to let her body take over. "You swear you'll stop if I tell you to? If you don't, I'll do everything in my power to castrate you."

"I'll stop," he assured her. "But just make sure that's what you really want before you say the word red.

She bit her bottom lip, and again, he waited while her mind and body battled within her. When she turned and lowered herself onto his lap, his soul rejoiced. He didn't move a muscle as she situated herself. His cock hardened as she shifted on his thighs, but there was no way he could control its response to her. Finally, she seemed comfortable, and he laid his hand on her thigh. She practically jumped out of his lap, and he placed his other hand on her back, urging her to stay where she was.

"Easy, Jordy, easy." He caressed her spandex-covered skin and spoke as if trying to calm a jittery horse. "Relax, baby. You're safe with me, I promise."

Gently, he made small circles with the palms of his hands as he murmured words of reassurance. Her head tilted to the side, and she studied his face with wary eyes. He slowed his breathing and pulse as if waiting to take a sniper shot. All his energy was focused on getting her to relax. His hand on her thigh stroked from her knee to the bottom of her ass. With each pass, it went higher and higher until it covered the swell of her ass cheek. Minutes went by, yet all he did was soothe her with his touch. The tension slowly left her, and her body melted into his. She was getting into the zone he wanted her in.

Palming her ass, he squeezed, then let go and stroked her again. He repeated that several times until her legs separated a scant inch. Trying not to smile, he was certain she wasn't even aware she'd opened a little to him, and he regretted the catsuit at that moment. A skirt would have given him full access to her sweet pussy.

Lifting his hand, he gave the luscious flesh of her ass a love tap—nowhere near as hard as he wanted to spank her, nor as hard as he knew her body wanted. Her breathing increased, and her legs shifted again, but she remained where she was. He started a new string of actions—well, just added to the one he'd already been doing. Stroke from knee to ass, squeeze cheek, circle palm, lift hand, and tap cheek, repeat. With every reoccurrence, he made the tap a little harder.

Jordyn squirmed on his lap. The wariness in her eyes had been replaced with heat—sensual, soul-bearing heat. What he wouldn't give to add thrusting his fingers into her pussy to the mix, but he could get close. After the next slap—they no longer could be considered taps—he ran two fingers between her legs and found her clit under the thin material covering it. Jordyn moaned. She was so turned on and had no idea why—but he knew.

"Are you okay, Jordy?" His voice was low, caressing her skin just as his hands were. "I know you're wet and hot—I can feel it. Do you want me to stop?"

Her hips bucked as her legs parted for him some more. Her grasp on his lower leg, holding her steady, tightened. She panted, reaching for the orgasm that was just beyond the horizon.

"Tell me, sweet Jordy, do you want me to stop or let you come? I can do that without even taking your clothes off. Tell me what you want. You have the control here—the choice is all yours."

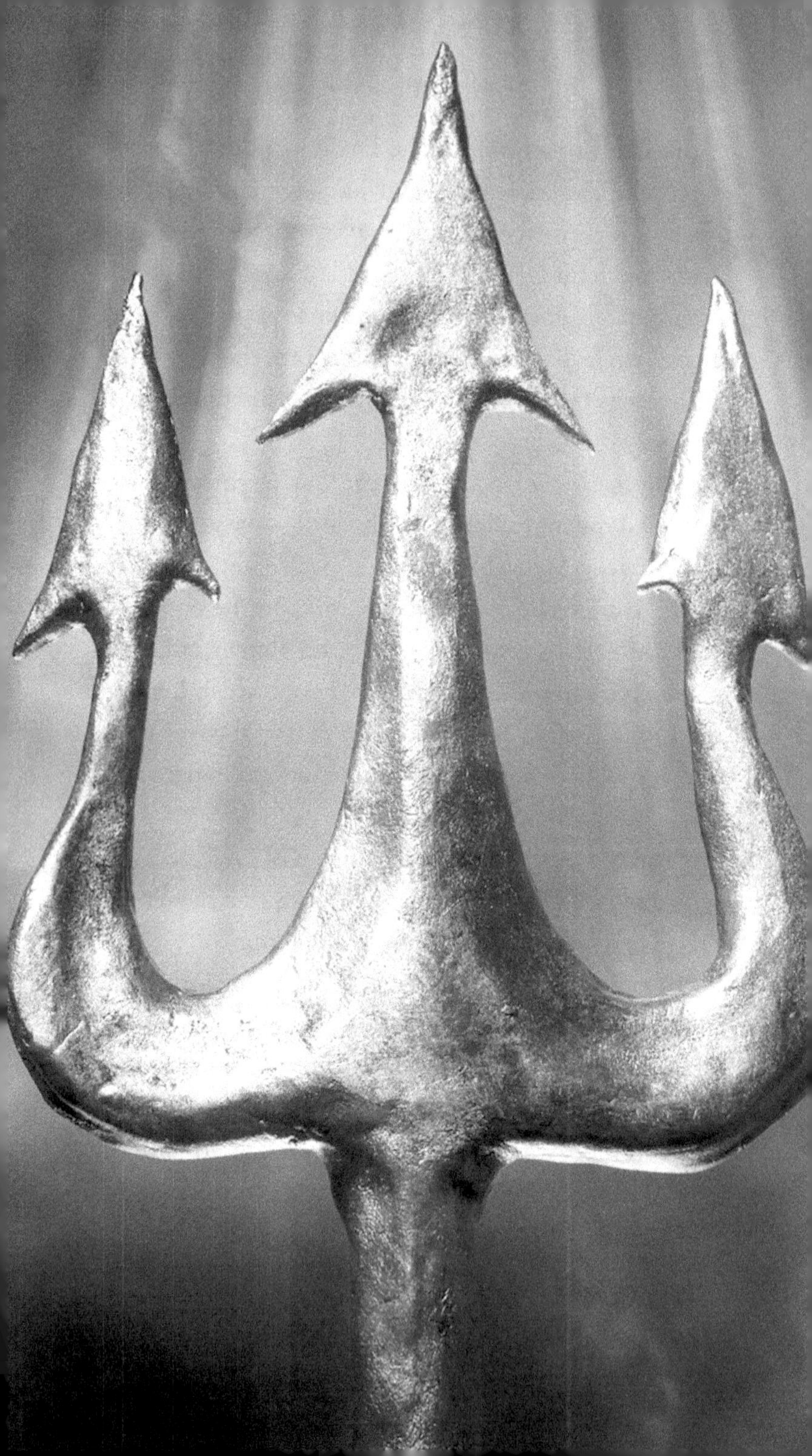

CHAPTER THIRTEEN

The war raging within Jordyn's body was one her mind was about to lose. Every organ, muscle, bone, nerve, and cell was beseeching her to do what Carter wanted so he would let her come. *Tell him. Ask him. Beg him.*

Her orgasm was just beyond her reach—all she had to do was open her mouth and say the words. Carter's fingers reversed direction as they circled her clit over and over. New sensations overpowered her, and a gasp escaped her. "Please! Don't... *¡oh Dios mío!*"

She felt the slightest hesitation in his torturous acts before he continued. "Don't, no, and stop are not words I'll heed, Jordy. Say red if you want me to take my hand away and let you stand."

"No! Don't stop!" She couldn't control her writhing as she tried to get his fingers to go faster—harder. Her breathing was so rapid that she was getting lightheaded. "*Por favor*... Carter, please let... let me come!" A sob tore from her chest. "Now! I need..."

His fingers picked up their pace, and he increased the pressure. She reached the peak of the mountain he'd taken her up. Suddenly, the hand on her back was gone and came down hard on her ass, sending pain through the nerves. Shocked, she couldn't say a word as the pain became pleasure, and she fell into an immense chasm. Her body shook with the force of the orgasm as she screamed her release. Wave after wave of hedonistic sensations tumbled over her as her thighs clenched around his hand, not wanting it to end.

Breathless, her lungs struggled to fill with oxygen again as the orgasm ebbed, and she sagged limply across Carter's thighs. Never in her life had she come while still fully dressed. Her muscles quivered with the last remnants of ecstasy as he turned her over and settled her back down on his lap. Her ass was sore, but for some reason, that made a flash of pleasure erupt from her clit again. Cuddling her to his bare chest, Carter placed a kiss on her head before tucking it under his chin. His hands massaged her arms and legs in firm yet soothing motions. "That's pretty much the extent of me *hitting* a woman, my sweet Jordy. Sometimes, it involves a flogger, but it always has the same end goal—my submissive's pure and complete satisfaction. How do you feel? Well, beside your sore ass."

She was confused but wasn't going to tell him that. "I don't know... I'm kind of lightheaded."

"That's subspace. Did you read about that on the website?"

"Uh-huh."

His hand went to the nape of her neck and her shoulders and kneaded the muscles there. "Your body released an overload of endorphins, which gives you the feeling of being drunk or high. Some describe it as that floating feeling you get from nitrous oxide at the dentist."

She buried her head in his chest, inhaling his scent. Her mind and body felt like he'd said—she was floating. Had she really been so wrong all these years? Unable to answer that, she filed the question away for later when she could think clearly—something she couldn't do in this man's arms. All she could do right now was feel.

How long they sat like that, she wasn't sure, but despite his massaging her limbs, some of her muscles began to protest the prolonged, motionless position. Stirring, she glanced up at Carter and saw him smiling down at her. It wasn't a smirk of satisfaction, she realized. Instead, his face held an expression of serene contentment—as if her orgasm was all he needed to enjoy himself. His cock was still hard and pulsating against her hip, and she trailed her fingers down his sculpted chest toward it.

Before she could pass his belly button, he grabbed

her wrist. "Not necessary, love. This wasn't about me. While I would love to bury myself in your sweet body, now isn't the right time."

Lifting her, he helped her stand before getting to his feet. He stepped away from the recliner and gently pushed her back into it. The brown leather held his body heat, and she snuggled into its warmth. It even smelled like him, and she reveled in the deliciously masculine scent she would always recognize as his.

Leaning down, he kissed the top of her head again. "I'm going to get changed, and then we'll go downstairs. By the way, did I tell you how beautiful you look tonight?" When her mouth ticked up in a lazy yet sexy smile, and she shook her head, he said, "Well, let me remedy that. You look stunning, and I'll have to beat both the subs and Doms off you with a stick tonight." He chuckled. "Although some of them will enjoy that."

With one last kiss, this time on her forehead, he strode to the closet, retrieved some clothes, and then handed her an ointment tube. "Put this on your ass and thighs. It'll soothe them. Unless you want to strip and let me do it, but I can pretty much guarantee if that happens, we'll wind up in that big bed for at least the next twenty-four hours."

Her eyes widened, and she silently shook her head at him. There was too much confusion bouncing around her mind for her to feel comfortable getting naked and letting him care for her sore buttocks.

"Didn't think so," he said with a wink before heading to the bathroom.

Once the door shut behind him, Jordyn released a heavy breath she hadn't realized she was holding. So much had changed in the last few hours. Things she knew—or thought she knew—weren't as clear-cut as she'd thought. She forced her mind to shift to Carter's revelation of his foster sister and nephew.

As far as she was aware, no operative at Deimos had family members who knew they were alive. In Jordyn's case, she'd had no family left who even cared if she were dead or not. There were a few aunts, uncles, and cousins in Argentina who'd stolen her estate out from underneath her feet after the homicide/suicide of her mother and father, and she'd been an only child. She'd gone from having everything a teenage girl could materialistically want to having nothing and facing eviction from the only home she'd ever known. Her mother's brother, Ignacio Alvarez, the family's black sheep, had taken her in after learning his fourteen-year-old, orphaned niece was penniless. A pickpocket, scam artist, and cat burglar, Uncle Iggy, had taught her the tools of his trade after illegally sneaking her into the United States since he didn't have her passport or birth certificate. She'd changed her last name from Cabrera-Alvarez to just Alvarez, not wanting to be associated with any part of the sperm donor who had destroyed her young life. This year was the tenth anniversary of Uncle Iggy's death in a freak car accident, and she still missed him terribly. Despite his life of crime, he'd been the sweetest man she'd ever known. With him gone, there had been no one to "mourn" her when she was allegedly killed in a boating accident off the coast of California.

Her brooding over the past was interrupted when the bathroom door swung open, and Carter came striding out. Her mouth dropped as she stared at him. His long legs were encased in black leather pants that laced up at the crotch. The material hugged his ass and groin, making her mouth water. A gray T-shirt now covered his bare chest, but it was snug enough to outline every muscle and contour. He went to the closet, retrieved clean socks and a pair of black leather motorcycle boots, and then sat on one of the dining table chairs to put them on. His long, dark-blond hair was pulled back into a ponytail again, tied off with a thin leather cord.

Pulling her gaze away from him, Jordyn stood and entered the bathroom, where she used the toilet, applied the ointment to her still-stinging ass cheeks, and cleaned up a bit before fixing her hair and face again. She always kept a small bag with an emergency makeup stash in her go-bag for situations like this—right next to her KA-BAR knife. She may be a sanctioned assassin, but that didn't mean she couldn't look good doing it.

Once her face was repaired and every silky strand on her head back in place, she took a deep breath and turned off the bathroom light as she walked out. Trying not to drool over Carter, she pushed her mind into mission mode. It was a good thing he'd given her that website to look over. While she still didn't understand the lifestyle—or her reaction to the spanking he'd given her—she'd read enough to, hopefully, fake it downstairs with convincing success. She could at least blame any negative reaction that might pop up as she was still a "newbie" to the lifestyle.

Carter adjusted the legs of his pants over the boots and then stood. "Ready, Mistress Jordyn?"

"Ready, Master Carter."

A sexy grin spread across his face. "Damn, I wish you were saying that from a submissive's point of view. But... anyway, you're going to see quite a few faces you'll recognize. One or two might recognize you, but they'll follow my lead. If I introduce you, they'll pretend this is the first time you're meeting them. It's common in the real world not to acknowledge knowing someone from the lifestyle, but here in D.C., it's not unusual for the reverse to happen. A few agents from MI6, Interpol, and other allied agencies are all networking while enjoying some kink."

"All right, don't let on I recognize anyone, got it. What happens if someone approaches me to... um..." She was at a loss for the right word.

"'Play' or 'scene' are the terms." Picking up his wallet from the table next to the recliner, he removed a flat card she assumed unlocked the door to this room and stuffed it into his back pocket. "If that happens, just act cool and indifferent and tell them you're not interested in playing tonight. The submissive should immediately back off. I'll be nearby if you get into a situation you're unsure about. Okay?"

Taking a cleansing breath, she let her inner alpha bitch come to the surface for tonight's charade. "Okay. Let's do this. Oh, what's my cover?"

"Use your advertising exec persona for tonight. You've been working on the campaigns for my import/export company, and we've become friends."

That was easy enough—it was the cover they'd used in Malaysia, and she used it for a few other missions with "members" of the company's board of trustees. "Okay. Sounds good. Jordyn Dominguez it is."

With one last glance up and down her body, Carter shook his head and opened the door leading to the hallway. "Let's go before my hard-on comes back with a vengeance and I forget why we're here."

They took the elevator back to the first floor, and when the doors opened, Jordyn felt like she was in another dimension. Two burly men stood outside the tinted windows next to the unassuming front door— the way the interior and exterior lights were adjusted, it was much easier to see out than it was to see in. Another two guarded the double doors leading from the lobby into the club. All four wore black dress pants and shirts with gold bowties. Paul and a petite, blonde woman were stationed at the reception desk. The male submissive now wore black leather pants and a gold bowtie sans shirt. The blonde was in a short, gold, pleated skirt that barely covered her ass, a sheer, black, lacy bra, and the same necktie.

But it was the patrons who drew Jordyn's gaze. Five men and women chatted in the lobby. Two of them, a man and woman, both nearly naked, were on their knees, heads bowed, next to two men who she assumed were their Doms. Leather appeared to be the popular choice for clothing if a person chose to wear any.

Pulsating music emanated from behind the double doors as Carter led her toward them. Jordyn pasted on a mask of indifference, as Carter had advised, and followed him into the devil's lair of sex and kink. The club's atmosphere had changed since they'd been inside earlier. The lights were dimmed, and acoustic rock music filled the air, along with moans, groans, shouts, and begging. The aroma of oranges mixed with the scents of perfume, sex, and sweat—surprisingly, it was an enticing combination. More of what she'd witnessed in the lobby was scattered about the club—men and women, Doms and submissives, in varying states of dress.

Trixie approached them, wearing an emerald green evening gown and sparkling diamond hoops hanging from her earlobes. "You look stunning,

Mistress Jordyn. I hope you found the clothes to your liking."

Running her hands over her hips, Jordyn smiled. "Yes, I do—very much. Thank you for ordering them for me. I especially love the boots—they're very comfortable."

"Toni has nothing but the best in her shop, darling. Let me know if you want to visit her, and I'll set it up. It's by invite and appointment only."

"Thank you. Maybe next time I'm in town."

Trixie left them to speak to another couple, and Carter pointed to the bar. "Something to drink?"

Oh, yeah. Something to calm her nerves. Despite her outward appearance, Jordyn was quaking in her five-inch heel boots. "A vodka martini would be great."

He gave her a knowing smirk and flagged down the bartender. "Beluga Gold vodka martini and a Guinness, Victor, please."

Holy shit! He'd remembered the high-priced vodka she favored while hobnobbing with the social elite. While it wasn't outrageously expensive, it was still over a hundred dollars per bottle in a liquor store.

When their drinks were delivered, she nodded her thanks to the bartender. Carter signed for the tab, then threw a twenty-dollar tip on the bar while Jordyn took a soothing sip of her martini. She wasn't a big drinker —needing to keep her wits about her while working— but it was times like this she was glad she'd developed a taste for vodka.

"Master Carter!"

The two of them turned at the female voice calling his name. Jordyn was surprised to see a very pregnant redhead waddling toward them, wearing a semi-sheer, black teddy with red trim, which hung down to her midthigh. Black, satin slippers covered her feet. The woman looked like she was going to go into labor at any moment. A flash of jealousy coursed through Jordyn when she saw Carter's tender expression and smile.

He leaned down and placed a chaste kiss on the woman's cheek. "Hello, Lucy. You look wonderful. The due date's getting close, isn't it?"

"Yes, Sir. Three more weeks. Although my doctor thinks it'll be sooner than that. I wanted to thank you for the presents you sent for the baby. You didn't have to do that."

"It was my pleasure, little one."

The redhead had been beaming at Carter, but she finally noticed he wasn't alone. Her eyes widened as she took in Jordyn's outfit and frown. Her gaze immediately dropped to the floor, and she became flustered. "Oh, f-forgive me, Mistress. I didn't mean to interrupt. I'm—I'm so sorry—"

Carter cut her off. "It's okay, Lucy. That was my fault for not introducing you. This is Mistress Jordyn, visiting from California. Jordyn, this is Lucy."

Jordyn knew Carter had been with this woman in the past— there was no doubt in her mind. But Lucy appeared ready to burst into tears over her perceived faux pas—it could be her hormones or something else, but Jordyn couldn't let the woman feel as if she'd wronged her. She pasted a welcoming smile on her face. "It's a pleasure to meet you, Lucy. And you didn't interrupt at all. Congratulations on your baby. Do you know if you're having a boy or a girl?"

The redhead's shoulders sagged in obvious relief she hadn't insulted a Domme. "We—my Master and I—decided we wanted to be surprised. As Sir tells everyone, it's one of the few true surprises in life."

"Indeed it is. Well, again, congratulations, and I hope the baby is healthy and happy regardless of the sex."

"Thank you, Mistress."

Glancing around, Carter said, "Speaking of your Sir, Lucy—where is Master Frank?"

Lucy turned and pointed to a nearby couch where three men sat and talked. One man had a cast on his leg, and crutches leaned against the arm of the couch next to him. "Sir fell off a ladder last month and broke his ankle. The cast comes off the week before my due date."

Carter chuckled. "I won't even ask what he was doing on a ladder." He grinned as he addressed Jordyn. "Lucy's Master can be a walking disaster when it comes to household repairs. Economics analysis, he's a whiz at. Hammering a nail, not so much."

As Jordyn laughed, Lucy giggled and nodded. "It's

true, Mistress. But that's probably why we fell in love —opposites attract. My father made sure I knew how to repair anything around the house. If you'll excuse me, I should be getting back. It was nice to meet you, Mistress, and it was wonderful to see you again, Sir."

"And it was great to see you, too, Lucy," he said. "Go back and tell your Master I'll stop by later to say hello."

"I will, Sir." The woman waddled—there was no other way to describe it—back to her Dom's side.

Before Jordyn could ask one of the several questions bouncing around in her mind, a skinny man, a few years older than herself, dressed in brown leather boy shorts and nothing else, knelt down next to her. His dark-haired head was bowed, and he appeared to be waiting for something. Jordyn glanced at Carter with a faint "help me" look in her eyes.

The bastard smirked, and she'd bet "told you so" was on the tip of his tongue. But, instead, he said, "Mistress Jordyn, this is Santos. I believe he has a question for you."

Fighting the urge to roll her eyes, Jordyn looked down at the submissive and channeled her inner bitch. "Speak, Santos."

"If Mistress is interested, I would like to negotiate a scene, please." His squeaky voice sounded like he was still going through puberty twenty years later, and it grated on her.

She spoke in a bored tone. "I'm not sure if I'm in

the mood to play tonight. If I decide I am, I may or may not come looking for you." She noticed Carter fighting back his laughter from the corner of her eye. Oh, he was so fucking enjoying this, and she was going to kick his ass when it was all over.

"Thank you, Mistress."

The submissive didn't move, waiting until Carter led Jordyn away. After sipping her martini, she murmured just loud enough for him to hear, "You're a dead man if you say one word about that."

Holding up a hand in surrender, he shook his head. "I won't say anything other than you handled that quite well. I'm starting to wonder if I have a switch on my hands."

"What the hell is that?"

"A switch? Exactly what the word implies. It's someone who likes to be the Dominant in some scenes and aspects of life, yet submissive in others."

As they strolled around the huge bar, he drank his dark ale and nodded hello to several members. His gaze zeroed in on a group of people, and Jordyn scanned their faces, seeing if there was anyone she recognized. One man seemed familiar, but she couldn't place him—from his stature and aura, he was definitely a Dom. When the man's eyes shifted and met hers, there was a subtle flash of recognition on his face before it disappeared again. He was quite handsome, with wavy, brown hair that matched the two-day-old goatee and mustache on his face. From this distance, she couldn't tell his eye color, but if she had to guess, they were also brown. Snug, black jeans hung from his hips, and the muscular physique of his torso was covered by a long-sleeved, blue Henley with the cuffs pushed up almost to his elbows. After an almost imperceptible nod in her and Carter's direction, beckoning them to join him, the man turned back toward his companions and their conversation.

Carter leaned down to whisper in her ear. "Adam Sparks, MI6."

So that's where she knew the man from. It'd been a few years since she'd seen the British agent at a social engagement in Milan. They'd both been undercover and rubbing elbows with the Italian political and business elite.

Steering their way over to the group, Carter continued to say hello to several people. Jordyn put some attitude in her strut, and it didn't escape her notice that many members of both sexes appeared interested in the new "Mistress" among them. Some stared at her in curiosity, others with lust. She and Carter were stopped twice for brief conversations. While he made the necessary introductions, it was clear to her that none of the people were his targets for the evening, and he expertly moved them along at the first chance he had.

As they neared Sparks's group, the man stepped away from the others, and Carter held out his hand to him. "Adam, good to see you again. Allow me to introduce Mistress Jordyn Dominguez, an associate and friend of mine from California. Jordyn, this is Adam Sparks."

After shaking Carter's hand, Sparks took hold of hers and brought it to his lips. "A pleasure, Mistress," he stated in a generous, British accent. "It is beauty such as yours that makes me disappointed you're a Domme."

Oh, my God! Could he lay it on any thicker?

"It's a pleasure to meet you, too, Master Adam," she cooed. "And I'm sorry to disappoint you."

She held back a smile when Sparks mouthed the word "liar" to her.

Clearing his throat, Carter said, "Adam, I was hoping to have a few moments of your time this evening. I have a new business venture I thought you might be interested in."

"Sounds intriguing. I was just about to go meet my sub for a scene. Would you care to join us as a third?"

A third? What the hell was he talking about, Jordyn mused. *As in a threesome? Holy shit!* She couldn't figure out why that appalled her and turned her on at the same time.

"I'd be honored. Do you mind if Mistress Jordyn observes? She's still very new to the lifestyle, and I'm sure she'll learn a thing or two."

What! Jordy was so stunned and flustered she didn't know what to say or do. Did he really think she was going to watch him and Sparks fuck some other woman together?

"I'm sure she will," Sparks answered, the amusement in his tone was unmistakable. He knew she was dumbfounded even as she hid it from the rest of those present. "I'll meet you in observation room number seven in about five minutes. Just going to the gents first, then grab something from my locker."

As the British spy walked toward the men's lounge, Jordyn glared at Carter. She lowered her voice, so she wouldn't be overheard. "What the fuck? If you think I'm going to sit there and watch you two fuck some woman, you better think again. It's bad enough I can tell you've fucked a bunch of the women in this place—"

"Enough, Jordy." He grasped her upper arm, sending unwanted electricity through her skin, and directed her toward a staircase leading to the second floor. His voice was as low and angry as hers, yet the relaxed expression on his face belied that to the rest of the room. "That's not what I'm asking you to do. Trust me, for once during this goddamned mess, instead of questioning everything. As for your other comment— yes, I've been with several women in this room. Did you honestly think I was a monk all these years?"

Well, the bastard did have a point. She'd been with a few other men since she shared Carter's bed. Sometimes it was to relieve the stress and adrenaline that came with the job. Other times she'd been looking for someone to make her forget what if felt like to be in the arms of a man she despised. "Fine. You can let go of my arm—I'm coming with you and won't cause a scene. As far as anyone else knows, I'm getting an education in being a Domme."

"Good girl." They began their ascension to the floor above them. "This is one of the two play floors. Don't let your jaw hit your knees as we walk through it. The observation rooms have floor-to-ceiling glass walls on one side, so people outside can watch the scene. But with a flick of a switch, the glass turns into a one-way mirror, so no one can see in. The rooms are partially sound-proof, so the music isn't as loud in them. We can have a meeting in there without worrying about being overheard. Adam's getting a scrambler from his locker, just in case."

"The place is bugged?"

"We're in D.C.—always assume a place is bugged in D.C."

True. She knew that already, but she was still rattled about everything that'd happened in the past twelve hours or so. Meeting the president. Carter kissing her in the White House. Him bringing her to a sex club. Her *being* in the sex club as if it was no big deal. Learning BDSM was not what she'd thought it was. Oh, and not to mention how Carter had made her come while they'd both been dressed. Yeah, her brain was a big pile of mush right now while her girlie parts were tingling, wanting to know what was going to happen when they got back to Carter's room later. If he asked, she wasn't sure she could say no to having sex with him.

When they reached the top of the stairs, Jordyn did her best to keep her eyes from popping out of her head. She'd seen pictures of what lay before her on the website earlier, but that was nothing compared to the real deal. Male and female submissives were on various pieces of equipment, being spanked, flogged, clamped, and tortured in general. And each one was begging for more. The screams and cries of ecstasy contradicted the moans and gasps of pain in her head.

One woman was belly down on a bench, being fucked from behind by some guy while another fucked her mouth. Had Carter been involved in threesomes like that? An image of him taking her from behind while Sparks's cock was in her mouth flashed through her mind and startled her. She didn't think she could be classified as a prude, but if she were honest with herself, her experiences with sex had been relatively vanilla—a word she'd found on the BDSM website earlier. In other words, it had been a bit on the boring side, based on other people's experiences.

While she'd had some hot sex with men before, she'd had no trouble moving on after leaving their bed the next morning. Jordyn didn't do relationships—at all. She'd never wanted to have one with any of the men she'd been with. They'd each been a temporary fling—a way to blow off steam—and after a few days had passed, she'd pushed them from her mind. The single exception was Carter—the only one who continually popped into her head whenever sexual urges and needs stirred within her. Thinking back, she realized he'd acted like a Dom that night—ordering her to do certain things. Things she'd ended up liking —a lot. But it was clear to her now, he'd been holding back. He'd asked her if she remembered every detail of that night, and she hadn't answered him. Like him, she could recall every time he'd made her come as if it had happened yesterday. And that just made her even more confused than she already was. What would sex be like with him if he didn't hold back? If neither of them did?

CHAPTER FOURTEEN

Leading Jordyn across the huge playroom, Carter fought the urge to deck every man who drooled over her. Damn, he'd almost punched Sparks for kissing her hand, of all things. He had to get his jealousy under control and focus on the real reason they were here tonight.

With his hand on her lower back, steering her in the right direction, he felt, rather than heard, every time her breathing hitched. While her outward appearance said the scenes they were passing were nothing new, her pulse had increased, and small shivers raced down her spine. And that had him wanting to strip her naked and claim her for himself in front of everyone.

The window to Observation Room #7 was crystal clear at the moment, and Isobel Shaw was behind the glass, kneeling in a perfect present position. Her head was bowed, knees shoulder width apart, and hands on her thighs with the palms up. The brunette beauty, dressed in shiny, red boy shorts with a matching bra, was Jordyn's age and one of the best MI6 agents in Britain's employ. She and Sparks had been part of the Washington D.C. business, political, and BDSM communities for the past three years, and Carter hoped they had some intel for him.

Opening the door to the room, Carter followed Jordyn in, then shut out the rest of the club. The thumping music dropped in volume by about seventy-five percent, making it much easier to hear each other. He pointed to the room's leather loveseat. "Get comfy, Mistress. Sparks will be a few minutes."

Jordyn's brow furrowed slightly, but she sat anyway. She had to be wondering why the submissive hadn't moved or acknowledged their presence and why Carter had basically ignored the woman. After Sparks arrived and they dimmed the window so no one could see in, he'd explain it to her. For now, he leaned against the wall next to the window, with his arms crossed over his chest, and eyed the activity out in the main playroom. There were politicians, busi-nessmen and women, and agents and supervisors from various alphabet agencies—some working, others just enjoying the lifestyle. There were members of the social elite and even the thirty-year-old daughter of the vice president. All their identities were safe there—the current advertising slogan for Las

Vegas also applied to this club. What happened there stayed there. But that didn't go for what was discussed that had nothing to do with the BDSM community. Intel was passed here nightly, whether intentionally or not.

The door behind Carter opened and closed, and Sparks flipped a switch on the wall. The window dimmed, but the room's occupants could still see out. However, they were hidden from everyone else's view.

Carter waited until Sparks showed him the scrambling device and nodded that they were clear. Stepping over to the submissive still kneeling on the floor, the US spy held out his hand. "All clear, Isobel."

"About freaking time." She grinned at him as she accepted his hand. "How are you, love?"

He kissed her cheek. "I'll let you know after we chat. Isobel Shaw, MI6, this is Jordyn Alvarez from Deimos, using the name Dominguez for her cover."

With every ounce of professionalism, Jordyn stood and shook the other woman's outstretched hand. "Nice to meet you."

"Same here." Isobel retrieved a glass of wine from a nearby table and took a sip before her gaze fell on Carter. "I'm sorry to hear about your agent."

His eyebrows shot up a notch. It wasn't a surprise the spy community was already talking about a death among the Deimos operatives, but it appeared the information wasn't complete. "Agent as in singular?"

Sitting on the loveseat, Sparks glanced back and

forth between Carter and Jordyn. "There's more than one?"

"Three, to be exact. Benito, Aldridge, and Aikman."

Isobel's jaw dropped while Sparks let out an angry curse. "Holy shit! What the bloody fuck is going on?"

"We were hoping you could help us figure it out. What's the chatter been like over the past week?"

The two British spies glanced at each other, but Sparks answered Carter's question. "Word is you have a target on your back, mate."

His eyes narrowed. "Me specifically or Deimos in general?"

Sitting on the arm of the loveseat, Isobel gestured for Jordyn to take the seat next to Sparks before she spoke. "You specifically. We heard it through channels two nights ago—not sure where the word originated from or if it's been confirmed, but with three of your agents dead, I would think there was some truth to it. Apparently, you pissed off Emmanuel Diaz."

Carter froze at the mention of the Colombian drug lord's name, and he noticed Jordyn did too. "Fuck me," he muttered. His recent past was coming back to haunt him, but how?

Jordyn mirrored his thought, her face paler than it had been moments before. "How the hell did he find out?"

"Find out what?" Sparks asked.

Running a hand down his face, Carter paced the small room. "About two years ago, I took out one of his

US contacts, who was also distantly related to him. There's only one person outside of Deimos who knows for certain I did the hit—and he was the one who ordered it. So it can't be him."

It had happened shortly after Devon Sawyer met the woman who would become his wife—Kristen Anders. The Trident boys and several other former SEAL Team Four guys had ended up on a hitman's list because the contact for Emmanuel Diaz's deceased brother, Ernesto, had turned out to be a US senator. Luis Beltram had been hours away from being announced as the Democratic party's presidential nominee when Trident had discovered he'd been involved in many dirty dealings with his Colombian cousins. One of the former SEALs had recognized him from a covert mission, and the senator, in turn, had ordered the hit on all the SEALs who could make the connection. Three of the seven retired SEALs from the op had been killed before the Trident team had figured it out. Unfortunately, Ian's goddaughter, Jenn Mullins, had lost both her father—one of the men from Team Four—and mother during the assassinations that'd taken place.

Isobel's eyes widened as she stared at Carter. "Are you saying someone in Deimos sold you out?"

He stopped in the middle of the room, fury running through his veins. His fist clenched, he fought the compulsion to punch something. "That's exactly what I'm saying."

"But—but who?" Jordyn was as shocked as the rest of them. "And why kill the other agents?"

"To make it look like Deimos itself was targeted and not just one operative," Sparks replied.

Carter nodded in agreement to the British agent's conclusion. They had a mole in Deimos—and now they had to figure out who it was before anyone else was killed. When Carter found the bastard, he was going to make sure he suffered a very painful death.

After a few hours of restlessness, Carter woke up exactly where he'd fallen asleep last night—on the couch in his room. Jordyn had needed space, not that she'd asked for it. He was sure her head was still spinning with all she'd seen and heard last night, between the activities in the club and the realization they had a mole in their agency. *His* head was still spinning. Jordyn had probably felt like Alice falling down the rabbit hole, and he'd opted for the couch last night for several reasons. Her decision to explore the lifestyle had to come without his persuasion. If he'd shared a bed with her, he didn't think he could've stayed there without pulling her into his arms and playing dirty pool by taking advantage of her body's reactions to him. And if he'd done that, his Dominant nature would have demanded her submission. All around him, things were spiraling out of control, and sex was at least one area where he could stay in command.

Stretching, he stood and went into the bathroom to use the toilet. The faint thumping of the club music had disappeared hours ago. After finishing the conversation with Sparks and Isobel, Carter got on the floor and did a hundred pushups. He'd needed to appear flushed and sweaty as if he'd just enjoyed partaking in the threesome. He and Jordyn had then roamed the club, speaking to a few more of his contacts. However, while some had given him the same intel the others had, no one else had anything to add.

His internal clock told him it was about 6:00 a.m. Before they'd gone to sleep last night, he'd sent Brody an encrypted email asking him and the other geek at Trident to start digging into the financials and backgrounds of everyone at Deimos. Right now, the only people he trusted were McDaniel and Jordyn. Deimos was their boss's baby, and he would never do anything to destroy it. As for Jordyn, if she'd wanted to kill him, she would have done the deed herself instead of using all this subterfuge.

When he returned to the main room, he noticed his cell phone was blinking, indicating a message had been left. Cracking his neck, he picked up the phone and dialed his voicemail. He was instantly alert when Joe Underwood's raspy voice came over the line. "Hey. Um... call me as soon as you can. The doctors say we have no choice—Justin needs another transplant."

Carter's blood ran cold. "Fuck," he mumbled. His plans had changed—the Deimos situation was on temporary hold. He needed to fly to California and see the one person in the world he didn't know if he could be in the same room with *without* committing homicide. The only thing that would keep him from doing it was Justin needed the bastard's organ.

Striding to the small closet in the room, he retrieved some clean clothes and replaced the dirty ones in his go-bag. He left the latter ones on the floor of the closet. He would text Paul later, asking the assistant manager to have them cleaned for him.

Behind him, he heard Jordyn moving around in the bed. "What time is it? You're leaving?"

"*We're* leaving." There was no way he was letting her out of his sight right now—he might be the ultimate target, but whoever had ordered the hit didn't know he was aware of that. Jordyn and the other agents from the stolen NOC list were still at risk. "Get up and get a move on, sweetheart. We're out of here in twenty."

She jumped from the bed, and he ignored that she wasn't wearing a bra under the blue lounge outfit she'd slept in. Hurrying across the room, she pulled clean clothes from her duffel bag. "What? Why? Where are we going?"

"California. Something I have to take care of," he said as he strode toward the bathroom again.

Jordyn's jaw dropped as she stared at him. "What the hell are you talking about?"

"Something personal—I'll fill you in later." Saying nothing more, he closed the door and turned on the shower. He hadn't wanted to shut her out, but there would be plenty of time to explain it once they were in the air.

Twenty-five minutes later, they climbed into the SUV. While Jordyn had taken a shower, he called Joe to let him know he received the message and was heading to California. Justin was stabilized for now, but he had tubes coming out of him and machines helping his kidneys work. Carter spoke to Vicki for a few minutes to reassure her he would take care of everything. Then he called one of his many contacts and arranged for a private jet to fly Jordyn and him out of a small airport in Virginia. They couldn't fly commercially with their weapons, and with someone targeting both of them, they couldn't go anywhere without being armed.

"Are you at least going to tell me where in California we're going?" Jordyn asked as he pulled out of the parking garage into the early morning D.C. traffic. "It's a big state, you know."

"Sacramento." He really wasn't in the mood to talk, as his mind focused on what he was about to do. His stomach churned, and he still had at least five hours before he came face to face with the devil.

"Look, we'll talk later, I promise. Just give me some time to deal with what's in my head first, okay?"

He reached over and squeezed her hand, faintly pleased when she didn't pull away from him. She stared at him for a moment or two, then nodded her head. "Okay. Later is fine. Have you checked in with McDaniel yet this morning?"

"No, but I have to talk to him about this trip anyway, so I'll call from the plane. If you need something to do, why don't you call Reardon or whoever's working the comms desk and see if they have any updates for us."

"On one condition." He raised an eyebrow at her in question, and she pointed at a bagel place coming up on their right. "Feed me, Truman."

A chuckle escaped him—the first one all morning. "Truman? Seriously? No, definitely not Truman."

"All right, not Truman, but I still want you to feed me."

"Yes, Mistress Jordyn." He pulled into a parking space in front of the shop.

She groaned and rolled her eyes. "Stuff it where the sun doesn't shine, asshole."

"With pleasure, sweet Jordy." He waggled his eyes at her. "With pleasure."

This banter was what he missed when it came to her, and he hadn't realized how much until now. They'd often flirted and busted each other's chops during her training and the few months following that. Maybe once all the shit storms had been taken care of, he could convince Jordyn to give him and his lifestyle a try.

As soon as the jet leveled off at cruising altitude, Carter undid his seat belt, stood, and pulled out his phone. Jordyn watched as he paced the length of the cabin, dialing a number and waiting for the call to be picked up. When it was, she listened to his half of the conversation.

"It's Carter. Jordyn and I are on our way to Sacramento. Justin's in the hospital. That favor I told you I might need at some point? It's time. I need you to clear my way into the penitentiary to see the bastard... I know it's a fucking bad time, Gene."

At least Jordyn now knew *who* he was talking to, even if she had no idea *what* he was talking about.

His nephew is in the hospital? What does that have to do with someone in prison?

"I don't care—get me in there... Yeah... Uh huh... Make sure it's a room with no cameras or mics. Three chairs, one table, nothing more. I'll arrange the rest... Yeah... We've got some intel for you, but not over this phone. I'll call you from a secure line from California. In the meantime, I have my contacts doing some digging... Right... I'll call you when we land."

He disconnected the call and then tossed the phone onto a low table in front of the couch Jordyn was sitting on. Taking a deep breath, he brought both hands up and ran them down his face.

Something inside Jordyn hurt for him. Clearly, he was facing something that scared him, and wasn't that a kick? She'd never known big, bad Carter to be scared of anything—the man was as tough and confident as they came. It was one of the things that had attracted her to him all those years ago. Things had changed in the past few days—her seemingly unjustified hatred toward him had faded as other feelings took its place. Feelings she didn't know what to do with.

Wanting to comfort him, Jordyn patted the open space on the couch next to her. "Come here, Double-O. Tell me what's going on."

The corners of his mouth ticked upward at the nickname she hadn't called him in years. He flopped onto the couch, his shoulder brushing against hers. "Where to begin?"

Jordyn turned sideways to face him, bringing her knee up onto the couch and resting it against his muscular thigh. "How about at the beginning?"

"Ha! Smartass. Right. The beginning." Lifting his chin, he rested the back of his head on the couch's cushions and stared up at the ceiling of the jet. "We've never talked about our pasts prior to Deimos, have we?" She didn't answer him, since it was a rhetorical question. "I spent twelve years in foster homes after my birth mother decided to abandon me in a Walmart north of San Diego. I was six years old at the time."

Jordyn gasped and unknowingly placed her hand on his thigh. "Six! Oh my God, how could she do that?"

Shrugging, he glanced at her hand and then laid his on top of it. "From what I understand, she had mental problems on top of drug use. I was eleven or twelve when the police came to one of my foster homes to let me know she'd been found dead in a homeless camp in the woods somewhere. There isn't too much I remember about her, but... anyway, I was shuffled from home to home—some abusive, others neglectful—until I ended up with the Osbournes when I was fifteen. I stayed with them until I enlisted on my eighteenth birthday—the Marine Corps."

As he spoke, Jordyn realized there was so much about this man she'd never known. Part of her wanted to know everything, while the other part was terrified that if she did, she might come to care for him—possibly even fall in love with him. And she couldn't allow that to happen. Their jobs, his lifestyle, and so much more stood between them. But despite her fear, she let him continue.

"That's where I met Vicki. She came about a year after I was living there. Her parents were killed in a car accident a few years earlier, and there was no family to take her in. She..." He snorted. "She was a hoot. Smart. Cute. Funny. I knew it was stupid to get close to anyone when there was always a chance I'd get moved to another home, but Vicki became the kid sister I never had. I decided to go into the military—not only for a better life for me, but for her as well. Once the foster kids hit eighteen, the Osbournes kicked them out—they were only interested in the state stipend for fostering which dried up as soon as the kids became adults. I wanted to help Vicki go to college. I wanted her to have a good life so badly, I even put her as my beneficiary in case anything happened to me."

Carter shut his eyes and fell into the past. "The day I graduated from boot camp, I hitchhiked the hour's drive to go see her. I was going to be shipping out to Hawaii on my first assignment three days later. When I got there, Marion Osbourne wasn't home, but Roland was. I... *shit*... I walked in on him raping Vicki."

"Oh, God!" Jordyn squeezed his leg as her other hand went to cover her mouth in shock.

"I honestly don't remember much that happened before the cops pulled me off of him. Apparently, the neighbors had heard all the yelling and screaming and called 911. I had beaten him within an inch of his life— probably would have killed him if a patrol car hadn't been a block or two away when the call came in. Next thing I knew, I was in an interrogation room at the police station, with bloody hands, looking at a prison term. But the cops left me there—no one came to interrogate me or get my side of the story. What I didn't know was I'd already been on McDaniel's radar for his new agency—my recruiter had passed my name on to him, then my drill instructors kept an eye on me for him. No family. Street smart. Picked things up quickly. Excelled in firearms and hand-to-hand in boot camp without any prior training."

"Ideal for black ops," Jordyn said, stating the obvious.

"Exactly." His eyes were still closed. "After being alerted by my fingerprints being put into AFIS, McDaniel showed up at the station and gave me the same two options you were given—jail or Deimos. I told him I'd sign my life over to him on two conditions. One—Vicki was placed in the Witness Protection Program, given the help she needed to deal with the rape, and her college education was paid for. And two —Roland Osbourne never stepped foot out of jail ever again."

Jordyn's mouth dropped as Carter opened his eyes and stared at her. She couldn't believe, at eighteen years old, he'd had the balls to demand that—but then again, yeah, she could. "He obviously said yes, and so did you."

He nodded. "Yup. I was 'killed' in jail the next day." With his index fingers, he made air quotes. "Vicki wasn't the only foster he'd raped. During the ensuing investigation, three more female victims were identified. On top of that, the Osbournes scammed both the foster system and the state disability system out of thousands of dollars. Marion Osbourne was given a pass if she testified against Roland. In the end, he was sentenced to ninety-nine-years-to-life."

"But—but how does Vicki know you're still alive then?"

His thumb started rubbing back and forth on her wrist, sending warm tingles up her arm. "Four years later, I'd tracked down where the marshals placed her in Montana. I had no intention of letting her know I was alive—I just wanted to make sure she was doing okay. What happened was pure coincidence—I was following her home from a college class when she was in a car accident. A little old geezer ran a stop sign and T-boned her. Without thinking, I ran to her car to make sure she wasn't hurt. She wasn't, but it was too late—she'd seen me. Once she got over her shock, I drove her home. It was then I found out she had a son —Justin. He was almost three years old."

Doing the math in her head, Jordyn gaped. "Oh, my God. He was the result of the rape." She couldn't imagine what the poor girl had gone through. Having her rapist's baby and keeping it at the age of sixteen.

Carter nodded again. "By the time she gave birth, Vicki hadn't wanted to give him up. The marshals placed her with an older couple who were also in the WPP. They helped her keep Justin and get her GED so she could go to college. They're gone now, but Vicki's doing fantastic thanks to their help. She's married to a great guy, who adopted Justin as his own."

"Okay, so why are we going to a prison in

California?" she asked. Reaching out, Carter picked up a few strands of her hair and rubbed them between his fingers. Jordyn tried to ignore how erotic that simple act felt.

"A few years ago, Justin was diagnosed with a kidney disease, and they went into failure. Vicki donated one of her kidneys. Unfortunately, his body is now rejecting it. He's got one of the rarer blood types, and the doctors say it's best if the kidney comes from a relative. I'm going to go see Justin's sperm donor in prison." His jaw clenched as revulsion and determination filled his eyes. "He's going to give me that kidney if I have to take it out of him myself."

Jordyn hadn't needed to hear the certainty of that statement in his voice or see it on his face to know it was true. She was now realizing he wouldn't hurt anyone that wasn't an assignment nor hadn't done him or his family wrong. All this time, she'd been comparing him to her father, who'd beaten his wife for the pettiest shit. But as Jordyn stared at Carter now, she knew he was nowhere close to the monster her father had been. That bastard had been out of control, whereas the man in front of her was doing everything in his power to maintain it.

Yesterday she'd read on that website that control and the exchange of power was a major part of the lifestyle, in addition to communication. When she'd first started reading, she'd thought the whole site had been a bunch of BS and those who'd contributed to it had been making excuses to justify their abusive behavior or the fact they were being abused. But then she'd started reading entries in the chatroom, and what she'd found there, among experienced Doms and subs, was something she could almost describe as beautiful and carnal. The submissives had been very articulate about why they enjoyed being spanked or flogged or whatever. Like Carter had said, everyone was wired differently. Jordyn still wasn't sure why her own body had responded to the spanking he'd given her or the erotic scenes she'd observed while walking around the club, but she could no longer deny they'd turned her on. And that scared the crap out of her even more. The big question was, what was she going to do about it?

CHAPTER FIFTEEN

Following the warden through the halls of the state prison in Folsom, Carter's hands fisted and then released repeatedly. His jaw was so tight it ached. After he'd spilled his guts to Jordyn, they'd spent the rest of the flight spooned together on the couch. He'd been shocked when she'd pushed him down, then laid next to him with her back to his chest and her ass snuggled up to his groin. While she'd fallen asleep for a few hours, he'd been unable to. His mind had been one big tornado of the past and the present churning together in chaos, and he hadn't been able to shut it down. So instead, he'd counted every one of Jordyn's breaths as he held her close—all 2927 of them.

Not wanting her anywhere near Osbourne or any other prisoners in this state dump, he'd told Jordyn to find them a hotel for the night. Once he got what he wanted, it would take a few hours to organize

Osbourne's transportation to Montana and get the transplant teams ready for both surgeries. Since a lot of this was not technically legal, it was being done all at the same hospital where the physician in charge was on the Deimos and CIA payrolls.

"This is highly unusual," the warden proclaimed as they were buzzed through another locked door. "What does a convicted rapist, who's been incarcerated for twenty years, have to do with national security?"

"It's classified."

The squirrelly man tsked and shook his head. Carter didn't give a crap what the guy thought about the clandestine meeting he'd been ordered to arrange, as long as it had been done to the spy's specifications. Somewhere in the bowels of the prison, the warden stopped at a door guarded by two men in uniform. Carter eyed them. "The cameras and microphones are turned off?"

The guard on the right answered, "There's none in this room. It's an old storeroom that's not used anymore. Only the one door in and out, no windows or one-way mirrors. We brought in a table and three chairs as requested."

Good, they'd followed the instructions to the letter. It was clear they were as curious as the warden but didn't ask him what was going on. Carter assumed it was because he probably looked like he wanted to kill the prisoner, who was already sitting in the room, and what they didn't know, they wouldn't have to testify to. At least they didn't have to worry about any weapons—the warden had insisted he leave them behind, and while Carter could have probably snuck one or two in without detection, he'd decided against it. The temptation to kill the prisoner might be more than he could resist.

Staring at the gray metal door, he conjured up all his black-ops and Dom training to center himself. He would need every ounce of control to get through this. When he was done, he'd find a punching bag somewhere and pound on it until his knuckles bled. Hell, even a brick wall would do.

Carter reached for the doorknob, ensuring his expression was a blank canvas. Before he turned it, he glared at the guards. "Under no circumstances do you enter this room until I come out. I don't care if it sounds like I'm killing him. I won't, because I need him alive, but that doesn't mean he won't be hurting by the time I'm done. Understood?"

The men glanced nervously at the warden, and when his head bounced like a bobblehead doll, theirs did too. Opening the door, Carter stepped inside and shut it behind him again. As requested, there was a metal, armless chair right next to the door, and he grabbed it, shoving the back of it under the doorknob since there was no lock. Taking a deep breath, he stood to his full height, and his barely controlled gaze fell on the man sitting at the table. Roland Osbourne, dressed in an orange prison jumpsuit, was twenty years older than the last time Carter had seen him and hadn't aged well. More wrinkles lined his face, and his arms were more muscular, but he still had that beer gut, resulting from the starchy, fatty foods here in the slammer.

Osbourne stared at him. "Who the fuck are you, and whatta you want?"

Taking deliberate steps, he strode to the chair across the table from his former foster father, turned it around, and straddled it. Now that he could see the younger man's face better, a lightbulb seemed to go off in Osbourne's head. His gaze narrowed as it scanned Carter's face. "You? *Harrumph.* Thought you were dead. What the fuck do you want?"

Below the table, Carter's fists clenched, his voice low and deadly as he spoke. "You have something I want, and you're going to give it to me."

The older man snorted. "Yeah? What's that?"

"Your fucking kidney."

"What? You're out of your fucking mind. What makes you think I'm going to give you a fucking kidney, or anything else for that matter?" Without waiting for an answer, he stood. "Sorry you made the trip for nothing."

Before Osbourne could move away from the table, Carter leaped up, grabbed his greasy, gray hair, and slammed his face, cheek first, into the table. Even in his rage, he'd known if he broke the guy's nose, with that force, it could've killed him. And, for now, he needed the bastard alive.

"Hey! Hey, get the fuck off me! Guard!"

Carter leaned down. "Shut the fuck up. They aren't going to save your ass." He grabbed one of Osbourne's flailing arms and held it straight to inspect the skin. Good—there were no signs of needle marks. He also didn't have that strung-out look junkies had. Thankfully, it appeared Osbourne wasn't one of the prisoners who partook in the drugs that were undoubtedly smuggled into the prison. Carter had also inspected the man's prison medical file. Aside from the usual injuries from fights, a few bouts of the flu and dysentery, and an appendectomy twelve years ago, the man was relatively healthy, as far as Carter could tell.

Shoving him back into the chair, Carter put his hands on the table and leaned toward the wary-looking man. "Here's the deal. First thing in the morning, you'll step outside this prison for the first time in twenty years. Enjoy it while you can because it won't last. You'll be blindfolded and transported to a hospital where you're going to be tested for everything under the sun. If the doctors say it's a go, then you're going to donate your fucking kidney to someone who needs it. If the doctors say your kidney's not good enough, I'm going to do what I should have done years ago—I'm going to fucking kill you—because you'll be worthless to me."

Osbourne stared at him, trying to figure out how he'd gotten on Carter's radar for a fucking kidney. "Who's getting it? Why me?"

"Because you're the right blood type."

"Not good enough. What am I missing? If you want my kidney so fucking bad, you'll tell me why."

Carter stood straight and ran his hand down his mouth and chin. He didn't want to tell this bastard he was Justin's sperm donor, but it might sway Osbourne to do this without a hassle. Crossing his arms over his chest, he glared at the other man. "The doctors say the best chance he has is someone who's blood-related."

"He? Blood…" A lightbulb must have gone off in his head. "That little slut had my kid?"

Flying across the table, Carter punched the guy in the face, sending him and the chair tumbling backward. He shoved the table out of his way, reached down, and grabbed Osbourne by the jumpsuit. The urge to beat the crap out of him was strong, but Carter forced it down. Instead, he hauled the guy up, righted the chair, and pushed him back into it. Getting in Osbourne's face, he growled. "Before you use that word again, let me tell you what I've been doing for the past twenty years. I've been torturing the scum of the earth into telling me all their secrets. I'll gladly give you a taste of that, without damaging your kidneys, if you use any other words to reference her other than 'that nice young lady.' Understand?"

Osbourne was now shaking in fear. His eyes were

wide as the realization Carter could and would make the next few hours very painful for him sunk in.

"Nod your fucking head if you understand, Osbourne."

The man did, and Carter backed off. He returned the table to its prior location, putting it between them. Otherwise, he might make good on his threat just for the fuck of it.

Using his knuckles, Osbourne wiped the blood seeping from the corner of his mouth, his wary gaze still on his assailant. "So, I'm a father. Go figure."

"No, you're a fucking sperm donor. The kid has a father who's been there for him for a long time now. And, like me, he'll do anything he can for his son. All you're going to do is give the kid your kidney and then come back here and rot for all I care."

Osbourne sat up straighter as if suddenly realizing he had a bargaining tool. "I give him my kidney, and you get me out of here. You've got to have pull to arrange all this. Get me out of here, and it's a done deal."

"You're out of your fucking mind if you think I'll help you join society again. Minimum security, and you stay in. Your other option is me inflicting enough brain damage for you to be still able to donate the kidney, and then you end up bedridden for the rest of your miserable life, drooling and fucking shitting yourself on a daily basis."

Silence filled the room as the man considered the

offer, which should've been a no-brainer. "Minimum security and I get to meet the boy before the surgery. What's his name?"

Carter fought the onslaught of rage coming to a head inside him again. "There's no way in fucking hell you're meeting him."

Feeling a little more confident, Osbourne leaned forward. "Let me meet him, and he can have both fucking kidneys. He doesn't have to know he's mine. I just want ten minutes with my only child."

Slamming his hands on the table, which sent Osbourne jumping back, Carter roared, "He's not your fucking child! You fucking raped his mother! You're a goddamned sperm donor and nothing else!"

"Fine! I'm his sperm donor." The man sneered. "Ten fucking minutes, and you save his life. You'll be the fucking hero again, and you won't even have to bust your knuckles to do it."

Carter didn't want to be a hero—he only wanted Justin to be healthy again. It went against everything in him, but he said, "If it's okay with his parents, you get five minutes and not a second more. I'll be in the room the whole time, and if you try to tell him he's yours, I'll be inflicting that brain damage. Understood?"

Standing, Osbourne had the audacity to hold out his hand. "Deal."

Snarling, Carter ignored the man's hand and strode to the door. Kicking the chair out of the way, he yanked the door open, startling the three men behind it. "Take him back to his cell. Warden, you'll be getting another phone call within the hour. Now, how the fuck do I get out of this pisshole?"

By the time he walked out of the last locked door and gate, Carter had his anger down to a simmer. Striding across the parking lot to where Jordyn was waiting for him in their rental car, he pulled out his cell phone and sent McDaniel a text, telling him it was a go, before calling Ian. It rang twice before the man answered. "What do you need now?"

"I still have chips you have to cash, dude. Deal with it. I need a four-man team to meet me in Sacramento and escort a product to Montana first thing in the morning. Then I need a second team to keep eyes on another product in Montana after the first is escorted back." He was speaking in generalizations, and Ian's teams would need more information than that, but Carter wasn't trusting Vicki and Justin's lives to a conversation that could be easily intercepted.

"Do you want me to blow up North Korea while I'm at it?" Despite his sarcasm, Ian understood there would be more intel forthcoming. "All right, I'll have Jake meet you with a team in Sacramento. Text him with the details of where to find you. Where's the other team going in Montana?"

"Missoula. Have them meet us at the airport. I'll get our flight info to you as soon as I have it."

"You got it. Anything else?"

"Egghead or Cook have any info for me yet?" He paused at the passenger door to the rental. Jordyn could drive them to the hotel she'd booked them in since he'd probably crash them into a tree in his current state of mind.

"They're still working on it. You really think this has to do with Diaz?"

"It's the only lead we've got right now. We—and that includes you—might be taking a trip down to Colombia in the near future. Can that be done?"

"Yeah, it can be done." Ian sighed heavily. "All right. Let me know if you need anything else."

"Will do, and thanks."

"Not necessary, jackass."

Disconnecting the call, Carter opened the car door and climbed in. Jordyn looked at him expectantly. "How'd it go?"

"We're set for the morning. Get me the hell out of here." His eyes were focused on nothing in particular, staring out the windshield in front of him.

She studied him a moment longer, then nodded and put the car in Drive. "Okay."

Without looking down, Carter reached over and found her hand. Pulling it to his mouth, he kissed her knuckles before interlocking their fingers and resting their joined hands on his thigh. He needed her now more than ever. "Thanks, sweetheart."

The tension rolling off of Carter filled the rental car as Jordyn drove toward their high-end hotel—if there was no need for a cheap motel, she wanted nice digs. But now, she wondered if booking them one room to share had been such a good idea. She'd been shocked when they'd returned to his private room last night, and he'd taken the couch instead of insisting on sleeping next to her. With each moment in his presence, Jordyn became increasingly confused as her attraction to him grew. The story of his youth and how he'd become a Deimos operative had helped her understand the man he was today and why he needed to be in control of every aspect of his life. The last few days' events had to be driving him nuts as everything spiraled in and out of his control. Yet, he was still gentle and patient with her—still the man who'd rocked her world in Malaysia all night.

The guilt coursing through her for believing all these years he was an abuser of women had settled deep in her gut. She should have known he wasn't anything like her father. She should have researched the lifestyle instead of jumping to conclusions. Yeah, she was sure there were people involved in BDSM for the wrong reasons and were hiding behind the veil of the lifestyle to justify their destructive behavior, but

Carter wasn't one of them. Jordyn still had so much to learn about it, but now her curiosity had her wanting to research it more. She didn't think it was necessarily the lifestyle that was drawing her in—instead, it was the dominant male currently holding her hand, sending bolts of electricity through her nerves to the junction between her legs. Was there a place in the figurative road where they could meet in the middle? Maybe, but first things first—make sure Justin received a new kidney and had a happy life ahead of him, then track down the Deimos mole and send the bastard to hell.

After pulling up to the valet parking at the hotel, the two climbed out of the vehicle and retrieved their duffels from the trunk. The sun started setting, and a chill was in the air. The weather in D.C. and California had been a little warmer than usual for November, and a sweater was all she'd needed. But if they were going to Montana next, Jordyn would need to do more clothes shopping. She should have insisted they swing by her apartment in Virginia before they hit the airport, but she hadn't thought about it until it was too late.

Carter followed her through the hotel to the elevators without a word. His face was blank, but his jaw was clenched. She couldn't think of anything to say to ease his apparent anger and frustration. It must have been hard for him to be in the same room with the man who'd raped his foster sister and not have killed him.

When the elevator doors opened on the third floor, Jordyn led the way to their room. If Carter wondered why they only had one, he didn't ask about it. Before she'd returned to the prison to get him, Jordyn had pulled up the hotel floor plans on his laptop they'd brought and plotted at least three escape routes. It was something he'd trained her to do no matter where she was.

Pulling the room key from the back pocket of her jeans, she unlocked the door to their room and pushed it open. As soon as the door shut behind them, Carter dropped his duffel to the floor, spun Jordyn around, and pinned her to the wall. Before she could ask what was going on, his mouth came crashing down onto hers. He kissed her with every emotion he'd been holding back all day. Bending his knees, he grabbed the back of her thighs and picked her up. Without rational thought, Jordyn dropped her duffel and jacket she'd still been holding, then wrapped her arms around his neck and her legs around his hips. His prominent erection rubbed against her core, and she moaned into his mouth at the contact. Their tongues danced as they kissed as if their lives depended on it.

Carter's hands lowered to massage her breasts as his body held hers against the wall. He licked and suckled his way to her jaw and neck. "Jordy... sweet, sweet Jordy. I need you... I need you to remind me there's something good and beautiful in this world instead of all the evil surrounding us." He ground his hard cock against her clit, and Jordyn almost came right then and there. "Please, I need to take control... to have you submit to me. Please say yes—I swear I won't hurt you, but it *will* be intense."

"Yes," she whispered, tilting her head to the side to give him better access to the sensitive spot behind her right ear.

His mouth left her skin as he pulled back just enough to stare into her eyes. "I need to hear you say it, sweetheart. There's no room for misunderstandings here."

His gaze bored into her soul, and butterflies took flight in her belly. There was no way she could say no. She couldn't deny him if she tried. "Yes," she gasped, trying to slow down her breathing to speak clearly. "T-take control. Tell me what you... you want me to do."

"Just listen and follow me. Let me do the thinking for both of us. All you have to do is feel... feel how alive we both are. If I do anything you're not comfortable with, say the word red, and I'll stop." One hand left her breast and tugged at the collar of her shirt. Bending his head, his teeth clamped down where her neck met her shoulder, and then he licked away the pain.

Shivers went up and down her spine as her eyes fluttered shut. "Yes... oh, God, yesssss." They'd barely started, and already she felt more alive than she had in years... since the first and last time she'd been naked in his bed.

"Say it, baby. Tell me your safeword."

"Um... I..." Jordyn couldn't think. She couldn't do anything but feel his body against hers. "I don't remem—"

"Red, baby." He lifted his head and cupped her chin with his hand. "Look at me, Jordy." Her gaze met his intense stare. She saw a storm raging within him in his blue irises—one she wanted him to unleash and consume her with. "Tell me your safeword—I need to hear you say it."

"Red... it—it's red."

"Do you trust me?"

Do I trust him? Yes, she trusted him to cover her six. If she didn't, they wouldn't be here. She trusted him here and now to bring them both pleasure and ecstasy without hurting her. But did she trust him with her heart? That was the one answer she couldn't give right now—thankfully, it wasn't what he was asking. "Yes, I trust you."

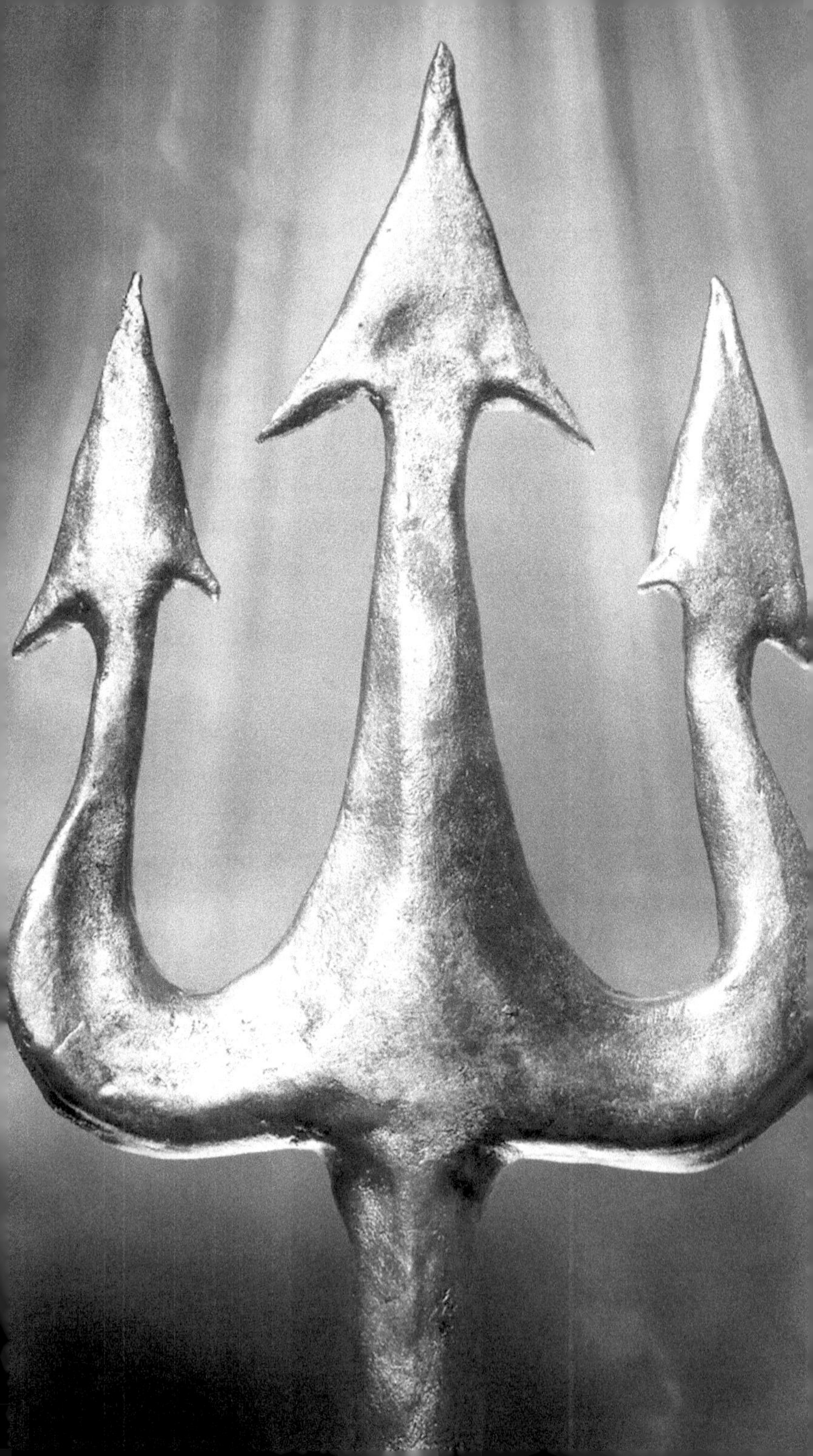

CHAPTER SIXTEEN

"Thank fuck!" Carter's hands went to the hem of Jordyn's sweater and dragged it up her body, revealing all the luscious flesh beneath it. "Lift your arms, baby."

When she did, he pulled the garment over her head and tossed it to the floor. His mouth found hers again, and he devoured her as he grabbed her ass, carrying her over to the end of the king-sized bed. It was at that moment a thought popped into his head. Pulling his lips from hers, he raised an eyebrow at her. "Is this your room or mine?"

Jordyn's cheeks flushed. "Um… ours."

"Ours? One bed? Damn, woman, you just made my day and possibly my year." Placing one knee on the mattress, Carter lowered her down, nibbling on her neck as he did. Reaching behind her, he unclasped her bra, but instead of removing it all the way, he slid the straps down her arms and then used them to tie her wrists together. When he was done, he ran his fingers under the bindings to make sure her circulation wouldn't be compromised. Instead of fear, he saw lust flare in her eyes, and that made his cock grow harder. He quickly relieved both of them of the firearms and knives hidden on their bodies and placed them in a pile on the nightstand.

Kneeling on the bed, he dragged her further into the middle by her armpits. It was then he finally allowed his gaze to drop to her bare breasts. He brushed his knuckles over the sensitive, mauve peaks and reveled in Jordyn's response. She shivered, moaned, and clenched her thighs together—that last part wouldn't do.

Carter glanced around. He didn't have any of his toy bags, so he'd have to improvise. "Stay there, sweetheart."

Standing, he strode to the closet and inspected the contents. An iron—*that would do.* He pulled open two drawers in the bathroom before finding a hair dryer. Grabbing it and two hand towels, he headed back to the bed. Stopping at the foot of it, he stared down at her. Damn, she was beautiful.

Jordyn saw what was in his hands, and her eyes narrowed in confusion. "What's all that for?"

Waggling his eyebrows, he replied, "You'll see."

Dropping the appliances and towels on the bed, he reached up and undid the snap and zipper of her jeans, then pulled them down her legs, along with her thong. He swallowed hard—she still kept herself bare, a fact he loved. Once she was completely naked, he took one of the towels and wrapped it around her left ankle, then looped the cord of the hairdryer over it. Jordyn watched him but didn't ask any more questions. Glancing down to where the dust ruffle hid the legs of the bed, he realized he still had a problem. "Scoot down, sweetheart. It's not quite long enough."

"Long enough for what?" she asked while doing as he'd ordered, which thrilled him.

"Keep coming." Once her ass was near the foot of the bed, he lifted the skirt and wrapped the hairdryer around the bed's leg. He quickly repeated the process for her other ankle with the iron's cord, then winked at her. "There. Now you're wide open for me."

Ever since she'd said she trusted him, the tension in his body had been slowly fading—well, what had come from his anger and frustration. His sexual tension, however, was skyrocketing. Pulling his shirt over his head, he tossed it on a nearby chair and then fell to his knees. "Hands above your head, Jordy, and keep them there. I want to see how many orgasms you have for me tonight."

Her eyes widened, and she tried to close her legs, but the makeshift bindings held her in place. Leaning forward, Carter nipped the inside of her thigh, causing her to yelp. "I said, hands above your head, baby. Follow my orders, and I'll let you come until you can't come anymore. Disobey me, and I'll teach you all about orgasm deprivation."

"Like hell! You wouldn't dare." Despite her outburst, she lifted her arms above her head.

He gave her an evil grin. "Good girl, keep them there. And yes, I would dare."

Peppering the inside of her thighs with kisses, he made the journey to her pussy torturously slow on purpose. She squirmed her hips, and he put a stop to that right away by wrapping his arms around her thighs and holding her pelvis in place. Her skin was so soft and delicious—he could spend a lifetime feasting on it. When he reached the junction of her legs, he flicked the tip of his tongue over her clit and restrained her hips when she bucked them. Using his fingers to expose her little gem, he gave it a thrashing with his tongue before closing his lips around it and sucking.

"Oh, shit! Carter!"

He loved making her scream his name and hoped one day to hear Master Carter fall from her lips with ease. He'd give her everything she'd ever dreamed of, and all he asked for in return was her submission and her orgasms—they were his and his alone.

Moving his mouth down to her pussy lips, he ran his tongue through them, which caused her to start begging. "Please!"

"Please what, baby?" He sucked, licked, and nibbled on the plump, bare flesh, savoring her taste. If he had his way, he'd be the last man ever to enjoy her bounty. "Please make you come?"

"Yes!" Her hands gripped the sheets above her head and twisted them.

"Not yet. I'm going to take you so high that when you fall, it'll seem like forever before you come back to earth. But don't worry, I'll be here to catch you."

Releasing her hips, he brought one hand to her breast and puckered nipple and the other to her swollen labia. As his mouth returned to her clit, he slid two fingers into her soaking-wet core and coated them with her juices. Pulling them out again, he dragged them downward between her ass cheeks, rimming her rear entrance. She gasped and bucked her hips again. Her thighs clenched as she unsuccessfully tried to close them.

"Tell me, sweet Jordy, have you ever let a man take you back here?"

Her gaze ran down her body until it met his. Lust was written all over her face, which was coated in a fine sheen of perspiration. "N-no. Never."

"Someday, I will. Your body is mine, and I'll mark my claim on every inch of it." He spit on his fingers and brought them back to her ass, lubricating her tight hole. "But it will take some preparation for that. For now, just relax and let my finger in."

Instead of relaxing, she tensed, and her ass clenched. "N-no."

"Jordy, trust me. I won't hurt you." His finger continued to circle the puckered hole while his other hand played with her nipple. "I'll take it slow. Don't say no just because you're scared. And remember, I won't accept no as your safeword. Do you want to say red?"

There was a long pause as he let her decide what she wanted to do—while she figured out what she wanted to let him do. The whole time his fingers stayed in motion while his tongue ran up and down her slit at a slow, soothing pace. Seconds passed, and he felt her relax a bit. Finally, she answered him. "No, I don't want to say it. But I will if it hurts."

"There shouldn't be any pain, baby. It might be a little uncomfortable, but that's normal for a virgin ass." He spit on his fingers again. There was no lube handy, so he used what he could to make sure he didn't hurt her. "One day, I'll introduce you to some more pain for pleasure, but not tonight." He attacked her pussy with his mouth, tongue, and teeth, wanting to give her a distraction. When she was squirming and moaning again, he pushed his finger into her asshole a scant millimeter, then withdrew. He did it again, and again, gaining a little more ground with each thrust. Whenever she tensed at the unfamiliar invasion, he distracted her with his mouth and his other hand until the muscles in her thighs and buttocks relaxed. Her gasps, cries, and begging increased as he took her higher and higher. While her mind might still be undecided, her body was totally on board with what he was doing to her. Her pussy wept with her juices, which he was more than happy to lap up. The sweet and spicy taste tantalized his taste buds, and he was certain he could survive the rest of his life by drinking nothing else but her.

When his finger was finally past her sphincter, he sensed she was right on the edge of the cliff he wanted her to fly from. His mouth left her just long enough to say, "Come for me, Jordy." His teeth bit lightly on her exposed clit, and she screamed her release. He wouldn't be shocked if someone in the room next to them called the manager about all the noise, but Carter didn't care. Watching Jordyn shatter for him was the most incredible sight he'd ever seen. And he swore he'd never take it for granted.

Standing, he quickly shed his pants and grabbed a condom from his wallet before tossing it aside. Grabbing her hips, he pulled a still-panting Jordyn to the edge of the bed. He really should give her a few more orgasms before he took her, but the need to be inside her was so strong that he couldn't wait any longer. He had all night to make it up to her.

After donning the condom, he lined his cock up with her slit and eased into her. Jordyn moaned. "P-please, let my legs go. I want to wrap them around you."

With his pelvis making slow plunges and withdrawing again, he lifted her right leg and then her left, sliding the towels and cords from her ankles. Her legs encircled him with her heels resting on his ass. Leaning over her, his mouth found her taut nipple as his cock fucked her core. Her body rocked in time to his as she met him thrust for thrust. The drag of her walls was the sweetest torture. His body, mind, and soul celebrated. Being inside her was where he belonged, and he was finally home. Never again would he let her run from him—and he swore he would never give her a reason to. But first, he had to convince her of what he already knew in his heart—she was the love of his life and belonged to him.

The room was filled with their combined gasps, moans, curses, and heavy breathing. The scent of sex filled his nose. They were joined in the most primal way they could be. She had been made for him. She'd been his from the moment she'd been born, even though it would be decades before either of them knew it.

A tingling started in his spine as he fucked his sweet Jordy faster and harder. Pushing up on one hand, he snaked the other between them and found her clit. There was no way he was coming without taking her with him. "Come for me, baby. Come for me now!"

Her channel squeezed and quivered around his shaft as she shrieked his name. Three more thrusts, and he roared, following her over the edge into a vast abyss. He couldn't stop his eyes from closing even though he wanted to watch her come apart. Black, white, and gray spots flashed behind his lids as he emptied his seed into the latex barrier. One day, he'd take her with nothing between them, but that would be a choice they'd make together.

When the last of his orgasm began to fade, he collapsed on top of her, doing his best to keep most of his weight on his arms. Sweat and deep flushes covered both of them. Jordyn's sated and exhausted gaze met his. "Damn, that was even better than I remembered."

Trying to catch his breath, he grinned. "I'm not too sure. We might have to do it again as soon as I recover, just to be certain. Any objections?"

"Not a single one."

At 6:15 in the morning, Jordyn was finishing up in the bathroom when someone knocked loudly at their door. Already dressed, Carter snatched his 9mm from the nightstand, then strode to the door. A check through the peephole had him relaxing and swinging the door open to let Jake Donovan in. Carter had sent him a text letting him know where to find them after he and Jordyn had taken a breather from their

marathon sex sessions last night and had dinner before some quick shopping for warmer clothes. "Thanks for coming, Jake."

"No problem. Gives me a chance to make things even with you. I owe you for helping with both Alyssa and Kat, among other things—it'll be a while before I can call it even with you." Jake had been guarding Boomer's fiancée when Russian mobsters had kidnapped her. Carter had put a bullet in one of the kidnappers' heads while a SWAT sniper had killed the other guy.

Handing Carter a secure satellite phone the spy had requested as he passed, the former SEAL walked into the room and glanced back with a raised eyebrow after he spotted the one bed, then heard Jordyn in the bathroom. "I won't even ask."

"Good. Because I probably wouldn't answer. Nick with you?"

Jake leaned his ass against the room's dresser and crossed his arms. Two inches taller than Carter, Jake was just as lean. With his brown hair and sharp, green eyes, he had movie star features that had many women hitting on him, but since Jake was gay, it never mattered to him. "Nope. He got called up two weeks ago. No idea where he is or when he'll be back, but they told the team to plan on missing Christmas. You know, it kind of sucks being on the other end of that." His submissive/boyfriend had less than a year left on his commitment to the Navy and SEAL Team

Three before joining his older brothers and Jake at Trident.

Snorting, Carter holstered his weapon at the small of his back. "I'm sure. You'll get through it, though." Jordyn exited the bathroom, and Carter couldn't help running his gaze from her head to her toes and back again, remembering every inch of skin he'd enjoyed last night. "Jordy, you remember Jake, right?"

"Yes." She smiled and held out her hand, which the other man shook. "Nice to see you again, even though last time was only for a few minutes. I heard Ian's brother and the girl are both doing okay."

"Yes, ma'am. Nick and Alyssa are doing just fine. I never really got a chance to thank you for your help. Alyssa means a lot to me, and she's leading a normal life now, thanks to you."

Jordyn waved her hand in a no-big-deal gesture. "Please, all I did was crack a safe. You and Nick were dodging bullets—or, in Nick's case, getting hit by one."

"Yeah, every time he leaves on a mission now, I remind him to duck a little faster if the bullets start flying," he said with a wry grin. "All right, fill me in. I've got three from my team waiting for us downstairs."

Running a hand down his face, Carter sat on the edge of the bed and looked up at his friend. "We're transporting a prisoner from the penitentiary, fifteen minutes away from here, to a private jet waiting for us at the airport. From there, we're heading to Missoula, Montana, where he'll donate a kidney to my nephew."

"Nephew?" Jake's eyebrows almost hit his hairline. "Damn, every time I think I've got you figured out, dude, you go and surprise me again." He paused. "Who's the prisoner, and why aren't they just taking the kidney from him here in California and transporting it?"

"The prisoner is Justin's sperm donor. The bastard raped my foster sister when she was fifteen, and Justin was the result."

Jake's jaw clenched. Alyssa had been a missing person case for him that had him turning the tables when he'd found out she'd been repeatedly raped by her father starting at age twelve. Jake had helped her and her mother escape, but the latter was murdered a year later when the bastard found out where they were hiding. Jake had come to Alyssa's rescue again, along with Nick and a few others from Trident. To say the man hated rapists, especially when the victim was a minor, was a huge understatement. Carter felt the same way.

"With the help of my boss, Osbourne is being released into federal custody. All the warden knows is it's classified, and he'll be returned when we're done with him. We're doing it this way because, otherwise, we'd have to get a court order, which could take weeks if not months—time we don't have. I also don't want Osbourne to know where all this is taking place. With official paperwork, he'd have all the details he'd need to fuck with her. The head of the transplant team is also on the government's payroll, and I've discussed this with him in the past—in case we had to go this route.

"It'll take about forty-eight hours to run all the tests on Osbourne to make sure he's a complete match and healthy enough. Then comes the surgery, which will take a few hours. Forty-eight hours after that, he should be released from the hospital but will need to remain local for a week in case any complications pop up. Honestly, after we get his kidney, I wouldn't care if he croaked—actually, I'd prefer that, but I'm sure the doctors would disagree with me. I'll arrange for a place where you can hole him up for the week. Then you'll return him to Folsom. At that point, the warden will have to be filled in because there's about a six-week recovery period they'll have to be aware of. Can't just return the guy minus a kidney and not let them know, I guess."

"Guess not," the man agreed. "Ian said he's sending a second team to Montana. All six of Omega."

Carter nodded his head. "Yeah. It looks like Senator Beltram has come back from the dead to bite me in the ass. Emmanuel Diaz wants revenge."

"Seriously? Fuck." Jake had been one of the men on the hit list Beltram had given his hired assassin. While the men at Trident hadn't known for sure Carter had pulled the trigger on Beltram, under orders from his superiors, they had to have suspected after it all went down. He trusted Jake would take that intel to his grave, just like Ian and the others would.

"Yeah. It looks like the security breach and hits on the other agents were red herrings. Problem is we've got a mole in Deimos. Until we figure out who that is, Diaz gets to keep breathing, then they'll both be eliminated."

"So until that happens, you want a team on your family," Jake acknowledged.

He nodded again. "Exactly." His gaze searched for Jordyn. While the two men had been talking, she'd been repacking her duffel and, to his surprise, his as well. "Thanks, sweetheart."

"Don't get used to it," she teased. "Next time, you get to do the packing while I sit on my ass."

Unable to stop the grin spreading across his face, Carter ignored the fact that Jake was in the room. He stood and pulled Jordyn flush against him. Bending down, he gave her a brief kiss that held a promise it would continue when they were alone again. He was pleased to see a blush on her cheeks, but now was not the time to celebrate it. "All right. Let's hit the road. The pilot was told to be ready by 0730."

After grabbing both their duffels, Carter followed Jake and Jordyn out of the hotel room to the elevators. They were all on alert for anything out of the ordinary. When the doors opened to the lobby, a man and a woman flanked them for the walk out to the parking lot, where another of Jake's team members waited to drive the eight-passenger van. Jake opened the back door, and his operatives climbed into the rear third seat, leaving the middle one for Jordyn and Carter. Getting in the front, Jake nodded for the driver to take off, then pulled up the address for the penitentiary on the GPS unit. Shifting around, the head of Trident Security West introduced everyone. "Jordyn and Carter, behind you are Riley Kramer and Rebecca Faraday."

The foursome shook hands over the seatback between them. After Ian, Devon, and Jake agreed on the new team members, they'd let Carter review the operatives' files in case he needed their help—he liked to know who had his back. Kramer was a thirty-four-year-old retired Green Beret. Five foot eleven, with brown hair and hazel eyes, he was the team's primary sniper. Faraday was a kick-ass woman in her own right. The pretty blonde with blue eyes was five foot eight and held a black belt in three individual martial arts disciplines, including Krav Maga. They'd snatched her up from the Seattle Police Department, where she'd been on one of their SWAT teams as well as their counter-terrorism unit. She smiled at both of them. "Nice to meet you. Please call me RJ."

"RJ it is. Thanks for the help," Carter replied.

"And in the driver's seat," Jake added, "is Tap Corrigan."

The black-haired, stocky, retired Marine and

former FBI agent met their gazes in the rearview mirror and nodded hello before following the GPS woman's voice instructing him to "turn left."

After a brief stop at a deli for egg sandwiches, bagels, and coffee, they arrived at the state penitentiary at 7:00 on the nose. Carter was the only one who hadn't touched his breakfast. His stomach was churning at the thought of being in a vehicle and then a plane with Osbourne.

They were flagged through the huge gate by one of the guards, and it closed again behind them. The vehicle was stopped over a narrow trench that was used to inspect the underside for bombs, weapons, or other contraband. None of them opened their doors while another guard approached the driver's window. Corrigan hit the button to lower it. "Hey, we're here to pick up a prisoner."

Carter handed one of his federal ID's with an alias, along with the paperwork McDaniel had faxed to the hotel for him last night, to Corrigan, who gave them to the guard. The uniformed man looked everything over as two other guards stood nearby with dogs that were probably trained to sniff out drugs, explosives, or other contraband. The guard at the window handed the paperwork back to Corrigan. "You'll need to hand these to the guards inside. They have Osbourne in a holding cell, all ready to go. I just need everyone to step out so the dogs can search the vehicle. Please keep your weapons holstered and wait over there." He pointed to the wall behind him.

Yesterday, Carter hadn't gone through all this because he'd walked in after leaving his weapons with Jordyn. This time, since their prisoner was waiting for them just inside the intake area, they didn't need to relinquish their firearms. They were back in the vehicle five minutes later, and Corrigan drove them through the interior gate. While the rest of them waited with the van, Carter and Jake entered the prison, where, once again, the former handed over the ID and paperwork. The warden was nowhere to be seen, but he'd clearly followed McDaniel's instructions to the letter. Through the plexiglass window of the holding area, they could see Osbourne, dressed in civilian clothes, waiting for them.

When the holding room door was unlocked and opened, the two men walked in to retrieve their prisoner. Carter stood stiffly, his fists clenched in a hatred that had been festering for years, as Jake instructed Osbourne to stand. The operative cuffed his hands behind him, then patted him down from head to toe. Just because the guy had spent the last twenty years in prison didn't mean he wasn't carrying some sort of weapon on him. When Jake nodded to Carter that they were all set, he pivoted and led the way out the door without a word.

Osbourne snorted as they approached the vehicle with the others standing next to it. "You need this many people to transport me? And two women, no less. At least they're hot-looking. Hey, babes—"

Whatever he was about to say was lost when Carter spun around and grabbed the bastard's throat, crushing it tightly, cutting off most of the man's oxygen supply. Osbourne's eyes bugged out, filling with fear, as Carter got into his face and spoke in a deadly voice. "Shut up, you piece of shit. Those two women know more ways to kill a man than you ever thought were possible. They also have permission to break any of your bones they see fit if you so much as look at them the wrong way. I don't want to hear another fucking word out of you for the entire trip unless you're asked a direct question. Blink if you understand me."

Osbourne opened and closed his eyes several times. When Carter let go of his throat, the man stumbled backward and gasped for air. Unsympathetic, Jake shoved Osbourne toward the van. Kramer pulled out a blindfold and put it over their prisoner's eyes, then helped him into the middle row after Jordyn and RJ climbed into the rear seats.

Carter held his hand out to Corrigan. "Let me drive so I have something to do with my hands besides strangling him." The man nodded in understanding and tossed him the keys.

The rest of them loaded up—Jake in the front passenger seat again, with Corrigan and Kramer flanking Osbourne in the middle row. Carter started the engine and drove them back out the way they'd come in. By the time they arrived at the airport, where the private jet awaited them, he'd gotten himself completely under control. Well, as much as he could be around a man who he wanted to beat into a bloody pulp.

It's going to be a long, fucking flight.

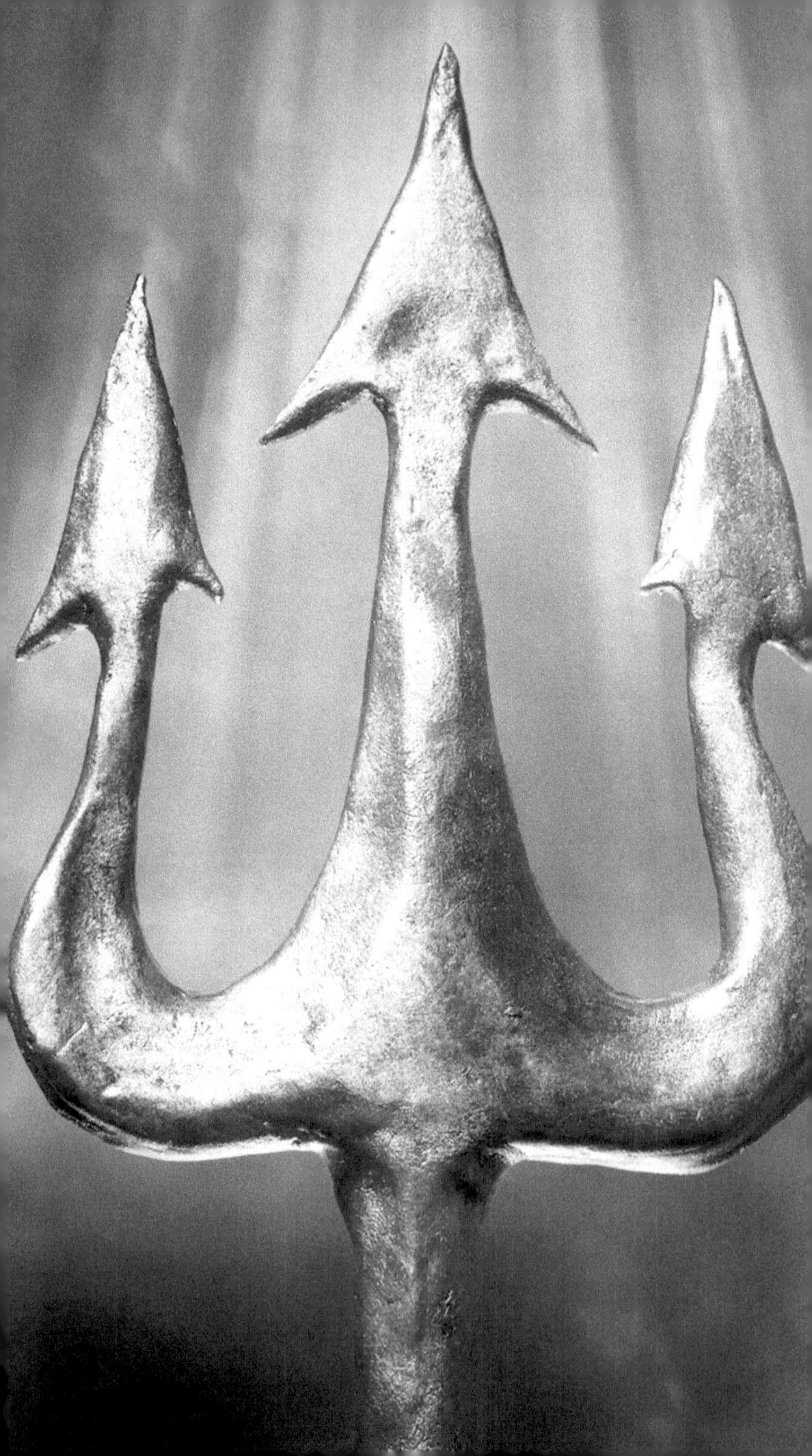

CHAPTER SEVENTEEN

Corrigan and RJ escorted Osbourne onto the waiting jet while the others followed with everyone's go bags. Once they were in the air, Carter would, begrudgingly, let them take off the blindfold and cuff his hands in front for a while, but he didn't want the bastard to know exactly where they were going. Jake's team would ensure no one at the hospital let Osbourne know what state Justin and Vicki lived in. It might be overkill, but Carter wanted to make sure they never had to deal with Osbourne again—his only other option was an unsanctioned kill—aka murder.

The pilot, who'd flown Carter and Jordyn in yesterday, had already done the preflight checklist, and within minutes of the cabin door shutting, they were rolling down the runway. Osbourne was strapped into a seat toward the front while Jake's team surrounded him. Carter sat in the back with Jordyn, waiting for the jet to gain altitude and level off. Once that happened, he pulled out the secure SAT phone and called McDaniel, filling him in about what they'd learned at Club X before adding, "So it looks like this has all been a farce to cover up a hit on me."

The realization that three good men had lost their lives for an assassination he'd been assigned to was eating at him more and more. "We've got a mole in Deimos—you and Jordyn are the only people I trust right now, so she and I are heading to Colombia—we'll be off the grid." Jordyn reached over and squeezed his hand, and he gave her a small smile in return.

"You'll need backup," McDaniel huffed.

"We'll have it. I know exactly who I'll call—again, people I trust with our lives. You know I have to do it this way, Gene, until we find the mole. I don't want anyone from Deimos down there on my six and me worrying if the shot will come from behind." It was a sad day when you didn't know which of your fellow operatives wanted you in their crosshairs.

There was a long pause. McDaniel knew he was right. The man was just weighing all the options—not that there were many. "Fine. But I'm telling you right now, I know Jacobs gave you the green light, but the mole changes things. Try not to kill Diaz until we find out who it is, all right?"

"I'll do my best."

"Let me talk to Jordyn."

Carter rolled his eyes and handed her the phone. Her brow furrowed, but she took it from him and put it to her ear. "Yes, sir?" There was a long pause, and then, "Yes, I understand." Their boss must have hung up without saying goodbye because Jordyn wordlessly hit the end button and placed the phone on the couch next to her. "He said I'm supposed to keep you from killing Diaz until the mole is found. Guess he doesn't trust you to do your best."

He grinned. "Knows me too well." Reaching down, he tugged on the lower halves of her pants, bringing her legs up across his lap. Pulling off her boots, he let them drop to the floor before massaging one foot. "So... we have a few hours to kill with not enough privacy to fool around. I told you about my crappy childhood yesterday, why don't you tell me about yours. I know some of your background, but not all, and definitely not from your point of view."

He half expected her to refuse, but then she settled deeper into the couch, propping a pillow under her head. "I guess fair is fair. Just keep doing that, and I'll talk."

"And here I thought I'd have to torture it out of you. Something tells me you're getting sweet on me."

"Don't push your luck, Thaddeus."

Barking out a laugh, he shook his head. "Not even

close, love. And I think that's a repeat from when I was training you."

"Damn." She took a deep breath and let it out slowly. "All right. My background. I'm sure you know about my parents—who they were and what... what happened." He nodded. "Mom was a beauty queen who fell in love with my father, a businessman, when she was twenty. They dated for two years and would have gotten married sooner, but then Mom wouldn't have been able to enter the 'Miss' pageants anymore. I don't know how long it was after the wedding before he started abusing her, but I don't remember a time there wasn't yelling and hitting going on. Mom got very good at hiding her bruises under clothing and makeup."

She paused, and Carter realized he'd stopped massaging her foot and was staring at her. "Shit! That's why you thought I was into abusing women, isn't it?"

Biting her lip, she nodded. "I assumed that's what the lifestyle was—just a curtain to hide behind—an excuse to beat up women. I'm sorry I—"

"Sh. No apologies, sweetheart. You're not the first person, nor will you be the last, who misinterpreted what BDSM is all about—I did, too, in the beginning." Her eyebrows arched at his confession. "I had no idea what it was all about until I ended up on an assignment at a club in Russia for a few weeks. By the time

I'd gotten what I needed from my target, I'd found a lifestyle that gave me that last bit of control I was searching for. After that, I trained under the best Doms in Europe and the US. I learned every form of play that appealed to me and how to ensure my submissive's safety at all times. I would be crushed if something I did resulted in a sub being physically, emotionally, or mentally damaged. Unfortunately, there are some people out there who *do* use it as an excuse to abuse others. Or don't take the time to train properly, which is just as bad." He massaged her foot again, trying to get her to relax a bit. "But let's back up a little—you were talking about your parents. Did your father abuse you, too?"

"No. Quite the opposite, actually—he doted on me. Because he was so nice to me, I grew up thinking it was normal for men to hit their wives. I went to private schools and had everything a kid could ask for —I was pretty spoiled. That all changed when I was fourteen." She swallowed hard. "I got home from school one day and couldn't figure out why none of the staff were around. I went from room to room—it was a huge mansion—trying to find someone— anyone. My dad apparently told them to take the rest of the day off an hour or so after I left for school. I found my parents in their bedroom—my father had shot my mother in the head, then himself. The police never found out the reason, and just like that, I was an orphan. My father's side of the family took every cent we had and left me with nothing. No one wanted me."

Her voice had gone flat as if she were reciting something tasteless she'd repeated over and over, but Carter knew, deep down, this was something she'd never told anyone. Maybe it was about time she did. He let her continue without any interruptions.

"I went from being a rich, spoiled kid to living in an orphanage until my mother's brother found out about three months later. Uncle Iggy was the black sheep of the family. He came and got me, then smuggled me into the US. As I'm sure you were told before McDaniel introduced us, my uncle was an accomplished jewel and art thief. He trained me how to pickpocket and bypass some of the best alarm systems out there. I learned how to crack open a safe before I could even drive a car. Not an Ivy League education, but he did his best to make sure I could survive in the world. He was actually a very sweet man."

"He was killed in a car accident, right?"

"Yes, a freak accident—a tree fell on his car during a rainstorm. That was ten years ago." She shrugged away the painful memory. "From then on, I was on my own. I'd been working a target for a few weeks and was about to break into the safe during a party when I ran into Benito. All hell broke loose at the party—a rival had crashed it, and bullets started flying—and he got me out safely but wouldn't let me go. He didn't believe me when I told him I was targeting the jewels kept in the safe, not the arms dealing intel he'd been after. He brought me to McDaniel, and you know the rest."

Pulling Jordyn into his lap, Carter held her tightly. She'd been through much more than he'd been aware of, and now he understood why she'd hated him all these years. Damn, so much time they could have had if he'd chased after her and demanded to know what was wrong. But his ego had gotten in the way. He'd been so used to submissive and non-lifestyle women throwing themselves at him that he thought it was no big deal if Jordyn wasn't one of them. He'd been so wrong, and he realized she was the one he wanted all along. He'd be deliriously ecstatic if she were the only woman for him for the rest of his life. Over the past few days, he'd fallen for her hard. Could he give up the lifestyle for her? He didn't think so—it was second nature to him now. But could he find a happy medium they'd both be comfortable with? Maybe—if she was willing to give them a chance. But how the hell could they do that with Deimos sending them to opposite sides of the globe for weeks or months at a time? *Shit.*

"So, who are you calling to back us up in Colombia?" she asked, bringing them both back to the present. Clearly, she'd understood his end of the conversation with McDaniel.

"Trident, for anyone Ian can spare on top of this detail, and Steel, which I'm not looking forward to."

She lifted her head so she could look him in the eyes. "Why?"

"Mic and the boys had a bad op down there, and I'm not sure how she'll take me asking her to return."

"She's tough... and loyal to you. I think she'd do anything for you, just like you'd do anything for her."

Carter stared at her, searching her face, trying to figure out her feelings. "Are you jealous of Mic?"

"A little bit," she admitted. "You have a deep, long-time friendship with her that I could have had with you if I hadn't jumped to conclusions. But she assured me it never went further than that, and she's very much in love with Chris."

Kissing her gently on the lips, he rubbed his hand up and down her back. "I may have a deep friendship with her, but what I have with you... what I *want* to have with you is so much more, Jordy. Even when I was on that op with Mic years ago, pretending to be lovers, it was *you* I wanted in my bed. I should have chased you back then... fought for you, but I didn't, and that's all on me. But if you give me a chance, I'd like to try and make up for lost time."

"It's not on you at all. I was the one who ran. Before I even knew about you being a Dom. I-I was scared about how you made me feel that night, and I ran because I didn't know what to do with that. I'd never felt that way before."

His lips brushed against hers again, and he whispered, "What way, love? Tell me."

She blushed. "Like—like I didn't want to let you go. I was scared it was a one-night thing for you and I was reading too much into it."

"Huh. Ironically, that's how I felt when I woke up alone, and my bruised ego wouldn't let me run after you. So much..." Another kiss. ". . . so much time we've lost. Can we start again, Jordy? Let's be open and honest with each other, and we'll see if this is something special between us. Because I think it is."

Jordyn followed Carter down the hallway toward the elevator. The rest of the trip had been spent discussing all the Deimos employees—agents and support teams. They had Brody Evans and Nathan Cook at Trident going through everyone's financials, looking for discrepancies. Carter had also called Mic and then Ian, asking them to hightail it to Colombia and set the groundwork for going after Diaz. They had to take him alive until they found out who the mole was—then all bets were off.

Mic hadn't been thrilled with going back to the South American country. However, she'd gone off on Carter when he suggested she stay behind and just send her team. Jordyn heard her screaming at him over the satellite phone despite the noise of the aircraft. She was pretty sure the woman had invented a few new curse words in addition to suggesting he do the anatomically impossible. Both teams planned to be wheels up within a few hours of his call, and Jordyn and Carter would meet up with them tomorrow in Colombia.

After they landed in Montana, they were met by the six Trident Security Omega Team members, who'd been waiting for them at the airport with two vans. McCabe and Mancini had been the only two she recognized, and they'd given her warm smiles, which she returned before Carter introduced her to the rest of the men.

Upon their arrival at the hospital, they'd entered through a rear security entrance with the blindfolded prisoner. The head of the transplant team, Dr. Howard Regal, had met them and escorted them to a private suite where Osbourne would spend his hospital stay. While none of them thought the bastard deserved a luxurious room, it was large and comfortable enough for his guards, and the hospital staff coming and going would be minimal. The TV had been disconnected from cable, so he couldn't watch the local channels, but to keep him occupied, a Blu-ray had been hooked up, and a dozen movies were available for him to choose from. When he was released two days after the surgery, the safe house the team would hole him up in was actually a rental cabin.

The Omega team introduced themselves to the head of hospital security before following Carter and

Jordyn to the transplant ward while Jake and his team stayed with Osbourne. From what Carter had told her, the hospital had had its fair share of clandestine patients and surgeries in the past, so security was used to having armed guards doing their jobs while trying to stay out of the way of the doctors and nurses.

As Carter hit the button for the elevator, Jordyn studied him. She hadn't answered him on the plane about starting over and giving whatever was between them a chance, and he'd been okay with that, asking her to think it over. Since then, it had been *all* she'd been able to think about—that and how good it'd been to be wrapped up in his arms.

Her feelings toward him confused her. She'd been on her own for so long, with no real friends, only acquaintances, and no boyfriends—just a few flings that never went past a three-day weekend. Jordyn didn't know how to have a relationship, at least not a healthy one. While she'd come to love her Uncle Iggy, he'd been more of a mentor than a father figure or friend. Her heart-to-heart with Mic had been as close to a girl's night out as she'd ever had that hadn't been part of a charade connected to an assignment. All she knew about marriage was she didn't want to end up like her mother. She'd sworn never to give her heart to any man because there was no way to know if he'd turn abusive like her father.

The ride up to the fourth floor was quick, and when the doors opened, Carter seemed to know exactly where he was going. He'd probably been here years before when Justin had received his mother's kidney. He entered a waiting room just outside a set of doors leading to the transplant ward.

A tall brunette with soft, brown eyes jumped from a chair and ran to him with her arms open. "T.! I'm so glad you're here."

Carter embraced his foster sister and held her tightly as a man approached and extended his hand. Without letting go of Vicki, Carter shook the proffered hand. "Joe, it's good to see you."

"Same here. Wish it was for a different reason, though." Joe Underwood stood about five foot eleven, about two inches taller than Vicki. A brown crewcut, sharp, hazel eyes, and a toned physique screamed former or current military. He appeared to be in his mid-thirties, maybe the same age as his wife.

"Me, too." Releasing Vicki, Carter reached back and grasped Jordyn's hand, pulling her forward. "Jordyn, this is my sister, Vicki Underwood, and her husband, Joe." He gestured from them to her. "This is Jordyn Alvarez, my coworker and... um... friend? I guess."

Jordyn let out a small snort at his hesitation because, apparently, like her, he had no idea what they were to each other. Their eight-year relationship had existed on so many levels that it even confused her. First, he'd been her mentor, followed by coworker, friend, and then lover. A few days later, she'd hated him—had wanted to castrate him. As for right now, they were coworkers again, and she wasn't uncomfortable calling him a friend. It was sticky, though, because they were somewhere on the border between lovers and being in love. She wasn't sure if she was in love with him and definitely had no idea how he felt about her. So what the hell else could they call each other? Smiling at the other couple, who seemed bemused by his last words, Jordyn extended her hand to Vicki and then to Joe. "It's nice to meet you, and I wish it were under better circumstances as well."

"How's Justin doing?" Carter asked the couple.

Vicki glanced at her husband for support, and he answered for her. "He's stable again now, but it was a rough night. Where's... uh..."

"In a room on another floor surrounded by a team I trust." He paused and scratched his head. "Listen, ah... Vicki, Osbourne wants... *shit*... he's demanding to meet Justin before he'll go through with it." The woman gasped and paled. Joe put his arm around her waist to steady her as Carter continued. "It's only for five minutes. I'll be in the room the entire time, and I threatened him with extreme bodily harm if he even suggests he's Justin's father."

Jordyn was as shocked as the others. She knew that small concession was killing him, but if that's what it took to get Osbourne's kidney, Carter would make it happen.

He cupped Vicki's cheek. "I know this is hard, sweetheart, but I promise Justin will think this is a stranger who happens to have the right blood type and is doing the right thing. Nothing more. Just think about it before you say no."

Before she could answer, the Omega team walked in. Vicki's eyes widened at the sight of them—the six men were quite an intimidating bunch. Carter cleared his throat. "And this is the other thing I needed to talk to you about." He took a deep breath and blew it out, his gaze fast on Joe's. "It looks like I have a target on my back."

Underwood's jaw clenched. "Worse than normal?"

"Yeah. Even though I've always ensured no one could connect me to you, it's not good for me to be here—but it had to be done. First thing in the morning, I'm going OCONUS and leaving a team on you both and Justin. Osbourne's being watched by another team. I'll check in with you every chance I get. As much as I want to be here for the surgery, it's best I'm not. In the meantime, guys, this is Vicki and Joe Underwood. Joe is the sheriff of Ravalli County, just south of here." He pointed at the teammates as he introduced them. "This here is Tristan McCabe, Darius Knight, Logan Reese, Val Mancini, Kip Morrison, and Cain Foster. I trust them completely because they know I'll kill them if anything happens to any of you."

As the team leader, a title he shared with McCabe, former Secret Service agent Foster stepped forward with a grin intended to put Vicki at ease and shook Joe's hand. "He's said that about nine times since we met him at the airport an hour ago. But don't worry, it'll never come down to that. You and your son will be safe at all times. From what I hear, I'm better off having Carter owe me than vice versa."

Vicki smiled at the man, the initial shock of everything starting to ebb. "Thank you. And yes, it *is* better to have him owe you. Unfortunately, I speak from experience."

And damn, if that didn't have the big, bad spy blushing a tad. He bent down and kissed Vicki on the cheek. "I told you a long time ago, we're even. Now, can I go in to see Justin? Foster will talk to the head nurse and introduce his team. Two of them will be outside Justin's room at all times, and one will go in whenever a staff member has to be there for any reason. Two more will be with Vicki. Joe, I know you can handle yourself—just watch your six. Foster will set up the rest of the rotations with you later."

His brother-in-law nodded, then turned to Vicki. "I don't want to rush you, little one, but if Carter has to leave in the morning, you have to decide about Osbourne. The last thing I want to do is let the bastard anywhere near Justin, but this will go a lot smoother if he's not under duress."

Vicki swallowed hard, and tears filled her eyes but didn't fall. "I know. Will you go with them?"

"If you want me to. We'll take one of Justin's guards, too, to make sure Carter and I don't kill the guy before we get what we need. All right?" His half smile said that had been a teasing but true statement.

"Okay. Five minutes and not a second more."

Carter held up three fingers on his right hand. "Scout's honor."

An unladylike snort escaped Vicki. "You were never a scout. Now, while you're taking care of that, I don't want to be anywhere near him. Jordyn, would you like to join me for a cup of coffee in the cafeteria?"

Her mouth dropped open as she glanced back and forth between the foster siblings. She hadn't expected the invite, but if that's what she could do to help, then what the hell? Chatting with the woman who knew Carter best would be interesting. "Um, sure."

Foster addressed his team. "Mancini and Reese, you're on the ladies. McCabe, do you and Morrison want to take the first shift with Justin? Knight and I will check out the cabin with Donovan or whoever from his team."

"Sounds good," Tristan responded, then nodded at Carter. "I'll cover your six in the room when it's time."

"Thanks."

Jordyn eyed Carter. He really was holding on by a thread over this five-minute meeting, but with McCabe, Joe, and him in the room, Osbourne would have to be crazy to say anything out of line. At least, she hoped that was the case.

A few minutes later, Jordyn and Vicki strolled into the cafeteria, with Mancini in front of them and Reese pulling up in the rear. While neither woman was hungry, they made themselves coffee and found a table away from everyone. Their guards posted themselves nearby but far enough away to give them some privacy.

"So," Vicki said with a smile after sipping her coffee. "What exactly does 'coworker and... um... friend' with a question mark mean?"

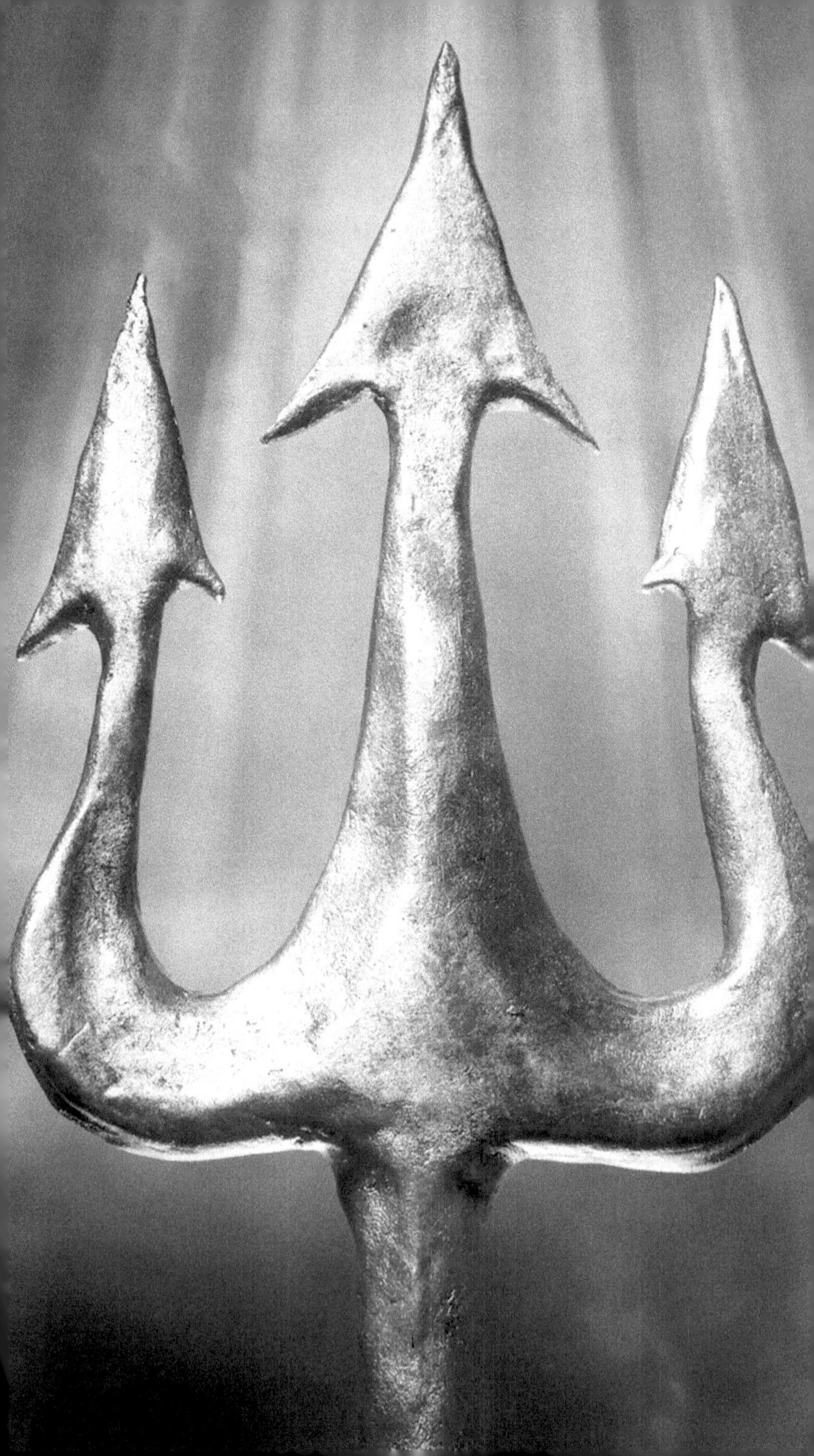

CHAPTER EIGHTEEN

Caught off guard, Jordyn chuckled. In that instant, she truly relaxed with Carter's sister. "Straight to Double Jeopardy, huh?"

"Yup, but you don't have to answer in the form of a question. In fact, I'd rather you didn't. Carter's never brought another woman here before, so that and how he introduced you makes me curious. You don't have to tell me if you don't want to, but I could use something to get my mind off everything else."

For someone who didn't do girlie chats, Jordyn was about to have her second one in three days. "I honestly don't know what we are."

"You like him, I can tell. And he definitely likes you. So what's the problem?"

Rolling her eyes, Jordyn settled back in her chair. "I'm confused—that's the problem." She took a deep, cleansing breath and forged ahead—if anyone knew the man, it was Vicki. "You see, years ago, Carter trained me. Despite a rocky beginning, we became friends, and one night, it went further than that. I got scared of my feelings for him and ran the next morning. Then something happened to change everything." It wasn't her place to let his sister know he was a Dom. "I've spent the last seven years or so hating him because of something I'd misinterpreted."

She was surprised when Vicki nodded her head in understanding. "You found out he was a Dom, didn't you? And not knowing anything about the lifestyle, you kind of freaked?"

Jordyn's jaw dropped. "How did you know?"

Smiling, Vicki brought her hand to the gold choker necklace she wore. "Because that was my reaction when I found out." She tilted her head. "Did Carter tell you about Justin... about how he was conceived?"

"Yes, and I'm so sorry you went through that."

"For years, I hated Osbourne. I'd thought it was odd the US Marshals put me in the Witness Protection Program after I'd testified against him, but the way they'd explained it to me, I believed them when they said it was for my safety." She shrugged. "I was fifteen —what did I know? I didn't have any family, and as a foster kid who'd bounced around, my friends were few, so I was happy to get far away from California. I was able to keep my first name, but I had a new last name. A childless couple, Brendon and Barbara Rush, took me in here in Montana—they were also in the program, so they taught me everything I needed to know about my new identity. They were great. They helped care for Justin while I got my GED and went to college. I was comfortable with my new life. Then, Barbara passed away from cancer three weeks after she was diagnosed. Brendon had a heart attack a few months later."

A sad smile spread across Vicki's face. "I wasn't surprised when he died so quickly after her. They were one of those couples who were so in love they couldn't live without each other. That was two years after I found out Carter was still alive and all about the deal he'd made with the government. At first, I was mad at him for signing over his life for me, but if he hadn't told them to take care of me, I honestly don't know what would have happened to Justin and me.

"After that, Carter came to see me whenever he could, and I loved that Justin had a good male role model to look up to as he grew. I was only nineteen, almost twenty when Carter came back into my life. For the next few years, my life revolved around Justin and my job as a high school social studies teacher. When Justin was ten, I tried dating a guy one of my friends set me up with. He was nice, but when he wanted to take our relationship to the next level, I just couldn't. I was so stressed out over it. Here I was, twenty-six years old, thinking I would never have a normal rela-tionship with a guy.

"One day, Carter was visiting, and I broke down

crying about it. At that point, he'd been in the lifestyle for a few years and thought I'd benefit from it." She snorted. "I thought he was bat-shit crazy. But then he had me research it for a few months and also hooked me up with a chat group where submissives interested in the lifestyle could ask experienced subs questions. I found quite a few of them were victims of rape, and they explained how the lifestyle gave them the control they'd lost." She took a sip of coffee, and Jordyn was in awe of how strong the woman was and the lengths Carter had gone through to ensure his foster sister was cared for.

"Once I finally agreed to try it, Carter vetted a few Doms who lived in the area and were looking for a submissive and introduced me to them. That's how I met Joe—we just clicked. At first, there was no sex— he showed me how I could release my stress with non-sexual play—exercise, yoga, meditation—and how to take control over my mind and body when it came to having a relationship. Over the months that followed, we fell in love, and I was able to overcome my fear of sex. Joe collared me a year later, and it was another year before we got married. There aren't many clubs in the area, but that was okay with us—neither of us wanted to practice among others in the community. We were content to keep it at home."

Vicki grimaced. "Wow, that was way more than you probably expected when I opened my mouth. Sorry. I just wanted you to know Carter is one of the most respectable, loyal, caring men in the world, and he would never hurt you. I would love for him to find someone special—someone he can truly be himself with."

Jordyn's mind was spinning again. Here was a woman who'd been violated in the worst way a woman can be, and she found comfort and love in the BDSM lifestyle. Jordyn's past wasn't the same, but the lack of control over her life had been there.

What would it be like to hand over all the stress of my past and my missions to Carter for him to ease? What would it be like to alleviate his stress too? Could I do that?

Jordyn wasn't sure, but for the first time, she was seriously considering it.

"You didn't have to come, Uncle T." Justin was pale, and the whites of his eyes were slightly jaundiced. Hooked up to IVs, oxygen, and a bunch of monitors, the kid was taking it all in stride. He should be hanging out with his friends, dating some pretty girl, and planning his future. Instead, he was fighting for his life.

Carter smiled at him while sitting in a chair next to the hospital bed. "Did you honestly think I wouldn't, little buddy?" The old nickname no longer fit the young man who stood six foot one and would be entering his twenties next year—God willing.

"No. You've always been there for me."

A knock sounded at the door, and Carter glanced over his shoulder. Jake stuck his head in. "Ready?"

He held up two fingers. "Give me a few, and I'll be out."

"'Kay."

Turning back, Carter nodded at Joe, who was standing on the other side of the bed. The man gestured with his hand for his brother-in-law to give Justin the news. Leaning forward, Carter laid his hand on top of his nephew's. "Listen, buddy. We... um... found a donor for you." He forced a smile and lied through his teeth. "He's a nice guy, works in a prison in California, and was on the donor list—he's sort of paying it forward."

Despite his weakness, Justin's face lit up. "Really? That's great! Wow, we didn't expect it to be that fast. Does Mom know?"

"Yes, she does... and it really is great. Anyway, instead of going to the hospital there, he decided to fly up here. He's... uh... outside and wants to meet you first. Is that okay?"

"Yeah, of course! Why wouldn't it be?"

Carter shrugged. "Just checking. Um... there's one other thing. You know about my job with the government, right?" As far as Justin knew, his uncle was an FBI agent. Carter hadn't wanted the kid to know he tortured and killed people for a living, so that was as close to the truth as he could get. When Justin nodded, he continued. "Well, this case awhile back... we think a guy wants to get revenge against me for putting his brother in prison." Yeah, another lie. "I wanted to make sure you all were safe, so I hired a private security company to watch over you until we find this guy. The owners of the company are friends of mine, and they sent up a few men to be bodyguards for you and your mom."

"What about Joe?"

The boy's stepfather grinned. "I've got the whole sheriff's department covering my six, kiddo, you know that. Like your Uncle T. said, we're just taking extra precautions. Hopefully, it won't be for long."

"Right," Carter agreed. "But this also means I can't stay for the operation. We have a lead on this guy, and I've got to check it out. Joe and your mom will update me every hour until I get back, okay?"

Justin shrugged. "Yeah. I mean, it's not like I'll be awake for it anyway, right? Yeah, Uncle T., it's fine. You just be careful, okay?"

"You bet." He stood. "I'm just going to check with the guards outside, and then I'll bring your donor back in."

"What's his name?"

Carter swallowed hard, averting his gaze so his nephew wouldn't see the hate in his eyes. "Uh... John Osgood. I'll go get him." Not even blinking at the fake name, Joe dipped his chin once, acknowledging he understood why Carter had given Osbourne an alias.

Striding out into the hallway, he saw Jake and Tap Corrigan flanking their charge, who had a sweatshirt over his cuffed hands, hiding them. McCabe and Morrison stood on either side of the door to Justin's room. Carter glanced around and spotted a linen closet. Grabbing Osbourne by the arm, he dragged the guy into it and shut the door behind him.

"What the fuck?" the bastard spat as he was shoved against a rack of clean blankets and sheets.

Carter got into the man's face, letting him see the hate and rage in his glare, yet keeping his voice low and deadly. "This is just a fucking reminder. You have five minutes, not a second more. You don't say anything about being related to him in any way, and you've never met his mother or stepfather. His name is Justin. I told him your name is John Osgood, you're a guard at Folsom, and you just happened to be on the donor list. Told him you were paying it forward for some reason—make up whatever you want. So help me, God, do not make me hurt you, got it?"

"Yeah, I fucking got it. John Osgood, prison guard, not related. Got it." He held up his cuffed hands. "You going to take these off? 'Cause they'll be a little hard to explain, don't you think?"

Opening the door behind him, Carter never took his eyes off Osbourne while raising his voice. "Reverend?"

Jake stepped into the doorway. "Yeah?"

"Got a key for these bracelets?"

The operative handed him a set of keys—the small, skinny one for the handcuffs was easy to spot. Carter gestured for Osbourne to hold up his hands. "Jake, this bastard makes one step in the wrong direction, shoot him in the fucking knee."

"No problem."

Osbourne smirked once his hands were free and followed Carter out the door, where Jake fell in step behind him. Opening the door to Justin's room, Carter walked in and held the door open for Osbourne. Jake and McCabe entered as well.

Justin eyed the three strangers, clearly trying to figure out which one was his donor. Carter made the introductions, pointing at the Trident men first. "Justin, these are my friends, Jake Donovan and Tristan McCabe. They'll be two of the men watching over you and your mom. And this... this is John Osgood... the man who is donating a kidney to you."

Smiling, Justin weakly gestured for Osbourne to come closer, then held out his hand. "Mr. Osgood, I don't know how to thank you... I mean, not many people would donate a kidney to someone they don't know."

Osbourne hesitated, and then, to Carter's and Joe's amazement, the expression on his face softened as he laid eyes on his biological son for the first time. It would also be the last time if they had any say about it.

Osbourne reached out and shook the young man's hand. "That's okay, Justin. I-I'm happy I can do it. How —how're you feeling? You seem to be hooked up to everything under the sun here." He indicated all the monitors and IVs.

Justin laughed. "Yeah, kind of like Wolverine in *X-men*."

"Ha! Yeah, great movie."

"I know! The original was the best, but they were all good."

Nodding, Osbourne sat in the chair next to the bed Carter had occupied earlier. The latter narrowed his eyes at the back of his former foster father's head but remained quiet as the man continued his conversation with Justin. "Totally agree with you there. So... um... I didn't hear how you... um... why you needed the kidney... I mean, what's wrong with yours?"

Justin didn't appear to notice the tension rolling off the other men in the room as he explained about amyloidosis, the rare kidney disease he'd been diagnosed with several years ago.

The two then chatted about baseball and Osbourne's alleged job at the prison—the man was, not surprisingly, skilled at fabricating a believable story. The five minutes went faster than Carter expected, and he cleared his throat when the time was up. "Justin, you're looking a little tired. Why don't we let you get some rest? Okay?"

Joe stood straight from where he'd been leaning

against the wall. "Yeah, son. The doctor said he doesn't want you pushing yourself. Your mom and I will check back in with you later."

"I am kind of tired." Justin nodded and then yawned.

Osbourne stood, seemingly reluctant to leave the room. Carter would have no problem dragging his ass out of there if necessary, but the man extended his hand to Justin. "Well, it was nice to meet you, Justin. I hope everything goes well."

Taking the older man's hand, the teenager clasped it with both of his. "You too, Mr. Osgood. Thank you. You'll never know how much this means to me."

Hesitating, Osbourne finally nodded and said, "I-I think I do, Justin. You just get well, you hear?"

"Yes, sir!"

Joe was the last one out the door when they exited the room. While Jake placed the handcuffs on his prisoner's wrists again for the trip back to his room, Osbourne's gaze met Joe's. "You're his stepfather?" The man nodded. "You and his mother did a good job with him. Glad he didn't inherit anything more than DNA from me. I'll go through with this without any more demands or problems. He's a good kid—he deserves it."

Whatever any of them had expected Osbourne to say, it hadn't been that. For the first time in twenty years, Carter didn't have the urge to kill him. Hell must have frozen over.

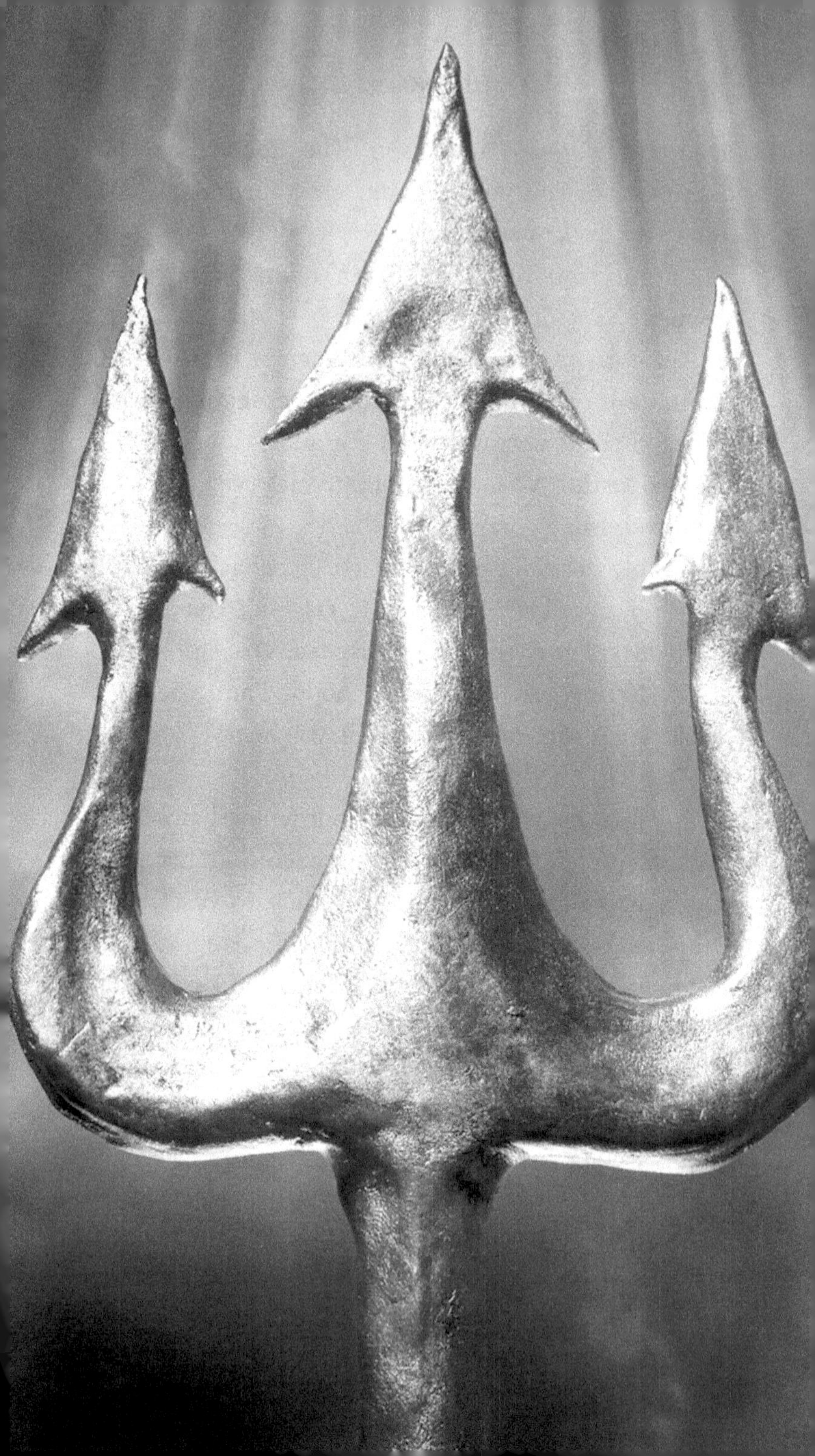

CHAPTER NINETEEN

As Jordyn, Vicki, and their guards rode the elevator back up to Justin's floor, Jordyn suddenly thought of something. "Vicki, you've known Carter for so long, you have to know his first name, right? All he ever tells everyone is it begins with a 'T' and he hates it."

Vicki laughed out loud. "Oh, no, woman. There's no way I'm telling you what it is. He'd kill me or, at the very least, not speak to me for a very long time. Sorry, but that's his decision if he wants to tell you. I owe him so much. I'd never betray him."

"Damn! I'll have to pick up my game and come up with new names. I've been trying to guess since the day I met him."

The elevator doors opened, and Carter was standing there waiting for them. He'd texted Mancini to let them know Osbourne had returned to his room, and the coast was clear again. Stepping out of the car, Vicki stared at him. "How'd it go?"

"Okay, I guess. He didn't say anything out of line, and they chatted about a bunch of stuff. Afterward, Osbourne said he wouldn't ask for anything else—he'll donate the kidney. Dr. Schofield has ordered all the necessary tests, and we'll know by tomorrow night if it's a go." His eyes shifted to Jordyn, then back to Vicki. "I'm sorry, Vic. We won't be able to stay for the surgery—have to chase a few leads on this guy after me—but I'll check in every chance I get. Hopefully, we'll be back in a few days. All right?"

"You're leaving tonight?" his sister asked.

"No. Tomorrow will be soon enough. I have someone checking stuff out for us, and we both need to get some rest. We've been on one plane or another for the past four days."

"Then head home, relax, and meet us for dinner later at Roberto's, okay?"

Carter's hand went to his stomach as he licked his lips. "Jordyn, you're in for a treat. Roberto's has the best Italian food outside of Italy." He bent his head and kissed Vicki on the cheek. "We'll meet you there at six o'clock."

"Perfect. Now go. I'm going to sit with Justin for a while."

After saying goodbye, Carter and Jordyn stepped onto the elevator, which had opened again to let two nurses get off. When they reached the first floor, he led the way to the security entrance where they'd come in. The four SUVs they'd rented were parked outside, and Carter pulled the keys to one of them out of his pocket. He clicked the key fob to unlock it, then held the passenger door open for Jordyn. Hopping in the driver's seat, he started the engine and steered them toward the main road.

When they passed the road to the cabin Carter had pointed out to Foster, where the teams would spend their downtime and take Osbourne when he was released from the hospital, Jordyn glanced at him. "We're not staying at the cabin?"

"Nope. We're going to my house."

"*Your* house? You have a house here?" Jordyn knew he had apartments or condos in several cities around the world, just like all the other Deimos operatives did, she hadn't expected him to have a *house* here in the middle of nowhere. She'd just assumed he stayed with the Underwoods when he was visiting.

"Yup. It's about thirty minutes from here in Florence. I designed it about eight years ago, complete with all the bells and whistles an international spy needs to feel secure. My property backs up to Joe and Vicki's, so they can keep an eye on it for me and use some of the acreage for their horses."

Jordyn gaped. "Acreage? How big is it?"

"Forty acres—same size as theirs. Joe has a nice breeding program for Appaloosas and a foreman who runs it for him so he can focus on being sheriff. It's an elected position, so he has to run for office every four years. He has a year left on his second term and plans on running again."

"Wow, he's young for that, isn't he?"

Shrugging, he stopped at a red light. "Joe's actually a little older than he looks. Forty-three. Bastard aged very well. Before he ran for office, he'd been a deputy for a few years—before that, he was in the Marine Corps."

"Is that how you met him? The Marine Corps? Or because of the lifestyle?" He raised an eyebrow at her, and she added, "Vicki told me how you introduced them and why."

"Really?" He grinned. "She must really like you already if she did that. Anyway, Joe and I met on a few ops in Afghanistan. After a while, I knew he was a standup guy and wasn't too surprised to find out he was in the lifestyle. He's originally from Billings, Montana, and I thought he'd be perfect for Vicki—turns out I was right."

For the rest of the ride, they discussed normal things most people who weren't government-sanctioned assassins chatted about. The weather. The Montana landscape and areas of interest. Movies. Current events. Sports. It felt weird yet familiar at the same time. With each minute and mile that passed, Jordyn learned more about the man she was falling for.

After her talk with Vicki, along with the BDSM

website she'd read through and the club, she finally admitted to herself she'd condemned Carter because of her ignorance of the lifestyle he enjoyed. She now understood the power exchange between a Dom and a sub, what safewords were all about, and even what was involved in negotiations. There'd been a hard and soft limit list on BDSM 101. Hard limits were something the sub or Dom had no desire to try, while soft limits were something they were willing to explore. After speaking with Vicki, Jordyn wanted to go back onto the website and read more. She had a few questions she'd been embarrassed to ask Carter's sister, but if she used an alias to sign up for the site, she could use that anonymity to find the answers she sought.

After leaving the highway and making several turns, Carter made a right onto an unnamed dirt road. Beyond the fence lines on both sides, dozens of horses grazed on green grass, with majestic mountains standing sentry in the distance. The scenery was so tranquil, and Jordyn fell in love with it. She rarely ended up in a place as beautiful and soothing as this, spending most of her time in cities or third-world countries.

The road bumped along until they reached a grove of trees. A quarter of a mile into them, a house appeared in a large clearing. From the main road, one would never know it was there. The beautiful, stained wood siding blended perfectly with its surroundings. Huge windows with tinted glass to prevent anyone from seeing in, yet letting anyone in the interior see out, ran along the wraparound porch.

Carter stopped beside an unassuming post with an attached gray, hard plastic box. Flipping the front panel up, he punched a few numbers on a keypad, then placed his hand on a scanner. Suddenly, the double garage door on the left side of the house began to roll up. He drove them inside and killed the engine. Climbing out of the SUV, he hit a button on the wall, and the door closed behind them again.

As Jordyn exited the vehicle, he opened another security box and repeated entering a code and scanning his hand. The door beside him clicked open, and he arched a teasing eyebrow at her. "Come into my lair, said the spider to the fly."

Jordyn smiled as she walked through the door. "If I remember that story correctly, the spider *ate* the fly."

"Lucky fly."

Rolling her eyes at his pun, she strolled into the state-of-the-art kitchen. Honey-colored cabinets were combined with black granite countertops. A huge island sat in the center with four stools tucked under one side of the counter, and on the outer walls were a large, sub-zero refrigerator, a six-burner stove, and a double-drawer dishwasher. It was a chef's dream, and she was surprised Carter had put so much into a home he was probably rarely in. The kitchen opened into a great room with a stone fireplace and a sixty-inch, flat-screen TV. The comfortable brown and blue décor fit the man perfectly. "Wow, this place is beautiful, Carter."

"Thanks." He opened the refrigerator and pulled out a bottle of beer. "Want one?"

"Sure, one won't hurt."

He handed her that bottle and then grabbed another for himself. "While I worked with an architect to design the place, Vicki did most of the decorating for me. Joe acted as a go-between while it was being built, so I never had to meet any contractors. A retired CIA tech designed the security and alert systems inside and out—but don't tell Brody that. He'll have a fit that I didn't use him, even though this was built a few years before Trident was ever an idea for the Sawyer brothers. The deed to this place is buried so deep, it can never be traced to me." He took a long pull on his beer. "Anyway, I'm going to take a shower, make yourself at home."

Jordyn opened her bottle and took a sip. "Kay."

Watching him walk up the staircase between the kitchen and the great room, she could tell everything still weighed heavily on his shoulders despite his relaxed outward appearance, and she wished there was something she could do to help. A small grin spread across her face as she stopped the beer bottle halfway to her mouth.

Maybe there is something I can do. At least it'll be fun to try.

Placing the beer on the counter, she left it there

and started up the stairs. There were three bedroom doors and one that led to a bathroom. The door at the far end of the hall to her right was partially ajar, so she assumed that was the master bedroom. She pushed the door open and found she was right. The sounds of a shower being turned on and a belt hitting the floor came from her left. Stripping down to nothing, she entered the bathroom through the half-opened door. Carter was already in the walk-in shower. Large glass blocks made a curved wall, so no curtain or door was needed. She could see his sinewy figure through the distorted glass. He was leaning on his hands against the tiled wall, his head bent as the water pelted down on him.

Skirting the wall, Jordyn stepped in behind him and put her arms around his waist. He didn't startle, clearly knowing she was there before she touched him. Resting her head against his broad, hard back, she let her hands roam his chest and abdomen. His muscles rippled and quivered under her touch, but otherwise, he remained still. Jordyn pulled on his shoulder and turned him around. Looking into his blue eyes, she saw numerous emotions he desperately tried to control, raging like a tempest at sea.

Jordyn ran her hands up his chest. In a voice just loud enough for him to hear over the shower, she asked, "Will you let me take control, just this one time? Let me take care of you the way you take care of your family and friends." She kissed the skin over his heart and felt him inhale sharply. "Just this once... Sir?"

His eyes widened as his nostrils flared. His hand delved into her long, wet hair, grasping and pulling it until her chin tilted up. He stared into her eyes for only a few seconds before slamming his mouth down onto hers. The kiss was hard and fast, and when he finally let her up for air, her heart beat faster as she saw his intense desire written all over his face. That man did things to her she never knew existed—made her want things she never knew she wanted. He bent down and peppered her jawline with nips and licks before reaching her ear. His voice was low and rumbling, sending shivers down her spine. "Just this one time, Jordy."

Even though she'd asked for the control, Jordyn was surprised he'd conceded. His hand left her hair as she pushed him against the tile. Holding his hips, she lowered herself to her knees. Her fingers curled, and her nails dug into his ass. His cock was hard and standing proud, waiting for her to do whatever she desired. Not wanting to rush, she licked and kissed the deep V of his abdomen and the creases where his hips and thighs met. She felt his fingers in her hair again, and she shook her head. "Hands against the wall. Just enjoy."

A soft chuckle came from him. "So bossy."

As soon as he obeyed her, she took his cock into her mouth as far back as she could. He gasped loudly, and his hips bucked off the tile before she pushed them back again. Her tongue swirled over and around his stalk, paying extra attention to the thick vein and notch below the tip on the underside. In and out, deep then shallow, again and again. Her cheeks hollowed as she sucked him hard. Her nails dragged over his lower back, hips, and thighs. She glanced up, expecting to see his head against the wall and his eyes shut. However, his chin was down, and those baby blues watched her every movement. The water cascaded over every peak and valley of his shoulders, chest, and arms.

Jordyn's head bobbed up and down. One hand snaked between his legs and cupped his sac, squeezing and rolling it gently. A moan escaped him, and his hands curled into fists as if fighting the urge to grab her head and control the pace she'd set.

"So fucking good, sweet Jordy," he murmured. "Please don't stop."

Running her tongue up his shaft, she sent him a wicked smile. "Beg me."

The corners of his mouth ticked upward. "You really might be a switch. Too bad I won't surrender to you like this very often." He inhaled sharply when she swiped the slit at the tip of his cock. "Damn, Jordy. Do that again."

"Uh-uh. Not until you beg me, *Master* Carter."

His hand reached out, and he ran a few strands of her hair through his fingertips as his sexy smile grew.

"Evil woman—you're killing me. All right, here goes nothing." He gave her a lost puppy look. "Please, do that again. I beg of you. And please don't stop." A smirk appeared. "Was that good enough?"

She licked him again. "Needs work, but it'll do for now."

Her lips wrapping around him again, Jordyn picked up the pace. Carter's breathing increased, and his moans reached her ears. Thighs and ass clenching, his hips made small thrusts in time with her movements. Taking him to the back of her throat, she swallowed.

"Oh, fuck, Jordy! Do that again... please, do that again."

More than happy to oblige him, she did what he'd begged for—repeatedly. She wanted him to lose control with her—the control he always managed to keep in place. His pleas became murmurs as his chin lifted until his head hit the wall. Using her hands, lips, and tongue, she took the power he willingly gave her this one time. His pelvis stiffened as he roared his release into her mouth. Swallowing, she drank every salty drop until there was nothing left.

Through heavy-lidded eyes, his gaze met hers, and he held out his hand to help her up. Pulling her to him, he held her tightly. "Thank you, baby. I needed that." Jordyn inhaled his scent as his hands caressed her back. They stood like that until the water began to cool, and Carter adjusted the temperature, giving them a little more warmth. Bending his head, he kissed her lips, then nibbled on the bottom one. Putting a few inches between her face and his, Carter's eyes twinkled at her mischievously. "Why don't we *rinse* off, *dry* off, hop into bed, and let me get *you* off this time? Sound like a plan, my little fly?"

For most of the flight to Colombia, Carter was on the phone or computer. After dinner with Vicki and Joe the night before, he and Jordyn had gone shopping for things they'd need. Their weapons were good, and Trident and Steel would bring anything else they needed. However, they'd desperately needed tactical clothing and gear and found almost everything they needed at a hunting store. Thank goodness hunting was a big thing in Montana.

While Carter was finishing up on another phone call, Jordyn was sitting on the jet's couch, using his laptop, and for at least the hundredth time today, he studied her. He couldn't help himself. Whenever she was in sight, his gaze automatically roamed over every curve of her body. Last night, as she fell asleep curled into his side, he realized he'd fallen hard for her, but the question was, would they ever be able to make a relationship work between them? While she'd finally accepted the lifestyle he enjoyed, how far would she be willing to explore it with him? If that question was answered, they had to deal with Deimos. For the past several years, they'd barely run into each other, and when they did, she hadn't wanted anything to do with him. If things had been different, would they've seen each other more?

"Dude, you listening to me?"

Brody's question penetrated his mind, bringing him back to the phone conversation. "Um, yeah, sorry about that. What were you saying?"

"Nathan and I completed the financials on everyone at Deimos except for the agents. Everyone came up clean for the most part. A few red flags popped up—gambling, family health issues, etc.—but digging further, we ruled them out. Now, for the operatives, it's taking longer to connect the dots. Everyone's got so many aliases—it's scary. But so far, we haven't found anything that stands out. While I'm down here in Colombia, Nathan's still at it back home. Hopefully, he'll get a hit soon. When are you expected to land?"

He glanced at his black, military-style watch to check the time. "About another hour."

"Sounds good. Boomer and Marco will be waiting for you at the airport. See you in a bit."

Disconnecting the phone, Carter flopped onto the couch next to Jordyn. Startled, she slammed the laptop closed. Eyeing her guilty expression, he arched his brow. "What don't you want me to see?"

She cleared her throat and set the laptop down on the other side of her. A blush stole across her cheeks. "Um... nothing. Just... um... women stuff."

Reaching over her, he snatched the laptop and opened it. "Yeah. I should warn you, 'women stuff' doesn't work on me. Being in the lifestyle, I've seen and heard it all before, so there isn't much that embarrasses me." The screen came to life, and he saw the site he'd shown her the other night. "BDSM 101, huh? User name: CartersMistress666." He laughed. "Seriously? My Mistress and the sign of the devil?"

"Yes, seriously, Trevor." Grabbing the laptop from him, she shut it again and tossed it over to the seat of a recliner, out of his reach.

Grasping her opposite hip, he pulled until she was straddling his lap. "Yeah, that's another one you've guessed before."

"Damn. How long are you going to torture me before telling me your first name?"

Leaning forward, he licked her exposed cleavage. "You've been trained to withstand torture, and you know how adept I am at doling it out, so it'll probably be awhile."

"Brat."

Squeezing her ass cheeks, he placed light kisses on the swell of her breasts. "That's usually my line." Lifting his chin, he rested his head on the back of the couch and stared up at her for a few moments. One thing he'd learned in the lifestyle was how to be open and honest with a submissive, so he decided to ask the question that had plagued him for the past two days. "When all this is taken care of, will you disappear from my life again, Jordy?"

She bit her bottom lip. "I-I'll probably have to... you know, missions and all."

"What if that wasn't an issue? We work well together, and there are plenty of assignments we can be partners on. It won't be all the time, but we can find a way to make it work for us. I can't help but think we have something special here—something I honestly never thought I'd find." He ran his hands up and down her sides. "But you need to think about it, sweetheart. I don't think I can leave the lifestyle behind, and you've only had a small taste of it. Is it something you can live with to be with me if we find somewhere in between that gives us what we both want and need?"

Cupping his face, she leaned down and brushed her lips against his. "I honestly don't know, Carter. I mean, I have so much emotional baggage, and I've also spent the last seven years hating your guts." He opened his mouth to say something, but she cut him off. "I know it was wrong, but... we're not the same people we were back then. How do we know this isn't just scratching a seven-year-itch?"

"I know because you're the only woman I've never been able to get out of my head. Because if all this hadn't happened, I was seriously close to breaking down your door and demanding you talk to me.

Because you're the only woman I've ever let take control, even for a short time, aside from when I was first training in the lifestyle—but back then, I had to." He pushed a few strands of her hair behind her ear. "With you... I wanted to. It felt right. I'll never be able to fully submit to you, but as you've read, it's the submissive with all the control. The sub sets the limits and uses her safeword, and the Dom accepts it."

She seemed to ponder his answer a few moments before continuing. "Can I ask you something?"

"Of course, sweetheart. Anything. Communication and honesty is what the lifestyle is built on."

"What do you get out of it? I mean, besides the control you crave. In the chatroom, there were many different answers to that, depending on the individual or couple."

Carter squeezed her ass again. He couldn't help himself because it was so delectable and fit right in his hands. "I get knowing that my submissive—which, by the way, you'll hold that title for me as long as you want it—my submissive. There will be no other woman for me while you're in my bed."

That was saying a lot. He'd enjoyed many women over the years, even some of his friends' women as a third during play. But he was starting to understand why Ian wouldn't allow a third in his playtime with Angie. The jealousy that popped up at the thought of any other man's dick in Jordyn had his blood boiling. Now, if she wanted to try a ménage with another woman, that he might get into. *Oh, hell, who am I kidding—I'd definitely be into it.* But he'd have to wait for her to complete her limit list before he suggested it.

"I get the satisfaction of knowing I've given you pleasure, comfort, orgasms, and anything else you need or desire. Many years ago, I figured out the lifestyle gave me the control I didn't have as a child. Most of the time, I was on my own—physically, mentally, and emotionally—despite having a roof over my head and food in my stomach. Vicki was the only person I had in my life that I took care of in any way—and if it weren't for her, I probably would have ended up on a path that resulted in me being dead or in prison. A club shrink I spoke to once said being a Dom gave me an outlet for my innate need to care for someone other than myself—to give what I never received as a child. If I wasn't able to do that, I'd have ended up self-destructing at some point.

"Now that you're back in my life, making you happy is my ultimate goal. I never want you to think you can't ask or tell me something. If you want something, I'll move heaven and earth to make it happen." He slid one hand around her hip and thumbed her clit through her jeans. Her breathing hitched, and her eyelids drooped but didn't close. "Seeing you smile or shatter as you come for me, and only me, is all I need to make me happy."

Using his other hand, he reached up and pressed the button to the intercom in the cockpit. The pilot, one of the former military contractors Deimos used, responded, "What's up?"

Still teasing Jordyn with his thumb, Carter said, "Come back here during the next half hour, and you're a dead man."

The other man's chuckle filled the air. "Yes, sir! Welcome to the Mile-High Club."

"Bastard." He flipped off the intercom and then cupped Jordyn's breast. "Have you ever had sex at forty-one-thousand feet above the Earth?"

Jordyn grinned as she arched her back, thrusting her chest forward. "Nope, but I'm looking forward to rectifying that... Sir."

"Good. Stand and strip for me, love, then lay across my lap. I think it's time you had another spanking." He smirked. "A pleasurable one, of course."

CHAPTER TWENTY

anding at a private airstrip north of Bogota, Colombia, they found Marco and Boomer waiting for them. Less than ten minutes after they'd touched down, they loaded into the black SUV the latter was driving and were on the road toward the small settlement of San Justino, an hour northwest of the city. The small, unincorporated town was about a thirty-minute drive to La Mesa, Cundinamarca, where the Diaz family headquartered its illegal businesses. From the backseat, next to Jordyn, Carter asked, "Got an updated sit-rep for us?"

Marco shifted in the front and turned to face them. "Costello, Devil Dog, and Flynn have eyes on the compound at the moment. We'll be rotating shifts." Lindsey "Costello" Abbott was another new member of the Trident team, filling in on sniper duties while Jake Donovan was on the West Coast. She and Jones,

Steel's sniper, would cover everyone else's six when the op went down. "Boss-man was able to get the floor plans of the house and grounds from when SEAL Team Four was here years ago and Emmanuel's brother Ernesto was running the family business. But it looks like some renovations have been done since then. Pierce, Rook, and CJ are pounding the dirt, trying to find someone who works for Diaz willing to provide some intel." Low-level servants usually had a beef with the cartel for one reason or another, however, convincing them to help was a completely different story.

"CJ?"

"That's what Ian started calling Chris Jordon, so there's no screwup. The kid hates it, so of course it stuck."

When they reached San Justino, Boomer drove them through the open iron gate of an adobe wall into a good-sized compound. About a dozen children were playing in a courtyard while several adults were doing assorted chores in and around seven rustic buildings of varying sizes, a large garden, and a water tower. Jordyn took in their surroundings. "Where are we?"

"A mission," Carter responded. "Years ago, I helped out Dr. Ramona Sanchez, who runs the place—she's remained a contact down here ever since. Missionaries are always coming and going from here, so extra people from the States won't stand out. She also has several armed guards who live here or nearby, so weapons are commonplace. Ramona's not a fan of guns, but she's smart and knows the clinic can be a target for the drugs and supplies."

Boomer parked next to one of the smaller structures, and everyone climbed out of the vehicle. A little boy, about seven years old, came running over as Boomer and Marco entered the building, leaving the other two standing there, stretching. "*Señor* Carter! *Señor* Carter!"

He ran into the spy's arms, and Carter picked him up and spun him around. "*Hola*, Mateo. *¿Cómo estás, mi amiguito?*"

"*Muy bien, gracias.*"

Smiling, Jordyn watched as Carter interacted with his little "chum," who told him about the snake he found this morning. A skinny, gray-haired, Caucasian woman in her sixties approached and said in a New York accent, "Carter, it's about time your sorry ass showed up."

Putting the boy down, he drew her into a hug. "Another member of the opposite sex who likes to reference my fine ass when she greets me. How are you, Ramona?"

"Good, as always." Stepping back, she placed her hands on her hips and glared at him, but her smile said she wasn't mad. "Are you going to tell me what has the troops descending on my little camp here, or am I better off not knowing?"

"Better off not knowing." Carter gestured to

Jordyn. "This is Jordyn Alvarez. Jordyn, this gorgeous creature is Dr. Ramona Sanchez."

The older woman rolled her eyes as she shook Jordyn's hand. "He's a crock of shit, isn't he?"

Jordyn laughed. "It's nice to meet you, Doctor Sanchez."

"Oh, none of that Doctor Sanchez crap. Please, call me Ramona. And it's a pleasure to meet you too. Now that the niceties are out of the way, dinner will be ready in about thirty minutes, and I'm sure you want to meet up with the rest of your gang. They're all in the classroom." She pointed to the small building Boomer and Marco had disappeared into, then took the hand of the little boy who was still babbling to his apparent hero. "Come, Mateo, you'll see *Señor* Carter at *cena,* and you can talk his ear off then."

As Mateo reluctantly waved goodbye, Carter and Jordyn strode into the one-room schoolhouse. Ian, Mic, Brody, Marco, and Boomer were scattered about the room, their gazes on maps, papers, or computers. The sound of one of the mission's generators hummed from behind the building. Maps of the Diaz compound and surrounding areas were pinned to the wall, along with other intel.

Carter shook hands with Brody and Ian, then turned to Mic. Before he could say anything, she gave him a pissed-off glower. "If you even think of asking me how I'm handling being in this shithole of a country, I'll kick your ass. Understood?"

He leaned down and kissed her cheek. "Understood, *Mistress* Bea."

Behind him, Jordyn must have given Mic a questioning look because the small but mighty woman laughed at her. "No, I'm not a Domme, but I fucking played one on TV. And before you ask, I'm not a sub either."

Ian clapped his hands together. "Now that we've established that, can we get back to fucking business?" He grinned at Mic. "And I still don't believe you're not a Domme. I can totally see you flogging CJ into submission."

As the woman gave Ian the finger, Carter grabbed the back of a rudimentary wooden chair, spun it around, and straddled it. "Hit it."

"Hit what? We've got shit." The head of Trident Security crossed his arms over his hard chest. "If we don't get some intel soon, we'll be flying blind. Word is there have been upgrades to the Diaz compound since Ernesto ran it. Dev reported there's now a heliport and some new features to the front entrance and the pool area out back. Canopies and additional landscaping are making it harder for them to get eyes on those areas. And that's just the stuff we can see. Who the hell knows what else has been added for security? I told Mic's boys to offer up everything except a ride to the moon on the Virgin Galactic. Hopefully, the promise of *mucho dinero* or a green card will get someone to open their mouth. I'll let your boss figure out the logistics.

"He'll be fucking thrilled."

Ian smirked. "Sarcasm gets you nowhere down here, my friend. We do know that Emmanuel is throwing some sort of party in three days. It's all hush-hush and by invite only."

From where she'd been studying the compound map, Jordyn looked over her shoulder at them. "Arms, drugs, or slavery?"

"Your guess is as good as ours," Ian answered. "While the drugs never waned, Emmanuel's been trying to reestablish the other two businesses, which took big hits when his brother was killed. Ernesto had been running them without much involvement from Emmanuel."

Carter stood again. "So what do you want to do, Boss-man? Wait a day or two, see if we can find some loose lips?"

"I don't see that we have a choice. There's too many new variables."

He eyed Mic. "You okay with that?"

Nodding, she answered, "I agree with Ian. None of us want to be down here longer than necessary, but hitting the place without more intel will be a crap-shoot. My team is good with waiting."

His gaze found the third person he wanted input from. Carter arched his brow. "Jordyn?"

"My two cents are the same as theirs," she replied without hesitation.

"All right. We wait."

Ian disconnected his cell phone call and faced the rest of the room. "That was Marco. He and Rook are bringing in a source. Looks like we finally lucked out."

It'd been over fifty hours since Carter and Jordyn had touched down in Colombia, and everyone had been taking shifts watching the Diaz compound, searching for intel, and strategizing a raid based on what little info they had. Carter's day had just gotten a little better for the second time. Earlier, he'd spoken to Vicki and Joe, who'd told him the transplant surgery had gone through without a hitch and Justin would be in the post-operative ICU for several days to be monitored for infection or organ rejection. Jake and Foster also reported that all was well with their respective charges.

Across the room, Jones glanced at his watch. "You'll have to fill us in later. We're heading out to relieve the others." Devon and Boomer would join him in the shadows around their target's compound for the next eight hours. Lindsey, Flynn, and CJ would crash in the bunkhouse as soon as they returned to the mission to rest up for whenever the others could throw together a plan of attack.

Ian pointed to Carter and Mic. "You two have the best experience with interrogation—not that I expect you to torture him from the get-go. You'll be able to read this guy better than the rest of us. If he's telling the truth, we can start planning. If he's not, feel free to do whatever's needed to get him to squeal. We've got to end this soon before we die of malaria or something from all these damn mosquitos."

To prove his point, he smacked his neck, killing another little bloodsucker. They'd all started taking the medication Ramona had given them to protect against the disease, but it was best if the daily pills were started before arrival in the country, which they hadn't had time for. Carter had told everyone to keep track of what supplies they'd taken from the mission's coffers, and he would replace them ten-fold, as he usually did after visiting Ramona. The clinic and school she ran there were the only medical care and education sources to which most people in the area had access.

Mic grabbed a wooden chair and placed it on the opposite side of the room from where all the maps and papers were on the wall. She spun it around to face away from them. "Pierce, can you see if Ramona has some sort of privacy screen we can borrow from the clinic? No sense in letting this guy see what we know so far."

"Copy that." The big man strode out the door with little Mateo on his heels. The boy was now in awe of all the team members and, instead of playing outside with his friends, had been helping out in any way he could. They gave him small chores to do and rewarded him with a few pesos or pieces of candy. Ramona had cautioned them against giving him or any other children more significant amounts of money as it would make the young ones targets if any of the less scrupulous men from the local village found out.

Shortly after, Pierce returned with a wicker tri-fold screen and set it in place. A few minutes later, Marco and Rook's SUV pulled up to the schoolhouse, and the engine turned off. They led a short, blindfolded man into the room and sat him in the chair Carter had pointed at. Rook pulled off the blindfold and then stepped away. The man blinked several times until his eyes adjusted to the light in the room.

Carter and Mic stood in front of him. The Deimos spy crossed his arms as he spoke. *"¿Habla usted inglés?"*

The man nodded. *"Si.* Yes."

"What's your name?"

"Carlos Palencia."

"You work at the Diaz *casa?"*

"Si, en la cocina."

The kitchen was perfect because the man would know more about the interior than a gardener or chauffeur. "Tell me about this party *Señor* Diaz is throwing tomorrow night."

The Colombian's gaze shifted from Carter to Marco standing nearby. The Trident operative nodded. "I told you—answer all his questions, and you'll get your money and green card. Just make sure it's the truth. You lie to him, and he'll probably stake you to the ground and let the *ratas* and *buitres* eat you alive."

As the man's eyes widened, Carter and Mic tried to hide their smirks. Marco's statement about feeding the man to rats and vultures was a little dramatic but had the desired effect. Every question Carter asked from that point on was answered. He started with simple questions that could be verified by the intel they'd already gathered—just to ensure this guy wasn't stringing them along. After that, he moved on to what they didn't know about the current details of the compound and its occupants. Some of it they were able to pass onto Jones, Dev, and Boomer to check out from their covert locations.

The "party" was as bad as they'd expected. It wasn't a party at all. Instead, it was an auction of captive women who had been kidnapped from various Caribbean islands, Central America, and even the US. They were probably all in their teens and early twenties and were to be sold into slavery to sexual deviants who would eventually kill them after they did despicable things to them.

It was after midnight by the time they finished. After getting as much intel as possible, Carter gave the man five hundred American dollars and told him to report to the Diaz compound at his usual time of 6:00 a.m. After they had his boss, they'd fly Palencia out of Colombia in the Trident jet and let him loose in the States with some cash and a green card. If he didn't show up for work tomorrow, though, it would raise a red flag—something they didn't want happening hours before the raid.

The team had decided to wait until the women were brought to the compound so they could also stage a rescue if possible. According to their new intel, the captives were being held off-site until a few hours before the auction, at which time they'd be placed in cells in the basement of the huge villa. The escape tunnel the operatives planned on sneaking in through would put them in the same area where the women would be held.

Sitting on the bench of a splintering picnic table outside under the stars, Carter ran all the intel through his mind again, looking for holes or anything that may cause a problem during the raid. There were a few undefined variables, but they were minor and could be worked around on the fly. They knew how many guards were expected on-site, and the rotating teams watching the compound had the guards' schedules down pat. Most of the household staff would be gone before the women arrived at the compound, except for four people who would be serving food and drink to the guests—otherwise known as the deviant perverts.

"You need to get some sleep."

A stirring in his groin and a fluttering in his heart had told him Jordyn was behind him before he heard her. Without looking, he reached back and, when she took his hand, pulled her to stand in front of him, between his knees. He wrapped his arms around her waist, holding her tightly and resting his head on her breasts. "I know this isn't the right time, but have you made a decision yet?"

He felt her swallow hard as her hands stroked the hair lying untied down his back. "I have."

Lifting his head, his eyes met hers. "And?"

"I'm scared shitless—not a common thing for me —but I honestly don't think I can walk away from you once this is all over. I've done some more research during my downtime over the past few days. I also talked with Polo yesterday."

"Really?" DeAngelis hadn't mentioned it to him, but the man was the most sought-after Dom at The Covenant. The subs were always going to him for comfort and advice. He had an innate gift for listening and saying the right thing to help them figure out what they were searching for. So it wasn't surprising Jordyn had approached and opened up to him about her feelings after she'd learned the Trident Alpha Team were all in the lifestyle.

"Yes, really. Did you mean what you said about easing into a Dom/sub relationship and finding a middle ground we're both comfortable with? I don't know how my limit list would compare to yours, but there are things I don't think I can do. And if we work together, I need to know you won't go into Dom mode on a mission. I've worked hard to get where I am. I need to be your equal out in the world, even if I submit to you in the bedroom."

He smiled. "When we get back to Montana after this is over, we'll sit down and discuss everything. I trained you, love, and respect the amazing operative you've become. I'll always ask your opinion on a mission. But if I have to, I'll dive in front of a bullet for you any day of the week. That's got nothing to do with you being submissive and everything to do with the fact I've fallen in love with you. Hell, I think that happened the moment I found out you picked my wallet without me knowing it."

"I think I fell in love with you when you laughed about it." She leaned down and placed a quick kiss on his lips before smirking. "You realize, though, now you have to tell me your real name. I can't be in a relationship with you and only know your first name starts with a 'T.'"

He gave her a playful glare. "I don't know about that."

Her brow inched upward. "Hmm. Then maybe I'll have to rethink my decision."

"Fine," he huffed. His mouth went to her ear, and he whispered the dreaded name.

Jordyn gaped at him. "Really?"

He rolled his eyes. "Really. Repeat it, and I'll be spanking your ass every night for the next five years."

CHAPTER TWENTY-ONE

As nightfall approached again, everyone had their assignments. Carter, Jordyn, Brody, Mic, and Rook would sneak in through an escape tunnel Ernesto Diaz had put under the compound years ago. It led to the basement of the huge thirty-room, three-story estate—opulence built on the blood and souls of others. Drugs, white slavery, arms dealing, and every other illegal product were the core of the Diaz fortune. Emmanuel had added new features to the compound after his brother's death, which included a heliport, a panic room, and landscaping that ensured he could sit out by the Olympic-sized swimming pool without worrying about a bullet piercing his brain. He'd learned from the mistakes of other cartel leaders and adjusted his life according to their failures—but that didn't mean he wasn't still vulnerable. The team just had to find and exploit those vulnerabilities.

If any of the five going inside gave Ian the signal they had trouble, Boomer, Pierce, and Flynn would set off explosives, blowing holes into the stone wall surrounding the compound. That would send the guards running right into the line of fire. Between the two snipers and other operatives stationed around the outskirts of the property, they would cause enough chaos for Carter's team to snatch Ernesto and get the hell out of there. They had to use caution so the hired help, Emmanuel's wife and children, and any other innocents weren't injured or killed in the attack. And, hopefully, they'd be able to rescue the women who were scheduled to be sold tonight.

While Jordyn's sniper skills were on par with, if not exceeding, the other two trained shots, Carter needed her eyes and ears inside with him. If there were any connections to be found to Deimos in there, he and Jordyn would recognize it before anyone else. He also needed her cat burglary skills to get them inside quietly.

Using their connections, the teams had acquired several SUVs they needed, but everything else—explosives, ammo, night vision goggles, and other gear had been flown in under the radar by Steel and Trident. Armed to the teeth, dressed entirely in black, and with faces darkened with paint, they loaded into the vehicles and drove to a spot that had been vetted earlier. It was a rarely used dirt road about three-quarters of a mile through the woods from the compound.

Apparently, since adding the panic room and heliport, Diaz had decided he didn't need to maintain the escape tunnel his brother had relied on, so it was a near-perfect entry point. He may have learned things from others' failures, but he'd become complacent in some areas like most men high on their power.

Once the vehicles were hidden under camouflage netting, the teams disappeared into the foliage, heading for their assigned positions surrounding the compound. One of Dr. Sanchez's guards, Rich Parsons, was ex-special forces from Canada and had volunteered his services. The plan was to release the captives, send them down the tunnel, and he would get them to safety. Parsons had followed the SUVs in the mission's unmarked van so he would have room for all of them.

Over the comm sets, Devon, the leader of the trio currently watching the comings and goings of Diaz's people, reported everything, for the most part, was status quo. The usual guards roamed the property while Diaz, his trusted lieutenants, and his family were inside. There had been little movement aside from the arrival of two vans filled with the female captives about an hour ago and two men who'd pulled up to the house about a half hour ago. One was a lieutenant under Diaz, and the other was an unknown entity.

Carter and his team located the metal door for the escape tunnel, and using machetes, they cleared the vines and foliage from it. Next to the door, set into concrete, was a covered panel, which Brody started to work on. It didn't take him long to get in and bypass the alarm system using clamps and wires.

"Damn, it feels awesome being out in the field again." Brody had been stuck back at the Trident compound since his release from the hospital after being electrocuted by his fiancée's stalker. He'd just recently gotten the doctor's approval to resume all activities.

While the light on the panel remained green for whoever was monitoring the compound's security, according to the geek's laptop, they were good to breach the door without alerting anyone to their presence. Carter knew better than to ask if the man was positive—it would just instigate a tirade about his superior tech skills.

Once Brody gave the all clear, Jordyn got to work on the door's lock. It was a little more complex than a standard lock, but she was pulling the door open within two minutes. Carter tapped the microphone of his comm set. "We're in. Might lose you in the tunnel between all the metal and concrete but should be back on at the other end."

"Copy that," was Ian's answer. "Everyone else report in."

One by one, the operatives confirmed they were in position as Carter's team entered the tunnel. Electrical wiring ran the length of it for both the alarm system and red lights, which were just bright enough that they didn't need to use their night vision goggles. Jogging at a comfortable pace, they made their way through the tunnel. According to their intel, another door at the far end dumped them out in the basement, where the women would be held until after the bidders had arrived. They would be held in cells with only one guard watching them if tonight were no different from past auctions. The others would be upstairs getting ready to frisk the bidders upon their arrival. The teams needed to get in and out again before there were more people they had to worry about.

When they reached the other door, Brody got to work on another alarm panel. After bypassing it, he used the wiring to hack into the security camera feeds. Selecting the camera for the cell area, he enlarged the picture. There were eight cells, but it was hard to determine if the women were together or separated since only one of them was close enough to the thick metal bars to be seen on the camera. The door to the tunnel was at one end, while the guard and the door to the stairs were at the other. The man's head bobbed in time to whatever song he was listening to through the earbuds attached to his phone.

"Excellent," Carter whispered. "They probably figured the women wouldn't be any trouble, so they put their dumbest fuck on duty."

Jordyn got to work on the lock. "Hopefully, with his tunes on, he won't hear the tumblers click."

"If he does, yank the door open, and I'll take the shot." He readied his silenced 9mm. "Brody, get ready to kill that feed and any others it doesn't look like we need. With luck, they'll think it's the system and not one camera."

The geek nodded as his fingers flew over the keyboard. Once the commands were in, his finger hovered over the enter key. "There's another feed from the other end of the cells aimed this way. Once you're through, I'll let that one pop back up. With the girls not in view, it'll look normal. Whenever you're ready, Jordyn."

"Two more clicks." As she played with the tumblers within the lock, the sound of them falling into place resonated loudly in the silence on their side of the door, but on the other, the guard didn't miss a beat with his head.

After the last tumbler fell into place, Jordyn nodded at Carter, who pushed the transmit button on his radio. "All right, we're unlocked and ready to go. Open mics for the insiders."

The other four tapped their microphones on so the rest of the team could hear everything in case anyone got into trouble and couldn't transmit in time.

"Copy that," Ian responded. "Ready when you are."

Jordyn grabbed the door's handle and stepped to the side, waiting for the go-ahead from Carter. Brody pushed the enter key, and the large basement feed went blank, along with three other thumbnail views from other cameras. Rook and Mic stacked up behind Carter. When everyone was set, he whispered, "Go."

Yanking the handle, Jordyn swung the door wide. Before the guard even realized their invasion, a bullet from Carter's gun nailed him right between the eyes, and he toppled to the ground. The team rushed in, Rook going to the guard's body and locating the cell keys. While Carter and Mic switched to their assault rifles and kept them aimed at the door leading upstairs, Jordyn and Rook opened the cell doors. A dozen scared young women dressed in lingerie for the auction eyed their painted faces warily until Jordyn spoke in soothing, unaccented English. "It's okay— we're here to rescue you. You need to hurry."

It didn't take more than that to convince the women to move. Despite being held captive, they appeared to be clean, healthy, and uninjured—they were more valuable that way. Rook pointed at the door to the tunnel where Brody was still watching the laptop screen while gesturing for the women to come his way. "Run to the end of the tunnel. There's a man named Rich, dressed like us, waiting for you." He then spoke to the Canadian through the comm set. "Rich, you've got twelve coming toward you. Load them up and take off for the mission. Shoot anyone who gets in your way."

"Copy," was the response.

Once the women were on their journey to safety, Rook closed the door to the tunnel with Brody on the other side. The Trident operative would stay there, monitoring the security system. As Carter, Jordyn, Mic, and Rook started up the stairs and were out of view of the one camera, Brody turned that back on and switched off the one at the top of the staircase. "Hallway above you is clear. I don't see Diaz on any of the screens, so he's either in his office or bedroom—both doors are shut." Their source had told them those were the only two rooms without security cameras, but the hallways leading to them appeared on the feeds. "You've got three people working in the kitchen and one in the east side living room. One guard standing at the entrance to the living room. Two guards at the front door and two more at the back door leading to the patio. All have sidearms but no assault rifles. I don't see Diaz's wife, but the two kids are in their bedrooms. The sick fuck was going to auction off the girls with an eight- and ten-year-old in the house. Bastard."

Mic eased the door open and led with her silenced weapon. The plan was for her and Carter to head for the office while Jordyn and Rook eliminated the interior guards before they could alert anyone to the intruders' presence. If Diaz wasn't in his office, then they'd head up to the master bedroom and find his ass.

Pivoting to the left, Mic advanced on silent feet

with Carter on her heels. The other two went to the right. Despite Brody monitoring the security feeds and letting them know where the guards were, the Steel Corps leader still did a quick glance around the corner of the doorway where the hall passed the dining room. Finding it clear, she hurried past it. As Carter followed, they heard Jordyn's whispered voice through their earpieces. "Brody, kill the living room feed."

"Done."

Seconds passed before Jordyn spoke again. "Living room guard down and out. Server sleeping tight."

They hadn't wanted to kill any of the workers unless they were a threat, so either Jordyn or Rook had knocked the guy out. However, the guards were a different story—they carried out Diaz's dirty work and knew what they'd signed on for.

As Mic was about to turn left down another hallway leading to the office, Brody sounded an alarm. "Two guards coming in the back door. Mic, Carter, you're about to have trouble."

Pivoting toward Carter, Mic pointed at herself and then down the hall away from their target room. She then indicated for him to continue onward without her to the office. Knowing they were running out of time, he nodded in agreement. She would dispatch the guards, and he would hopefully find Diaz behind door number one.

They headed in opposite directions. When Carter

reached the office door, which was still closed, he paused to listen for any voices or movement behind it. Hearing the low murmur of two male voices, he was about to open the door and shoot everyone who wasn't Diaz or an innocent, but shouts from behind him had him pausing.

"Fuck!" Mic's voice was loud in his ear, followed by gunshots. "Two down, but cover's blown. Son of a fucking bitch!"

Yeah, she hadn't needed to state the obvious. As Ian gave the order to blow the charges at the perimeter, Carter lifted his foot and kicked the door in. There was no point in being subtle now as the ground shook with the three nearly simultaneous explosions outside. Movement to his right caught his eye, and he fired his gun at two men a split second after confirming neither one was Diaz. As they dropped dead where they'd stood, Carter scanned the room, leading with his weapon, but he'd missed someone who'd been partially blocked by the swinging door. A hand chopped down on his wrist, forcing it to lose its grip on the gun.

Bringing his hands up to a defensive position, his eyes focused on the assailant, and shock raged through him. He didn't have a chance to question why he was fighting a dead man as a fist came flying toward his jaw. Ducking the punch, he tackled Glenn Aldridge—the Deimos operative who'd supposedly been blown to bits in a car bombing.

They landed hard on the floor and rolled several times, each trying to gain the advantage. As badly as Carter wanted to kill the bastard, he had to try and take him in. Aldridge would still be a dead man before the week was out, but not until after he was tortured into spilling his guts about why the fuck he'd become a traitor and who else was involved.

Rolling again, Aldridge ended on top, but Carter was able to get a leg between them. Kicking out, he sent the other man flying back onto a low coffee table. Outside the office, more shouts and gunfire reached his ears, and he realized he'd lost his comms earpiece, so he had no idea what his team was up to. The whine and thumping of a helicopter's engine and rotors starting up came from the heliport—someone was making a run for it, and it was probably Diaz.

Spinning to his feet, Carter's gaze searched for his gun, but it wasn't in sight—it'd probably gotten kicked under something. Aldridge was also searching for a weapon as he also stood. From the intel they'd gotten, Carter knew Diaz didn't trust anyone other than his own guards to carry guns in the house. Outsiders were frisked and relieved of weapons before being allowed anywhere near the cartel boss. Clearly, Aldridge hadn't earned the man's complete trust yet.

The traitor snatched a sharp, metal letter opener from the desk and held it like a switchblade. This wasn't an ordinary foe Carter was facing—they'd both been trained by the best, so it would come down to which one of them was faster on his feet and had the dirtier tricks up his sleeve.

As they circled each other, Carter got his first good look at his comrade-turned-enemy. Aldridge's eyes were bright and jumpy—he'd obviously been partaking of the cartel's cocaine stash. Carter growled as he searched for an advantage. "So what did Diaz offer you? Drugs? Money? What was so fucking tempting for you to screw over your country and sell out the agents who always had your back?"

Waving the letter opener, the other man kicked pieces of the destroyed coffee table out of his way. "You self-righteous bastard. Diaz wanted revenge on you and made me an offer I couldn't refuse. You really mean to tell me you haven't gotten tired of working in the worst shitholes on this planet, doing what we do, without any recognition beyond a fucking pat on the back?"

He stepped forward and swung the makeshift weapon at Carter's throat but missed as the latter dropped and rolled out of the way and back onto the balls of his feet. More shouts and gunfire sounded inside and out of the large villa, and from the sound of it, the helicopter had taken off. "Recognition? You knew damn well when you signed up that there wouldn't be any fame or glory. You did this because your ego got too fucking big. Too fucking greedy. Hope the money and nose candy were fucking worth dying for. And I don't hate telling you you'll be buried in an unmarked grave I'm going to piss on every chance I get."

That insult had the desired effect as the other man lunged at him. Instead of moving away, Carter used the man's forward momentum and grabbed his wrist, yanking hard and sending him flying onto the floor. But Aldridge countered faster than expected and kicked him in the knee, forcing him to stumble to the side. When Carter recovered and spun around, he found himself face to face with a 9mm Aldridge had pulled out of one of the dead men's side holsters.

Fuck! Point blank range and no cover to duck behind. He was fucking screwed. Maybe if he could get the bastard to talk, Jordyn, Mic, or Rook might be able to save the day—and his fucking life. "So, who was in the car you blew up?"

Aldridge smirked. "Some fucking homeless guy. All I had to do was get a DNA sample from him and swap it out with mine in the database. Now, how many others are out there?"

"Not as many as it sounds." There was no sense in lying since the man wouldn't believe an entire platoon was out there. "But they're still the best, so either you walk out of here with me, or you won't make it off the property."

"Fuck you, Carter." As Aldridge squeezed the trigger, Carter dove for the large desk, but not in time as a bullet slammed into his upper arm with searing, white-hot pain. Sliding over the top of the desk, he sent everything that had been on it flying before he rolled off the far side, crashing into the chair and falling into a heap on the floor. His body was in agony as he struggled to right himself before the bastard came in for the kill shot.

"Carter!"

Jordyn! Why wasn't she shooting? He looked up and saw her beautiful face etched with fear as she rounded the desk, her 9mm in her hand. Her body sagged with relief when she saw he was alive. "Oh, thank God!"

He slumped against the wall and brought his good hand to his wound. The bullet had hit where his upper arm met his shoulder, and it hurt like a son of a bitch. "Al-Aldridge?"

She dropped to her knees and holstered her weapon before pulling out a knife and ripping the sleeve of the bloody T-shirt to reveal the gunshot wound. "Fucking road kill. I shot him at the same time he pulled the trigger." That and the adrenaline would explain why he'd only heard one shot.

Jordyn moved his hand out of the way, then rolled her eyes. "That's it? A fucking scratch? You've got to be kidding me?"

It didn't feel like a fucking scratch. Inspecting it, he saw she was right. It was a deep gouge that would require stitches to close, but the bullet had missed entering his flesh by centimeters.

Mic appeared behind Jordyn, and it was then Carter realized the gunfire and chaos had been silenced. The Steel Corps leader frowned at him. "Seriously? A fucking scratch? You're slacking. By the way, the list of women who've saved your sorry ass is growing."

"Thank God for that," he grunted while Jordyn pushed the desk chair out of his way so he could stand. "Who took off in the helicopter?"

"Diaz," Ian spat as he strode through the door, taking the entire scene in with one glance. "Who gave you the boo-boo?"

Carter snorted. Yeah, he was going to hear about this injury for a while. He pointed to Aldridge, who'd taken Jordyn's bullet in the head. "Glenn Aldridge. The agent who supposedly was blown up in his car. I'll explain later. What happened with Diaz?"

"Fucking bastard and his pilot used the wife and kids as shields. Jones and Costello couldn't risk taking the shots. We'll have to wait until he pops up again somewhere to take him down. For now, the hostages are safe, the innocent workers are shaking in their shoes but alive, and the guards are either dead or wishing they were. Aside from you, the team is uninjured. I'll make sure Ramona gives you a lollipop when she's done stitching you up." Ian turned on his heel and headed for the door again. "Now, call your cleanup team, and let's get out of this hellhole."

That was the best suggestion he'd heard all day. Jordyn pulled out her cell phone. "I'll call Gene."

Nodding, Carter holstered his gun, which Mic had found for him. "You and your team are better off disappearing before the cavalry arrives. Thanks for the help, Mic."

She smiled at him. "Anytime." Her head tilted toward Jordyn, who was deep in detailing the day's events to their boss. "She's a keeper. I expect an invite to the collaring ceremony even though I'm banned from the US. I've never seen one, so if you can, have Egghead stream it to Scotland."

A grin spread across his face as he leaned down and kissed her camouflaged cheek. "You got it."

Her brow shot up, and he realized she'd noticed the absent endearment he'd always given her, whether she liked it or not. "Never thought I'd say this, but I kinda miss you calling me 'sweetheart.' But I'm glad to pass the torch onto someone who deserves it."

"I'll have to tell Chris to come up with some sappy nickname for you."

His chuckle turned into a flat-out belly laugh as she gave him the finger on her way out the door. Turning toward Jordyn, he watched as she disconnected the call. "All good?"

She nodded. "Gene has everyone scrambling. We just have to hold down the fort until the first wave gets here to secure the place. Should be within an hour or two." She sidled up to him and wrapped her arms around his waist. Anyone not involved in the world of black ops would think she was crazy when she asked, "Think your shoulder can survive a little nookie? Cause I'm horny as hell right now, Double-O."

Gotta love adrenaline.

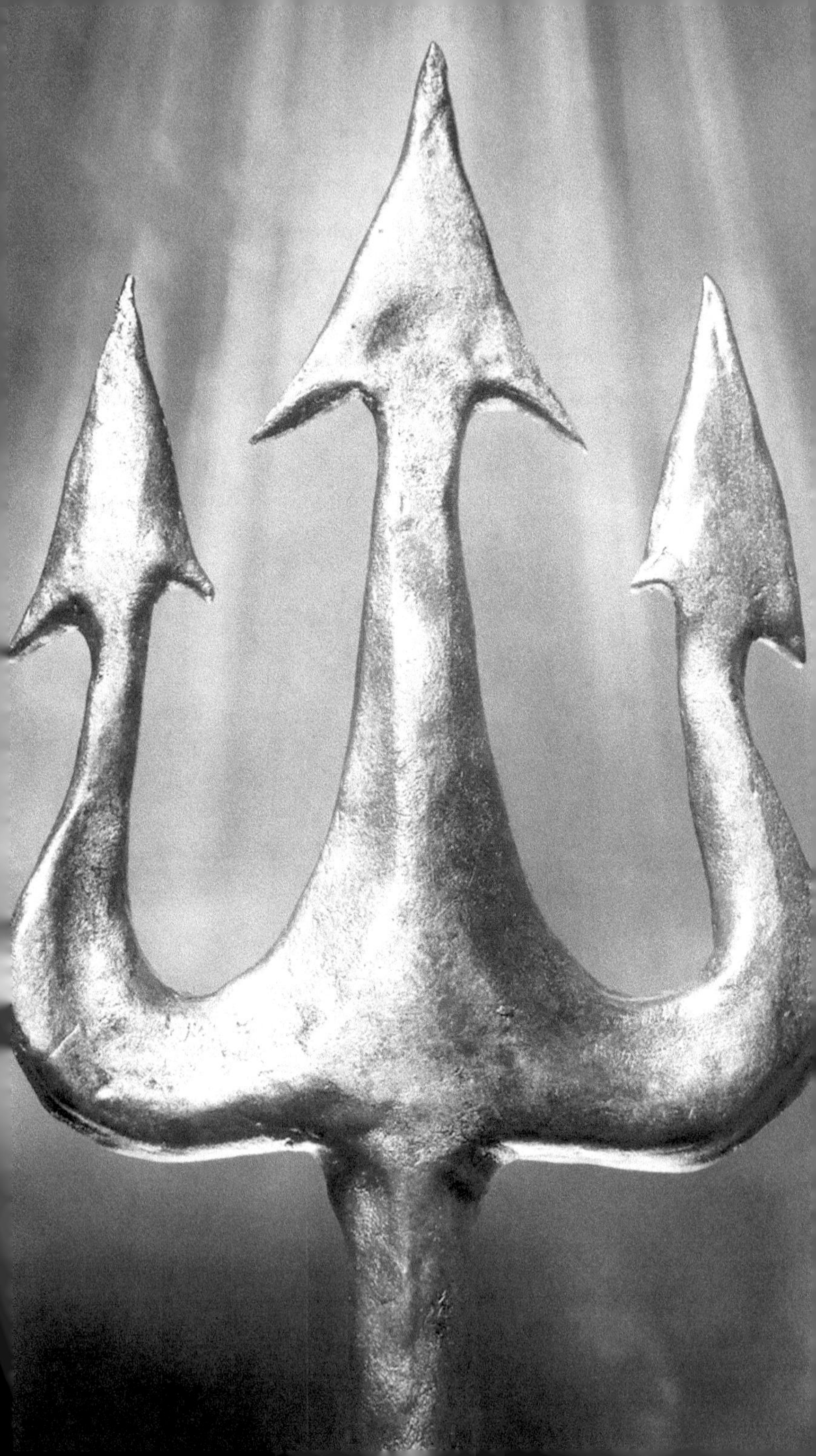

CHAPTER TWENTY-TWO

Striding out of the elevator, Carter squeezed Jordyn's hand. His shoulder still hurt like a bitch, and would for a few more days, but he'd declined the pain meds Ramona had tried to get him to take. With Diaz flapping in the wind, he needed to stay alert—they were still trying to find where the bastard had disappeared to with his family, but so far, they were coming up empty. Brody had assured him the cartel boss's computer system had been fried from the virus the geek had planted after downloading a shitload of information from it.

After Jordyn had notified Gene McDaniel, Deimos agents, and a cleanup team had been flown in to go through the now unoccupied compound with a fine tooth comb. The only other place the NOC list had been found was in an office safe Jordyn had cracked into. Hopefully, that meant the remaining agents were protected once again. The support techs had been busy ensuring an additional firewall was in place to prevent further hackings despite figuring out how Aldridge had managed to bypass the others. They were also burying Carter, Jordyn, and the others' NOC list information even deeper, adding several more layers of protection for them. Carter was confident they would do their best.

Arriving at the transplant ward's waiting room, they found Vicki and Joe having coffee while Foster and Mancini were on guard duty. When Vicki saw them, she ran over and hugged her foster brother before pulling Jordyn into an embrace. "Thank God you're okay. I know you said so over the phone, but I wouldn't believe it until I saw you."

She hadn't been given the details of what had happened and had missed Carter's grimace when she'd squeezed his upper arm. Her husband had noticed but wisely kept his mouth shut—Vicki had enough to worry about.

"How's Justin doing?" Carter asked.

"He's doing well," Joe answered, shaking his hand. "My folks are in with him now. It's the first time the doctors let someone other than Vicki and me in, so that's a good sign. You'll have to wait an hour before going in, though."

Vicki turned back to Carter and took his hands in hers. Concern filled her face, which made his gut churn. She licked her lips as she stared into his eyes.

"You should know, I went to see him this morning... Osbourne."

His eyebrows shot up. That had been the last thing he'd expected her to say. Taking a deep breath, he glanced at Joe and then back at Vicki. Not wanting her to think he was passing judgment, he tried to keep his voice neutral. "Okay. And?"

"I told him I forgave him."

Now Carter couldn't keep the anger inside. "You what!"

Jordyn placed her hand on his arm in a not-so-subtle warning that he'd crossed the line. "Let her talk... Sir."

At that last word, Vicki gaped while Joe grinned. "I told you, little one. You owe me an item off your yellow limit list tonight." To Carter and Jordyn, he added, "My bet was Jordyn would be calling you Sir by the time you returned from the mission—Vicki said it would be at least a week after you got back."

"Nice to know you were betting on my love life, but right now, I want to know what the hell you were doing letting her talk to Osbourne," Carter said with a growl.

Joe's eyes hardened slightly at his brother-in-law. "She's your sister, T., but she's my wife and submissive. She told me she needed to do this, and I was right there while she did it."

Taking a cleansing breath, he nodded and controlled his anger again. He'd stepped on the other man's toes big time. "You're right, Joe. Sorry. It's all right, Vicki, you just caught me off guard. What did Osbourne say?"

"Nothing," she answered quietly, clearly trying not to upset him further. "I told him I had to say my piece and didn't want to hear anything from him. I told him I forgave him but would never forget what he did to me." Her eyes were pleading with him to understand. "How can I not forgive him when because of him I have Justin? And now my son has a chance at a healthy life again. I thanked him for saving Justin, and then I walked out."

Carter swallowed hard. He always knew Vicki was a strong woman, but once again, he was in awe of that strength. Some women would have aborted the baby or given it up, not being able to acknowledge the product of rape. But his sister had chosen to claim her son as her own and raised him to the best of her abil-ity. And Carter could not imagine a life without Justin in it. He pulled Vicki into a warm embrace. "You're right, sweetheart. I never thought of it that way."

An hour later, he brought Jordyn in with him to visit Justin and introduced the love of his life to his nephew. The kid looked well despite being hooked up to every monitor possible. His color was good, and his eyes were bright. Seeing the vibrant young man returning to normal, Carter completely understood why Vicki had felt she needed to see Osbourne.

They couldn't stay long, just ten minutes, but it

was long enough for Carter to feel confident the boy would completely recover. It would be a few weeks before he'd be released, but as soon as he was able to leave the ICU and transfer to a regular room, visiting hours wouldn't be so restricted. His friends would be allowed to visit, which would really help his spirits.

"Uncle T.?"

"Yeah, buddy?"

"Can you thank Mr. Osgood for me? Mom said he was discharged already and went back to California. I don't know how to contact him."

Carter cleared his throat. Joe had told him Justin wanted to get in touch with Osbourne after he was feeling better, something they hadn't thought of before this—they'd been too worried about the operation. Usually, recipients didn't learn who their donors were for a full year, but this case was far different from most. Vicki, Joe, and Carter had come to a decision about it while talking in the waiting room, and Carter had asked them to let him tell the kid if the subject came up. Vicki would've been too emotional for the conversation, and Joe hadn't been there all those years ago. It was in Carter's dominant nature to want to deal with it, and he hated doing it now, but they'd lied to Justin long enough. Things would just get worse if they kept it going because whether they liked it or not, they were almost certain he would find out someday.

"Yeah, about that, kiddo." He pulled one of the two chairs in the room closer to the bed and sat so he was on eye level with his nephew. Jordyn placed her hand on his shoulder in support. "I... um... kind of lied about Mr. Osgood."

Justin's eyes narrowed at him. "Lied? What do you mean?"

Taking a deep breath, he let it out. "Osgood isn't a guard at the prison. He's an inmate. When you got sick in the beginning, and we were all getting tested to see if we could donate, I made some inquiries, just in case, and found someone who could donate."

Silence filled the room as the young man processed that. "What... what's he in prison for?"

"Assaulting several women... including your mom."

Several emotions ranging from confusion to understanding passed across his nephew's face. He was old enough and smart enough to figure it out without hearing the word rape. A flash of anger and horror appeared in his eyes. "Holy fuck! That's why mom never wanted to talk about my real father. She just always said she barely knew the guy, and he was gone from her life before I was born."

"Yeah. Please, don't be mad at your mom and watch your language around women—Joe and I taught you better than that."

Although the young man was clearly annoyed, he apologized. "Sorry, Jordyn."

When she gave Justin a forgiving smile, Carter continued. "Look, kiddo, we just never knew how to explain it to you while you were young, and then as you got older, I guess we kept trying to sweep it under the rug. It's not exactly dinner conversation. There's a lot more to it, but none of it is close to the bombshell I just lobbed at you, so we can talk about it more after you're out of here. But know this... your mom loves you more than you'll ever know. She had the strength and courage to give birth to you and raise you herself. She is one of the very few amazing women I know, and everything she's done for the past twenty years has been for you. This morning, your mom went to see Osbourne... his real name... and she forgave him."

Justin's mouth dropped open, and he shook his head. "Forgave him? Why the hell—heck would she do that?"

"Because of you. If it hadn't happened, she never would have had the son she loves more than anyone else on this Earth."

Silence again hung in the air, and a bell rang from the nurses' desk. Carter stood. "It's time for us to go. Are you going to be okay?"

"I-I think so." His gaze flicked to the ceiling and then back to Carter's face. "Uncle T.? I love my mom. I could never be mad at her for protecting me. And she's right—no matter what happened back then, she still raised me to be the best person I could be. So, can you do me that favor and thank Mr. Osgood... I mean, Osbourne for me? I never want to see him again or have any contact with him, but I do want him to know that, despite him being my birth father and giving me his kidney, I'll never be like him."

After leaving the transplant ward, he left Jordyn to visit with Vicki and Joe and drove to the cabin they were using as a temporary safe house for Osbourne while he finished recovering. Jake and RJ were in the living room area of the two-bedroom structure, and the former shook his hand. "Ian called me and gave me the update. Glad you're all back in one piece, and don't worry, we'll nail Diaz soon, I'm sure."

"So am I." He nodded to the closed door. "How's he doing?"

"The doctor said he'll be released from his care in another five days if he remains stable. A nurse comes daily to monitor his vitals and take blood and urine samples. We've been with him every time someone had to be in the room with him, and he's only been allowed the DVR, no live TV. If he found out where we are, it's been through osmosis."

"Good. I'm going to talk to him."

Jake raised an eyebrow at him and smirked. "Talk, not kill, right?"

"Ha! Yeah, I intend to talk, but you may want to keep an ear open for me killing him, just in case."

As the other man laughed, Carter pushed the door open and stepped inside before shutting out the rest of the world. Osbourne lay on the only bed in the room. One of the Jason Bourne movies was playing on the TV, but the volume was barely audible. The man was doing a crossword puzzle in a paperback book and looked up as Carter approached. One corner of his mouth ticked up slightly. His voice sounded tired as he spoke. "You here to kill me now that you got what you wanted?"

Carter stopped a foot from the bed, crossed his arms, and set his feet shoulder-width apart. "Thought about it. And until I spoke to Vicki a little while ago, it was still a crapshoot whether or not I would when I got here."

Osbourne nodded, and a somberness fell over his face. "She was here. Said she forgave me. Why, I don't know."

"Because she's one hell of a woman, and even though you assaulted her in a way no woman should be, you also gave her Justin. And by the way, he knows who you really are and never wants to see you again but asked me to thank you for going through with the surgery."

"*Harrumph.* He's a good kid." The man's eyes flickered toward the window. "I was a bastard. I could try to make excuses about why, but they'd just be lame attempts to cover up the fact I was a selfish bastard. She didn't deserve that—none of them did." He paused. "If it makes you feel better, I now know what I put them through. The first few years in Folsom weren't pretty for me."

If Osbourne sought sympathy or absolution for his sins, he wouldn't get it from his former foster child. "I didn't think they would be. Most prisoners find rape, especially of a minor, the vilest crime you can commit." He let out a long breath. "When the doctor gives the okay for you to go back, you'll go to Avenal." The level two security prison was halfway between Los Angeles and Sacramento. While there were still armed guards and a secure perimeter, the inmates had more freedom and programs to take part in. As long as he stayed out of trouble, Osbourne would finish out his life sentence with a little more comfort than before.

The older man's gaze returned to Carter's. "Thanks. I know it was hard for you to keep up your end of the bargain."

He wouldn't deny it, but after talking with Vicki, he felt better about having Gene arrange the transfer. "This'll be the last time you'll see me—on one condition. If you ever try to contact Vicki or Justin, you'll be dead within forty-eight hours. Understood?"

A smirk spread across Osbourne's face, and he let out a soft snort. "Forty-eight? Why do I get the feeling it would be more like twelve?"

Turning on his heel, Carter headed for the door. "Probably because you're right."

Later that night, Carter had Jordyn strip where she stood in his kitchen. After dinner, she'd cleaned up while he went to his bedroom—actually, now, it was *their* bedroom—to prep for the scene he wanted to do with her. Although they still had to go through her limit list, he'd cleared all but one part of the scene with her. There was one thing he wanted to surprise her with, and he highly doubted she'd object. He hadn't come across a single submissive who hadn't enjoyed a suspension play scene. There was a range of what could be added to it, but until she did more research and club observation, he'd keep it to a simple sex swing.

While he'd never brought another woman to his house for play or any other reason besides Vicki, he hoped he would one day. But the woman had to be special—she had to belong to him to be allowed into his sanctuary—and Jordyn was exactly that woman. In anticipation of finding his other half one day, he'd instructed Joe to make sure a few things were added to the design of the house. The feature he'd be using tonight was the hidden hooks for the suspension swing.

"What are you waiting for... *Sir*?"

Carter hadn't realized he was just standing in the kitchen, staring at his submissive's scrumptious body. "Why do you always pause before you say 'Sir,' my little subbie?"

Shrugging, Jordyn responded, "Just a little reminder of who's really in charge... Sir."

The corners of his mouth ticked up in amusement, but he used his annoyed Dom voice to respond. "Brat."

"You wouldn't have me any other way."

She was one hundred percent right about that, but he wouldn't tell her that now. "It's time for you to learn what happens to bratty submissives who want to push their Master's buttons. Turn around."

When she did as he ordered, he stepped closer, put a blindfold over her eyes, and tied it behind her head. After it was in place, he reached down and gave her a swift slap on her right ass cheek, which caused her to yelp. He chuckled at her grumbling that followed. "What was that, my sweet Jordy?"

"*De nada... Señor.*"

He loved that she wanted to play. Bratty subs had always been his favorite because it meant he could get inventive with their scenes. "I think you need a bit of discipline before pleasure tonight. Bend over and hold onto the counter."

Jordyn hesitated only a moment before following his orders. He knew she was still scared of the unknown, so he would continue to take it easy on her until she became more accustomed to the lifestyle. But that didn't mean he would let her top from the bottom. Pulling open a utensil drawer, he grabbed a wooden spatula and ran it up the back of her bare thigh. "I think five smacks will remind you that I'm your Dom, and you're my submissive. What's your safeword?"

"R-red."

"If you say it, I'll stop, but then we won't scene tonight at all, *¿comprendes?*" When she responded that she understood, he added, "Count for me out loud, my love."

Without waiting for an answer, he pulled the spatula back and, with a flick of his wrist, let it land on her right buttock with a resounding slap. Jordyn squeaked and went up on her toes. "*¡Mierda!*"

Her hand reached back to protect her flesh, but Carter grabbed her by the wrist and put it back where it belonged. "Hands on the counter, baby. Concentrate on the heat that follows the pain. Breathe deeply."

When her fingers gripped the granite countertop again, he let go of her wrist and covered the spot he'd struck with the palm of his hand. Squeezing gently, he asked, "Are you green, baby, or do you want to use your safeword?"

She took several deep breaths, then said, "I-I'm green... *Sir.*"

Shaking his head, he flicked the spatula against her left cheek. Again, she cursed and went up on her toes, but this time, she kept her hands where they were. "You're supposed to be counting, Jordy. I've been accused of failing math before, so you may want to make sure I stop at five."

"Two! That was two, Sir."

He couldn't help the grin that spread across his

face because she hadn't paused that time before using his title. "Good girl."

The next two smacks were in rapid succession on her sit spots, where her thighs met her ass cheeks. "¡*Mierda!* Three! Four!"

Carter was hard as a rock, needing to move this along so he could get his cock inside her. No other woman had ever sent his control spiraling before Jordyn, but she tested his limits without even knowing it—and that made him want to test her limits, too. He made contact with the utensil against her skin again, hitting both cheeks simultaneously, then tossed it onto the counter. His hands gently rubbed her pink skin, and then he dipped the fingers of one between her legs, thrilled at what he found there. She was soaked for him. Gathering up some of her juices, he grabbed her hair and tugged her head up. His wet fingers went to her mouth and ran over her lips. "This is what my discipline did to you, my love. Your body craves and responds to it. Lick my fingers and taste yourself."

Her tongue snaked out and lapped at his fingers. She moaned as the spicy flavor hit her taste buds, and the sound went straight to his groin. When she was done, he spun her around and hauled her up into his arms, ignoring the pain in his shoulder and wrapping her legs around his waist as he carried her to the master bedroom. Hanging from the ceiling in the corner was the leather swing. Setting Jordyn down next to it, he said, "Stand still. I'm going to put something around your legs."

She nibbled on her bottom lip but did as she was told. It didn't take him long to wrap the straps around her thighs and attach them to the chain above her head. He then lowered the four-inch-wide strip of leather for her to sit on, yet leaving her ass exposed. The piece was for her comfort now while he continued to prep her, but when he was done, it would be removed. She would then be supported only by the thigh and arm straps and him. "It's like a swing in a playground." He stabilized the seat as she sat and wriggled her hips until she was in a safe position. "Comfy?"

"Um-hm. I mean, yes, Sir."

Next were the two straps he slid over her hands to her wrists. "Grab hold."

Once she was secure, he pulled on the chain attached to a pulley system. Jordyn's feet left the ground, and she gasped at the weightless feeling as he lifted her into a sitting position. Slowly, her thighs spread apart, and when her sweet pussy was at the right level for him to fuck her from where he stood, he locked the chain in place so that she wouldn't drop.

"This is interesting," she giggled as she shifted a little to distribute her weight properly.

"It's about to get much more interesting, my sweet." He quickly stripped his clothing off. Stepping over to the bed, he picked up a tube of lubricant and a basic string of anal beads. He would have to purchase a starter kit of plugs to begin stretching her ass to take him someday,, but this would be a good introduction to anal play for her.

Standing between her legs, he put some lube on his fingers and the beads. Reaching around her hips, he ran fingers over her virgin hole, working the lube into it. The more he played back there, the wetter her pussy got. She moaned and tried to close her thighs to get some friction where she wanted it the most. He smacked the anal beads against her thigh. "Stay still. I wouldn't want to deny you your orgasms tonight while I took my own."

"Y-yes, Sir." While his index finger pushed into her hole, his thumb dipped into her vagina, and a shiver went through her. High-pitched whimpers filled the room. Removing his finger, he replaced it with the beads. Each one gradually increased in size as he advanced them into her ass. Her hips bucked as the last one popped past her tight rim. He tapped the finger loop, which lit up the nerves of her rectum. "*Mierda*! Oh, shit!"

Carter chuckled as he continued his sensual torture. "I didn't need the translation, sweetheart. You already know I can speak quite a bit of Spanish."

"*¡Jódete!*"

"Screw me? Oh, no, sweetheart. I'll be the one screwing you... and you're going to enjoy every minute of it. But first, let me clean up a minute. Don't go anywhere... oh, that's right... you can't."

"Evil bastard," she said with a growl. "If I wasn't so fucking horny right now, you'd have a fight on your hands."

Laughing as he stepped over to a basin filled with water, soap, and a towel he'd set up on a small folding table, Carter loved how she continued to challenge him. Most submissives he'd played with over the years had yielded to his every command, which was fine if that's what he was in the mood for. But when he wanted something more, he sought out the bratty ones, knowing each would have a breaking point where their snarkiness turned to begging. He was looking forward to finding Jordyn's point of no return, and he was certain it would be different every time they played.

After washing his hands, he turned back and stopped to study his submissive hanging from the ceiling in the swing. Her legs were spread wide apart, her pussy weeping for him. Her dusty rose nipples were taut, begging for him to play with them. Tonight, he was going to take her without any barriers between them. For Deimos, they had to go through a full physical every two months or after a mission if the other wasn't an option due to being undercover. They were both clean, and Jordyn was protected from pregnancy with the birth control shot. As he stepped toward her, he envisioned her ripe with his child someday and knew she would be even more beautiful. That was something they'd have to discuss in the future. Neither of them had experienced an ideal childhood, and being international spies and assassins wasn't exactly conducive to having a traditional family. They would figure it out as they went, though. If it was meant to happen, it would, but for now, they could have a lot of fun practicing.

Running his hands up her thighs, he spread them a little further. Her pussy was soaked, and he thumbed her clit, which made her moan. His cock twitched toward her core, and he was convinced it knew where it belonged. "My sweet Jordy, I can't wait. This will be hard and fast. Then we'll take it slow later. I just need you so badly right now."

"And I need you... please hurry!"

"Hold on tight. I'm removing the strap under your ass." With one hand around her waist, he released the leather support and let it drop to the floor. Lining his cock up with her slit, he grabbed her hips and swung her forward, impaling her.

"Oh! Oh, fuck!" she screamed.

Using the swing's motion, he slid in and out as her walls tried to keep him in. He fucked her hard and deep. Her head fell back as she gave herself to him and took everything he offered her. Skin slapped against skin, faster and faster. Leaning down, he flicked his tongue over one and then the other nipple, but that caused him to lose the angle he needed. Standing straight again, he drove her higher and higher, chasing her up the cliff. Her whimpers, pleas, gasps, and curses urged him on. His thumb found her clit again, and he pushed down on it while the fingers of his other hand tapped on the end of the anal beads. Jordyn screamed as she came, and his fingers and cock didn't let up, extending her orgasm as long as possible. When another one crashed over her, she took him with her. It'd happened so fast that it almost caught him by surprise. Pounding on her pussy, streams of cum shot from him, deep into her core, marking her. She was his, and he was hers—his heart would never belong to another for as long as he lived.

Later, as they lay in bed, wrapped up in each other's arms, sleep was drawing them in. Before darkness overtook him, Carter kissed her forehead. "I love you, my sweet Jordy."

"I love you, too... Master Templeton."

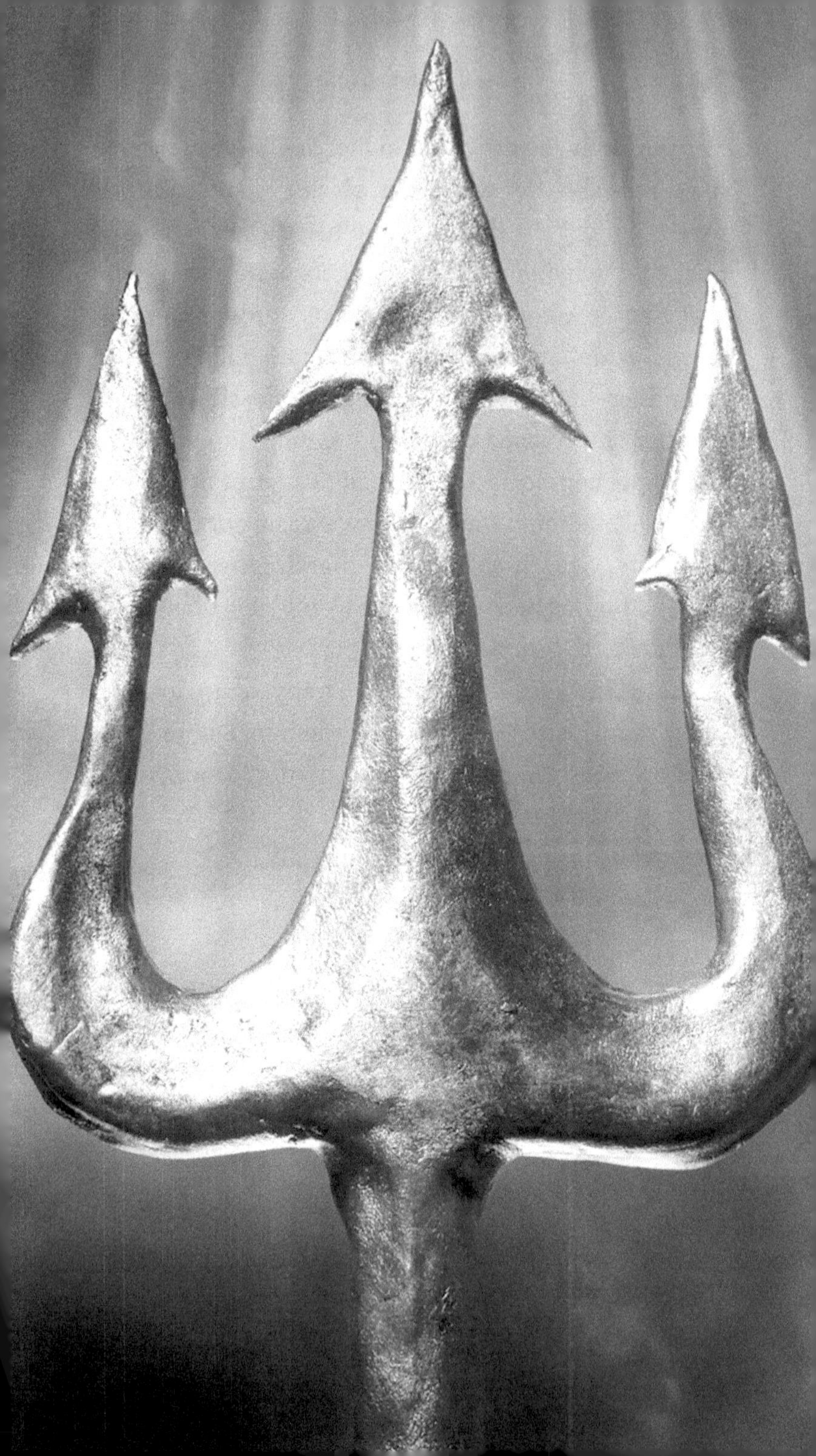

EPILOGUE

Three months later...

Fingering the gold collar Carter had given her in a ceremony the last time they'd been in Tampa, Jordyn glanced around Ian's Oasis, the grassy retreat between two converted warehouses at the Trident Security compound. The large, makeshift backyard was filled with people. They were celebrating the announcement that Ian and Angie Sawyer were expecting a baby, in addition to Boomer and Kat returning from their honeymoon in Hawaii.

Smiling, she realized she was starting to think of these people as her friends and family—something she hadn't had in a very long time—just like Carter did. They'd welcomed her with open arms, and she felt more comfortable having girlie chats with the other men's wives and girlfriends.

Apparently, parties like this were commonplace for the extended Trident family. It was mid-February in Florida, and the temperature was hovering around seventy-eight degrees, which felt like one hundred to Jordyn since she and Carter had flown in the day before, leaving temperatures well below freezing in Montana.

Lively conversations took place all around her. Thankfully, she'd excelled in remembering names and faces over the years. There were the six members of the Omega team, plus sniper Lindsey Abbott, who was still filling in for Jake Donovan on the original team. Jake and his fiancé, Nick, hadn't been able to fly in for the party but had checked in a little while ago by Skype on the big, weatherproof TV that hung next to the outdoor kitchen.

Marco DeAngelis was with his wife, Harper—they'd tied the knot in a very small ceremony this past Christmas Eve. They were talking with Brody Evans and his fiancée, Fancy Maguire, and Devon and Kristen Sawyer. Alyssa Wagner, the teen Jordyn had helped, and a pretty, blonde woman, Ian's goddaughter Jenn, were playing with little Mara DeAngelis, but the latter's eyes kept flashing to one of the contract operatives Trident used on occasion. Doug Henderson seemed oblivious to the younger woman's crush on him as he talked shop with Calvin Watts, head of the local FBI Hostage Negotiation Team, and Trident's mechanic/chopper pilot, Tempest "Babs" Van Buren.

In another area, Boomer's parents, Rick and Eileen Michaelson, sat with Chuck and Marie, the heads of the Sawyer clan, and Will Anders, Kristin's cousin.

Sitting over by the koi pond, Shelby and Parker Christiansen, with their dog Spanky at their feet, were chatting with Charlotte "Mistress China" Roth and Travis "Tiny" Daultry, head of the club's security. The man's moniker was a drastic contrast to his actual size. Two D/s couples, Reggie and Colleen, Trident's attorney and office manager, respectively, and Roxy and Kayla London stood nearby, also deep in conversation.

More people had recently arrived, but Jordyn hadn't met them yet. This was the third time she and Carter had visited Tampa together and stayed in one of the spare rooms above the Trident offices. Gene had accepted their relationship and took advantage of it by assigning them to missions together if the situation warranted. Sometimes, they'd have to go off independently as before, but those assignments wouldn't be often.

She really liked visiting Tampa. Maybe one of these days, they'd get an apartment or condo in the area. However, their security requirements were stricter than for an average couple. But their main residence was in Montana. They took a roundabout route each time they arrived in or left the northern state and did everything they could to ensure their professional lives didn't interfere with their personal ones. Vicki had wanted them to spend as much time as they could with her family, and, like Carter, Jordyn found she couldn't say no to the woman.

While learning the lifestyle, she accepted it more and more. Carter had been so patient. When they'd gone over her limit list after the op in Colombia, he'd added a column to the green, yellow, and red limits. Usually, yellow meant an activity the sub had wanted to try but had not experienced yet. Carter had included an "orange" column. In it went the activities that weren't exactly hard limits for Jordyn, but she still didn't know how she felt about them. They differed from the yellow limits in that he wouldn't randomly pick one of them to push her past her comfort zone. Instead, they were there for her to choose if she wanted to move one over to her soft limit list someday. He did everything he could to open her eyes to new experiences, yet not make her feel like she had no choices. It wasn't all or nothing with them—as long as they remained faithful and honest with each other— and that was all she'd ever wanted. Well, that and his love and the orgasms he gave her regularly.

Ian strode over and handed them fresh drinks. Despite being thrilled about becoming a father, she could tell the man definitely had things on his mind that were bothering him. To Jordyn's amusement, Carter, who was holding baby JD, noticed it too. "All right, my friend. Spill it."

Swallowing a mouthful of his beer, Ian grimaced.

"They found the latest missing submissive this morning—that makes nine so far. I swear, when I find out who this bastard is, you two won't have to give me lessons in torture. I've already thought up a few painful ways to kill the guy myself."

She'd learned that the Doms of The Covenant fiercely protected the submissives in the lifestyle, whether they knew them personally or not. From what she'd been told, the FBI was involved. A profiler, Dr. Suki Ralston, and an agent specializing in tracking serial murderers, Colt Parrish, had been working with the local federal office, Tampa PD, and Trident to find the killer. The UNSUB had been kidnapping and viciously torturing the women involved in the lifestyle before killing them and disposing of their mutilated bodies in public places.

"Nothing new in the search?" Carter asked.

"No. The profiler thinks he's in the lifestyle, not just playing a role to get closer to the subs. He's been picking them from clubs all within a two-hour drive from Tampa, but it's possible he's not going into the clubs. You know how it is—between experience and how most subs dress, picking them out when they walk to their cars isn't hard. Aside from Heather, none of them were collared long-term."

Heather had been one of the first women killed and a former member of The Covenant. So far, none of the victims had been a current member of the Sawyers' elite club on the other side of the compound.

But it was probably only a matter of time before one of their subs went missing unless the killer was caught.

Angie strode by, running her hand across her husband's back as she passed. He winked at her before turning back to Carter and Jordyn. "I promised my wife I wouldn't talk about the killings for more than a minute or two, and only if someone asked, so let's move onto another subject before she makes me sleep in Beau's bed tonight." The company's trained lab/pit mix picked up his head from where he lay at Carter's feet. Anywhere little JD was, the dog was rarely far away from his new charge.

On Carter's shoulder, the baby yawned, which had the man smiling. "Where's Mitch?"

"Las Vegas for the weekend. Tori and Tyler were going to a wedding, and her cousin was recently uncollared by her Dom. Things didn't end well, and the guy will be there, so Tori asked Mitch to escort the girl to the wedding." On previous visits, Jordyn met Mitch Sawyer and the D/s couple at The Covenant. Mitch co-owned the place with his cousins and managed it while they ran their security business.

"Oh, before I forget, I wanted to ask you something," Ian said to his friend. "But I need it between us for now."

Carter arched his eyebrow as he shifted JD to his other shoulder. "What's up?"

Subtly pointing toward Shelby and Parker on the far side of the grassy expanse, Ian said, "They've been trying to adopt, but with her two-time cancer history, no US or international agency will talk to them. Parker told me they tried to go private, but nowadays, there isn't the same stigma there used to be for being sixteen and pregnant. Birth mothers request thick portfolios from the prospective parents and pick the ones they like best. So, again, the cancer thing is a negative, and they have to disclose it, according to Reggie. Our laws here are stringent, but some other countries aren't. They also discussed using a surrogate, but Shelby being Shelby, she'd rather adopt an orphan than bring another baby into the world. So, here comes my question—do you have any connections outside the US that can help them bypass all this crap?"

Jordyn's face lit up. "I do!"

Shelby had such a bubbly personality that Jordyn had liked her immediately during her first visit to the club ten weeks ago. When the two men stared at her, she explained, "After my parents died, I ended up in an orphanage in Argentina. I was there for three months before Uncle Iggy found out and came to get me. After I learned," she shrugged, "how to be a successful thief, I started sending Sister Patrice money whenever I could. Since Deimos, I've gone to visit her several times too. She was so nice to me—I never forgot her."

A soft smile spread across her face. "She used to sing me to sleep. Anyway, I'm sure she'd help out. Nothing would make her happier than finding homes for her kids—I know her cousin has connections in the

Argentinian government. He's helped her place kids with good parents other agencies turned down due to similar circumstances." She gestured toward the childless couple. "Let me contact her before you say anything to them, though. I don't think there will be a problem, but just in case."

Putting his unoccupied arm around her and tucking her close to his side, Carter kissed her temple. "My sweet Jordy, just when I think I couldn't love you more—bam!—you prove me wrong."

Ian was about to say something but was interrupted by his ringing cell phone. He checked the number, and his brow furrowed. "Shit. It's Parrish. I hope this doesn't mean someone else has gone missing." Pressing the call button, he brought the device to his ear. "Sawyer... What? Who?"

He paused, and then his eyes went wide. "Are you fu—" He stopped short when he noticed Jenn was nearby with little Mara. The toddler's ears picked up everything, which she would then try to repeat. "Are you kidding me? That's insane!"

Everyone else went silent as his voice grew louder and angrier. "All right. I'll be there in twenty. Don't start the interrogation until I get there... Parrish, you can wait twenty frigging minutes! I—"

Ripping the phone from his ear, he glared at it. "Bastard hung up on me." He looked up to find everyone staring at him. His gaze searched and found Reggie Helm and then Calvin Watts. "Need you both to come with me. Parrish said they made an arrest in the serial killings, and you'll never freaking believe who it is because I sure as hell don't."

IMPORTANT INFO!

If you're following the best reading order of the Trident Security series and its spinoff series, then up next is *Double Down & Dirty: Doms of The Covenant Book 1.* **Keep reading for a preview chapter.**

For the best reading order of the Trident Security series and its spinoffs, check out the printable list on my website - www.samanthacolebooks.-com/pages/best-reading-order. This will ensure you find out who the Kink Killer is without spoilers for other books.

Want to know what's coming next? Join my Facebook Group -
Samantha Cole's Sexy Six-Pack's Sirens...

Or sign up for my newsletter -
samanthacolebooks.com/mailing-list

The characters of Steel Corps have been lovingly used with the permission of their creator, J.B. Havens. Please check out her website - jbhavens.wixsite.com/author - for more from Mic and the boys!

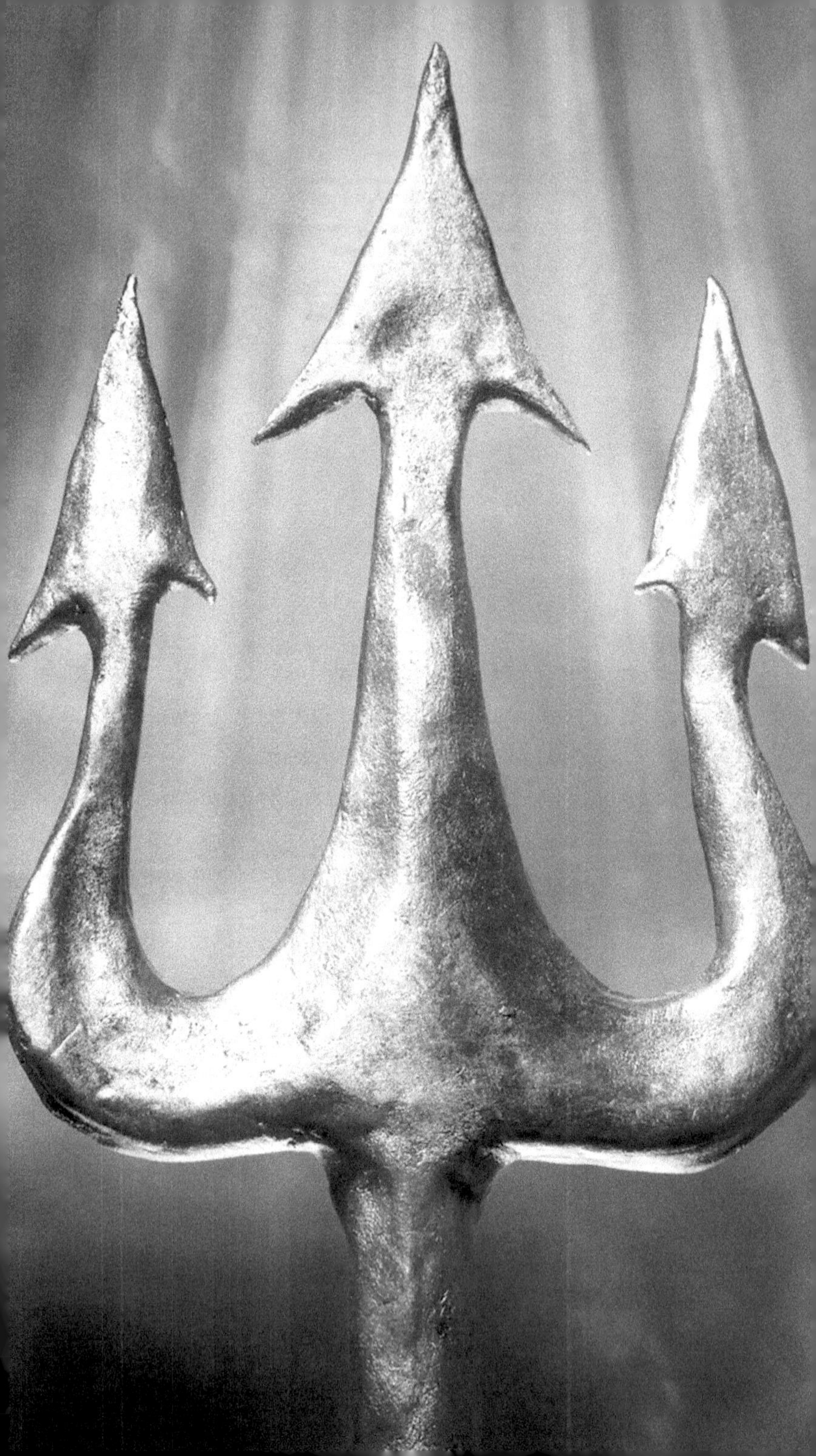

**Double Down & Dirty: Doms of The Covenant
Book 1**

"Abby, hold all my calls."

"Yes, Mr. Mann." Startled by his sudden appearance, scowling face, and barked order, Abigail's heart pounded as her employer, Grayson Mann, strode into his office without a backward glance and slammed the door shut. Well, actually, he was one of her bosses—the other was his fraternal twin brother, Remington, who was currently out of town on a business trip to Miami. It was just after seven-thirty in the morning on the twenty-first floor of Black Diamond Records in Tampa, Florida, and she hadn't expected Gray in before nine today. He'd been scheduled to attend a breakfast meeting with the record label's branding development team on the third floor. Gray and Remi were the producers of some of the world's hottest bands and solo artists. No genres were excluded—performers of rock, country, classical, rap, easy-listening, gospel, and more had found international stardom thanks to the Mann brothers.

Abigail had been the CEOs' personal secretary for six months after working for the vice president of marketing for a year. Remi and Gray's longtime secretary, Liz Carpenter, had resigned to work for her husband's booming law practice and had recommended Abigail as her replacement after the two had become friends.

She'd been shocked at the huge promotion. While she loved the increase in pay and benefits, part of her wanted her old job back. Not that her new bosses were difficult to work for because they weren't. The problem was they were gorgeous—total dreamboats —and she tended to be flustered around them. Both were well over six feet tall, with solid physiques, dark brown hair, and adorable dimples, but that's where the similarities ended. Remi had soft brown eyes, while Gray's hazel ones were harsher—not that he was mean or anything, he just didn't relax or smile as often as his brother did. Why they'd given her the job as their secretary when she always seemed to stutter in their combined presence was beyond her. But once they were behind their respective closed office doors, she did her duties with complete efficiency, so they obviously overlooked her flaws.

While Gray remained in his office, Abigail finished off a stack of correspondence Remi had left on her desk before departing for Miami late yesterday afternoon. She'd just sent the last letter to the printer when the door to the CEOs' reception area opened and Chad Crawford walked in. The head of the recording studio division was dressed in his usual khakis and a green polo shirt with the Black Diamond Records' signature BDR logo. He also wore a huge smile as he sat on the edge of her desk.

"Hey, gorgeous. How are things going today?"

Abigail blushed. Chad was sweet, good-looking, and a huge flirt—at least he was with her. He'd asked her out on a date when she'd first started working at BDR, but she'd turned him down, not wanting to have an office romance. Although his disappointment had been clear, they'd become good friends. He even consulted her now about what to wear or where to go on his dates, and she hoped one day he'd find Ms. Right because he really deserved her—she just wasn't Abigail.

"So far so good. Just finishing up a few things. How was the blind date last night?"

He rolled his eyes. "I was ready to run ten minutes into it after she started planning our wedding."

Abigail's hand froze over the paper she was about

to pluck from the printer. "Oh, my God! Are you serious? What kind of woman does that?"

"Yup. A desperate one, I guess." He winked at her again. "You know, one of these days, you should put me out of my dating misery. Oh, that's right, you don't date."

She rolled her eyes. "I date. I just don't advertise that I date."

"Uh-huh. When was the last time—"

Whatever his question was, it ended up being cut off by Grayson's door flying open and the man storming into the reception area. His face became thunderous, his beautiful, hazel eyes flaring in annoyance at the sight of Chad sitting on her desk. "Crawford, is there a reason you're here other than to flirt with my secretary? If not, get out."

Oh, boy, he really is in a bad mood, Abigail thought.

With an apologetic glance at Abigail, Chad leaped up. "Uh... sorry, boss. I... uh... just wanted you to know we're done with the final mixing of Aurora's latest album. She really knocked it out of the park with this one."

Aurora Locke was one of Black Diamond Records' top-selling artists of all time. She was also a stuck-up bitch, in Abigail's opinion. The twenty-six-year-old woman had no concept of what the word humble meant, among other things. She treated everyone at BDR like they were miles beneath her feet, except for

Grayson and Remington—who also happened to be her boyfriends for the past three months. Yup, the Mann twins shared their women, a concept Abigail knew nothing about other than what she'd read in the fictional romance books she loved. She'd always been too embarrassed to ask Liz what she knew about it, and there was no way she was asking either of the two men. That was far too personal. She was their secretary and nothing more. But that didn't stop her from having dreams of being sandwiched between the hunky twins.

"Give it to Tessa to approve."

While Abigail hid her surprise at that statement, Chad's shock was clear as day, his jaw almost hitting the floor. Tessa Mann was the twins' younger cousin and in charge of all new album releases the CEOs didn't handle personally.

At six foot three, Gray towered over the shorter man by a good six inches. His eyes narrowed as he placed a thick file on top of Abigail's inbox. "Problem?" he barked.

"Uh, n-no, boss. I just figured you or Remi would handle Aurora's release."

Gray turned on his heel and strode toward his office. "You figured wrong."

The door slammed shut, and Chad raised his brow and whistled at Abigail. "Trouble in paradise?"

"I have no idea." And even if she did, Abigail would never discuss it with her bosses' employees. What happened in that office stayed in that office. "But it's not my concern—nor yours." She reached for the file Gray had left. "Looks like I'll be busy for the rest of the morning."

Chad headed for the door leading out to the main reception area. "And I've got to track down Tessa now. See you later, my little chick-a-dee."

Shaking her head, Abigail let out a light chuckle. He really was a sweet man—she just didn't feel an attraction to him. At least not like the one she felt for Gray and Remi. Those two men only had to walk into the room, and her heart beat out of control, her mouth went dry—which was the complete opposite of what happened between her legs—and butterflies took flight in her stomach. But she was far from their "type" of woman if the celebrity gossip magazines were to be believed. Those women were just like their current girlfriend, Aurora—tall, blonde, skinny, with huge tits. That was a far cry from mousy, brown-haired Abigail's five-foot-six, size twelve frame. Even her 38-Bs were lacking. She wasn't even close to red carpet material. Therefore, both twins were way out of her league.

The rest of the morning flew by with Abigail answering a few dozen phone calls and putting out several figurative fires, in addition to all her other duties. It wasn't unusual to have people calling, demanding to speak to one or the other CEO, with a so-called emergency. Part of being a good, efficient personal secretary was knowing which ones truly needed her bosses' attention and which problems could be easily handled by the appropriate department heads. Abigail had become an expert at weeding the latter out and, today, had successfully avoided bothering Gray behind his closed door.

It was twenty minutes before noon when the glass door to the executive offices flew open and Aurora Locke burst in, sheer fury written all over her face. As always, she was dressed as if she were going on stage at any moment. Who wore black, leather pants, thigh-high boots, and a see-through shirt over a satin bra to an office in the middle of a Tuesday morning? *Someone with a body to pull it off,* Abigail thought wryly as she stood up quickly. "Can I help you, Ms. Locke?"

Without a glance or word to the secretary, Aurora stormed into Gray's office, slamming the door back against the wall where it bounced closed again, but not completely, which meant Abigail could hear every word. The woman's hard voice was a far cry from the melodious one her fans heard daily over the radio. "You son of a fucking bitch! I've been calling your cell phone all fucking morning! Why the hell were all my things delivered to me this morning in fucking cardboard boxes? Does Remi know about this?"

Gray's voice was also hard, but in contrast, calm, low, and deadly. "Of course he knows, Aurora. He also knows you spent Sunday night in another man's bed." Something light slapped down on his desk. "The private detective didn't get your good side in these photos, but it really doesn't matter, now does it? They're not exactly *People* magazine material—more like *Playboy*."

"Holy shit," Abigail muttered to herself as she stepped over to subtly close Gray's door the rest of the way. As much as she wanted to eavesdrop, she'd heard enough to know the other woman would no longer be sharing a bed with the twins. And the last thing she wanted was someone else to walk in and hear the screeching and sputtering from Aurora, which although still audible, was now sufficiently muffled.

Sitting back at her desk, she couldn't help the perverse satisfaction that came over her knowing the snotty bitch had fallen from the "current girlfriend" column to the "ex" column. Maybe the next one would be a lot friendlier.

Gray watched as Aurora marched out his office, madder than a wet hen. He was certain once her anger at being booted from their personal lives subsided, she'd be groveling and begging for them to take her back. And that wasn't happening. While he and Remi had known their ménage with the superstar would one day fizzle out, like they all did, they hadn't expected it to be so soon. And definitely not because she'd been cheating on them with her fucking body-guard of all fucking people.

Leaning forward, he punched a button on his desk phone. "Abby, please get Ian Sawyer on the line for me."

"Yes, sir."

He sat back in his chair and tried to ignore how those two words flowing from his secretary's pretty, plump lips made him feel. While he and Remi had no trouble dating their contracted artists, the employees of Black Diamond Records were off limits. And damn, didn't that suck when it came to sweet Abby Turner. Everyone but the twins called her Abigail—Gray and Remi preferred the shortened moniker, and she'd never suggested she was unhappy with it.

With sensual, womanly curves, Abby made his dick twitch just by entering the room. But his brother and he had agreed long before she came to work for them that office romances—or brief trysts—were not an option. They didn't want to put any woman through the company's gossip mill; they valued their employees and would hate to see anyone hurt for being involved with the big bosses.

It wasn't well-known, but his and Remi's sexual proclivities veered toward the dark side. He was certain the beautiful, young thing who ran their offices with excellence would flee into the night, screaming if she knew what they wanted to do to her. Being Dominants in the BDSM lifestyle for years, they enjoyed sexual play that tended to be frowned upon by mainstream society, although many people's misconceptions had changed in recent years thanks to popular romance novels featuring the subject. In fact, Ian's sister-in-law, Kristen, was a famous author whose last few best sellers took place in a BDSM club similar to the one the Sawyer brothers owned, where Gray and Remi also happened to be members. The Covenant was the top, private lifestyle club in the Tampa/St. Petersburg area, and the elite membership was contingent on a strict background check.

"Ian Sawyer is on line three for you, sir."

God, what he wouldn't give for her to call him Sir during a scene where he and Remi made her come over and over. Pushing the delicious thought from his mind, he picked up the phone. "Ian?"

The Covenant and Trident Security co-owner's voice rumbled over the line. "What's up, Gray? Did you take care of that problem?"

"This morning. Thank Boomer for getting those photos to me so quickly. Aurora is officially a thing of the past." He'd suspected the woman had been cheating on them for a week before finally calling in a favor and having her followed. Ian's employee and teammate had gotten up close and personal with a long-range, zoom camera lens the vultures who made up the paparazzi would drool over. The Trident operative had come to the house Gray shared with his brother last night with the 8 x 10 glossies. Ten minutes later, Gray had been packing up all the woman's shit she'd left at the house and sent it by private courier this morning with a simple "fuck you" note attached. Petty, yes, but damn, it'd felt good. There was a list of things he wouldn't tolerate in his woman and cheating was at the top, second only to disobedience when it came to safety.

"Good, and I will. I've already removed her from the club's approved guest list." If Aurora had been an actual member of the club, it wouldn't have been so easy to blackball her, but she'd only been approved as a guest of Remi and Gray. Because of her guest status, she hadn't been allowed to play on the premises, but it had let them explore possibilities for scenes at home with her. "If it's any consolation, my wife says most of the submissives hated her, and, as a result, won't be buying any more of her music." He paused, then added wryly, "Well, since that's a loss of money for you, too, I guess that's not anything to celebrate. Anyway, I spoke to Chase Dixon last night, and he'll be firing the guard—he's as strict as I am about guards messing with clients. And on that note, Dev and I have decided to expand the personal protection section of the business, so we won't be contracting out the bodyguards as much anymore. One of Chase's men, Doug Henderson, has signed on to oversee that division with us."

"Glad to hear business is booming."

"Always a good thing, right? So, are you and Remi

going to be attending the races next Saturday? We're trying to get a head count."

Gray laughed for the first time all morning. December's theme night was coinciding with the opening of the new wing at The Covenant. While the members knew a few basics of what was being added, a week from Saturday was the big reveal combined with the annual Christmas party. And to celebrate, A Night at the Reindeer Races was the theme. He could only imagine what that entailed, but like everyone else, he'd been left to speculate until then. "Yeah, we'll be there. I'm sure we'll find a single subbie to keep us entertained for the evening."

"A new training class is finishing up, and they'll be available as of this weekend, so I'm sure you'll find some poor woman to fall for your charm." The man's amused grin could almost be heard over the phone. "Listen, I've got to run. If there's nothing else…"

"Yeah, we're good. Send the bill to our residence."

"You got it. Talk to you soon."

Hanging up the phone, Gray spun his chair around and stared out over the Tampa Riverwalk. Behind him, he heard the door open, and Abigail cleared her throat before speaking. "Do you need anything before I go to lunch, sir?"

He didn't turn back to face her. If he did, he'd be hard as a rock within seconds. "Abby, how many times have I asked you to call me Gray when we're alone in the office?" He wanted to hear her call him by his first name as much as he wanted to hear her use the title Sir in a D/s setting. But, alas, he'd have to settle for the former because the latter would never happen.

"I—um—I... a f-few times, sir... I mean, Gray."

A satisfied smile spread across his face. "Thank you. Have a nice lunch."

"Th-thank you, sir... I mean, thank you, Gray."

The door shut, and the brief sunshine that had brightened his world dimmed again.

Double Down & Dirty is now available!

Grayson and Remington Mann—fraternal twins, the CEOs of Black Diamond Records, and Dominants in the BDSM lifestyle who enjoy sharing the same woman.

Abigail Turner—the Mann brothers' personal secretary and an innocent woman who's off limits... or is she?

Gray and Remi have been craving the woman they see every day at the office, but their strict policy of not dating employees puts a huge crimp in things. That is, until they discover Abigail has a naughty little secret.

Now, there's nothing holding the men back as they set out to show her how they can both love her and she can love them in return.

Come meet the Doms of The Covenant and the submissives who bring them to their knees.

***The Doms of The Covenant series is a spinoff of Samantha Cole's popular Trident Security series.

OTHER BOOKS BY SAMANTHA COLE

***Denotes titles/series that are only available on select digital sites. Paperbacks and audiobooks are available on most book sites.

THE TRIDENT SECURITY SERIES

Leather & Lace

His Angel

Waiting For Him

Not Negotiable

Topping The Alpha (MM)

Watching From the Shadows

Whiskey Tribute

Tickle His Fancy

No Way in Hell: A Steel Corp/Trident Security Crossover (co-authored with J.B. Havens)

Absolving His Sins

Option Number Three (MMF)

Salvaging His Soul

Trident Security Field Manual

Torn In Half

Burning For Him

***HEELS, RHYMES, & NURSERY CRIMES SERIES**

(WITH 13 OTHER AUTHORS)

Jack Be Nimble: A Trident Security-Related Short Story

***THE DEIMOS SERIES**

Handling Haven: Special Forces: Operation Alpha

Cheating the Devil: Special Forces: Operation Alpha

THE TRIDENT SECURITY OMEGA TEAM SERIES

Mountain of Evil

A Dead Man's Pulse

Forty Days & One Knight

THE DOMS OF THE COVENANT SERIES

Double Down & Dirty (MFM)

Entertaining Distraction

Knot a Chance

Finding His Forever (MM)

Reclaiming His Soulmate

THE BLACKHAWK SECURITY SERIES

Tuff Enough

Blood Bound

MASTER KEY SERIES

Master Key Resort

Master Cordell

HAZARD FALLS SERIES

Don't Fight It (MMF)

Don't Shoot the Messenger (MFM)

Don't Burn Bridges

THE MALONE BROTHERS SERIES

Her Secret

Her Sleuth

Her Savior

LARGO RIDGE SERIES

Cold Feet

*****ANTELOPE ROCK SERIES**

(CO-AUTHORED WITH J.B. HAVENS)

Wannabe in Wyoming

Wistful in Wyoming (M/M)

COCK & BULL SERIES (M/M)

Scout

Rico

STANDALONES

Where the Broken Bloom

Scattered Moments in Time: A Collection of Short Stories & More

Sweet Revenge

The Sugarplum Fairy (M/M)

*****The Bid on Love Series**

(with 7 other authors!)

Going, Going, Gone: Book 2

*****The Collective: Season Two**

(with 7 other authors!)

Angst: Book 7 (M/M)

Special Collections

Trident Security Series: Volume I

Trident Security Series: Volume II

Trident Security Series: Volume III

Trident Security Series: Volume IV

Trident Security Series: Volume V

Trident Security Series: Volume VI

ABOUT SAMANTHA COLE

USA Today Bestselling Author Samantha Cole is a retired police officer and paramedic who now writes heart-pounding romance in multiple forms—MF, MM, and ménage. From military heroes to rugged cowboys and small-town heat, her stories blend passion, loyalty, and danger in perfect balance.

Awards:

Wannabe in Wyoming (co-authored by J.B. Havens) won the bronze medal in the 2021 Readers' Favorite Awards in the General Romance category.

Scattered Moments in Time won the gold medal in the 2020 Readers' Favorite Awards in the Fiction Anthology category.

Where the Broken Bloom (formerly *The Road to Solace*) won the silver medal in the 2017 Readers' Favorite Awards in the Contemporary Romance category.

Sexy Six-Pack's Sirens Group on Facebook
Website: www.samanthacolebooks.com
Newsletter: samanthacolebooks.com/mailing-list

facebook.com/SamanthaColeAuthor

instagram.com/samanthacoleauthor

bookbub.com/profile/samantha-a-cole

goodreads.com/SamanthaCole

amazon.com/Samantha-A-Cole/e/B00X53K3X8

tiktok.com/@samanthacoleauthor

youtube.com/@SamanthaACole-bp6yu